X-Ca

The Absurd Legend of Cantiger the Wizard

❊

The first book of
the world-renowned, hitherto unknown,
Orsonian Legends

❊

Mark F. Parker

ROBINSON
London

Dedication

*For the Honourable Boss Gerard Noel, loyal friend, and of course, for Sir Thomas Malory, magical romancer, thriller-writer, father of our myths and of my profession, progenitor of the greatest artefact since the mouldboard and Baptist to the Master – with love, much worship, and many, many apologies from: **M.F.P.***

Constable & Robinson Ltd
3 The Lanchesters
162 Fulham Palace Road
London W6 9ER

First published in the UK by Robinson,
an imprint of Constable & Robinson Ltd 2000

A copy of the British Library Cataloguing in
Publication Data is available from the British Library.

ISBN 1-84119-106-X

Printed and bound in the EU

10 9 8 7 6 5 4 3 2 1

Prologue

STORIES are wild. They thrive best where other life forms fail. You do not get witches in orderly turnip fields, nor dragons in suburban gardens, much. You do not even get many stories, not real stories, in the seething cities. Order drives out stories.

Perhaps that is why so many stories have started in Loonis. Forest did OK there – dark snarled-up forest full of gurning roots and sweating, flaccid flowers that looked as though they'd sell you postcards of orchids being rude. And then, on either side of the forest, there was blasted heath, with stunted trees that did not want to be there, and then gawdawful, think-I'm-going-out-in-that? heath, and then *#@*$~*!!! heath, and then cliffs which looked very, very experienced.

And at the last, there was the ever-changing, ever-bombarding, never-yielding, very rough and surprisingly wet sea.

Stories do well in all of these habitats, but best of all they thrive in shadow, in the deep darkness of the groaning forest. In there, they have plenty of time to get seriously misshapen and disorderly before emerging to frighten the pants off people, most of whom were better keeping them on.

Chapter One

THE SHE-WOLF did not slaver as she followed Cantiger through the forest. She was provident and always laid in an elegant sufficiency of food long before slavering became necessary. Besides, she hated stereotypes. Stereotypes had massacred wolves in their thousands. If she wanted to eat a little girl, *then* she might slaver, in the certain knowledge that the brat would come closer to her than to any cooing, clucking *grandmother*. Grandmothers could consume you alive. Wolves just ate.

No one knows better than a wolf that clichés are death.

She slunk along the ditch, belly low, hunkers bunched and swaying, eyes fixed upon this appealingly scuttling meal. She smelled his fear. That was appetizing. She approved, too, the strange, happy little burbling sounds that proceeded from him. Other wolves might eat any old junk. She did not hold with meat processed by sunlight to yielding, tasteless pulp. "Fresh is best", she had always insisted. A modest shriek or death rattle was her sell-by label.

Cantiger was, in fact, far from happy. It was a bright autumn day, but it was dark in the forest. Every sound made him start. There were lots of sounds in the forest. His eyes jerked to left, to right, then swivelled round to scan the path behind him. His neck ached, and twice his head swerved so violently that he overbalanced and slithered to the muddy, mossy ground.

This was Loonis the remotest corner of Logris and less populated than most areas. For all that, there were animals aplenty, many of them heavy, many of them hostile. There were birds, too, which shrieked and cackled like jubilant hags. For defence, Cantiger had only a thickish branch wrenched from a passing larch and the hymns and spells that dribbled from his trembling lips.

The hymns were tuneless and all embracing, all appeasing:

Kill my foes, rip off their somethings,
Something, Lord Cernunnos, please!
Something also, sweet Rosmerta,
Anu, give the buggers fleas!
Something, something, thingy, thingy,
Hear thy servant who adores (nay implores!)
Save him from their maws and jaws and claws!

As for the spells, they too were more speculative than formal. Cantiger did not actually know any spells. He just sort of vaguely hoped that he might happen upon one: "Um, *abeste infideles*, bog off, beasties, thuraze chair . . ." he drooled, having read other people's books, usually over their shoulders, and overheard them reading. He gulped. "Um . . . oh, God (and, of course, any devils or demons if you're the right people to be talking to about this) . . . If I survive this, I really never will sin again (or, if you're a demon, I'll become a really great sinner) – and I'll never have impure thoughts again (or I'll plunge into reckless debauchery, whichever you fancy). Honest! *Veni creator spartacus* . . . Ohdearohdearohdear . . ."

"Oh dear . . ." was, in fact, the only component of this monologue that featured in currently effective spells.

On its own, however, it had no effect on the wolf. She scampered silently to within ten feet of the man.

As for the aurochs that stood around the corner just ahead of Cantiger, it was not even motivated by precepts of good husbandry.

An aurochs was the best advertisement yet invented for vegetarianism. A giant ox standing eight feet high at the shoulder, it just sort of liked charging and tossing and goring. For fun.

It was good at it. That was the thing. As with a trained soldier, that was as near as it got to a reason, nor did it seek further – well, that and the fizzing, popping crossfire of electric signals inside its giant head, the urgent surgent hormones in its pulsing veins.

It shook its head as though to sort out the mess in there. It did not work. The fizzing and popping continued. It lowered its head and dug a furrow in the ground ahead. It too heard

Cantiger's babbling. It smelled soft mammal. Here came diversion.

"O, tempora, o, morons! Arse longer, feet are briefer . . ." Cantiger whimpered.

The wolf slithered up on to the track. She darted forward to within four feet of Cantiger's heels.

Cantiger turned quickly – then turned quickly back again.

In the twilight his gaze had missed the crawling beast but he knew that there was trouble back there. Something swarmed up his spine. His voice climbed in pitch to a husky little squeak as he stumbled forward.

He resorted to poetry. "Bullock starteth, bucky farteth, I lick queer armour . . . Um . . . I sing of a midden that is mackerelles . . . um . . . Tim or Mort is bugging me . . . oh, Lord (or Lady), please, no . . ."

He swung around the corner. He saw the aurochs. He slithered to a halt. He moaned, "Oh, shit," somewhat sadly.

The wolf hunkered back.

And leaped.

It was a first-class leap, made all the more impressive thanks to Cantiger. Had he stood still, it would have been interrupted at its apex and so would have lost distance and been messed about with splattering and such. As it was, it continued in a perfect parabola, losing style marks only for the downward lunge of the wolf's head and the snap of teeth where Cantiger's neck had just been.

Cantiger's performance was even more stylish. He stuck a foot out to the right, ducked down, then plunged fast to his left. He sprawled, and slid in the mud to find his head overhanging a deep ditch half filled with chortling water the colour of milky tea.

The wolf found to her surprise that a fat little man had suddenly changed into a luxury, real-hide-upholstered, careering, laden wagon with sharp, curvy, sticky-out bits.

Cantiger eyed the water beneath him. He sighed. He said, "Oh dear" again, and pushed himself down the steep bank.

The water gulped as he slid into it. The wet and slime slithered beneath his linen shift. When at last he extricated himself from the wet (the slime was still wriggling downward –

and, more alarmingly, upward – on his skin), he peeked above the ditch's brim.

He was privileged to witness a rare confrontation. The wolf was now attached, growling and waffling, to the aurochs's throat, the aurochs striking with its great white forefeet and bobbing its woolly-fringed head at its assailant.

The wolf swung, but held on.

Cantiger knew little of such things. Natural history, for him, was just the unavoidable prehistory of dinner. His money, however, had he ever had any, would have been on the aurochs.

This assessment was based on his own experience. Cantiger was used to being small and, attempting, rather vainly, to be predatory. He had never willingly taken on anything bigger than a weasel, which had hurt him really quite badly. Nonetheless, certain big people had taken *him* on, for practice, so it seemed, or because they did not like the shape of his neck, or because they did not like his taking their property, even when he obviously intended putting it back when he got round to it.

These encounters had always left him feeling and looking worse than when they started.[1]

Whilst Cantiger's sympathies, then, were with the wolf, his putative money rode with the aurochs.

He'd have been wrong either way.

There was the pudder of hooves and the jingle of harness from the direction from which he had just come. There was ragged male laughter and the clank of armour. Cantiger reluctantly turned from the fight. He ducked further down. Two brindle-and-white greyhounds bounded into view, snapping and grinning playfully at one another as greyhounds always beautifully will, then two grizzled and ticked black alaunts,[2] burlier by far than the greyhounds, though as long in the leg.

---

[1] Nor had he experienced that sense of cameraderie which, he was assured, existed between two men who had fought one another. Somehow, after one minute of one man's snarling, "Stand up and fight, scum!" whilst the other whimpered, "I like it down here, sir, honestly!", followed by a few more during which Man 1 grunted in order to assist his pummelling and Man 2 said only, "Ooh, no, sir! Please, sir!" and "Ow", followed by silence from Man 2, you just did not seem to feel that enduring bond forged by shared experience.

[2] See Glossary, Appendix 2.

Their expressions were serious and resolute. Cantiger's bowels contracted at the sight of them.

Then in danced a small pack of beagle-like brachets, nuzzling at one another and padding along on fat feet. Cantiger knew little of anything. He was frightened even of these. He made it a rule to be frightened of everything that he had not previously and successfully bullied, and even then he sometimes got a nasty surprise.

When the Riders hove into view, he was very frightened indeed. There were six of them, big men in black who looked all the bigger for their armour and their crested helms. They rode on glossy big horses at a steady canter, roaring conversation at one another. The swords at their sides rattled.

"Biggest collops I ever saw!" Cantiger heard.

"Full comely, she was, and well bisene, wist what I mean?"

Behind the Riders came a motley group of pilliers, who rode in silence. Behind these . . .

"'Call that a hart?' I says. 'More like a by-our-lady stag, you ask me. Still, with redcurrant jelly . . .'"

"So quoth this wight, 'Fair damosel, wouldst tarry?' and the damosel said . . . Hey. Helloo!"

"Avaunt!" cried another of the Riders as the greyhounds flashed past Cantiger's hiding place, the lymers, or boar-hounds, hard on their heels, and the brachets, somewhat belatedly, gave tongue and streamed towards the embattled aurochs.

The wolf had already decided that pre-prepared foods had their merits after all and that this area was going down in the world fast. When next the aurochs tossed its head, therefore, she let go. She flew, twisting in the air, into the bushes by the side of the track. A few wise brachets peeled off to give chase. The rest followed the bigger dogs' lead and attached themselves to bits of aurochs.

But Cantiger was not watching the battle above him. His eyes were fixed upon the Rider who rode alone between the pilliers and the crossbowmen who brought up the rear on foot. He was not just big. In fact, it might be that he was little bigger than the other Riders, just as an eagle may be little bigger than a goose. He just gave an impression of confidence, ease and unassail-ability that would occasion awe and admiration in some but only terror and dislike in Cantiger.

The man wore no helm, and his legs were clad in gleaming leather rather than in hardware. His greying black hair also shone. It was slicked back and tied in a ponytail. His thick moustache was paler grey. He grinned a one-sided grin and he did not need to shout to be heard above the clatter of the men, the yelping of the hounds and the snorting of the ox. "Back," he ordered. The word rattled through the trees.

He held out a gauntleted hand. A huge lance appeared from nowhere, as it seemed. He grasped it, easily swung it down to the horizontal, fewtered it and laid it across his horse's neck.

He clicked his horse into a trot but, after a few paces, frowned. His hounds, when not flying off into or whimpering in the bushes, were fastened to various cuts of beef. One lymer even had the aurochs by the nose and was engaged in a solo tug-of-war. He could not see clear leather.

The Rider nodded. He held out the lance. A pillier was on hand to take it from him. The Rider dismounted. He drew his sword as he strode along the track. He was grinning again – rather disgustingly, Cantiger thought.

The ox became aware of the man in the centre of the track ahead. It tired of the nose-tugging lymer and jerked its head hard to one side. The great grey dog found itself somersaulting. The ox snorted. The other dogs at its back and neck were mere irritations. It wanted the grinning man.

It surged forward, head down, trailing dogs.

By the time that it reached the Rider it was travelling at speed. The man stood absolutely still, his weight on one foot. He did not even lift his sword until the beast was upon him. Then things happened, but Cantiger was never sure what those things were. The man was suddenly somewhere else. The blade flashed. The ox stumbled and stopped. The man was somewhere altogether elsewhere again. The blade flashed, slicing downward this time.

The ox stood considering what had happened. It appeared confused, which was unsurprising, really.

Its head had already bounced on the track and rolled into a rut.

Blood spattered Cantiger's face.

He did not hear the aurochs say, "Aha!" before it crumpled, but he would swear that that was what it was thinking.

"One thing I can't stand," said the Rider, "it's a burger with attitude."

Half a mile down the track, Princess Marina Lamaya stood at the topmost window of the tower, gazing out over the Forest of Loonis. Her trunk[3] was packed. Her diplomas and her report were in her reticule. She shifted eagerly from foot to foot.

It was the end of term.

She was a tall and slender girl of some sixteen summers. She was no beauty, but she radiated health of the sort described (usually, alas, inaccurately) as "rude".

Her brown hair, held back in a pearled net snood, was glossy as syrup, her skin fresh and unblemished. Her eyebrows swooped like twin rockets' trails above gin-clear eyes. Her shoulders were broad, but everything to southward tapered nicely and in proportion. She was unconventionally dressed in a corslet of softest beaten leather covered with a stiff leather cuirass, a broad studded black belt from which hung a dagger, black leather breeches and knee-length boots.

Again, it was the dogs, now spattered with mud and blood and happily panting, who first emerged from the umber of the trees. Marina gasped, "He's here . . ." As the six Riders, spears aloft, rode into the glade and took up their stations on either side of the track, Marina jumped up and down and waved her handkerchief. "Hi, Sadok!" she called. "Hey, Driant, hi! How's the back?" The Rider gestured. Marina winced. "And the front?"

The pilliers formed up behind their masters. Then the forty men-at-arms emerged at the trot, tramped in step up the avenue of Riders and took up flanking positions. They kneeled, their crossbows raised to their shoulders.

"He's coming . . ." murmured Marina. She clapped her hands

---

[3]This is "trunk" 2, "a strongbox for travellers", rather than "trunk" 3, "the body excluding the limbs", or "trunks" 4, "undergarments". Her trunk 3 and trunks 4 were merely nicely filled. She did not have a trunk 5. I hope this is clear.

in Girlish Glee. They still did Girlish Glee in Forms I and II back then. It was hard to forget.

Marina bethought herself of the old woman and the beautiful young girl in the room behind her. She glanced swiftly back at them. "Oh, Dame Iseult," she said sweetly, "and darling Garnish, I am sorry to be so excited. I really will miss you, and I'm so, so grateful to you both . . ."

"Nonsense, girl, nonsense," croaked Iseult of the White Hans (so called on account of a pallid young Hun whom she kept downstairs for unspecified purposes). "It's been a privilege to have you. We'll miss you terribly, of course, won't we, Garnish?"

"Well, I know I will," purred the girl in a voice that made tonsils tickle. "I'll never have another friend like you."

"Ah, you'll be able to visit," consoled the old woman. "Oh, and by the way, the White Hans is feeling poorly, but he asked me to wish you good luck. No, time moves on, my dear. You have work to do, and you've learned as much as I can teach you – excluding the arcana, of course . . ."

"Of course."

"I have never had a pupil like you. I am confident that you will make your mark on the world and be a credit to my academy. Your dear father should be very proud of you . . ."

"Oh, thank you, darling Dame Iseult!" Marina turned back to the window. "Oh, look! It's him, it's . . . ! Oh, no, it's not. It's a damp, dirty villein carrying a big cow's head. What's he doing? Oy! You!" She leaned out. "Bog off before I turn you into a sentient mushroom!"

Bedraggled and bewildered, Cantiger looked up. He had been soaked in muddy water and blood, half licked to death by ravening dogs, then laughed at by some large men. Now a nice-looking woman was bellowing threats and abuse at him. It was extraordinary how history repeated itself. Daily, at least.

"Sorry. Are you Dame Iseult?" he called up. "I'm the new apprentice."

Marina did not hear him. "Daddeee!" she called. "My daddee!"

The Rider with the ponytail rode into the glade, once more smiling his lopsided smile. His right hand held a rope whose other end was bound around the hind legs of the gutted aurochs His horse pranced like a faithless firewalker. He waved up to his daughter. "My baby," he said proudly. He shook his head, incredulous and admiring. "My little baby girl . . ."

When Marina and her father had embraced at some length in the vestibule, punched one another and slapped one another on the back and shoulder and exchanged guffaws, Cantiger found history behaving like a pickled onion yet again. First, he became aware that his new mistress was not, after all, the limber young girl who had threatened him, nor the comely damosel who held her hand, but the scowling, stooping, squinting pale old woman in the black cloak. Then he was thrust forward with the still-bleeding aurochs's head. The old dame was all coquettish with the ponytailed Rider. She writhed. "For me, King Cobdragon? Oh, your savagery, you shouldn't!"

"Nothing, nothing. Thought it might look good over the fireplace. Or perhaps you'd like to play with it. I know how you girls are with brains and things."

"The eyes might be good for the lunar thaumatropic epidiroscope,"[4] suggested Marina.

"And we can always use freshly dead brain tissue in the gamma-wave storage batteries,"[5] said Garnish.

"Or in hotpot," said Iseult, a practical dame.

"There," said Cobdragon. "Knew you'd have uses for it. Fees reach you, I trust?"

"Yes, boss," said Iseult. "Gramercy."

"Keep the cart."

"Oh, Ruthlessness, gramercy indeed!" Iseult squirmed.

"No, no. You've looked after my girl very well. Rest of the beast is outside, if it's any use to you."

Cantiger was impressed. An aurochs, anatomized, salted, smoked and potted, represented a year's food for a large family.

Cantiger had been the victim of this sort of profligacy. He thought it wonderful.

[4] A very useful implement for transcribing astral and zodiacal patterns direct from the heavens.
[5] A very useful implement for conserving emotional energy – so often dissipated.

"Right, you, villein," said Iseult. She leaned forward and glared at him. One of the glaring eyes was a jelly, the other a cloudy blancmange. "Are you really 'Bright, punctual, talented, pig's trotter, liquamen, butter, agrimony two grains, dose dog, oh shit and learned'?"

Cantiger sighed. His mother's habit of writing letters on shopping lists had got him in trouble before now. "I try," he said.

"Oh, gawd. Right, off to the kitchen with you, and start chopping."

"Chop, chop, chop! Just like me!" bellowed Cobdragon amiably. The slap on Cantiger's back propelled him across the circular room. His knees hit a bench. His forehead hit the wall.

"Sorry," he said to the wall, just in case.

"Now," said Iseult to Cobdragon, "sit down and tell me what's been happening. Still no overlord, I hear? I do hope I can help . . ."

"No. Realm's stood in great jeopardy long while, I'd say." Cobdragon pursed his lips and sat on an iron chair. "Every Rider that is mighty of men makes him strong, and many ween to be king."

"Fancy," said Iseult.

Cantiger shook his head, reeled a little, then pulled himself up on the bench. No one was paying the least attention to him, save Marina, who kicked him as he headed for the basement kitchen.

Already he felt quite at home

There were people who did not like Cobdragon. Quite a lot of these – the ones who had bumped into him and believed that it was "good to talk" – tended to be dead.

There were others, however, who disliked him more or less as a matter of principle. They did not even need to know him personally. They did not like his habits which, if gregarious, were unsociable. Like most successful warlords, he just wasn't the sort of man that you asked around for a nice little chat over a fig roll.

Strangely, Cobdragon did not seem to worry much about such disapproval. He slept well at night, admittedly with the assistance of large quantities of mead, and loved nothing better than a good joke[6] with his chums.

He was very much at ease with himself, was Cobdragon.

"So, you naughty daddy," said Marina as she rode beside him towards their home. "What have you been up to?"

"Oh, you know, the usual." His eyes were permanently narrowed, permanently shifting this way and that as he rode. "Conquering, that sort of thing."

"Great. How big's the kingdom now?"

"Well, we've got all of Dumnium, Somnium and most of Withershire now. That chap Herminde yielded himself and one hundred knights to me."

"Oh, well done!"

"And then Clegis slew a couple of lordlings up in the Marches and won us two thousand acres, two hundred Riders – most of them useless, but . . . and three nice castles. Rent of about seven hundred a year. I've put him in charge."

"It was time he had some lands of his own."

"Yea, and now he's got his warhammer technique sorted out he's pretty much Grade One. He should be able to hold the lands. I can't see any of the Premier crowd wanting them. It's rough territory."

"All the same, territory is territory," said Marina firmly. "Any losses?"

"Oh, nothing significant. Bersules beat Cobbledick, but I went down there and rased off his head."

"Quite right. Got to show that you'll put up with no nonsense." Marina was smug. "You *have* done well, Daddy. Is ours the biggest demesne now?"

"I'm not sure." Cobdragon cocked his head to consider. "I think it should be. There's this young chap Lynch making a bit of a name for himself out east, but yea, I reckon we're number one. Now, if you were to marry this Lynch fellow . . ."

---

[6]These jokes tended to be of the direct and practical, rather than of the delicate and verbal variety. The Snake in the Sandwich was a hoot, the Boat with a Plughole a classic, the Top-Storey Garderobe with a fake floor of ferns almost as riotous as the Whoopee Cushion. It was the facial expressions that Cobdragon and his men particularly cherished.

"What about the siege?" asked Marina quickly.

Cobdragon barked. "Still going on! Poor old Hammer! Hasn't got a clue. Wonderly wroth. Stamping and swearing and executing his Riders . . ."

Marina smiled. "Serve him right. Moist goat's crotty."

"Now, now," corrected Cobdragon. "Language . . ."

"Well, I'm sorry, but he really is a crotty. Anyhow, just wait till I get to his . . ."

Cobdragon's head jerked round. "Yes?"

"I've got a few new tricks of my own now," said Marina slyly.

"Aye, I'm sure you have, but you know the rules." Cobdragon was stern. "Start using maladies and plagues and thunderbolts, you never know where it will end. Hammer's got his sorceresses, too, you know. Things can escawhatsit."

"No, no, I know. But I've developed a whole new technique. They won't even know that it's magic."

"Hmmm," said Cobdragon gravely. "You just be careful, my girl."

"Don't worry, Daddy," Marina soothed. "I know what I'm doing."

"That," said Cobdragon, "is exactly what I'm afraid of. Anyhow. Grown-up now. Time to get married, have babies. Boys, mostly. I've put out the word. Suitors queuing up. Lucky girl."

Marina said nothing. She simply sighed and glared at a rabbit that was grazing on the bank fifty yards ahead.

"Be nice for dinner, that," said a man-at-arms when he came upon the rabbit.

"I wouldn't," said his companion. "It might have died of something nasty."

But some people never listen to advice. The man-at-arms was off sick for two weeks.

You have to consider the position of a feisty, funny girl at this time.[7]

As a younger son, Cobdragon had started out as an errant Rider with only a few handpicked men-at-arms and pilliers. In a kingless country, in which the only law was that of the sword, he had quickly won large territories and restored the ruined

[7]Well, you don't have to, but it's quite fun.

Weird[8] castle of Hennamucus on the north Hornwoggish coast. At the last, he became so mighty a warlord that, when King Hammer of Hornwoggle sent his usual representative to demand truage, Cobdragon sent him back most artistically rearranged, with a succinct and unRiderly message fastened to his cuirass.

Hammer sent his very best Riders to demand fealty. But they came back, if at all, far lighter than when they set out.

Last year Hammer got *really* wroth *and* wood, and led an entire army to Hennamucus. But so complete was Cobdragon's mastery of the sea, so many and complex the tunnels from castle to beach, that the hard-of-hearing within the walls did not notice for more than six months that they were being besieged at all.

Winter was setting in. Hammer decided that he would darned well make them notice.

One thing that Hammer was not short of at the time was dead horses, so he wheeled up his grandfather's three great trebuchets, loaded them with horses and fired them over the castle wall.

The people of Hennamucus noticed that. You do, when a dead horse descends from the sky and lands with a thump and a prolonged fart close at hand. It's one of those noticeable things.

They noticed it, however, even before the poor beasts were fired. They watched their trajectories with great interest, and laid bets as to which would land first.

They then butchered the horses and smoked or salted the meat against weather too stormy for fishing.

Hammer shook his fists and his jowls and swore vengeance on Cobdragon, his progeny, their dogs and their parasites. People get like that with vengeance. They favour the compendious approach.

And therein lay Marina's problem. Habits like her father's made enemies. And she was sole heiress to his lands *and* his enemies.

---

[8]The people of the time knew little of those who had lived before the Great Hiding. They knew a few of their legends, and they recognized that they had constructed astonishing buildings of stone, some of which still stood. They could not imagine what sort of people might or could have built thus, but they referred to them as "Weirds".

Armour was the all-important difference between Riders and villeins and men and women. Armour made you invulnerable to all save other Riders, but armour was both rare and heavy.

Ironically, there had been a time, recorded in wistful songs and legends, when the entire land was littered with metal. But that was in the time of darkness, the Great Hiding, when people skulked in caves or hollows, rarely venturing forth for fear of the White Sickness. By the time that they emerged, all that metal, which might have armed every villein in the land, had rusted and fallen to dust.

What, then, with mining, smelting, battering and tailor-moulding, a suit of armour was a pricey bit of kit.

I would like to be able to say that it cost, say, twelve common men's annual incomes. But common men did not have incomes. In barter terms, then, a modest, serviceable suit of armour could be traded for the annual yield of seventy-two well-husbanded acres, nine and a half fit young bondswomen or two bears' gall bladders. Even then, you still needed a sword, which cost almost as much again, several lances, laboriously wrought and polished from specially grown elm trees, a shield, a well-trained horse and a pillier to keep the horse fat and the arms and armour in working order.

And then, too, even if, like some burgesses, you possessed the price of all this equipment, you had to know how to use it, which was not something that could be picked up in a correspondence course. People like Cobdragon were born into the warrior caste and trained from birth in the skills of war.

As for girls, the weight of armour and the difficulty of panel-beating accurate cup sizes meant that even the richest of the sex, like Marina, were at a disadvantage. A bright, ambitious girl, therefore, one who wished to get on in the world, had to find other means.

From the cradle onwards, whilst boys of the Rider class learned the skills of arms, their sisters trained in the skills of other bits. Each had to matriculate in the noble arts of Comeliness and Deportment, Withering Scorn, Loathing, Disdain, Woe-is-Me-and-Lackaday, Eyelash Management, Pretending to Love Babies and, of course, Wiggling.

Marina learned all these in the nursery, but they did not suit her. She was a difficult, headstrong sort of girl. She preferred knife-throwing, archery and fencing, at all of which she was brilliant. Still, she could not wear armour or wield a broadsword. Cobdragon assumed that, once her studies were finished, she would marry some likely young warrior who would protect the family lands when Cobdragon no longer could. He thought that magic was just one of those little accomplishments that adorn a marriageable young lady, like wiggling.

Marina did not see it that way.

She had no intention of marrying any great lout. She had plunged into her studies of sorcery with a passion. Magic, high magic, laughed at arms and armour, and she was going to master it.

She had proved an adept. In no time (which was a good trick in itself), she had collected diplomas in Transmogrification and Personal Metamorphosis, Clairvoyance, Advanced Telekinesis, Telepathic Communication and Poisoning. And her Cordon Bleu. Iseult of the White Hans was just the last of the tutors engaged to instruct her.

And now her education was at an end. She was ready to face the world.

No one had asked the world how it felt about facing her.[9]

[9]The world, in fact, shuddered violently, but everyone put that down to the great god Lugh's having eaten a bad star. Obviously.

Chapter Two

THREE YEARS passed, in what was generally agreed to be the correct order.

Cantiger laboured in the basement kitchen, where Garnish took peculiar pleasure in tormenting him. Down there, preoccupied only with herbs and the rude bits of divers beasts, he was all unaware of the chaos that to-rove the nation. Everywhere, Riders seized lands by main force and named themselves Kings or Petty Princes.[10] Everywhere the sons of their victims swore vengeance. Some invited foreigners – Deedongs, Ochties, Sotis and others – to fight their battles for them. Many of these mercenaries were unpaid. They did not like being oxymorons, so they marauded and pillaged.

Gods were invoked on so many different sides that some committed suicide by mistake. Others forsook Logris for sunnier and calmer climes. Olympus was a favourite destination. The nectar was dirt cheap, even if it did taste of aftershave.

Cultivation all but ceased. Nature reclaimed the land with stonying speed, smothering buildings and whole cities which the Weirds had intended to endure for ever. Libraries were regarded as log sheds; tapestries served as bandages or makeshift beds; domestic animals went wild and fought amongst themselves like men, and so grew in stature and ferocity as they bred selectively. Giant cats killed men once more. Stray dogs reverted eagerly to feral type and scavenged or hunted in packs.

Riders – the successful ones – did not spend much time in thinking. Thinking slowed the sword. In the end, however, even lemmings, never renowned for wit, yield to the will of a collective and instinctive mind. So the Riders, weary of

[10]Petty princes did not last long, mainly because they said things like, "I'm not going to fight today. I did the washing up, so it's your turn."

fighting and of sleeping with at least one eye open, began – in passing, as it were – to express doubts as to the desirability of life nasty, brutish and short.

Well, "nasty" and "brutish" were tolerable, if not inevitable. It was "short" that they objected to.

Now it was that Lugh stepped in.

At Greatwen Abbey one bright autumn morning, the Archbishop was addressing the Press. The Press consisted of a gnome with a quill in his hand and a cigarette hanging from his lower lip. "We're all of us in the marketing business nowadays," said the Archbishop. "If Lugh were alive today, which, of course, he is in a figurative sort of way . . . well, I say, he'd be exceedingly old, wouldn't he?"

"Even after all these years, St Loa's is still the fifth oldest church in the country. This must change. It is also large. 'Old' and 'large' are negative marketing points. Old, large things don't move very fast The cathedral's got to be nimble. It's got to keep up with the times, and the times, they are a-changing, as that cool new hot song says.

"My intention is to let the transepts and chapels as residences. When people go to church, they only need one church at a time. Attaching chapels to a church is a serious planning mistake. I can't think how they didn't see that at the time.

"The various supernumerary chapels will make luxurious apartments. They are all ornately decorated, and many of the tombs make excellent and eye-catching beds.

"The nave, of course, must remain sacrosanct. There has been a lot of carping about the use of the west end as an all-weather pitch-and-putt course, but it's bringing people to church, isn't it? It is very noticeable that not one of those criticisms has come from anyone else with an all-weather pitch-and-putt course in their nave. I think that tells its own story, don't you?"

The gnome nodded. "Our readers are more interested in your enactment of the Seven Deadly Sins on the high altar last week," he said.

"I am totally baffled by the furore this has caused," said the Archbishop smoothly. "We are engaged in a ministry to make spiritual values more real. It's all very well using abstract terms such as 'sloth', 'lust' and 'greed'. When the audience saw myself and the church-ladies actually practising them, I believe that their eyes were opened wide. Well, having charged twenty pounds a head to watch lust, we didn't actually need to do greed, but that in itself was a valuable moral lesson, don't you think?"

"Er . . ." said the gnome, shifting uncomfortably in his pew. A figure had just materialized by the Archbishop. It was a giant figure clad all in leaves, with a face and hands of gnarled, lichen-covered bark.

". . . It went so well that I am considering making it a weekly event. After Dame Butterwick's unfortunate indisposition, we will, of course, place a rug on Lord Addledeigg's tomb in future," said the Archbishop.

"Um . . ." said the gnome. The giant green figure was tapping the Archbishop on the shoulder.

"Excuse me, I am busy," said the Archbishop, without turning. "No. I am a devout Lughian. I totally repudiate charges of venality. Every day I clothe the naked and I feed the hungry. Then, after breakfast, I concentrate very hard on my office – desk, chair, secretary, all that. If Lugh were alive today – which, of course, in a very real sense, he is – gosh, he really would be old, wouldn't he?"

At last he turned to the figure at his shoulder. "All right," he snapped. "Oh. There *are* standards of dress in church, you know. Very well, what is it?"

Back at Hennamucus, Cobdragon stared out at the moon behind its caul of silver cloud and, way below, the serried ranks of breakers. "What does one do with a girl?" he demanded.

Behind him, his old friend Bane grunted as he tossed a tree into the fire. He had children, and was used to instructing them. "Well, now . . ." he said sleepily, "girls are different . . ." Suddenly he remembered where he was and to whom he was speaking. "What do you mean exactly?"

"A girl like Marina. I've locked her up, denied her food, even stopped her beer . . ."

"She'll magic that," mused Bane.

"D'ye reckon?"

"No force. Or the Riders'll smuggle it into her."

"They wouldn't dare!" Cobdragon gaped at the thought.

"Oh, I wouldn't be so sure. They worship her. Or dread her."

"Oh." Cobdragon could not get used to the idea that his little girl inspired more dread than he. "So what am I meant to do?" he growled. "I mean, it's not natural. She's nearly twenty. I'm fifty-eight . . ."

"Sixty-one . . ."

". . . Whatever. And I can't go on for ever. The wounds don't heal as quickly. My arms get tired. One day, some young Rider comes along, has a bit of luck . . ."

"You don't need to tell me," Bane sighed.

"Yea, but you've got a son. He's already taken over some of the work. Suppose – this Lynch guy is meant to be of much main, and Hammer's nephew – what's his name? The one who's always hunting?"

"Woborn."

"Right. He's supposed to be pretty hot too. OK, so I don't lose, but it is . . ." He struggled with the hitherto unthinkable. ". . . It is . . . possible . . ."

Bane knew how much this acknowledgment must hurt. "It's always possible," he admitted softly.

"And then what? A mere damosel could not hold my kingdom. I mean, yes, if there were a prepotent overlord, if there were laws, like in the old days, but today . . ."

"She has got magic," Bane reminded him. 'She's higher-rated than old Iseult now, I hear."

"Sure, sure. Magic's useful, but you can't use the hard stuff in war, otherwise there'd be anarchy . . . plagues . . . ghosts . . . unseen enemies. Use that stuff and you're dead, however good you are."

"I know, I know. She got rid of old Hammer, though, even with soft magic."

"Yea, certes. All his men started itching, bats flew in the faces of his Riders, gulls attacked his camp even after he'd banned buns, and the camp's chickens all marched into a foxhole. Good stuff. Bad for morale. But stuff like that isn't going to worry this Lynch person, or Warhawk, or any of the big fellows. Sure as umber wouldn't stop me. No, Bane. She has got to marry, and it's got to be one of the Premier Riders."

"So marry her off!" Bane shrugged.

"Marry her off, he says!" Cobdragon swung round and paced on the rushes before the fire. "I've had the best Riders on live come seeking her thingy . . ."

"Hand," supplied Bane.

"Yea, and the other bits. And what happens? She laughs at them. She refuses to go dallying because she spends all her time with her fleas. 'Terribly sorry,' she says, 'but the bat-fleas need feeding.' It's not the sort of thing that persuades a suitor that she'll be a social asset. They ride off at the wallop."

Cobdragon was not accustomed to being thwarted. On the rare occasions when people had tried it, he had slain them. This had become a reflex. His fist opened and closed as he looked around the empty room for a suitable candidate. There was none. He groaned. A large chunk of rough ruby lay on the table at his left hand. He picked it up and hurled it at the giant mirror on the wall. The mirror shivered into fragments and sloughed tinkling scales for a full twenty seconds.

Bane did not even turn. He just gazed sadly at the fire.

Cobdragon breathed heavily for a while as he struggled to subdue his anger. At last he looked up at the high, dark ceiling. "I mean, my brother, Leo," he sighed. "OK, we haven't always seen eye to eye, but he's sib. If his son Mortmain – if he *is* his son – had come to anything, he could have taken over, but I'm told he mixes with painter chappies and *actors*, and wouldn't raise a sword to protect his own sister for fear of getting his hands dirty . . ." He shook his head sadly at the thought of such degeneracy.

"Right," he panted at last. He started pacing again, and chewed on a knuckle. "Right. She leaves me no choice . . ."

"What are you thinking, old friend?"

"Your boy, Kid. He's Premier now, isn't he?"

"Yes. Moved up last year. Slew that Saracen, Cantharides, and made Housewolf yield him to him."

"Right. Send for him."

"What? Why?"

"Six months' training. He comes up to the mark, stands for me, he inherits the lot. She can marry him or go hang."

Now Bane was awake. He stood and stared into the shadows. "Are you sure, Cobber?"

Cobdragon was once more gazing out at the sea. "I need an heir, Bane," he said. "I haven't fought this hard to have the whole lot destroyed by some . . ." He thought about it. "Chit of a girl" just was not a phrase that you could use about Marina without invoking laughter. "By some damn' damosel."

The two men did not notice – or, what with the rushing and hushing of the sea, dismissed as a trick of the ear – the curious ringing in the granite walls.

But then, they belonged to a different school, and a different generation, from Marina's. They thought of witchcraft as a harmless hobby involving pins and newts. They were unaware that Marina had moved on to high-tech.

Now turn we to South Woggle, where Orson and Kes, two young gentlemen of the Rider class, hit one another repeatedly on the head in order to improve their minds.

They stood on the meadow beneath their father's castle, panting and reeling and plumed with the vapour of their breath. A girl of fourteen or fifteen sat on the bank above them, watching their endeavours with an eye that frequently wandered away, with somewhat more interest, to study instead the birds that pecked and pulled at the turf or the deer that roved about the fringes of the woods below.

Orson – the tall one on the right – pulled himself upright, raised his sword high, cried "Ha!" and brought it down hard upon Kes's helm.

Kes, in reply, said "Ouff!"

The girl's eyes wandered briefly back to Orson. She picked a pale purple scabious, twiddled the flower beneath her nose, and smiled.

Orson sagged and propped himself on his sword He puffed. At last, from within the steel helm, there came a hollow voice that buzzed in the armour all the way down to his feet. "Now . . . now will ye yield thee as . . . overcome and . . . recreant?"

"Wha—?" demanded Kes, looking all about him. Then, locating Orson at last, "Pah! I had . . . liefer . . . die."

With that, he staggered towards Orson, half fell, half threw himself at him and, with one arm around his waist, bore him to the ground.

Above them, Boss Buller Delamere Maudite emerged from the great gate and took a deep breath of the bracing air. He looked down at his sons, who were now punching one another's heads. "Hard at it?" he said. "Excellent. Keep up the good work." Then, to the girl, "Oh, hello, Cress." He turned and strolled back within his castle walls.

Orson appeared to have got the better of the scrap, for he now sat up astride Kes. He flung off his gauntlets and cut the leather thongs that tied Kes's helm. "Now!" he said. "Yield thee as overcome or I will smite off thy head."

"Yay!" called the girl. "Go on! He doesn't need it!"

"Shut up!" Kes snapped. His head turned so that his already red cheek lay against the wet grass. "Go away! Why must we always be followed by that impertinent little villein?"

"Well, she's Cressy, isn't she?" said Orson as though speaking of an unarguable because inexorable force of nature. "Her choice, isn't it?" He shrugged with a great clank of his armour's scales as they settled one upon the other. "Now, excuse me. As I was saying, yield thee as overcome or I will smite . . ."

"No, you won't," said Kes, whose entire face was very red and shiny. "Get off! I'm bored."

"Oh, all right," Orson sighed.

Kes was soon to be "knighted", or blooded as a Rider. He could not wait. He had enjoyed his schoolwork less and less of late, and had become ill-tempered and snotty because, where once he regularly outfaced Orson at jousting and swordplay, Orson had lately won five times out of six.

Despairing, therefore, of besting his younger brother, Kes had taken to jeering and sneering at him about his origins and his prospects. This, of course, made Orson angry and more than ever determined to win.

The boys dusted off the grass and limped stiffly back across the ditch to the castle gate. John Dory, the gatekeeper, peered through the Judas, grinned a gummy grin and unbolted the postern. Kes gestured to the villeins standing within the curtain wall, and Orson, as was proper, fell in behind him whilst the villeins in turn followed Orson.

Cressy fell in at Orson's heel. Only now did her heaving, bobbing limp become apparent She was a slim but sturdy girl with thick dark eyebrows, wide eyes and a wide mouth, a small bust that she bore with natural but rare insouciance rather than as an adornment or a blemish, and hips as yet narrow. "Thank Lugh all that boring stuff is over," she sighed. "Can we go for a ride now that you have finished pretending that we haven't invented the tin-opener?"

"Cressida?" called a voice from a gallery at their left.

Orson grinned at her. "I'd like to. I'd like a swim, actually. Hold on. I'll have to see. I'll find you at your place or at the gates."

"Cressida, *will* you come here?" called the woman on the gallery, a plump, pink-faced woman with arms like alabaster balustrades. "There's eggs to be collected and bread to be proved and I don't know what all else," she announced to her neighbour, who was beating a sheepskin. "And there she is, mooning around like a princess ... I don't know. Cressida ... !"

Cressy nodded to Orson and half hobbled, half scampered off towards the stairs.

Now this castle was not so much a large house as a medium-sized village. Within its walls were many dwellings, for fowl, falcons, horses and cattle no less than for humans. The usual human residents were not just Boss Buller's extended family, but servants ranging from men-at-arms to ostlers, from austringers to cooks, from tutors to priests, from scullions to water-carriers. In times of war such as this, the people of the outlying areas of Buller's lands, the uplands herdsmen and their flocks, the hermits and the friars, guest errant Riders and other itinerants had also gathered under their lord's protection.

The extraordinary thing about this castle was that it was mobile.

There were two sorts of castle in those days – the great old forts, left over from the days of the Weirds, which the foreigners avoided and feared, and the mobile sort, like this one.

Mobile castles consisted mostly of earthworks, not stone. No one built stone castles like they used to. It just took too long to cut and face stone, chop down trees for beams and mix up the gloop of clay, water, straw, horsehair and dead cats that served as plaster when at any moment, a ravening band of Deedongs or Ochties might hove into view, intent on pillage.

The great landowning Riders like Buller, therefore, travelled when they had to with their staff and entourages, guarded at every point by men-at-arms. They set up their castles where it pleased them, and lived in them sometimes for years, sometimes for mere days.

Naturally enough, they liked to keep their work to a minimum. They always chose an elevated site, and, save for the superstitious, there was no elevated site better than one already built defensively by the fairies – long before even the Weirds – with steep ramparts and often ditches surrounding them. Sometimes there were even fairy stones already set on these sites for defence against arrows and quarrels.

Such was the castle that Kes and Orson were now entering.

It was a circular plateau high on the downs with a ditch around it. Fling up some wooden palings, with others beneath pointing outwards to impale invading horses, lower a stout retractable hurdle for your drawbridge, chuck up a few bent beams of willow and fling some skins over them for warmth, and – bingo – there was your castle.

Of course, if you stayed long enough, you inevitably got the urge to do a bit of DIY – an extension here, a chapel there – so more timber was brought in, and occasionally even stone, though timber was more easily managed.

All over the castle compound people were doing what country people have always done at leisure. Men were whittling wood, children were playing in the dirt, two women were playing "strangle the chicken" with a chicken that did not seem to want to play.

Dogs – alaunts and greyhounds who huddled together for warmth, brachets and curs who skulked about the great pit in which the castle's food was cooked and occasionally broke into a flurry of snapping and snarling – were careful to keep out of the two lads' clanking way as they strode through the camp.

They now entered the central edifice. It was smoky in here, for a fire burned at the house's centre and there seemed to be no chimney but only an aperture high above. The villeins busied themselves with disarming Kes and Orson. This was a lengthy process, particularly in the cold, involving a deal of fumbling with straps and knots tied too well. At last, however, both young men stood clad only in buckskin breeches and long shirts of cambric.

Orson was perhaps sixteen, Kes a year his senior. Where Kes was strapping, with mottled cheeks, broad white shoulders, chubby legs and an incipient paunch, Orson was tall, lean and gangling, with sandy red hair and a freckled face on which his smile drew a broad diamond.

Orson had dressed and was bustling out to join Cressy when he was checked by two new arrivals. "Ah, Orson, my boy," said a gruff male voice, and a heavy hand slapped on his shoulder. "Been looking for you. Haven't met Boss Brastias, have you? Brastias, my younger boy, Orson."

Orson shielded his eyes.

Before him he saw his foster father, Buller, a bewhiskered man of advanced years – forty-five or forty-six at least – and a dark-visaged Rider in his late twenties. This man had a deep widow's peak that echoed the swooping line of his eyebrows, and a savage scar down one gaunt cheek. Both men were dressed in close-fitting leather, with ballock-knives at their hips and poker-worked high boots on their feet.

"I am enchanted," said Brastias, though he sounded anything but. By way of a smile, the corner of his thin lips beneath the scar just tucked itself momentarily into the fold in his cheek.

"I am honoured," said Orson, with a bow.

"K in there, is he?"

"Yes, Boss," Orson answered.

"Good. Come along, then. We have news, important news." Buller swept into the house, followed by Brastias. Again, Orson brought up the rear.

"And this is Kes, my first boy, soon to be knighted. K, Boss

25

Brastias. Heard of him, no doubt. Did great deeds of arms at St Uncumber's. Slew a whole lot of those Ochtie brutes. That right, Brastias?"

"It happened me that I won me some worship that day," drawled Brastias smoothly.

"You did, indeed. Now, K, Orson. There's been a thingy, so Brastias tells me."

"A summons," supplied Brastias.

"That's it. Very thing. The Archbishop has let cry a blitz. Says we've all got to come to Greatwen, every Rider of the realm and gentleman of arms, by Yule, on pain of cursing."

"Mother's Night, Buller, please," Brastias sighed. "Call me old-fashioned, but I can't stand these new-fangled foreign feasts."

"No. Quite right, of course. Anyhow, never been there myself. Hate those Weirds' cities. Own a few acres of it, of course, but I just take the rent and thank God I don't have to have much ado with the place. Anyhow, yes. You tell them, Brastias."

"Blonk," Kes muttered imperiously to Orson.

Orson humbly moved over to the firkin of wine and the wooden goblets where they stood on a great oak chest. Whilst Brastias spoke, Orson filled three goblets, spilled them, refilled them and bore them to the other men.

"As you know to your cost, men," said Brastias, accepting his goblet with a small bow, "this land has been in great jeopardy long while. As if it were not bad enough having to defend ourselves from disgruntled bands of redundant mercenary soldiers, invasions from the north and such, we've wasted a lot of blood and effort in fighting amongst ourselves. For myself, I have no desire to be king, any more than has Buller here. Unfortunately, many of the minor kings and princelings are rather more ambitious.

"Well, some of us have been doing thinking. Tough, I can tell you. And the Archbishop's been doing praying. Not my thing, I must say. Not enough time, and a dismally one-sided business, I always find. Still, the Archbishop has the knack. Chats away to Mithras and Cernunnos and Lugh and Caturix and fellows like that full-time. Anyhow, one of these god guys has announced that we must all go up to Greatwen, and apparently the whole business about who should be overlord will be sorted out there. No idea how it's going to work, but it has to be worth a try."

K's eyes sparkled. "You mean, any one of us could be king? Like a sort of raffle? Let the gods decide, sort of thing?"

"That seems to be the general idea, yes," said Brastias.

"Gor!" K flushed. "Sounds just like my sort of thing, that."

Buller was a Rider of culture. He deplored the decline of bards in recent years and the destruction of so many books and manuscripts in the wars. He had, therefore, recently engaged a scribe named Snugsnuffler, an itinerant freelance whisky-taster, so he said, to transcribe the great classic stories of world literature in portable form and with sufficient succinctness not to exhaust the attention span of the average Rider.

In his office, Snugsnuffler sipped his muse and dunked his quill.

> *There once was a fellow named Oedipus Rex,* he wrote,
> *Who fought with his dad and had very nice sex;*
> *So what? Where's the drama?*
> *The sex was with mama,*
> *Which made it a little . . . complex.*

Snugsnuffler appraised his work. He appeared to have omitted nothing important . . .

He picked up the leatherbound *Plays of Sophocles*, the last known copy in the world, and tossed it into his out-tray, which was in fact a log-basket. Burn lovely, that would.

"So it seems that some brave soul will have to be overlord," Orson explained to Cressy as they rode down the banks of the stream towards the forest. There were willows here, beeches and hazels, and rowans heavy with fruit, whilst woundworts, deadhead nettles and many a fern and fungus tussled for space on the ferny bank beneath, but there was not cover enough for embushment – not, at least, with the eyes of the castle-guards scanning the valley from the ramparts.

"Well, someone's certainly got to do something," Cressy agreed. "I know people just think we're gullible, but I really do believe the old Weirds' stories. People really did live peacefully like that. I mean, of course they had their wars, their smugglers, their burglars, but not this . . . this mess. At least you knew who your enemies were. You didn't go for a walk and find yourself being murdered without knowing why or who was doing it. A good overlord could make it like that again."

"No. I'm sure you're right, Cressy. It is possible, but Lugh, what a job! All those squabbling Kings and Riders wanting to challenge you!"

The boy and the girl rode on in companionable silence. Cressy, though a villein, had been the companion of his childhood whether he wished it or not.

Frequently, to be honest, he had not wished it, and, like K, had told her to go away. But she was nothing if not persistent. She had won Orson's love by laughing at him when he stumbled or dropped things, which made him furious, by staying up through the night with him to tend sick or wounded birds or animals, by riding and swimming, for all the difference between the lengths of her legs, as well as he, and by sharing his love for the old stories.

Cressy was an oddity. She detached herself at once from the pomp and posturing of Riders and the snivelling and toadying of villeins. She was unimpressed. Her mother chided her with "having ideas, and an idea never cured a pig, my girl", but was obscurely proud, too, of a daughter who read, and who laughed at serious things – indeed, the more serious they were, the more Cressy seemed to laugh.

What exactly was to become of such a daughter, of course, was another matter altogether.

It was a worry.

She could no more marry one of her Rider friends than a cat could marry a tiger (though with some of the cats reported to have been seen lately on the moors, you'd never know these days), and she had none of the skills in nor enthusiasm for housework that villein men expected in their wives.

Her legs, too – the work of a male midwife with "ideas" who had broken the ankle by which he had wrenched her into the light – were against her. Villeins liked their women strong and capable.

Cressy was, in fact, both. But appearances counted for much, and most boys went in fear of her tongue, and so mocked her.

They alit by a pool and swam and splashed as the autumn sunlight grew orange and the hill above them seemed almost to throb in its glow. They played naked without modesty or fear. Either reflex would have been as inappropriate as its opposite between them. Orson's sword, however, and Cressy's bow lay on the bank, never more than two swimming strokes away from them.

At last, they climbed out and, as they dressed, resumed their conversation. "So I'll have to go up to Greatwen with K," Orson told her. "And then, who knows? I suppose there might be all sorts of trouble, whether they find an overlord or not."

"And you'll have to travel wherever he goes?"

"Yep."

She pulled weed from her straggly hair. "I suppose I might miss you a bit," she said.

Orson frowned at a six-bearded trout where it jumped beneath the far bank. He too dreaded the new life that awaited him. "I'll miss you, Cress," he told her. He found his voice failing him as he gazed into those dark brown, loving eyes.

A familiar horn sounded the curfew. Orson and Cressy, cursing and hopping, pulled on their jerkins and boots and untethered their mounts. Orson paused with his left foot in the stirrup and caught Cressy's eye. "I wish I could make time stop right here and now," he said.

A smile twitched the corner of Cressy's lips. "Like umber you do," she growled. "Plenty of 'dearmosels' for you to moon over up in Greatwen." She swung herself up into the saddle and turned the palfrey. "Come on," she called. "Race you to the castle!"

She leaned forward and flapped at the horse's 'quarters with the reins. And she was walloping towards the castle before Orson's arse had hit the saddle.

It was a nasty job, thought the man-at-arms who stood at the bottom of the garderobe, but somebody had to do it.

He found this thought strangely consoling. Of course, if

someone had asked him "Why does somebody have to do it?" or "What would happen if nobody did it?" he might have had a minor breakdown. But there was no one at Hennamucus of such subtle philosophical acuity.[11]

Princess Marina had said that it was necessary, and Princess Marina had eyes like fairy grots and legs from Here to There and lips like crimson velvet lined with slippery silk, so she should know. And she had promised unspecified delights should he succeed and had hinted at unspecified horrors should he fail, and, given the choice between horrors and delights, the man-at-arms knew which he preferred. He was not thick. Not him.

The garderobe was a chimney the height of the castle. At every level were the holes that served as the castle's lavatories. Over the past eight hours, therefore, the man-at-arms had viewed humanity from a sobering point of view. He had developed a cricked neck. He had also danced quite a lot within his confined quarters.

His instructions were explicit. Should his view of the clouds be blocked at the topmost level of the castle, he was to raise his bow and shoot.

He liked his orders simple, and you couldn't get much simpler than that.

At the topmost level of the castle, King Cobdragon was irate.

"You were warned, my girl!" he roared. He thumped the dining table so hard that his stale-bread trencher jumped and rattled. "You were given every chance. Every chance. All you had to do was marry one of the Riders. You could have set tasks – deepest rivers, highest mountains, golden apples from the valley of the sun – all that girlish guff. That's no mastery. Sort of thing the Premier boys do without blinking. But no. No one's good enough for you. You'd rather muck around with fleas. My daughter with fleas! Me, now, I've always been lusty, as many a villein goodwoman in these parts will tell you. Oh, yes. It's the meat that does it, of course." He held up a bloody chunk of flesh. "That and my rude health. Very rude, some

[11]Or dreary nit-picking pedantry, depending on your point of view.

would say, though I'd like to know where they think they came from. No, but there are a hundred fruits of my loins running around these parts . . ."

"I know, Daddy." Marina was sullen.

"Fruitful, that's me . . ." Cobdragon mused. He chomped for a while on the meat, quaffed and refilled his goblet, then rediscovered ire. "I mean, bulling, OK! Happens in the best of families. Girlish fun. Doesn't stop the old breeding business, does it? But fleas? I don't side with the small, but if you're spurning the mightiest Riders in the world for fleas . . . well, I . . . Those poor little buggers! You've brought dishonour on the family, girl. And I'm sorry. You just ain't gonna see Paulie no more."

Marina said, "What? Who's Paulie?"

"Oh." Cobdragon grimaced. He licked his lips. He said, "What the umber did that mean? Is someone putting words into my mouth?" He breathed. This was, perhaps, unsurprising, but he made much of it. "Look, doll," he said, "you've got one last chance here. I love you. You're my own baby girl. I'm proud of you. But we've got two fat moons now before an overlord is chosen, and I've worked – Lugh, have I worked – no fun, no leisure, just hew, smite, quaff, pillage, day in, day out to make our demesne the biggest in the country. But if I have no heir . . ."

"You suffocate," said Marina.

"I suffocate. That's right. What? No, no. *Heir*. With an 'h'. No, so it is resolved. Kid stands for me at the great blitz in Greatwen. He inherits the lot. He'll be here tomorrow. You marry him, or it's a hovel on the clifftops for you. Fleas . . ." He pondered briefly, then yelled, "Fleas!"

"Daddy," cooed Marina, "I'll marry the poor schmuck."

Cobdragon angrily tossed back a goblet of blonk. "It's not natural . . ." he drooled. Then he stared. "You will?"

"Sure. Sounds nice. No force."

"Oh, well, that's great!" Cobdragon wiped his dripping moustache, then licked the wiping hand. "It is meet," he announced.

"Of course it is. Venison."

"No, no. It is meet and fitting. Thing they say."

"Oh. OK. It is meet and fitting. My fleas could rule the world, you know, but . . ."

"Forget fleas already!" Cobdragon squealed. "Think babies! You'll have babies?"

"'Course I will, Daddy! Shoals of the little brutes . . ."

He reached across to lay a hand on her forearm. "You've made an old man very happy."

"You must need the loo, Daddy darling," said Marina.

"Nah." Cobdragon frowned. "I can wait."

"No point in waiting," sighed Marina. "Go on."

"You really will marry Kid?"

"Of course I will, if that pleases you. No force. Go on, Daddy."

"I must admit, I am busting . . ."

"Of course you are, darling. Two roebucks take it out of a man. Take a copy of *Rattler*. Relax."

Cobdragon took Marina's advice. All, at last, was well.

"Daddy?" she said as he staggered through the doorway to the garderobe.

"Hmm?" He unbuttoned his pants.

"You do know that I love you?"

"Of course, baby." Cobdragon hummed happily as he squatted. "And I love you, too."

"Well, that's all right, then," said Marina.

The man-at-arms beneath had been thinking for some time, *No one, but no one does that to me again.*

So it was with some force and urgency that he raised his bow. And fired.

Chapter Three

THAT WAS one king less in Logris, soon to be replaced, unsurprisingly, by a brand new queen.

There were many kings at the time, but few of them looked like kings as we are accustomed to kings in nursery rhymes. Merry old souls with one wife, one pipe and three fiddlers apiece were the products of plenty. In the time of which I am, alas, compelled to write, they were few, and most of those few were soon translated from their castles to subterranean residences or ravens' stomachs.

Minor dynasties had sprung up where warriors bred true, but not one was more than three generations old. Kings were parvenus and, although all of them could hold a knife, few would have recognized a fork, save as in "I clove him from his brain-pan to his fork", which, though containing four culinary terms, actually referred to a social encounter wanting niceties – or any ties at all, come to that – or sauces.

Most rulers were pretty rude, if truth were told.

There were, like Buller, a few cultured Riders and Rulers – men who warmed their hands before grasping things, regarded curtains as different from napkins and even checked on the rules of engagement before engaging. They had some strange inherited, barely understood notion that life could be better if might was not the only right. They believed – and this belief is important in the progress business – that mankind as currently available had fallen from grace in a careless moment and that grace was still around and available with effort and expense.[12]

In the wilder parts of of the country, however, things really were rude. I mean, look at Warhawk and his brothers as they rode at the head of their tribe into the dark, huddling grey town of Holmsworth in the borders. They were behaving, to be frank,

---

[12]She was too. She lived, unsurprisingly, in a tavern in Dumnium. She was never quite the same after mankind fell from her.

like very, very naughty wolves on the raven. Not "raven" as in the previous paragraph – the sleek black bird that taught John Hurt to talk and likes a nice intestine for breakfast – but the other kind, as in "ravening", as in "hordes", as in, "It's safer with pillage, dears, honest!"

Look at them. They whooped, they hollered. They walloped in built-up areas. They smote off several heads without a thought.[13] They then repaired to the pub.

Actually, wolves don't do any of these things, even when on a raven. But they would, one feels, if they could. Most pubs do not even serve wolves. Speciesism.

They swaggered, raucously laughing and hitting their heads on the low rafters, leaving head-shaped holes in the beams and causing the pub to lurch. Did they request a well-hung Siamese fillet and a sup of a fine vintage as you or I might do? Not they. They swaggered into the place, wiped their blades and axes carelessly on the corkindrill-finish leatherette bonkettes, told the landlord to take a rest, temporary or permanent, as he chose, gorged themselves on mutton and ale, laughing riotously and raggedly the while, played chess with undue and disrespectful violence to bishops, and, when a small man in striped pyjamas came down to ask them to be quiet, flung their rooks at him, penetrating his forehead and rendering him quite seriously dead.

Most disgracefully of all, they burped without covering their mouths and slopped their ale everywhere.

This was really rude behaviour. But they did not seem to care at all.

At all!

Warhawk was the youngest of the brothers. His was, however, easily the most impressive figure. He was big and broad and roughly six foot seven in height, with shoulders like hams and thews the thigh . . . Well, I wouldn't like to hazard a guess at his thew-thighs. Thixteen at least.

His brothers were also large. These things, of course, are relative,[14] but you would relate their size to, say, middle-aged oaks and redwoods rather than aspens and apple trees.

Warhawk was the biggest of them and the best bisene, and

[13]This is the accepted and usual way of smiting off heads.
[14]Size, I mean, not brothers, though they are too . . .

the only one with black hair and teeth in his head. The others had red hair, and their teeth were mere debris or memories. Ger, the eldest, made funny little twittering noises to a lobster in his hand.

"Ainochslop arran splichen bastard, fotten macdesty gocker morran!" announced Warhawk, and laughed. He poured his ale over Ger, who also laughed.

"Blasten flocken cresset bollom machen anti-banana spoch poggle ponk enter bruin cprylopsis!" roared Ger, with a woeful disregard for punctuation. He absently brought his fist down on Housewolf's head.

"Ay . . ." Warhawk quaffed from another tankard. He shook his head and spat. "A gurdle splech teapo pasty bastard unter blogger fockle glenty. Bollogy mantis enter glooamin clock, urk?"

"Urk," the others concurred.

And indeed this was not the first time that the brothers had had to ride down to Holmsworth from their Northern Isles stronghold in order to remind the inhabitants of the deep reverence and affection in which they held their lords. They were like that, villeins, they found. Forgetful. They swore you fealty and paid truage for a few months, then they started singing disrespectful songs and telling jokes at your expense. They offered hospitality to other Riders, who were sometimes rash enough to try to claim the lands for their own. Then the taxes stopped coming in. It was all very tiresome, but the brothers knew their duty and spent most of their lives riding around their vast, desolate terrain jogging people's memory by rasing off a few other people's heads.

"Hear they're trying to establish an overlord," said the subtitle at Warhawk's groin.

"Pah. Let 'em try," Housewolf jeered and spat. A gob landed on the "y" of "try". "We'll not have anyone lording it over us, thanks."

"They're hoping for some magical revelation sort of thing. Otherwise it'll be decided by blitz. Under Greatwen rules, of course, with taradiddle, but we'd still stand a chance . . ."

"Four chances. Good chances," mused Housewolf. "There aren't many Riders down there can vanquish us."

"If any. They don't get the practice we do, see."

"Urk," said all four brothers, and swilled.

"Ger, just think of the fun we could have down there. Vassals, damosels, all that Deedong blonk . . ."

"Gurky poo yuk muk,"[15] said Housespider.

"Urk."

"Still, it would be fun. Only thing is, Ger, if we go, you will have to behave."

"Oooza coochy woochy wiggle darling?" said Ger to the lobster. "Sparky is, dat's who." He turned. "Whassat then?"

"You remember. No killing because you don't like the shape of someone's neck. Say 'please' and 'thank you' before and after stealing something . . ."

". . . And 'What a nice face' before pinching anything . . ."

". . . And 'I am interested in your brain' to damosels, without opening the skull to examine it in detail . . ."

". . . And 'Just a little' when someone offers you an aurochs."

"Or a pig."

Ger took exception. "'Just a little' when some mean bastard offers me a pig? A pig *is* just a little! Gor!" This time the spit slithered down that "G".

"The tavern doors swung inward and flapped. A man stood on the threshold, his arms hanging loose but bent, his fingers flexing. His eyes were mere slits. He chewed on a singa from which smoke barely slithered. He wore a strange cape of goat's wool over his armour.

"Billa bocken gurgle turd?" asked Warhawk.

"I hight the Nameless Rider," declared the Nameless Rider. And he should have known. He had a foreign accent.

"Je m'appelle le Chevalier Anonyme," said the subtitle.

"Oh, yeah. Enter?"

"Enter . . . *And* . . . you have had ado with some friends of mine. They were unarmed . . ."

"Entre . . . et . . . vous avez eu affaires avec mes copines. Elles etaient sans armes . . ."

"Downright silly, I call that," said Ger. He tucked the lobster into a pouch at his waist.

[15]Subtitles were curiously omitted for this observation, whose meaning therefore wholly eludes us.

36

"Yeah, asking for trouble . . ."

"And I . . ." The man gulped. ". . . Well, I don't like it. Not one little bit."

"Et moi, ça ne me plait point. Pas du tout."

"Oh?" Warhawk's drunken grin was somehow, suddenly, something different. He leaned forward, a glint in his eye. "So what do you intend to do about it, missy?"

The man flung the cape back over his right shoulder. He chomped on his singa, which bobbed. "Go on," he drawled . . .

"Allez . . ." read the subtitle.

"Make my d—"

"Faites ma journee . . ."

They did.

I was a day that the stranger Rider would never forget.

Nor remember.

They really were rude, those boys.

But then, if you find yourself in the wrong century and you want to keep your head, it's as well to keep it down.

"Look, this is really unfair, Garnish, old girl," Cantiger objected to the seat of a chair. He held the chair between himself and a woman with a glittering knife in her right hand. "I mean, *nil bonum sed intenta jubilee sana,* don't you know?"

The woman did not seem to know, nor, extraordinarily, to care. Both in her attitude, which was unfriendly, and her aspect, which was unorthodox, there was ample reason for Cantiger to keep her at chair's length.

It was not that she was not in many regards personable. She was of average height. She was slender. The convexities beneath her green satin gown were entirely conventionally positioned and delightfully proportioned, whilst the satin hinted at equally well-ordered concavities.

It was the head that posed the problem.

It might appeal to some, of course. We make allowance for the wide diversity of tastes in the matter of physical beauty that ensures that the grossest amongst us, for better or worse, somehow contrive to breed.

This head, however, would constitute a potent contraceptive in all save the least discerning circles.

And, of course, in Florida, which was just now a steaming bog peopled only by corkindrills and dragons.

It was that of a giant snake.

"I didn't mean to do it, did I?" Cantiger gabbled. "You should consider what a person means, you know, not just the consequences."

The woman hissed. She ducked and lunged beneath the chair at Cantiger's nethers. He jabbed downward with the chair, striking her scaly silver brow. His hips jerked sideways, revealing unsuspected limberness. "Now look," he babbled, retreating, "you're overreacting. It's unconventional, sure, but there are nightclubs where it'll go down a treat . . ."

The voice that emerged from the snake's head was a gargling gas leak. "A serpent's head! No man will ever look at me . . ."

"Oh, I wouldn't say that," Cantiger soothed. "No, I really wouldn't say that. Anyhow, who wants men looking at you? Nasty, dirty things. No, find yourself a nice anaconda and settle down, that's what I always . . . Ow! Whoops! No, really. Please. Here, what's that shaking? What's that noise?"

Even the woman, who, unaccustomed to her new tongue, was slavering long strings of spittle, desisted from her vivisectionist pursuit at the violent tremors that now shook the room. There was a deep rumble, a splitting sound, the clatter of failing masonry, then, closer at hand, the smashing of glass and earthenware as phials, crocks and bottles tumbled from their lodgings on to the stone flags.

Cantiger gulped. He said, rather sadly, "Oh," then "Whoops," again.

The woman's yellow eyes gaped. Her lower jaw dropped to her breastbone. "Oh, no. You didn't . . . ?" she gasped.

"I only read it!" Cantiger had to shout now and hold on to the great oak table that, on a perilous camber, slid with a terrible grinding and groaning towards the far wall of the turret. "I was only trying to memorize it! I thought it might come in handy at hotels and things – 'Spell to pourvide that a lodging be to-rove in sunder' – I was studying! I'm meant to study, aren't I?"

But his squealed pleas were drowned by the cacophony as stout beams were wrenched from their niches and giant granite blocks ground one against the other, smacked and purled.

Cantiger saw Garnish now standing in the window frame. For a moment, she paused. Then, with a rather poignant yelp, she launched herself into the void.

As for Cantiger, his actions were swift and decisive. With a weather-eye for falling debris, he plucked up a sack, scampered to the shelves at his back and scooped in as many papers and artefacts as he could find there. Clutching these motley gleanings to his chest, he dived under the great table a mere second before the roof and the weather exploded in.

There was a lot of weather today, but, to Cantiger, it seemed that there was a lot more roof.

Blinded by dust, he now found himself taken on a rare (and therefore perhaps pardonably jerky) elevator ride.

His room – or rather, his platform – descended abruptly to the next floor, then, almost at once, to the next. There it rested for a few seconds, as though recovering its breath, before tilting still more violently, decanting Cantiger, now entirely unsupported, through a gaping, jagged hole of broken laths on to what appeared, from the feel of it, to be some sort of bench or settle.

This, having struck his coccyx really quite viciously, shattered. In a last brave gesture of defiance, spotting a well that opened up like tearing fabric between their several feet, it flung itself and its assailant forward and downward.

Up till now, Cantiger had had his arms wrapped around the back of his head. Feeling himself falling helplessly through emptiness, and assuming, *a priori*, as he might say, that this state of affairs could not continue indefinitely, he extended one hand, and had the satisfaction of finding his assumption triumphantly borne out by another stone floor which hit his hand, broke his wrist, slammed into both his knees at once, struck him firmly on the forehead and, sportingly, showed no further resistance when once he was prone.

He now remained prone for quite some time.

A few remaining blocks fell to the ground about him. An oak beam finally released its moorings way above and came to land with a thud about six feet from where he lay. A flock of bats, disturbed in their sleep, flickered about for a while before deciding to put up somewhere warm first and settle their claim later. The snow swirled and pattered about the stonied man.

Save for the want of ivy, in fact, the whole scene was now such as might move a Romantic poet to dash off a rapid rhapsody, or a painter to pull off the mittens and pluck a passing badger in anticipation of Christmas-card royalties. You had your picturesque ruin, your pony and trap patiently waiting, your snow, your sparkling icy waters in the moat, and, of course, within minutes, your publicity-hungry robin trying to hop in on the act.

Like a demented ping-pong spectator, this particular robin shifted its head this way and that, looking, no doubt, for a camera, a painter, a holly-sprig or a spade-handle. But, finding none, it hopped over to where Cantiger lay noseling in the dust. It cocked its head to examine his face. As it did so, Cantiger opened one brimming, baleful grey eye.

To this eye, it was the jauntiness of the bird that offended. As many a hangover-sufferer can testify, there is nothing so distasteful as jauntiness to one in pain and aware of indignity. As for bob-bob-bobbing jauntiness . . .

"Piss off," Cantiger mumbled.

The eye closed again, and a series of groans, echoing those of the wind, now emerged from Cantiger before at last he roused himself. He winced as he pulled himself to his feet, then did some bobbing and hopping on his own account. Initially, he did it with his left hand to his tailbone. When the pain bit at his right wrist, he hopped a bit more, clutching that. Then he slipped and sat down and suddenly remembered his tailbone again, and roared.

All this the robin watched with the polite interest of one stylist appraising another.

It was the awareness of an audience that finally made Cantiger forget his pains. He stared at the bird for a while. His face contorted. He looked about him, selected a suitable chunk of castle and, with a string of interesting silver-period curses, flung it at the bird, which hopped out of its path. Cantiger growled, stood and shouted, "Shoo! Shoo!" The bird nodded and cocked its head. Cantiger set off in lumbering pursuit. The bird removed itself to a wall six feet away, said "Twit", and shat.

Recognizing at last the futility of this confrontation, and sufficiently recovering his wits to realize that, should Garnish have had the relative good fortune to land in the moat and to escape, she and her far more terrifying mother might at any moment return, Cantiger set off to find his sack of goodies.

He picked his way through the wreckage, occasionally stooping to pick up some article and thrust it into the pockets of his linen shift. He found his glasses. They were twisted and shattered. There was a cup here, which glinted gold, another crucible of malachite there, a brass instrument of great complexity and indeterminate use, various articles of silver, and, at the last, a Thing.

This Thing, which Cantiger examined, bemused, before shrugging and thrusting it down the front of his garment, was long, thin and black, with a disc-shaped protuberance and a curved wiggly bit at its centre.

He found the sack at last, only slightly soiled, beneath the debris of the garderobe. He picked it up delicately, between finger and thumb of his undamaged hand, and dragged it across what had once been the hall – and the dining room, and the bedrooms, and the solar, and the laboratory. And the roof.

Cantiger trudged, clattering, to the pony-trap. On his way, he found a maroon gown of samite. This too he picked up and rolled into a cushion for his aching tail. He pulled the long black thing from his habit and cautiously placed it and the sack beside the cushion.

Very, very delicately, then, he climbed up on to the trap and lowered his person on to the gown. With many a hiss, he picked up the reins, let off the brake and clicked the palfry on.

It is an aphorism of someone-or-other that, if we can leave any enterprise without shedding a tear, we have been wasting time. Sad to relate, Cantiger looked back entirely dry-eyed at his *alma mater,* now veritably to-rove in sunder, as it vanished behind the swirling strobe of snow.

Cantiger had proved a seriously lousy magician.

Although he had now been studying for nearly three years under Iseult of the White Hans, still he contrived to mis-spell the simplest spells and to render beneficent potions maleficent and *vice versa.*

Iseult, a supreme mistress of her trade, had described him as "as asinine an alchemist and astronomer as breathed, blithering, by-our-lady blunderer and dumb, dithering dolt," only occasionally, for variety, abandoning alliteration to dub him (anachronistically, but then, Iseult was widely travelled in time and space) as "about as much use as an ashtray on a motorcycle" or "as a chocolate fireguard".

To be fair to Cantiger, he never avowed any expertise nor (actually, exactly, in strictest legal terms) claimed aptitude.

An only child, much cherished by his widowed[16] Brownie mother, he had, it was true, worn spectacles from earliest childhood, not because he could not see, but because he was a craven, weak-bowelled, despicable physical coward. He had hoped, somewhat vainly, that he would thus escape the trials of the street and the playground.

He had also developed a language that, to those who knew no better (such as his mother), sounded vaguely like Latin.

Cantiger's destiny, as ordained by the circumstances of his birth, was to labour as a villein on a great lord's land and, just occasionally, to go to war in that same lord's service. Cantiger had an innate conviction, however, founded upon his minimal experiences of haymaking and his considerable experience of being beaten up by schoolfellows, that he was somehow just not cut out for work or war – nor they for him.

Most people, he told himself, enjoyed that sort of thing. Sweating, bleeding and the like. His was a higher, harder destiny.

Cantiger's real talent was that of the improvisational actor, and he had actually managed to persuade his mother of his gifts. A midwife by trade, she had bullied and chided, tugged and spanked, scrimped and saved and been exceptionally nice to their landlord, and finally, with a set of forged references, had contrived to have her son apprenticed to Iseult.

Aside from ineptitude and deviousness, Cantiger's principal characteristic was ambition. He had rapidly discovered that he liked roast partridges and lampreys and fair damosels and

---

[16]"Widowed" is a term here used loosely, as was "married" nine months before Cantiger's birth. Two days after the "marriage", Cantiger's father's coracle went down "with the loss of all souls". Cantiger, who had not quite grasped this concept, still hoped daily, however, to inherit some recently recovered halibut.

feather beds, preferably in conjunction and in quantity. He had also soon realized that he was never going to win a master magician's diploma from Iseult but would be lucky if he so much as kept his lowly position as *commis*-magician, chopping ingredients, cleaning the pots and crucibles, being the subject of experiments and being jeered at by Iseult and Garnish.

When, therefore, Iseult drove off with the White Hans on a litter behind her, leaving Cantiger and Garnish alone for a couple of days, she strictly enjoined Cantiger not to go near the laboratory, but . . .

Well, yes. I'm wasting my time, just as she was wasting her breath.

Cantiger had tiptoed up the winding stairs that morning to discover the secrets of the Higher Sorcery. The first thing that he perceived on arrival in that turret sanctum was Iseult's burglar alarm – a basilisk.

Now, to look on a basilisk is death. I am afraid, therefore, that you will have to do without a detailed description. The creature was monstrous, grotesque, repellent – all that, of course. That will have to suffice.

Luckily for Cantiger, his unnecessary glasses prevented him from seeing the basilisk as more than a sort of basilisk-shaped, spitting blur, so he was immune to the deadly horror of the thing. He simply picked it up and put it into his pocket, where it writhed for a while but was soon still.

Legend affords an image of Cantiger as lean, gaunt and wispy – but then, he created the legend. In fact, he was soft and flabby, with a shock of black hair that would soon turn iron-grey, a pendulous, juddering lower lip, twin chins and a sagging belly. The next thing that he did, therefore, was to clutch at a chair and sink on to it with a noise like a punctured bladder.

He knew this room, of course. He had pulled himself up the stairs and slithered back down again many times in the course of his work for Iseult, carrying water, tallow, newly gathered herbs and animal parts for the witch's potions. A large part of Cantiger's duties had been the collection and preparation of these frequently revolting ingredients, which was why the pony and trap had been placed at his disposal. Never before, however, had he had leisure to examine the room as now. He enjoyed himself.

All around the stone walls were the store shelves. There were all the usual bits and bobs – corkindrills' tongues, gryphons' tails, cameleopards' willies and suchlike, pickled and neatly labelled in jars, together with other staples such, as toad juice, tiercel gleat, mandragora, hemlock, truffles, *amanita muscaria*, *amanita phalloides*, *nux vomica*, senna, agrimony (of course), cochineal, sun-dried golden apples, dog suppurations and hundreds-and-thousands. Then, on a higher shelf, were stored the rarer and more precious articles such as distilled maid-spittle, maids' blood, unicorn emissions and cocoa. (It was, I am afraid to say, Cantiger's job to collect these, too – all save the cocoa.)

Beneath these, there ran deeper shelves – what we would refer to as work surfaces. Here stood the pestle and mortar, the great scales with their weights of brass accurate from peck to grain, the many knives and scalpels, the astrolabe and globe, the mirror, the racks of phials, the glass still and other instruments too arcane for our[17] comprehension.

And beneath these again were stored the jams, the marmalades and the gin.

All these ranks of shelves were interrupted just four times – once by the door through which Cantiger had entered, once by the window through which Garnish was soon to precipitate herself, once by the great chimneypiece, in which, at waist height, ashes still smouldered beneath a blackened marmite, and once by a large panelled door.

It was in the contents of the cupboard behind this last that Cantiger sought his passport to freedom and to wealth, for here Iseult kept locked her finished potions and the secret recipes of her craft.

Now, it must not be assumed that a mistress magician relied only on lock and key – though lock and key there was. But Cantiger had long since cast the key in tallow and fashioned a replica.

It so happened that it had pleased Iseult one day to conduct on Cantiger an experiment in anaesthesia. She had reasoned that a draught of mandragora and poppy seed, mingled with a

---

[17]All right. Mine.

pint of fermented and distilled potato juice, supplemented by a sharp blow to the head, would induce a state of catalepsy or unconsciousness such that no pain would be experienced for a while after.

As so often with this remarkable woman, she had reasoned correctly.

Over a period of six hours following this treatment, Garnish, with a pair of pliers and a gleeful grin, had removed six of Cantiger's toenails. Only the last of the extractions had caused him the least discomfort.

In fact, in that by then he was wide awake, it had caused him a deal more than the least discomfort. But as Iseult so often observed, apprentices were born to suffer as sparks are destined to fly upwards, and that was all there was to it.

What Iseult had not realized was that occasionally the anaesthetized, while to all outward appearances out and with the net curtains drawn, may in fact be in, and aware.

Cantiger, feeling, it was true, no pain, had been able to hear throughout the operation. He had heard the giggles, the crunching and the arrow-nock "pht" as each nail was drawn. He had also heard, and memorized, the words with which Iseult disarmed the principal deterrent to intruders into her safe-press when she went in there for the Lapsang Souchong. These he now intoned as he arose from the chair, squeezed past the table and turned the key in the wards:

> As I serve Apollyon,
> As I honour the old one,
> Yea, and Pluto's pantheon,
> Do my will!
> Thou who rid'st a goat upon,
> Arsy versy proteron,
> Angra Mainyu, Abaddon,
> Be thou still!

This formula was simple and obvious enough even for Cantiger to remember without fluffing it. The door opened and, within the cobwebbed closet, he saw the most precious, private and arcane of Iseult's possessions.

He was, frankly, disappointed. There were more jars, these labelled "WRINKLE CREAM", "FOR HAEMORRHOIDS", "CHARLIE" and suchlike.

There was a sheaf of quite interesting woodcuts showing that the White Hans had considerably more energy than would be supposed.

There was a stuffed cat, a pincushion embroidered with forget-me-nots, a besom and the body of a young Rider, quite recently deceased, hanging from a hook in the ceiling with a stupid look on his face.

There was a human skull, too, its orifices plugged with gold and amethysts so that it could be used as a drinking vessel, a length of sheep's intestine – at least, Cantiger assumed that it was sheep's – and a picture of Caernarvon Castle in a pretty frame.

Aside from these, there were just two books, standing side by side between two earthenware jars that, being examined, proved to contain pickled organs. Nor could the books be properly described as such. They were folders, rather, of stained vellum, bound about with pink ribbons. Cantiger pulled out the first. He turned back to the room, placed the folder on the table and, with tremulous hands, untied the ribbon and turned back the cover.

"*An Efficacious Nostrum for to be rid of Warts,*" the first page was headed. "*Take of dandelions blanched two pecks . . .*"

Cantiger scowled and impatiently turned the page.

"*To be delivered of child without pain. Take two goats, two human childer and a quantity of esquires of noble blood. Slay the goats . . .*"

"Yes, yes," murmured Cantiger, and turned the page again.

"*To make a noix of dough with comfiture cached therein . . .*"

The whole book was filled with such wholesome receipts. Here the eager student might learn to heal cankers and sores, colic in horses and childer, dropsy, ague, dog bites, falling sickness, sleeping sickness and the king's evil ("*take one king . . .*") the French pox, the small pox, dandruff, dysentery, diphtheria, distemper and any number of emissions and eructations.

Here too were mouth-watering receipts for mint, quince and neat's-foot jelly, green sauce for boiled meats, grosaille sauce for roasted meats, syllabubs, flummeries, marchpanes, cheeses white, green and blue, cider and apple brandy, to name but a few. Here, had Cantiger but known it, was the first reference in the literature of modern cuisine to "ye rowes of sturgeon" as a delicacy, here the most thorough guide to indigenous fungus in our history.

Cantiger has been credited with prodigious foresight, but he did not foresee the renaissance of, and the world had long forgotten, the days of celebrity chefs and leeches who charged an arm and a leg for saving a toe. He was impatient. He wanted power and pleasure, preferably without labour.

It was with exasperation, then, that he returned this precious volume to its place on the shelf and withdrew its companion. Again he opened it eagerly, again scanned the first page with greedy eyes.

Again he was disappointed.

"For to make languish thy neighbour's kine" was a useful and nasty enough spell in its way. But poisoning cattle was hardly high magic, even if accompanied by a deal of mumbo-jumbo, nor was *"For to assail thy foe with the worms"*, the subject of the next page. The spells grew nastier and nastier, but all of them demanded a certain amount of cooking as well as incantation. Cantiger pulled out a few pages which might one day prove useful – *"To make a man of surpassing might"* was a good one, as was *"To make one wood for very love"*, but Cantiger was idle. He wanted just to murmur a word or two and to have the forces of magic at his disposal, be they dark forces or those of light.

He found them at the very back of the book, behind a page bearing nothing save the legend CAVE painted in huge letters gules edged with or.

"Yes!" Cantiger breathed, and grinned as he saw the headings: *"To transform men into beasts"*, *"To slay men with a curse be they never so far"*, *"To conjure spirits of right main"*, *"To see what is to pass ere it passeth"*, *"To render edible ye Turkey bird . . ."*

Here was power, real power, hard won, no doubt, by Iseult, but won with triumphant ease, with stonying daring, by the young, the ingenious, the now insuperable Cantiger!

He grasped the page headed *"To be translated to other places in a twinkling"*. He pulled.

No sooner was the sheet of vellum outside its binding than the writing upon it vanished. Cantiger took it to the window. He squinted at it from various angles. It remained blank.

"Aha!" said Cantiger, who had learned from the aurochs all those years ago. He returned to the open folder on the table and slipped the page back in. It remained blank.

"Aha!" said Cantiger. He closed the entire folder, bent and, with some undignified wriggling, stuffed it up the front of his habit, securing it by tying tight the rope at his former waist.

He walked to the door with a little giggle of glee.

He walked into a wall of glass.

He picked himself up and tried again, this time with his hands extended. His hands hit the invisible screen. He pummelled at it with his fists. It was impermeable. He groped for its outer edges. There appeared to be none.

"Oh," said Cantiger, "bugger."

He untied the rope at his middle, pulled out the book and laid it once more on the table. Very tentatively, he walked back to the door. He passed through it without let.

This was depressing.

He would have to memorize the spells that he wanted to retain. But Cantiger was no good at memorizing, nor did he know how long he had to learn these spells uninterrupted.

One thing he did know. The term of his employment with Iseult was now drawing to its close. She was sharp. When once she found the blank page in her spell book and the basilisk gone, Cantiger would be history, which would make a change.

This, then, was his one and only opportunity.

He started to read the spells aloud. The first that he read was a spell for turning men into beasts. He read it three times, then sat back and attempted to recite it from memory.

Now, this sort of liturgy always has an *"N"* for *"nomen"* at its midst. Substitute a name for that *"N"*, supply the spell with an address, as it were, and the sprites so charged will bear it, reliable as the Posts, to its intended recipient. Then it is only malicious, and malice can be agreeable, comprehensible – even morally acceptable in certain circumstances. When undirected –

and Cantiger merely babbled "Whatsit" or "Whatsisface" when he came to that *"N"* – it is evil unconstrained, evil undirected, evil random as a breeze-blown microbe.

Of the three men and one woman who travelled in a chariot through nearby Newton, two of the men and one of the women became aurochs, whilst the remaining man became a free man and a farmer and his grandson was given a barony which endures to this day.

Overall, a good result.

Next, Cantiger had a go at a first-class persuasive number – *"Spell to pourvide that a lodging be to-rove in sunder"*. Again, he assumed that he must do something other than merely speak the spell. Again he was, as he was to discover, quite seriously wrong.

Cantiger never did memorize those spells, but he spoke six of them before Garnish appeared. Thus was Loonis separated from the mainland, to the short-lived surprise of thirty short-lived cattle and twelve short-lived people. Thus did a poor peasant in a nearby field find himself showered with gold, which killed him, but his widow married the newly self-appointed Lord of the Isles, so that was all right. Thus did a laidly worm, thirty feet long and daily growing, come into being and take up residence in a cave beneath Hennamucus, where it was to cause a lot of nuisance before meeting Lynch some years later. And thus did Garnish, Iseult's daughter, who had until then been a right comely damosel, have a makeover that displeased her.

A good day for some, a bad day for others. Such is life.

On balance, though, not Cantiger's day.

Anon, therewithal, intuitively persuaded that Iseult would be rather wroth with him, Cantiger too headed for Greatwen.

Now, there was once a time when heading for Greatwen from Hornwoggle was very different.

Then, we are told, it was swift and easy. You would simply spend half an hour shouting at the children before climbing into the carriage in the early hours. You would then reach Dumnium and turn back again to pick up the child or dog left behind. You would proceed at ninety miles an hour on the windy country lanes and at ten miles an hour on the broad highways before stopping at Gordoneau in order to buy food and drinks for the children to vomit down the back of your neck at a later stage.

You then came to a halt just outside Birstow and remained there for some three hours, during which the children and you would climb in turn on to the verge for a pee, because no sooner did your stream flow than, by a curious law of nature, the stream of traffic would also do so.

At or near Sludge, as a general rule, a lot of exciting things would happen all at once. Your spouse would decide that the marriage was at an end and assault you, whilst the children would screech and several loris swerve across your path mere yards ahead. This would usually prove the point at which the vomit came into the equation. And so you would come to the metropolis shortly after midnight.

Things were not so swift or easy in Cantiger's day. To start off with, most of Logris was now thick, dripping forest, haunted by wild animals, wild phantoms, wild men and, still worse, women. The few roads ran along high ridges. These "roads" were rutted tracks, frequently swampy[18] and deeply potholed. On the other hand, there were no loris, and Gordoneau – and, indeed, most of the Land of Summer, save in high summer – was deep underwater.

All this, however, Cantiger at present had to look forward to. His first concern and his first problem was simply to escape the Kingdom of Loonis before Iseult could return and let seek for him. Iseult was very thick with King Toon of Loonis, having solved his mole problem for him, and Cantiger, who did not hail from these parts, had little hope of mercy when once the alarm was raised.

Unfortunately for him, he had accidentally detached several large chunks of Loonis (soon, unjustly, to be dubbed "The Silliers") from the mainland of Hornwoggle, and the boat-building and ferry trades had not had time to be established in what had hitherto been an area devoted to mining and to agriculture.

Fortunately for him, however, the russet-haired mistress of a passing trireme from Dunmoanin spotted him where he stood

18 Out of the rutting season.

desolate on the strand and, having lost her bearings, asked for directions. If she would take him on board, he would undertake to direct her helmswoman to St Ia's, where, the woman declared, her intentions were to rob and murder, in either order, some burgesses, to worship piously at the shrine of the late virgin and to look out for some likely young men.

Thus did Cantiger hitch a ride to mainland Logris.

Iseult was not to be so lucky. Together with her dwarf, Bogwhistle, and the White Hans, she would come to the new channel even as Cantiger set sail from Loonis. She would find sea where it should not have been, stamp her foot and set herself to work out a spell to get her home. In the end, she travelled with Bogwhistle on a large leaf, towing the White Hans on a half-submerged litter behind her. This proved slow. Long before she reached New Holeland, she had decided that there must be some better way of making the journey. And she may well have been right, though no one has thought of one yet.

Hornwoggle was relatively prosperous and civilized at the time, and Cantiger's swarthy, half-Brownie features attracted no attention as he drove the pony along the rough clifftop paths of the North Coast.

He lodged where he could, posing as a tinker at one mining settlement near Rustrue, and paying for stargazey pie and his bed of straw with Iseult's gown. At Steinstown, he begged refuge at a monastery. As soon as he heard that the abbot called himself Pet Rock, Cantiger knew that he was on to a good thing, and, by posing as a holy idiot won himself a cell and a farewell gift of two shillings.

At Hennamucus, however, he made his first big mistake.

Pet Rock had kept Cantiger talking throughout undorne, so it was late afternoon when Cantiger caught sight – just over there, to the left – of the sagging columns of smoke that indicated a village.

The snow was thick and the road strangely icy. His pony's hooves slipped.

This, though Cantiger did not know it, was because a certain giant laidly worm, which, since being mysteriously called into being a few days ago, had been asking itself what that strange aching sensation in its belly might be, last night concluded that its nocturnal visions of damosels might have something to do with it.

No worm of which I know ever got a degree, even at the University of Kynke Kenadonne, but certain instinctive imperatives are irresistible. So this worm had ventured forth from its cave, wriggled up a cliff path and slithered along this very road in search of a damosel or, failing that, one of those woolly white things that had also featured in its dreams, and its warm belly had impacted and slicked the snow.

The worm had left the road on scenting a farmstead, in which, as it happened it discovered a damosel, a farmer, a sheep and some clotted cream (which goes, as you probably know, terribly well with damosel) and so gorged itself that it fell asleep and would not now return to its cave until tomorrow morning.

At this point, there was a wall of drifted, fluffy snow. Cantiger drove his ("his" was, for Cantiger, always a relative term) pony stumbling and plunging over and through this, but, at the last, had to dismount, unhitch the cart and, slinging the sack containing his few possessions over his shoulder, lead the pony towards the village surmounted by a mighty castle.

If Cantiger had only known that the said v. surmounted by an m.c. was in fact Hennamucus, he might have stayed with the cart, lit a fire and invited a rabbit, more in faith than hope, to supper.

Things had been rough and ready in Logris of late, however, and signposts drew attention to dwelling places and so had all but disappeared from the land,[19] which was one of the best things to have happened lately. Cantiger, in many ways like the worm of his creation, had a very clear picture in his mind of a damosel, buxom for preference, and with buxom dumplings, serving him a mutton stew, as above, by a blazing fire. As now he foundered in snow-drifts and his clothes become drenched and the swirling snowflakes all but blinded him, that picture became ever more vivid and compelling.

When at last he found himself in the narrow, rutted main

[19]No "Child on board", no "Passing place", no "Stop", no "Viewpoint", no "Farmer Giles's Agrarian Experience" . . . Landscape was unlittered with idiots' orders or bloodsuckers' blandishments. How they survived, I do not know.

street of the village, therefore, he did not hesitate to knock on the door of the first house in which firelight showed. The houses here were permanent, thatched buildings because they were under the protection of the adjacent castle. Cantiger anticipated a good standard of living and of conversation.

As is usual in this vale of tears, it was not a buxom damosel but a mittened crone who appeared blinking on the threshold. One of her eyes was still and cloudy blue. The other, bright brown one skittered suspiciously over Cantiger's face and body. She held the door open a mere crack. She scowled from under her fringed scarf and the timeworn architraves of her eyebrows. She shrilled, "Yes?"

"Hello," Cantiger beamed. "Cold day." He looked about him as though just checking. "Snow," he concluded.

"Yes?" The crone obviously agreed.

"I was wondering," said Cantiger, encouraged, "whether I might find shelter in your lowly hovel."

"Yes?" she said again.

"And perhaps a scrap to eat?"

"Yes?"

Cantiger stood grinning inanely and shifting from foot to foot. The woman glared back. She still made no move to open the door. Cantiger concluded that the woman was insane or deaf. "Sorry!" he shouted. "I was wondering . . ."

"Yes, you said that," intoned the woman. "And?"

"Well, may I?"

"Oh, aye. Free to wonder. Wonder away. No law against wondering. Why d'ye have to drag me out here to tell me about it?"

"No," said Cantiger from between gritted teeth. He had taken an instinctive dislike to this woman. "May I come in?"

"Ooaaow!" she squawked. "Why didn't you say so? What do I want to stand here for, listening to you gibbering about wondering? It's cold, in case you hadn't noticed. Snow."

"Sorry," said Cantiger fiercely.

Still the woman did not step backwards. "You got money?" she asked.

"Of course, of course!"

"Emmuch?"

"What?"

"Emmuch?"

"Oh, how much? Well, seeing as you're a poor gaunt old crone, doubtless saving for emergency cosmetic surgery, I'll give you a whole lovely sixpence for a good mutton stew and a bed."

"Shilling."

"Outrageous."

"Shilling, and it's cat today."

"What's cat?"

"The stew. With dumplings."

"Oh, all right," sighed Cantiger, who quite liked cat, as it happened. "A shilling."

At last the woman stepped back. The door creaked open. Cantiger pounced in, dragging the pony behind him.

"And don't drip," ordered the woman as she walked back to her fire. "Can't abide people dripping."

Cantiger looked down at his sodden clothes and tried to work out exactly how he was meant to abide by this house rule. There was already a substantial puddle about his feet.

He looked up.

As his eyes accustomed themselves to the darkness, he made out three people sitting around the table, staring at him in silence.

A totally bald man with a thick white beard sprouting from his cheeks, his chin and his throat sat closest to the fire.

At his either side sat a tall, startlingly beautiful girl of sixteen or seventeen. The one at his left had short, spiky green hair – a fashion which Cantiger had noted on his travels – and large green eyes. She was slender as a wand of willow, save for the nestling turtle-dove things that girls always kept down their fronts. The one at the man's right looked exactly like her sister, though she had thinner lips, her green hair flowed to halfway down her back, she had downy stubble on her cheeks and no nestling turtle-dove things. She was, in fact, a boy.

Cantiger obviously felt that he should break the silence, not least to disguise the sound of dripping. He clapped his hands and rubbed them vigorously together. "Well!" he said. "Well, well, well!"

This gambit, though common, is not Grandmaster stuff and rarely augurs victory. Or, indeed, an interesting game. Though mere pawns, albeit with green hair, the opposing pieces merely stared, unmoved.

Cantiger released the pony's rope. The pony sniffed at the rushes on the floor, sank heavily to its knees and rolled over on its side. "Now!" said Cantiger, stepping over its legs. "Cat! Great! Got a lot of cats around here, have you?"

The bald man looked up at the crone as if for permission to speak. "Some," he answered in a soft voice.

"Some. Good! Yes, lots of places have some, I find. And dumplings! And what do you do, my good man?"

"Many things," said the man.

"Many— Right! Great!" said Cantiger, increasingly desperate. "No, good! Me, I'm a magician. Cantiger's the name, sorcery's the game. Yes indeed. Spells, herbs, incantations, that sort of thing. Boring technical stuff. Base metal into gold, all that. Won't bore you with the details." He sat on the bench next to the green-haired boy.

The boy looked at the girl. She nodded. Both looked at the man. He nodded. He looked up at the crone. She stirred the pot and crooned.

"Come far, have yer?" she asked suddenly.

"Oh, yes. Yes, quite a way. I'm bound for Greatwen. And you guys?" he beamed at the young people. "I must say, I like the hair. Oh, not you, of course," he gulped as he turned to the man, "but the green. Great. You till the fields, I suppose? Ah, well, we can't all. Always admired the honest labour of the lowly Logrian peasant, me. Great."

"They um . . ." said the crone, walking over to the table. "I think I'll have my shilling now."

"Oh," said Cantiger, affronted at such haste, "all right." He reached into his pocket and withdrew the coin. The woman's mittened hand grasped it with the speed of a falcon binding to. "They— What were you about to say?"

"They um . . ." she snapped. "And sixpence for the pony."

"Shickshpthuth?" Cantiger spluttered. "You didn't say anything about sixpence!"

"It'll pay for the dripping."

"What?"

"I told you, clear as day, no dripping in this house. You're both doing it. Been doing it since you came in. Drip, drip, drip, non-stop. Look at you. Disgusting, I call it."

"Madam," Cantiger explained, "it haps us that we are wet."

"That's as may be, but there's no call to go dripping. Can't abide that sort of thing. Sixpence, or out you go."

"Too right out I go!" Cantiger decided outrage to be the only course. He stood and pointed. "Give me back my shilling and I will leave at once, thank you! There must be someone around here who is sane!"

The man winced as he considered this statement at some length. "I don't think so," he concluded.

"And what do you mean, 'They um'?" Cantiger demanded, "You are all barking mad!"

"You'll not get your shilling back. Not after all that dripping. Sixpence for the pony, or on your way."

"This is daylight robbery!" Cantiger squealed. "Give me back my money! And stop those children making that dreadful noise!"

"That's 'umming," said the man. "We did tell you."

Cantiger had to acknowledge the justice of this. The two green-haired youngsters were indeed humming. They were staring into one another's eyes and making a noise so vibrant, so even in pitch, so steadily and constantly swelling in volume and intensity that he would have supposed it to come from a tuning fork, many times amplified, or from a skilfully pummelled gong.

"And why are they humming?" he demanded, raising his hands to his ears.

He did not hear the woman's next remark, but he could read her outstretched hand and her thin lips. "Sixpence," she said. "Quickly."

The door banged open. The wind pounced in with a *woof* and snuffled in the corners. Snow pattered on the walls and floors. The woman's face fell. "Oh, drat," she said with a sigh, and turned away.

Cantiger turned. There was a clatter and a metallic glint but the view was obscured by the pony that, with a prolonged grunt, now scrabbled to its feet. It reversed towards Cantiger. Its strawberry-roan rump shoved him back against the bench. His coccyx hit the table. He yelped.

Then there were male faces glowering at him, gauntleted male hands grasping his forearms (Cantiger screamed this time), dull swords with glinting edges at his either side, and an interesting, if distorted stereoscopic view of himself silhouetted against the fire in two black breastplates.

"Cantiger, magician," said one of the Riders, spitting out the word "magician" in chunks which plainly tasted foul. "You are under arrest. Queen Marina would speak with you."

"Oh," said Cantiger. Then, "Oh, um." Then, warming to and finding variations upon his original theme, "Oh, um, Queen Marina. Right. Of course." He swallowed a large chunk of sharp-edged air. "Oh. Queen Marina of Hennamucus, would that be?"

"The same, matey," said the man. "She likes magicians."

"Well, I'm not really . . . Just, as you might say, a hobby . . ."

"Good ones, that is. Bad ones, or those who don't share their secrets, she does funny things with."

"Funny?" Cantiger's voice emerged strangely high-pitched.

"Yeah. *We* think they're funny, anyhow. Difficult, comedy. Subjective."

"Nothing more subjective, I always say."

"'S right. Like the one she turned into a gull, eh, Sadok?"

"Yeah," laughed the other man. "That was a good one, Ondslake. Laugh? We nigh passed around the agrimony pellets!"

"A gull . . ." Cantiger prompted.

"Yeah . . . yeah, listen to this – it's priceless. He was flying away across the cove, thinking he'd got off lightly . . ." Laughter became too much for the man. It dribbled from him, and he doubled up, wheezing.

"And she suddenly said . . ." Sadok burbled. "Oh, I can hear her right now. She suddenly said . . ."

"Oh, dear . . ." Ondslake honked. The tears were now streaming from his eyes and he clutched his belly. "She s-s-said, 'I seem . . .' Oh, God, it's just too good . . . !"

"Yeah. She said, 'Oh, dear, I seem to have forgotten

something!'" The two Riders were now leaning against one another for support as laughter shook their frames.

"And what had she forgotten?" asked Cantiger softly.

"And— No, be serious, no, wait, no, oh, God! And suddenly, woof!"

"Su-hu-huddenly . . ."

"Suddenly, a str—

"A string . . ."

"With a bloody great pianola . . ."

". . . piano-o-o . . .!"

". . . nola appeared attached to the gull's . . .'

". . .'s feet, 'n 'e plummeted . . ."

". . . lummeted! Gawd, his face!"

"His face! Oh, God! Wonderful! On to the rocks below. S-m-m-m-ashed to smithereens!"

This was altogether too much for the two men. They flapped their arms, then looked down at their feet with expressions of surprise, then they indicated falling with great movements of their arms, then they whooped and giggled and cried until they had to sit down.

Cantiger smiled and spoke faintly, "Very droll," he said. "What's a pianola?"

"Droll? Oh, she's droll all right, Queen Marina," Sadok nodded vigorously. "Laugh a minute! Then there was the one she turned into the bridge. He was a magician, wasn't he, Ondslake? Yeah. Thought so. Still get a giggle every time I ride across him, and it must be five years now . . ."

"Six, easy . . ." gasped the other.

"Flat on his back, mouth wide open and his hands fastened to one bank and his feet to the other, and him all stretched out, and every time we ride over him he always says the same thing!"

"S-s-sssame thing!" chorused his friend as laughter punched him again.

They mimicked, too, in falsetto chorus, " 'Thir Rider, fwee me fwom thith duranthe vile. Rathe off my head, I pwithee!'"

" 'What?' I always say. 'And lose a good bridge that costs us nothing?' Nah."

"Mind, he does cost us . . ." Ondslake pointed out.

"True. A raw ram's testicle and a handful of nettles every

time we pass, popped in his mouth to keep him on live. Fair toll, I always think . . ."

"Cheaper than some . . ."

"Dearer than some."

"My wife always says you can get across the Tarmac cheaper, but who wants to ride all the way down to Holegate? No, he's useful. That's Queen Marina for you. Thoughtful. Thinks of our needs. And funny."

"Oh, funny. That's for sure," Sadok panted. "More rusted gussets at Hennamucus than anywhere in Logris, I'll be bound. Anyhow," he announced with a deep sniff. "Yes. Can't stand here laughing. Work to do. Come along now, Mr Cantiger. No tricks. 'Least, not till we get there. Like a good trick, of course. We all do . . ."

"Yeah, but you do tricks on our way to the castle, we'll get nervous, see? And when we get nervous . . ."

"Well, it's training, isn't it?"

"Course it is, Sadok. Honed to it"

"Hew first, discuss it later."

Cantiger decided to show some interest. "Who's Hugh?" he asked.

Sadok frowned. "Who's who?"

"Hugh. Who's Hugh?"

Ondslake seemed mystified. "Hugh who?"

"I don't bloody know!" squealed Cantiger. "You said . . ."

"Now that's quite enough of that," said Sadok, suddenly stern. "Owl impersonations come under 'tricks' in my book. Don't you agree, Ondslake?"

Ondslake frowned. "I don't know. Haven't looked. I suppose if the book's in alphabetical order . . . It wasn't a very good owl."

"All the same," said Sadok firmly. "One more lark like that . . ."

"It was a bloody awful lark," said Ondslake.

" . . . and it'll be hew slash slash hew bye bye, Mister Magician. Got it?"

Cantiger had not only not got it, whatever it might be – he hadn't even grasped the dot on its "i". The conversation over the past minute had bemused him, but this final, stupendously intricate outburst was of a degree of incomprehensibility that caused him to look about him, just checking that the other constant laws of life – gravity, flames burning upward, people standing on feet and so on – were still in force. His jaw had dropped, which was a good thing.

Had he asked who Hugh / / Hugh Bye Bye was, Sadok might have got really shirty.

Cantiger had, of course, seen Riders before, usually from the vantage point of a ditch. He had seen them arriving at Iseult's, then riding away with their love philtres or whatever. This, however, was the first time that he had enjoyed dialogue with that lofty class of personages, and "enjoying" was not the word, nor, save in the very loosest sense, was "dialogue". If these two were representative, he found Riders intimidating, coarse and incomprehensible and wanted as little to do with them as possible.

"Ready, then?" asked Sadok. He picked up Cantiger's sack. "I'll take this. You take the pony," he ordered.

Cantiger took the pony's rein and followed Sadok to the door. He was aware of Ondslake close behind him, sword in hand.

"Thanks for the hum," called Sadok back into the hovel as the three men stepped out once more into the snow-plump street.

Cantiger might not have liked the company of Riders, but he would quite happily have stayed in that hovel, sharing their depressing reminiscences, sooner than take a step towards Hennamucus castle.

For it happed him that, after his spell at Iseult's, Cantiger knew somewhat of Queen Marina. And that what was anything but consoling.

It would take Cantiger some ten crunching, slithering minutes to reach the great gate of the castle, a full five minutes to be admitted and a further ten to reach the turret that clung to the outermost corner of the castle above the beetling cliffs, which again, just as the plummeting stone or person gratefully thought that it had reached terra firma, plunged rugged and ragged, but essentially sheer, to the sea.

Here ground level became a variable. When the tide was in, the dry, plummeting person or pianola hit the water, then sank three interesting, prawn-flicked, coelocanth-nuzzled fathoms or more, wet. When the tide was out, the journey still ended three fathoms down, but without the falsely reassuring interruption, and dry.

Let us take advantage of this brief lull in Cantiger's affairs, then, to study the very best of contemporary architecture. The entire building, you will note, speaks of its purpose, which is the preservation of the status quo. What is in should stay in. What is out should remain out.

To these ends, note the boldly innovative curtain wall,[20] stabbed with loopholes and buttressed by towers every hundred yards or so. Within that, a steep and rocky hill climbs to the mighty inner walls, on which life-size lead soldiers stand silhouetted against the sky. Within these again is the dairy – down there to the left – the stables, the mews, the armoury, the great hall and, above it, really quite delicately arcaded and surrounding a small garden, the solar. That big round tower thing in the middle with a door halfway up it is the keep, with the castle's plate and jewels and so on secreted not very secretly within. There are a lot of other granite buildings in there, all of them, once locked and defended, looking pretty much unassailable to the earthbound.

Our attention, however, does not acknowledge gravity. It should proceed apace to the turret at the outermost corner of the inner wall, which overhangs nothing save the rushing, hushing, crashing, rattling, thundering, lacy, silky sea, way, way below. For there is no curtain wall here. There is hardly need.

When Marina sent postcards to her friends, it was the small window in this turret that she marked with a little arrow and the legend, "My room", or, just occasionally, when she had been at the cooking-mead, "Li'l ol' me!"

After all the cold weather and rough living to which we have been subjected, this is really quite an agreeable surprise. Oriental rugs, a zebra skin on the divan, drapes of diaphonous lilac chiffon, a throbbing fire, a bowl of fruit, glittering goblets and ewers of gold . . . This is altogether more like it.[21]

[20]Absolutely characteristic post-Mankh.
[21]Whatever "it" may be; but, if this apartment was more like it, we like "it" quite a lot, and there's been precious little "it" so far . . .

The only problem is that Marina, inconsiderately, is not in her bower, so our attention must once more don its muffler and its nice woollen mittens and go hunting around this cold and creepy castle in search of her. Look at that picture on the wall. Tasteful, I call that. The way the line of the woman's arm is echoed in the stream of blood from the severed head, the way her smile finds a simulacrum in the curve of her scimitar. Lovely thing. We could always let our attention wander, or lie down in front of that fire, until tomorrow morning, say . . . ?

All right, all right. Yes, she is in the solar, which, of course, with its arcades of windows on either side, is freezing.[22]

It is a long room, a sort of gallery, with arched windows at regular intervals down to our right and our left. There is a key-pattern frieze up by the ceiling, and there are strange rectangular patterns in the polished stone floor. The moonlight makes them eerie. Statues line the wall, casting elongated shadows that shift and slide in the flickering lamplight.

There is humming going on here, too. It sings and rings in the vaults and the window frame before streaming, refined to a thin, silvery whine, out into the cold darkness.

Marina sits at a table, also of stone, in a shiny, satiny gown that looks to be dark green. Her hair has auburn lights and is scooped up, like before, into a net snood at the back of her head. Her complexion is still fair and unblemished. She is talking to herself. In front of her on the table there stands a large glass box in which there seem to be a lot of levels linked by ramps.

"He didn't," she is saying to no one. "Hey, that's amazing. What . . . ? With a rolling-pin . . . ? God, sounds uncomfortable, but he always was an oddball . . . No, well, I would have been there, darling, but I've been dashing about earning my crust, you know how it is . . . Yes, mostly boring old stones. There's been a positive rash of them at the moment – ginormous, some of them – popping out of the ground ruining perfectly good

[22]Whilst we're on the subject, how exactly do you get a job writing about "it" and things like it? Sultry damosels in the Bahamas, for example, with fewer scruples than clothes, and balmy nights redolent of frangipane, and lobster and champagne? They need their chroniclers, don't they? But oh, no. It's "bloodshed, terror and persistent discomfort in winter? I've got just the man for the job . . ."

fields, and, of course, I'm the only person who . . . Oh, it pays all right. The problem is storage. No, you can only have so many circles, and with the quantity we're getting at the moment . . . Sadok was up in Withershire the other day and he met and sort of slew some chap called The White Rider of the Black Down or some such thing . . . Oh, you knew him, did you? Nice chap? Well, these things happen. Anyhow, that's brought me a few hundred acres up near Swinesdown . . . Oh, is it nice? I haven't seen it. You didn't . . . On a tumulus called *what?* You're a very naughty girl. Anyhow, Sadok says there's some sort of fairy castle that would be perfect for stone-storage, which should help. What . . . ? Oh, I'll try, darling, I promise . . . Don't. It's too tempting . . . Well, just you tell him to leave his rolling-pin behind. Greatwen? Oh, I don't know. I might make it for the blitz, but I am terribly busy. Look, sorry. I must dash. Some funny magician has turned up in the village . . . and I've got to instruct the fleas before he arrives . . . What? Don't be silly. He'll probably turn out to be some useless little backwoods herbert . . . I will. Lovely. Right. No problem. Yes. OK. Byee. Yes. Byeee!"

She draws herself to her feet, says, "That's enough humming, thank you," and bends to her glass box.

The humming suddenly stops, and one of the naked statues bows low and scuttles to the door at the far end of the room.

Marina waits until he or she is gone, then places her lips to the glass box and softly murmurs, softly croons.

Cantiger's two companions were plainly suffering from that sense of emptiness that follows excessive laughter. They were silent now, and brooding. They shoved him, and tutted when he stumbled. He stumbled quite a lot.

They had tethered the pony at the foot of the stairs and now, after what seemed to Cantiger an endless climb, they came to a little door. Sadok opened it. Ondslake pushed Cantiger in.

"Ah," said Marina, and her voice rang in the ceiling, "the magician. Good." She emerged from the shadows, one long leg circling the other as she walked. "Always revere magicians round here, don't we, boys?"

" 'S right ma'am."

"And it wasn't a gull, Sadok. It was a puffin."

"Oh. Sorry."

She looked down on Cantiger. For a moment, curiosity flickered across her face. "Have I seen you somewhere before?"

"Oh, no. No, certainly not," Cantiger hastened to assure her. "That was someone else. I remember it clearly. Definitely someone else. You remember, don't you? Never been anywhere, done anything, me . . ."

"Cantiger . . . the name rings bells . . ."

"Oh, no. Never. Not even the slightest tintinabulation. Lowly stock. Maybe another Cantiger. Quite a few of us about."

Marina continued to frown. "Oh, well," she said at last. "Perhaps not. Very well, Sadok, Ondslake. If you will leave his effects and wait outside . . ."

The two Riders bowed as they withdrew. The door rattled shut behind them.

"Do sit down," said Marina, gesturing to a joined stool. "So, what discipline do you follow?"

"Um, I studied in, er, Little Logris," Cantiger improvized as he sat. "Deedong absurdist transcendentalism. Existence precedes essence, I always say, particularly in the case of vanilla, *quod erat demonstrandum*, *dodgy toe ergo shtumm* sort of thing, you know. You?"

Marina winced. "I was privileged to train under Dame Iseult of the White Hans at her academy of Loonis, before developing my own entirely novel methodology – pulvicovectoral telekinesis, I call it."

"Nice," said Cantiger.

"It is founded, you see, on the simple premise that smaller beings influence larger. So, for example, a man may master an elephant, yet will die in the service of a woman, whilst a woman will devote her best years to a small unappreciative child. This principle may profitably be extended *ad infinitum*. And what small companion do we all have – chickens, rats, bats, dogs, cats, men, women? Fleas."

"Indeed," said Cantiger sagely.

"So much of traditional magic is based on wishes," said Marina dreamily. "Wishes! Ha! The word is onomatopoeic. Wishes are soft and wistful. They barely stir the leaves on the trees. To work magic, you must want, crave, hunger, single-mindedly. Thus you can flatten forests. That's the trouble with humans. They seldom want properly. Oh, they'd like to be in the Bahamas, but they'd also like to be in the barmaid; they'd like to go to the ball, but they also quite fancy a night in, washing their hair; they'd like to have wealth beyond the dreams of avarice, but they'd also like to be loved. If they really really wanted anything, they could do magic alone . . ."

"Absolutely," said Cantiger, who tried really really wanting to be in the Bahamas right now, but the image of the barmaid kept getting in the way.

"Of course, this is commonplace stuff," Marina went on. "But I therefore reasoned that what was needed was a telepathically receptive and potent creature with an uncluttered mind. The flea is such a creature, and is famously easy to train. If, therefore, a Rider wants to do yucky things with a comely damosel, say, there is no longer a need for philtres or potions. I merely train a flea to want to move from the Rider to the damosel, and the flea will transmit this desire to other fleas and they in turn to the two humans, causing them to wish to be close to one another. Very simple."

"Self-evident," said Cantiger.

"These are my love fleas here . . ." She indicated one compartment of the glass box. "Equally, if a flea on a hen, say, very much wants to be on a fox, the hen can be prevailed upon to enter a fox's earth. With standing stones, which are always popping up everywhere these days, I merely work on the minds of moles and earthworms. These are my sarsen fleas here. Of course, I am only telling you this because you are going to die. So anyhow, that is how I am going to be made Queen of all Logris next week. Such fun. Neat, eh? Would you like a drink?"

"Fascinating," said Cantiger. Then, working backwards, "Yes, please. I mean, no, thank you. Queen of all . . . ? Did you say 'die'?"

"Hmm? Oh, yes. The beauty of fleas is that they operate upon the minds of their hosts almost imperceptibly . . ."

"When you say 'die' . . ." said Cantiger.

"As in 'dead' sort of thing. Yes. Of course, the lifespan of the average flea . . ."

"I'd really rather not," said Cantiger. "I mean . . ."

"'Well, you shouldn't go round pretending to be a magician, should you? And casting spells on my best friend. It's Not Sensible."

"Oh." Cantiger's mouth was suddenly very dry. "You heard."

"I hear everything, dear. It doesn't cost much to keep in touch. About two shillings a day for a skilled hummer, in fact Dame Iseult would never forgive me if I didn't kill you, you know. *Noblesse oblige* and all that. Sorry. Sure you wouldn't like a drink?"

Cantiger badly wanted a drink, but even more badly wanted not to be poisoned. "No, thank you. How did you . . . ? How am I going . . . ?"

"To die? Not that it makes much difference really. People do get fussed about the most ridiculous things, don't they? I mean, the end result is the same, isn't it? You never hear wormcasts shouting, 'Oy! It should have been the axe not the rack!' Now do you? But I think I will have to consult with Dame Iseult and my beloved Garnish about that. It should be something fairly deeply unpleasant, don't you think?"

"Um. Not really . . ."

"Oh, yes. People do have the funniest deaths here at Hennamucus, you know. One man-at-arms the other day stabbed himself in the back at the bottom of the garderobe, would you believe? Gross."

"Sounds it." Cantiger shuddered.

"It was the very same day that my dearly beloved daddy died of a flux . . ." Her voice quavered. She sniffed, and wiped a tear from her eye. "Sorry," she said at last. "Silly, sentimental girl. So, if you wouldn't mind waiting overnight in a dungeon . . ."

"Oh, no, no . . ."

"Then tomorrow morning we can attend to it. Make a bit of a show. The Riders always like that."

"Yes," said Cantiger, anxious to avoid giving offence, "I imagine they would."

"And I'm sure you'd like to give a little pleasure . . ."

Cantiger considered this. "Not a lot," he said at last.

"Sadie!" Marina called. "Ondy! Oh, good. Take this peculiar

little person down to the dungeon, would you? No need to mollycoddle him, but keep him on live till tomorrow, if you would."

"Not going to do the puffin thing again, are you?" grinned Sadok.

"No, no. Far too predictable," mused Marina. "And far, far too quick."

Cantiger was not a selfless soul. He was not one of those people whose misfortunes are diminished by the good cheer of all around. In fact, his view was that, if he must be miserable – and it appeared that this was a necessary condition of his existence – he would rather that everyone else suffered with him. He was companionable that way.

It offended him, therefore, to hear the raucous carousing of the Riders as he sat in a dungeon whose walls gleamed in the darkness with a ghastly phosphorescence. If he wanted to sit, it had to be on wet rock, with rats scuttling over his bare legs. The wetness too was suspect. It somehow did not have the fresh, invigorating aroma of the sea.

Although stimulus was in short supply, he had a great deal to think about. Dying, for example. He knew, of course, that a lot of people did it. He just thought it wrong that he should have to, and even wronger that it should be tomorrow. He resented the way that fate had treated him. He had never eaten the rowes of sturgeon, which sounded good, nor had ado with the nestling turtle-dove things that women kept in the front of their robes, which looked interesting. He felt that he should not have to die before those experiences had been attended to.

Cantiger had an acute sense of fairness, and he thought that it would be fair for anyone – everyone – else to die sooner than him. Everyone else had deserved it, but all that he had done was to try to persuade people that he was a great magician and then had a little accident with a tower and a girl's head whilst trying to borrow some spells. You didn't die for things like that. You should die for . . . being big and noisy, for example, or for having too much money, or having nestling turtle-dove things in the front of your robe and not showing them to magicians.

Everyone singing up there in the refectory should die, for

being cheerful and not thinking about Cantiger. That would be fair. They were cheerful, so they should do the dying. He was miserable, so he should live. Obvious, really. Simple justice. He could not see why the world could not see it.

Outrage, fury, resentment, envy – Cantiger entertained all of them that night, but none was sufficiently entertained to hang around for long. In the end, only self-pity proved to have real staying power. Cantiger sat huddled on the floor, trembling in the bitter cold, and he howled.

He very intensely and single-mindedly did not want tomorrow to come.

But that doesn't work with time.

It was tomorrow.

This is one of the most irritating sentences that I have ever read, let alone written.

It cannot have been tomorrow because tomorrow is, well, tomorrow, and cannot be in the past. On the other hand, it really was tomorrow. The one that Cantiger had wanted not to come.

But it did, as it daily does. Though tomorrow can't do anything daily. It is only tomorrow for twenty-four hours, then ceases to exist because it is today, then it becomes yesterday, the other day and finally, oh, ages ago. And I need a lie-down.

Anyhow, it was dawn on the morrow of the evening of the day before, as it is every day . . .

Oh, God. Excuse me.

Now.

The new day dawned. Well, of course it did. And what else can dawn except a day? "I say, darling, those new socks just dawned"? And how can an old day dawn? Only this is an old day, because it happened a few years ago now, but it was obviously new when it was actually dawning.

Someone must have an aspirin.

Look, Hennamucus Castle, Int. Morning. Right? And how come scriptwriters get paid so much?

"Morning, magician!" Sadok thumped on the door. "Big day, eh?"

Cantiger sobbed and keened.

"Cheer up! Should be good. I heard Queen Marina. They're

talking bulls and albatrosses. Or sea cucumbers. Wayhey! Or planting strangler-figs in your hair. Nice one, that. Or stuffing with live rats and spit-roasting, which we've seen before, but it's always good. You'll enjoy that. Or . . . Oh, well. Surprises are best, aren't they?"

Cantiger whimpered and drooled.

"Thing is, this is your big chance. Agony. That's what we want. No such thing as overacting when you're being tortured to death. You can really go for it, lad! Show some guts!"

Cantiger did not want to show any guts. He had always liked to keep them modestly covered. His whine trembled violently, like an airliner warming up in an earthquake.

"Good stuff," called Sadok "One hour to the half, mate. Break a leg!"

His footfalls rang and receded, ringing.

Cantiger sobbed violently. He did not like life much, but what was the alternative?

On serious reflection, he did not want to know.

Chapter Four

ORSON GASPED. "Now that," he breathed reverently, "is what I call a marvel!"

Many a visitor to Greatwen had had cause to stop and stare as did Orson, nor was the "Wow!" that emerged from his awestruck lips the first to echo in the niches in the Abbey's great west front.

The Abbey was merely an abbey – ankhiform, Mathic, with Early Gnomic additions and Thuringian coruscations and a great square tower designed by Waddle. It had taken, it was said, four hundred master masons and stone carvers, together with a further seven hundred dwarves named Snotbucket,[23] a total of forty-seven years to build it to the greater glory of the gods.

Buller had two very similar at home.

What Buller did not have, however, was a lawn like the one at which Orson gaped.

The grass was smooth and even as moleskin and green as emerald. At any time it would occasion comment. At present, in a city otherwise under a quilt of snow, it drew the eye more than ever.

Orson squatted to investigate the texture of the grass. He touched the fine fronds with the palm of his hand. At home, of course, there were meadows cropped by scythes, rabbits and geese, but they were nothing like this. This would make bowls boring . . .

"No, no, no, sir!" a cracked voice shrilled. "Oh, dearie me, no. Oh, absolutely no. Oh, veritably, positively no, sir, no!"

A little man with gleaming glasses and a splash of orange hair was bustling across the lawn as fast as he could. This was not

[23]It was a closed shop.

very fast, as his feet were fastened to things that looked like sticky[24] bats, wrapped in wool.

"You haven't injured it, have you?" The man nodded eagerly as he crouched to examine the turf. "You haven't occasioned irregularities?"

"I – I don't think so," said Orson.

"No. No, it's all right, thank Lugh." He looked up at Orson with wild but grateful eyes. "Oh, it's too much for me," he moaned. "The nervous strain of it all. With all these people around. I haven't slept a wink for six days and nights. Myself and Mrs Potter – that's my wife, if you don't mind, sir – have killed twenty-nine dogs, forty-eight cats and eight thousand, two hundred and thirty-two pigeons. And we're lifelong vegetarians. And then there are all these Riders and their corsages wandering around, all prodding, prodding, prodding. I mean, why prod? If you want a rough and scrubby patch of mud, fine, just walk all over it, prod away, but if you want a sward, a proper sward, look but do not touch."

"Absolutely," said Orson. "I am sorry."

"Sorries mend no broken blades," snapped the man, more from tetchy habit than anger.

Orson was always interested in skills that he did not possess. "So, you tend this lawn, do you?" he asked.

"I have that honour, young sir. Hector Potter, guardian of the sward. Man and boy, rolling, brushing, pricking, shaving, keeping the grass to seven twelfths of an inch height at a distribution of seven blades per square inch horizontal."

"Hard work," Orson observed.

"Aye," the man agreed, "but worth it. They get in your blood, do swards. Fascinating things. I had a plantain here once."

"No!"

"Aye. Exciting, that was. It was rooted out and executed at the Tower of Greatwen. We've had Bedwetters, too. And it's no good just cutting them down. You have to delve deep, find the very root of the root, take it far, far away and destroy it utterly. Delicate surgery. We don't want nature around here, thank you."

[24]"Sticky" or sphaeristica was a popular game played, we understand, with bats, a net, frilly knickers and a ball.

"Ah. No, indeed." Orson was familiar with the megalomania of gardeners back home. "Well, it's a remarkable achievement. Lovely thing."

"You running for overlord, are you, sir?"

"Me? No, no. Just a Pillier, me. No, it'll be some mighty Rider. I just hope it will be a wise one."

"Amen to that," breathed Potter. "No sign of a god-given trial yet?"

"No. Portents, of course, but nothing obvious. It looks as though it'll be decided by the Blitz next week."

"Unsatisfactory, that. Some great lummox'll win, and all the other Riders'll want to take him on all the time. What we need's a king who's strong and wise and kingly. And likes grass."

"Well, Mr Potter. Pray for it," Orson advised. "We're all praying for it. It's not going to be easy." He patted the little man's shoulder and went on his jaunty, shambling way.

Orson was a boy of the champaign and loved the champaign's pleasaunces and agremens – hunting, fishing, gardens, jolly wenches and decent eggs – but he had to admit that Greatwen was fun, particularly, as now, when it was *en fête*.

Riders and their entourages had come from all over the country. Exotically painted Riders had arrived from the northernmost points in Ochtieland, Brownie Riders from Gales and Little Logris, and great blond giants from Sotis. With them had come their wives and daughters, their pilliers, cooks, artisans and villeins. Some Riders, like Buller, had lodgings in the town. Others simply set up pavilions in squares or on commons. There were glorious silk pavilions, tasselled and tipped with gold, and simple pavilions of hide, but all kept their cooking pits filled and their spits turning, and ever made guests right welcome.

Marvel it was to see and meet the passing good Riders from distant lands, to see their fashions and to hear their songs, intriguing too to see the legendary stars, the Riders of whose prowess tales had spread far beyond their areas of influence. Lynch, Buller's younger brother and a marvellous good man of his hands, had spent some time with Orson and taught him a new trick with the short-sword. The flower of Riders and the hardiest man of arms on live, talking to him, Orson, as though they were equals!

And the girls!

The bare-breasted Ochtie girls, the wild-dancing Sotis girls with their gleaming green eyes and slender wrists and ankles, the foul-mouthed Greatwen girls who hitched their skirts at you and kept pace with your drinking . . .

Orson had a roving eye at the best of times, but in the last few days it had not so much roved as skittered, scurried, scampered like a demented gerbil over contours and crevices.

That, of course, was before last night.

Last night he had met Geneva.

Well, "met" was overstating the case, he admitted as he drifted back to the Golden Cow. "Seen" was nearer the mark. "Seen" and "been insulted by" answered the case to perfection. "Where I come from," she had said in that beautiful, ringing, terrifyingly grand voice, "pilliers sleep in the stables."

Orson cherished each beautifully modulated word.

She was beautiful. She had long golden hair like seaweed and perfect eyebrows and eyes the shape of Dover soles and a nose like – well, a perfect, slightly retroussé nose – and a mouth like a mousetrap made of wet rose petals, or sea urchins, and a neck like a – well, oyster flesh came into it somewhere. As for the rest of her, it did not exist. It was sacred. She had no baser functions, no glands or organs. She was an ethereal being, and anyone who insulted her by suggesting that she had legs or a bottom would jolly well pay for it.

Of course, Orson knew that she was a princess – her father was King Leo – whilst he was a mere pillier. His passion, therefore, was destined to be unrequited, and that was how he liked it. He longed to write odes that she would tear up, to lay roses at her feet, to lick the lace of her hem when she had thrown the gown away, to save her life at the expense of his own on a daily basis.

Well, he *was* very young . . .

Warhawk and his brothers rode into Greatwen that morning with sneers on their faces. They had been challenged six times on their journey south. On each occasion, the Rider-in-

73

question's last words had been of disapproval for their methods.

Well, what the brothers always said was, "We're riding off with a new suit of armour and a horse and some gold, and you are dead, minus a suit of armour and a horse and some gold, so who are you to criticize our methods? I mean, they *work,* don't they?"

The thing was, down here they were soft and went in for taradiddle. And if there was one thing they did not put up with in the Northern Isles, it was taradiddle – words and suchlike. Someone armed comes up to you and says, "Fair Rider, what be thy name?" You say, "Bog off," pull out your sword and cleave off a vital bit or two. Logic.

I mean, "Fair Rider . . ." What sort of talk is that? Next thing you knew, he'd be asking about who cut your hair, and who knew where that sort of thing would end?

It didn't bear thinking about.[25]

And then, when he'd done his poofy "Fair Rider" bit, and you'd done your "Bog off", he would say, "That is unRiderly said. I would have ado with thee," which did not mean, as in the Northern Isles, "Let's buy a few bottles and get slaughtered together," but, "Excuse me for a moment while I powder my nose and polish my lance so that I can try to kill you."

People had tried and tried to explain to the Riders of the Northern Isles that this was the right way of going about things. They didn't see it. Seemed to them, if someone was going to fight you, you should kill him before he had a chance, not prink about talking taradiddle.

Life was too short for taradiddle, said Warhawk.

And, to his enemies, at least, he proved it again and again.

"Blostoch bollom gurdlestock roggly turd," said Ger disdainfully as now they rode into the bustling streets of the capital.

"Now, now," said Warhawk. "Logrian subtitles please, and mind your language. We don't want trouble."

[25]An extraordinary phrase, much used at the time, which meant, in fact, that a specific brain would not bear the thought. Thoughts invariably bear thinking about without suffering the least strain.

"Why n[26]?" Ger puzzled.

"I can't remember . . . Oh, yes, because if we are going to rule the kingdom, people have to like us."

"Why? They don't like us at home."

"No, but that's different. At home we are the only Riders for five hundred miles around. Here there are loads of Riders of much worship and prowess and whatnot, and if they all got together against us, we'd probably get very tired. We might even get vanquished."

"Us? Vanquished???" Ger was incredulous. "In a bloggen morkpot, marran!"

"It can happen," said Warhawk sternly.

"Nah . . ." Ger spoke distractedly. His eyes were following a shapely damosel with a basket of prunes on her head. "Gor!" he growled. "Cop dem gullopy rouncers!" He drooled. Spittle slithered from the corner of his mouth. He spurred his horse forward.

"No, Ger!" Garech leaned over to grasp his reins. "We got to be civilized! We told you! No rouncers, however gullopy, unless you're invited."

"Ah, poo!" Ger's face fell. He pulled out his lobster. "Likes our rouncers, dun' us, Sparky? And prunes," he reflected, as the girl fell behind the Riders. "Oy! Am I allowed prunes?"

"Certainly," said Warhawk. "But you have to pay for them. With money."

Ger nodded. He had heard of this process. He turned his horse back. The others stopped and watched him apprehensively. He reached into his saddlebag and pulled out a pouch. He tipped twenty huge gold coins at the girl's feet. "That's money," he said. "Giss prunes."

"No force," quoth the girl. Her eyes sparkled. She handed over the entire basket. Right so in all haste she scrabbled in the street for the coins. " 'Ere," she panted up at Ger. "You're a real gentleman, you are." She forced the coins into the folds of her skirts and stood. "Wouldn't like to see me rouncers, would you? They're really lovely and gullopy today."

Ger's whiskers splashed and he grinned a ragged grin. This

[26]He almost certainly said "Why not?" but his horse snapped at the letters at its nose.

civilization lark was a doddle. Easy as 3.141592. Whatever that was.[27]

Cantiger was shoved into the Great Hall. Silence fell. Knives were laid down and kidneys left to cool on their trenchers. Men and women turned to watch the condemned man as he was led on to a stage at the end of the room.

"Er, don't mind me . . ." he murmured. They stared at him but spoke not a word.

"There's been some sort of mistake," he tried again. "I'm someone else, actually . . ."

"Silence!" ordered Marina from the head of the table. The vowels slapped at the barrel-vaults. The sibilants hissed around the walls.

"This will have to be quick," said Marina. "I have to go to Greatwen today. I have discussed this matter with Dame Iseult, whose tower you to-rove in sunder, destroying her spells, and my dearly beloved friend Garnish, whom you most foully transformed into the guise of a serpent . . ."

There was a murmur about the table. Cantiger thought that he detected some respect in the watching faces.

"They give it as their opinion that you are a treacherous, idle, deceitful, vainglorious toad, a cheat, a blight upon the kingdom and, Garnish says, a pangolin turd. In the light of this last, it has been resolved that you will die by putrefaction and the agency of insects. You will be taken from hence, stripped naked and fettered to the floor. You will be fed maggots and other larvae. You will daily be spread with scalding molten sugar and cattle slurry and slowly consumed from inside and out by a selection of ants, fleas, scorpions, bluebottles, wasps, hornets and other bugs. You will receive visitors. Garnish has declared her desire to see you in pain and to remove certain intimate appurtenances to your person, and my Riders will come daily to goad and kick you and feed you still more larvae."

"It's not fair!" Cantiger whined. "I hate insects!"

[27]They still taught this at schools, and it was proverbially easy. The only problem was, no one knew its significance any more. It had something to do with pies, but intensive research by piemakers had yet to bear fruit. Except plums.

"Good. Was that six words, Ondslake?"

Ondslake counted on his gauntleted fingers. "Seven, if you count the 's' in 'It's'."

"Very well. Seven buffets."

"OK," said Ondslake cheerfully. He spread his legs, formed a fist and slammed it into Cantiger's solar plexus. Cantiger tried to double up but found a fist in his way, rising fast. He tried to fall over backward then, but the fist hit his stomach again. So it went on until Ondslake stood back and he was at last free to fall to the floor, writhe and whine.

"Have you anything to say before sentence is carried out?" asked Marina.

Cantiger had indeed. He said, "Ow."

"Very well, gentlemen . . ."

At that moment, the wall of the Great Hall brast inward, showering the gathering with stones and glass. Marina was struck on the head by a block of granite, and Cantiger, despite his pain, had a remarkable experience of *déjà vu*.

Now turn we to the worm that had awoken with a groan at the farmstead and surveyed the remains of its meal. It had been a good meal, and there were few leftovers, but worms are never tidy eaters so there were a few scraps that it had quickly lapped up.

It had glanced regretfully around the hovel, vaguely hoping that a whole new family, preferably carrying a churn of clotted cream, might materialize. At last, recognizing the vanity of this hope, it had mentally shrugged non-existent shoulders, licked its maw in conceptual fashion and slithered once more into the open air.

Very little research has been done into the psychology of the laidly worm. We know, of course, that the species tends to be solitary and to inhabit damp, dark spots, venturing forth to seek a diet consisting almost exclusively of young human females. This, zoologists believe, is largely due to the worm's underdeveloped molars. The front fangs are, of course, curved and sharp, but the grinding back teeth are squat, blunt and peculiarly prone to cavities. The lack of fur, the softer, less fibrous flesh and more frangible bone of the juvenile human female, requiring less mastication, are thus perfectly adapted to the worm's natural requirements, and the subcutaneous fat helps the meat to slip more readily down the giant gullet.

Nature knows what she is doing.

This particular specimen had eaten largely and, whilst the damosel had been easily digested and the worm's long rest had seen the smallholder and his wife largely broken down by the stomach acids, the sheep, which had been swallowed all but whole, lay heavy in the poor creature's stomach. The beast had burped repeatedly as it slithered across the snow-covered heath towards its home beneath Hennamucus. Indigestion undoubtedly contributed to its irascible mood.

Then, too, worms' longsight is poor, and various rationalists have tried to argue that the worm that morning simply lost its way. Research, however, has shown that, by scent or magnetic guidance, laidly worms can find their way back to their lairs over more than one hundred miles, so this thesis simply will not stand up.

I think that we have to accept that Cantiger's distress communicated itself to the creature that owed him its very existence. This is far from unprecedented. Five years ago, in a well-recorded incident, an Ochtie wizard was rescued from his wife by an Arctic Tern that he had conjured mere days before, whilst no one, I think, needs reminding of the sensational, accredited story of Princess Helge of the Dournochs, the sea lion and the cucumber.

However that may be, the worm brast into the Great Hall and set about it with a will.

The trouble with being a damosel-eater is, of course, that you usually have to get past several indigestible men in order to get at your meal. Several Riders were that morning crushed or slashed by the worm's fangs before it found its first damosel, which it gulped down swiftly, increasingly irritated by the sometimes really quite uncomfortable blows of swords on its hide and by the screaming and shouting all around. It lashed its great tail, and men went flying.

The worm found a trencher full of kidneys and absently ate that before sniffing another damosel and setting off in pursuit.

Cantiger looked up to see a giant pink, gleaming creature

with savage fangs and disgusting breath heading straight for him. "You'd think just once I might get a lucky break!" he complained as he ran towards the nearest door. "Oh, no. Vicious women, beastly men, dirty great worms . . ." He slammed the door behind him. There was still a lot of screaming in the room behind.

He found himself in a stairwell, and was about to run downwards when he heard the tramp of footfalls heading upwards at the double. He turned and bounded upwards taking the steps two at a time. He could not afford to be seen in these parts. His face was already too well known.

He staggered into the solar. His sack still lay on the flags. He snatched it up and ran towards the other end of the room where, he knew, there was another tower and another staircase. As he careered past Marina's glass case, he stopped. He grinned. He reached into his sack for the hard black Thing that he had found in the ruins of Iseult's tower. He swung it. The glass shattered with a satisfying smash. Cantiger leaned in and scooped out vegetation and, he assumed, fleas, which he threw into his sack.

He took a couple of handfuls from each section, picked up the long black Thing with the wiggly bit and, holding the neck of the sack tightly closed, ran on.

He hurtled down the stairs, bouncing off the walls, and emerged in the cold, clean fresh air. For a moment he could make out nothing as his eyes accustomed themselves to the dazzling brilliance of the snow. Then he saw the pony.

Cantiger had never ridden in his life, but the worm had plainly satisfied its hunger and was nosing out through the far wall of the Great Hall. At the moment, the milling people over there were concerned only with not being eaten, but once the worm had gone, they were likely to remember what they had been doing when it arrived.

Cantiger untied the pony, pulled himself over its back and somehow slithered into something like a sitting position. He swung the lead rope to hit the animal's rump, then, in some surprise, lay down on his back as the beast spurted forward. "Ohdearohdearohdear," he keened.

"The corpulent porcupine ate my auntie's nightie, didn't it?"

said Marina. "Who's the fat fellow with the yellow toes? Take him hence and thrust a pineapple up him. Noses should not be lit after dusk. It disturbs the pigs. See to it."

"Yes, ma'am," said Sadok. He glanced quickly up at Ondslake, then back at Marina's bandaged head. "You just relax now."

"Garnish has a long forked tongue," she drooled, and giggled. "The dog said nothing, you will note. Look! There is an unclothed nostril! Do I have to attend to everything? No, Daddy! It wasn't my fault! It disagreed with you! Cut off its head. Blood steams, streams, splashes, plashes. The whinny shall prick thee tae the bare bane. How should I love, and I so young? The maidens came . . . The lily, the rose, the rose I lay . . ." She sat up suddenly and pointed. "There shall be no pollen on the sweet and sticky pudding. Enact it now!"

"It shall be done, ma'am. Please rest," Sadok soothed.

He stood and walked side by side with Ondslake to the window. "She cannot go to Greatwen like this," he murmured.

"I know, and the stone is already on its way."

"How long will this condition last?"

Ondslake shrugged. "Who knows? You know how it is with head injuries. A week? Two?"

"But the trial will be over and done with!"

"Not if no one can move it, and no one else can."

"But they won't wait indefinitely. They'll resolve it by Blitz, whatever the stone says, and all our plans will be ruined!"

"Iseult," said Ondslake. "We must get her. If anyone can get her thinking straight again, it's the old woman. Send for her now."

"Yes. OK. And the daughter. I'll ride up to Greatwen with the chosen ten and make sure that everyone knows about the stone!"

"What happened to that villein, by the way? The one who was to be executed?"

"Dunno. I think he was eaten," said Sadok. "Little runt vanished, anyhow, and good riddance."

"I wonder . . ." Ondslake mused.

"What?"

"Could he have been cleverer than we thought? He's at

Iseult's, the building falls down. He comes here, the Great Hall is demolished. You don't think . . . ? Nah. He was just a berk, wasn't he?"

"A total berk," said Sadok. "We've got bigger things to worry about than him. Like I want to be Lord Chancellor and you want to be Seneschal. Let's get going."

"Oh, God!" shrieked Marina, plainly in distress. "The melon gnashes, the oyster bites, the fig burns! I have a gentle cock, and I really haven't seen Paulie in ages!"

Sadok paused on his way to the door. "Paulie?" he winced. "Who the */$@? is Paulie?"

Cantiger retrieved his cart and went a soft amble along the coast. At the Bede's Haven, he sought out the Bede on Chapel Rock and passed a noisy night amidst the breakers, sustained only by raw mussels, samphire and a crock of mead.

From Bardanstapol, he struck westward into Dumnium, wisely skirting the Waste Lands, and so, within the week, came to the Land of Summer.

Which was where the trouble started.

The previous night, Cantiger had for the first time failed to find a refuge. First he tried to terrify a farmer's wife into taking him in by posing as a mighty magician and threatening to change her into a pig. She chased him with a pitchfork. Her dog chased him unarmed, and bit his left buttock.

He then lost his way.

The Land of Summer was so called because its levels were deep, treacherous swamps that dried out only in the summer months. The paths through these bogs were narrow and, as darkness fell and mist closed in, increasingly deceptive. Cantiger dared proceed no further. He therefore hobbled the pony and climbed into the back of the trap.

The night was cold, the moon a mere white thumb-smudge behind the shifting veils of mist. There were many sounds – strange squeakings and creakings, cracklings and shrillings from close at hand, sudden thuddings, barkings and howlings from further afield. And then the light-show began. At first there was merely a throbbing phosphorescent flush about the sparkling grass and reeds, but soon the flickering started.

Tongues of purple and pink licked at the marshes. The whole swamp seemed to seethe and rustle.

Cantiger was, as has been stated, a coward, but few on this occasion could blame him for passing most of the night sleepless and shaking. He had been reared in the hills of South Gales and, although he was to conjure many such effects in order to scare others in years to come, he had no experience of Jack o' Lantern and was convinced that these were sprites sent by Iseult to torment him before closing in and consuming him in a sheet of flame.

Slowly, however, the light of dawn suffused the mist, and creatures of the light began to scurry about the cart's wheels. As soon as he could make out the path ahead of him, Cantiger untied the pony's legs, once more climbed into the driver's seat and clicked the animal on.

Many were the illusions on that milky, misty morning. The gnarled willows of the bog seemed grotesque giants or assailants awaiting Cantiger's coming, and often he was upon them before they loomed from the fog.

Once he was certain that he saw a man hanging from a gibbet not six feet from him. A second glance showed that it was in fact a man hanging from a gibbet not *four* feet from him. He started.

More than once he heard the murmur of conspirators hard by his path, beneath the plashing of the hooves. Once some giant creature lumbered, puffing with every stride, across the winding causeway, and vanished, crashing and splashing in the reeds and the mire.

When Cantiger set out, he eyed the shadows ahead with apprehension. Within an hour, he had become accustomed to breathing a sigh of relief as they revealed themselves to be mere trees or timbers. When, therefore, a great helm-shaped island loomed out of the white mists and marshes at his left, he dismissed it as another illusion. As for the towering dark figure up ahead, that, he was confident, would prove to be a blasted tree above a bush.

He drew nearer. The blasted tree seemed to move but that, no doubt, was the effect of a stray wind. Once, the bush snorted, but that would be the creaking as the sun's paltry heat penetrated the timber. Suddenly the trunk of the blasted tree toppled. All that remained was the bush beneath, which looked remarkably like a large man upon a horse.

"Well, well," said the bush. This caused Cantiger to jump. This caused Cantiger to land. This caused Cantiger to howl and writhe. By the time that he had completed this manoeuvre, a lance tip was no more than a foot from his nose.

"Hello," stammered Cantiger. "Nice day. *Dies irae, dies illa, policarpus in capilla,* what I always say."

"And what sort of lower-than-human life form be this?" sneered the bush, now clearly visible as a Rider clad all in black. He had raised his visor. Cantiger could make out a face that was mostly beard and eyebrows.

"Please, Boss," said Cantiger in his most unguent tones – and Yardley could not do unguent like Cantiger could – "I am, um . . ." He briefly considered tinker, tailor, leech or holy man, but settled instead for ". . . a poor man."

"No doubt," the Rider bellowed. "And or ye quit these marches, methinketh ye shall be poorer. An 'e be Rider, none may pass this way but 'e mun' joust with me. An 'e be churl, 'e mun' yield unto me his chattels. Or," he said as an afterthought, "'is feet."

"His . . . feet," echoed Cantiger. Briefly, he thought about taking the basilisk from his pocket. But he no longer had his glasses, and basilisks, as offensive weapons, have disadvantages. They can, for example, backfire by turning to look at their bearers. Cantiger decided to strike up a friendly conversation instead. "Any particular reason why feet?"

"Not really." The Rider shrugged. "I just likes feet, I reckon. We all on us 'as our little gimmicks, see. Boss Bruce Sans Pitie – that's me – 'im's the foot man. Ask anyone. An' – I dunno – people usually seems to want to keep un's feet."

"Yes, I can see that." Cantiger nodded intelligently. "Well, jolly good. Very interesting. I'll be seeing you, then . . ."

"Hold!" roared the Rider. The lance tip prodded Cantiger's chest. "Yield unto us thy chattels, churl!"

"Ah, yes. Sorry. Forgot. Chattels. Certainly. Silly of me." He picked up the sack at his feet. "Here we are. Chattels. Definite chattels."

Bruce spurred his horse forward so that Cantiger sat between the lance and his person. That person smelled strongly of stagnant water and fish. He reached across to take the sack, and, propping the lance in its rest, peered in. "What be this? Parchment? No use for parchment. Think I'll tek the feet. More use in a foot. Oh. Arr. That be more sib!" He pulled out the gold chalice. "Ah, yes. Gold! Splendid! Did 'ee steal it?"

"Oh, no," Cantiger assured him, "I was . . . left it."

"Good. Us dun' like thieves. Well, very nice. Grand. Please keep ee's feet."

"Thank you," said Cantiger.

"Don't mention it." Boss. Bruce leaned forward and frowned down at Cantiger's feet. "'Ere!" he said. "What be yon thingy?"

"Er . . ." Cantiger picked up the black Thing. "I'm not sure, actually. It has a sort of waggly bit here, and a hole at one end, and . . ."

Cantiger was never quite sure what happened next.

The Thing bucked violently in his hands, striking him a great blow on the breastbone and flinging him backward into the cart.

A moment later, there was a report like the sound of a thunderbolt in an empty granite well. It rang and rippled through the marshes, and was followed by the flapping of a thousand birds as they took fright and flight in rapid succession.

Equally simultaneously, both Cantiger's pony and Boss Bruce's horse reared and squealed, whilst, with similarly admirable co-ordination, Cantiger crossed and wet himself. He then lay for a full three minutes in a foetal position on the cart, groaning and trembling as he recalled and repented all his sins, which took far less time than he would have liked.

Somewhere, a horse's hooves puddered and splashed until its footfalls faded into silence.

Suddenly, Cantiger was aware of writing on the terrible, magical Thing where it lay at his side. It was faint and worn, but Cantiger was able to make out an "X", a dash, and the letters: "C-A-L-I-B-R-E".

At last, Cantiger raised himself on to his forearms and peered out over the marshes. To his surprise, not much appeared to have changed. The sky was a little brighter, the mist a little clearer, but earth was still beneath and sky, apparently, above.

The pony was fretful, but the brake on the cart had held, and Boss Bruce and his horse were gone.

Or at least, the horse was gone.

As Cantiger's ears stopped singing, they registered a grievous groaning from near at hand and, clambering back on to the driver's seat, he espied a gleaming armoured leg amidst the rushes.

"Er, is that you, Boss Bruce?" asked Cantiger cautiously.

"Ooooh," moaned the leg. "Arr. Ooh. By Lugh, but that was a mighty blow. Us din' even see un' comin'. Ooh. 'Urt us full sore, that did. Marvel it was to see. Proud to be felled by a blow like that. Good man. Never did lance or foyne of sword give us so great a stroke. I be all forbled, so I be."

"Yes, well, that's what comes of robbing people," said Cantiger smugly. He climbed down, attended to pressing matters of personal hygiene, then – nervously, for fear of tricks – approached the prostrate Rider. "Disgraceful, I call it."

"Ah, yon's just a bit of fun," creaked Boss Bruce. "No 'arm meant. Man's got to live, 'a'n'e?"

Cantiger plucked up his sack very swiftly and stood over his vanquished foe. "Well, I don't like it," he announced.

"That me repenteth," Boss Bruce panted, "for I am come to mine end an this wound be not staunched."

"Nonsense," said Cantiger. He squatted down and studied the clean hole in the Rider's breastplate. Blood bubbled up through the black steel just inches above the heart. "On the other hand . . . Trouble is, I'm not much good at staunching wounds."

"There is a hermit," gasped Bruce as a paroxysm shook him, "on yon island of Glass, hight Avalon, which is the Isle of the Dead. Bear us thither, for 'im be a great leech and will make us 'ole if any can."

"Hmm," Cantiger considered. Then, "And what's in it for me?"

"Forty pound, and a fine palfry, and safe conduct wheresomever thour't bound."

"And a coat of silk," said Cantiger, who had been doing some dreaming *en route*.

"All right!" Bruce winced and hissed.

"And a pointy hat?"

"Yes! Yes!"

"And two geese and a cat for dinner?"

"Dollops, collops!"

"And woolly socks?"

"Yes!" Bruce groaned. "And as many feet as 'ee likes!"

The deal was done

So it was that Cantiger dragged Bruce Sans Pitie into his cart and thence on to a boat moored nearby, and rowed in several circles, and thence to the Isle of Glass in the Land of Summer, and there he abode four days until Boss Bruce was made whole.

If there is one thing that nature is not, it is organic.

It rests for long whiles, then jumps.

And sarsen stones, for millennia buried beneath the earth, suddenly decide, like shrapnel working its way over decades out of the flesh, to emerge and stand proud.

No one, then, should have been surprised when Greatwen was awoken by the shrieking of Hector Potter, but everyone was. That too seems to be nature.

"The sward!" he shrieked. "My lawn! There's a dirty big stone in the middle! It's destroyed! Ruined! Desecrated! Violated! Buggered altogether!"

So Riders, Ladies and Pilliers, Men-at-Arms and Villeins dragged themselves out to the Sward to study this latest marvel.

And there was, indeed, a giant, almost triangular standing stone.

It was not until the next morning that someone noticed the inscription at its base: *"Whoso removeth this stone from this patch of grass is rightwise king or queen od - sod it - of - Logris"*.

"My lawn!" sobbed Potter. "My lovely, lovely sward! All that work! Mrs Potter will need palpating! Get that stone off my lawn! At once!"

But the greatest Riders and men of most might in the world looked at the huge chunk of rock and simply sighed.

Cantiger quite enjoyed the rest of his journey. He had a grandstand view of Logris and of several interesting encounters, yet was put to no danger or discomfort. Boss Bruce and his brother Boss Bertelot, who had to be in Greatwen for the trial anyway, saw off a band of brigands near the escarpment of the downs, a small but decidedly unfriendly worm that emerged from a cave near Weland's Bourne, a hesitant lioness on Swinesdown and one Rider who had no interest in Cantiger but merely saw it as his duty, or, at least, essential to his *amour propre,* to try his strength against the interloper Riders.

The brigands were a doddle. Although there were thirteen of them, they had about as much chance of penetrating a Rider's carapace as would a pack of wolves of storming a tank. The two Riders shrugged off this futile assault with characteristic roars and guffaws, and Cantiger watched, admiring, as they hewed a few dispensable extremities from the unwise bandits.

Cantiger knew nothing about fighting, but Boss Bruce, having been bested by him, regarded him with awe and timorously sought his approval. "Ye knows yon foyne which made the blood to brast from the green churl's shoulder?" Boss Bruce asked as he fell in beside the cart again.

"Um . . . er . . . Oh, yes. Fine foyne. Never saw a foyner fine – I mean, finer foyne," said Cantiger.

"But methinks mayhap us should 'ave smote 'im a buffet . . . ?"

"Oh, no, no. I don't think so. Just the moment to foyne, I reckon."

"'Ee really thinks so?"

"Absolutely," Cantiger assured him, without the slightest idea what he was talking about.

"Did 'ee ever 'ave ado with a lion?" Rider Bertelot enquired later as he and his brother rode back to Cantiger, having pursued the beast into the forest.

"Oh," said Cantiger airily, "I've dealt with a few. By magic, of course."

"Of course," Bruce said approvingly. "An we meet another, us'd like to see yon. Us'll let you kill 'un."

"Oh, no. Honestly. No, really," Cantiger said quickly. "No, I like to see you doing your crude deeds of arms. Honestly. So quaint, you know. And I took an oath to my dying grandmother that I would never use my magic thunderbolts save in direst need . . . on Thursdays . . . in the morning."

Bruce considered this gravely. "Fair enough," he concluded.

And so they came through an endless foaming sea of rustling, snow-laden trees to Sludge. Here, on the banks of the river, they found a shield of green and white chevrons slung on the lowest branch of a great oak that overhung their path. Beyond the shield, in a glade, a horse stood cropping grass beside a pavilion of pine fronds covered with hides, surmounted by a green and white pennant.

"Yonder is one'll joust," said Bertelot, a giant, shaggy man with a bulbous purple nose, "Wilt dress 'ee to 'un, brother?"

Bruce Sans Pitie shrugged. "As 'ee wills, Bertelot, but I have but lately suffered a grievous hurt, and would liefer as 'ee tookst the honour."

"So be it," said Bertelot, and spat into the snow before drawing his sword, standing in the stirrups and striking the shield a mighty blow with the pommel.

The men waited.

The wind swooped and scurried amongst the trees. Some ducks on the river thrashed, honking, into the air.

There was movement up at the pavilion now. The pine branches stirred. The hides bulged. There was some clanking.

At last one of the hides arose, and a dwarf dressed in grey and blue plaid knee-breeches and cross-gaitered woollen puttees stepped briskly across the snowy bank.

"Fair Rider," he addressed himself to Bertelot. "Why smote ye down my master's shield?"

"For I would joust with 'im," announced Bertelot sturdily.

"It is well said," pronounced the dwarf, "for there may no Rider ride this way but if he joust with my master. Dress thee then, fair Rider, and save thee. Haven't got a fag, have you?"

Bertelot shook his head. The dwarf strode very busily back to the tent.

Bertelot now concerned himself with preparation for the fight.

He had Cantiger's cart removed from the woodland track. His pillier checked the fastenings of Bertelot's armour, then dismounted to tighten the courser's girth and to cram the hooves with butter to prevent balling snow. He fetched Bertelot's shield – a bend argent on a field sable – and handed it up to him. Bertelot slung it around his neck. No sooner had he done so than the Rider of the pavilion stepped out, armed at all points. His armour was burnished to a bright silver, and he wore a crest of feathers upon his helm. His dwarf and his pillier helped him on to his mounting block and thence into the saddle.

All this time, Bertelot's pillier watched and murmured. "A big Rider and well bisene," he said to his master, "and well breathed, I'll be bound. That crest might prove his downfall an you can hit it, squire, and his courser will be cold while yours is hot-sinewed. Ah," he said as the Rider took a spear from his pillier. "The great spear. Same for you, squire?"

"Ay," said Bertelot, "and stop calling me 'squire'. It confuses me."

The pillier ran back to his own horse and, from a selection of four lances slung from his saddle, he withdrew the longest. He handed it up to his master, who raised it aloft as boatmen ship oars. "Good luck, mate," whispered the pillier.

"Slaughter 'un," urged Bruce simply. "Kick 'un. Lay yon bugger low."

Bruce and the pillier retired amongst the trees and hoved under the wood shaw whilst Bertelot spurred his horse forward until the two horses' heads were just six feet apart. "So, Rider," he bellowed, "what be tha' name?"

"As for that," said the other smoothly, "I will be avised, for that me concerneth."

"That be discourteous said," bawled Bertelot. "Then save 'ee, for I will 'ave ado with 'ee."

With that, he wheeled his horse and set it to go a gentle hack-canter some two hundred yards back along the track. The other Rider also withdrew a fair distance, though not so far as Bertelot. There was a moment's silence then as each turned to face the other, save for the jingling of harness and the snorting of the horses as the spears descended and were lodged in their fewters, the leather-lined pouches behind each Rider's right arm. Then both Riders leaned forward, and clicked on.

This jousting business served many purposes, and was performed with widely varying degrees of seriousness and passion. It was sport, of course, and a means at once of practising the skills of war and, as it were, establishing precedence within the league of warriors.

As with all contact sports, however, there was an element of risk. A Rider might be struck an unhappy stroke on some unarmoured part of his body, or the point of the spear might pierce the helm and break his neck as he fell.

Then, again as with all contact sports, there was always the risk that tempers would be lost and a friendly joust turn into a deadly battle. In general, however, such encounters as these were similar to modern steeplechases in their ferocity and their element of risk.

At times, however, jousting was an altogether graver business. A discourteous Rider might dress against a young greenhorn or a wounded opponent, in which case it was little short of legal murder.

Then there were Riders who sought to claim a patch of land, perhaps with a few villages attached, for themselves. Such lands would provide them with wealth, wives and position, but such a Rider had to continue to fight to keep such holdings against belligerent neighbours and passers-by. A beaten Rider who yielded to another had to yield too his lands, his followers and his rents, and hold them, if at all, only by the grace and under the patronage of the victor, or become a Rider errant once more. So a strong and doughty man might rapidly expand his estates and his power, until all travellers would pay a toll or skirt his lands sooner than meet with him. Until another hungry young Rider came along.

Then, of course, there were the most serious jousts of all: those in which a woman's honour or that of the Rider depended upon his prowess, or, almost as grave – almost synonymous – those in which a woman's life or that of the Rider hung in the balance. There mercy was neither given nor accepted, for a clean death in the open air, with some worship, was preferable by far to a shameful one in a stinking prison or by fire.

This afternoon's meeting, then, was at the lower end of the scale – the fencing bout rather than the duel or the grudge match.

It did not look so to Cantiger.

Both horses started slowly, but their Riders spurred and chivvied, and soon the combined weight of horse and Rider gave impulsion, so that, as with a charging bull or a wild pig, no deviation was possible without a tumble, and to check were to slide forward on the horse's knees and, perhaps, to break the necks of both horse and Rider. With every stride, the saddles creaked and the horses puffed steam from their nostrils with a sound like cymbals clashing.

Bertelot aimed, quite properly, at the body – or, rather, the shield – of his opponent, but a great spear is, at the best of times, an unwieldy article, and it wavers a bit on the back of a walloping horse. The Rider of the silver armour and the green-and-white shield seemed, to Cantiger's untutored eye, to possess greater strength and balance than his opponent.

The two Riders' feet thrust downward in the stirrups. The men lunged forward. Bertelot yelled, "Ha!"

They met. If that was the word.

With a disappointingly dull "clunk", the stranger Rider's lance hit Bertelot's shield and slewed him round in the saddle. Bertelot said, "Woof!" A split second later, his lance tip slammed into his opponent's shield head on, bearing the stranger Rider backward over his mount's croup. His gauntleted hands on the reins and the sudden shifting of his weight caused the horse to slither back on to its hocks, then, with a grunt, on to its rump. The Rider toppled backward and, with a great clanking, fell into the snow. He said, "Unngh!" then, "Whoops!" then, "Sod it!"

Bertelot, meanwhile, though hanging at an alarming angle, was still on his wheeling, snorting mount. He regained the saddle, shouted, "Ha ha!" and, before the other Rider had a chance to attain his feet again, spurred his horse over his prostrate foe.

"Er, isn't that unRiderly done?" asked Cantiger, a little nervously.

"Ha!" yelled Bruce, whose family's vocabulary was limited. "Serves 'un right!"

"Yes, but shouldn't Bertelot be, um, lightly avoiding his horse and drawing his sword sort of thing?"

"Nay," scoffed Bruce as his brother, seeing the fallen Rider pull himself up on to his elbows, once more rode him down. "An 'e do that, 'e may be put to the worse. Silly, new-fangled notions. I dunno. Get a man down, do 'un, says I."

"Oh," said Cantiger. He ruefully admitted the practicality of this philosophy.

"'Ere!" Bruce hollered to the other Rider's pillier, "what be thy maister's name?"

The pillier, eyeing his master with some concern and Boss Bertelot with some disapproval, stammered, "Would you mind asking yon Rider to stop that, Boss? It's not nice. It's nasty. It's . . ."

"What be 'is name, lad?" bawled Bruce.

"Um, King Skinner. Please don't do that."

"King, be 'e?" Bertelot giggled as his horse once more struck and trampled the fallen man. "Ooh. Pardon me, Your Majesty. Was that thy royal bonce? Shame. My brother might want tha' feet. 'Im's funny that way. Want 'is feet, Brucey? Got any kings' feet, 'ave 'e?"

"Oh, one or two," Bruce acknowledged as he rode forward. "Better specimens nor 'ese 'uns. Nah. Leave 'un be. 'Im's proper stonied, and 'ese 'ere beggars nigh Greatwen 'as all sorts o' fancy friends. Honour. Worship. All that guff. Mind, some on 'em can smite a bit. Shew 'un mercy. Be bountiful, brother."

"Oh, bountiful, is it?" said Bertelot as he continued pensively to dent his foe. He raised his own visor. His nose was by now a detailed map of an area thickly netted with arterial roads. Sweat trickled down its wings. Pendulums of snot swung from his nostrils. He wiped them off on his gauntlet, and said, "Ow! I's always doing that!" before resuming his musings. "Bountiful. I dunno. What's wrong with yon 'ere modern Riders? Bountiful – bah! Never 'ad a belly full o' bounty keep us warm of a nasty night."

"Like Pitie, bain't it?" Bruce guffawed. "Never 'ad no Pitie mysen'. 'S why they calls me Sans Pitie, see? On account of I ain't got none, 'sans' bein' the word for not 'avin' none, in Sussex and 'em Deedong parts. Never knew what Pitie was, truth to tell, but I never 'ad none, nor never missed 'un." He rode over King Skinner a couple of times himself. It seemed to aid thought. At last, he hit his brother a fierce, friendly blow. "All the same. This Skinner guy might 'ave some clout. Let's be goin', bruv."

"Arr." Rider Bertelot pulled himself upright. "Not a lot o' clout down there. Still. Bountiful, me, today. Oi! You! Wizard! We'm off!"

"What?" Cantiger started, then smiled as the word "wizard"' permeated his skull. "Oh, right. Yes. Absolutely."

And so the two Riders and their pilliers again flanked Cantiger on his cart as they rode from the glade where Skinner's pillier and his dwarf kneeled over their fallen master, fanning his brow.

And so, in time, they came syker and sure unto Greatwen town.

Chapter Five

NOW TURN we again.

"He is on live!" declared Iseult. She looked up from the multifaceted, ice-crystal model of a dragonfly's eye and pushed back the yellow builder's helmet in order to slap her brow. "The foul creature is on live and in Greatwen! How can so pestilent a creature live? Everyone wants to eradicate him. At first sight, he inspires a natural urge to disembowel that increases with every subsequent encounter, yet no one seems competent to do it! He cannot fight! He has no brains! He is a craven coward! Yet he has riven two great castles in sunder and thwarted two of the sorceresses of most might in the world. He is against the rules."

"Is that America or a mosquito?" puzzled Marina, peering from the battlements towards the sea. "It buzzes."

"It's all right, darling." Garnish stroked her friend's forearm. "Oh, I do hope the lotion works. No, he must die, Mama. Look what he has done to me, to Marina, to all of us."

"And I don't like the way he's got himself up to Greatwen," mused Ondslake. "Queen Marina should have been Queen of all Logris by now, but with that brute up there and Marina down here, anything could happen."

"Yes," said Iseult. "He must be stopped. Oh, woe, alackaday and buggery. I have so few spells left . . ."

"What about the rabies one?"

"Mmmyes, yes, I'll do that, and we can conjure some ectoplasmic assassins, and we could visit an attack of birds – always effective – and maybe a wild boar, and of course the usual curses, though at this distance there are no guarantees. Once we are actually in Greatwen, of course . . ."

"No, he must die now," said Ondslake.

"And what about the fleas?" asked Garnish.

"They're all mixed up." Iseult shook her head sadly. "I've isolated the love ones by experiments with villeins. I'm working on the suicide ones right now, but we have to stop these people jumping from the parapet. Once they're in the sea, we can't recover the fleas."

"I'll see to that," said Ondslake. "Anyone topping himself must do it indoors, by order. Or else."

"Or else what?" asked Garnish innocently.

"Er . . ."

"Naked as a needle was she, and either clipped we other soft and long . . ." droned Marina.

"Marina!" squealed Garnish.

"Sorry."

"What did you say?"

"I said sorry." Marina frowned. "Here, what's been happening? Where are the fleas? What happened to that toerag? What's going on? Who broke my hall?"

"It worked, Mama!" Garnish clapped her hands together and jumped up and down on the spot. "It worked. Oh, darling, darling Marina. We were so worried . . ."

They soothed her and explained the events of the past week. "And what day is it today?" demanded Marina.

"Milsday. The first day of the Blitz."

"Has the stone arrived?"

"Of course, but no one's even tried to move it."

"Thank Lugh. But the fleas. You say they're all mixed up?"

"I can't tell them apart," admitted Iseult, "but all this Pulvicovectoral stuff is new to me."

Marina barked orders. "Ondslake! Call the Riders together and get the horses saddled up! Garnish, come with me and we'll sort out the fleas. Dame Iseult, can I leave wiping out the Cantiger creature to you?"

Iseult rubbed her dry white hands together and cracked her knuckles. "It will be my pleasure," she gloated.

Warhawk and Bros proved a success in Greatwen. Although no one could understand a word that they said, their desires were all such as could readily be conveyed by gesture and farmyard noises, and they found that, for the first time in their lives, they did not need to threaten or to fight in order to get what they wanted.

In their domain, people had little use for discs of shiny yellow stuff. Down here, they found, all you had to do was make the appropriate noise and gesture, thrust out a fist full of discs, and everyone was scurrying around to do your bidding as though you had said, "Goolloken gurk bogger toopuck" and raised your warhammer.

It was really quite restful, just for a change.

Unfortunately, old habits dying hard, they had accidentally razed a chophouse to the ground, but everyone agreed that this was not really their fault, and the chophouse owner was well satisfied with the coins that they had already paid him over the past days, which allowed him to establish a whole chain of stalls selling lark in deep-crumb and battered cod-pieces, which were strangely popular with the ladies.

It happened because Housewolf took it into his head to give the chef a lesson in cookery.

For two days, he had put up with the curious customs of Greatwen. They drank water, for example, from bowls on stems, alongside their beakers of blonk, and used implements with which to convey their food from trencher to mouth.

Housewolf considered this primitive and peculiar, besides the fact that water was famously dangerous stuff.

On the third day, therefore, in a fit of benevolence, he indicated that he wished to demonstrate the correct method of eating. With suitable gestures and noises, he tipped the contents of the small water bowls into larger bowls, and demonstrated to the astonished diners that it was possible to eat the food in the fingers, then wash the hands in the water, thus doubling the beakers available for blonk.

Next, he attended to the traditional methods of cooking. In general the brothers were content with the large piles of hefty lumps of pork and beef placed on their chargers, but they yearned for the familiar savours of home. Housewolf therefore brought to the chophouse two barrels of hoosgabath, or life-water, and poured it over the vast quantity of flesh laid out for them. To the bewilderment of all present, he then rushed outside, lit a taper from the square's log, ran back in again and flung the flame into the spirit.

The result was dramatic. Housewolf and his brothers, of course, invariably practised this style of cooking outdoors. They were also well accustomed to the smell and the heat of burning cots and crofts. Everything therefore seemed to be going quite well to them as the flames at last subsided and they helped themselves to the delicious, charred chunks of meat. They took the cries of the assembled company to indicate admiration, and could not understand why, through the smoke, they saw diners throwing that disgusting water stuff into the pit.

They were fierce slow on the uptake, these Greatwenners. The *fingers* went into the water, the *hoosgabath* into the meal.

Aside from this petty little incident, and the need to fight one another for a few hours every evening,[28] just for practice, they found Greatwen really quite agreeable. As Warhawk said, "Educate the inhabitants a bit, get rid of a few of the buildings (which really were excessive), and it was the sort of place where you wouldn't mind being king at all. You wouldn't want to live there, of course, but . . ."

So was his resolve and that of his brothers hardened. They were missionaries, colonists. The people needed their example . . .

Now turn we again.

Orson strolled along the embankment of the Thuinne, the great brown river that glided through the heart of Greatwen. He was, on balance, content. Tonight he would see Geneva again. She and her parents were bidden to a little "entertainment" called by Buller at his inn, the Golden Cow. If he was really obnoxiously doting, she might even insult him again.

And tomorrow the Blitz began.

It was universally accepted that this was not the best way of deciding the overlordship but, since the gods had offered

---

[28]It had to be the evenings, because Warhawk's strength increased as the sun arose and dwindled as it sank. Some said that this was because he drank hoosgabath from midday onwards. No one said it to him, however, and certainly not round lunchtime.

nothing more than that stone on the lawn, which even the mightiest of Sotisians could not move an inch, they had had to fall back on simple trial by combat. After all, any man who could move the stone must be a giant, and giants were not exactly renowned for wit and savvy. Combat involved more skill and subtlety than weightlifting.

It would, at the least, be a memorable few days' sport. Orson hoped that K might win him some worship, though, to be honest, it seemed unlikely that he would get past the first round. There were just so many Classic Riders in town at present . . .

And then, Orson supposed, it was back to the countryside, and the usual round of County blitzes and occasional battles with varlets, trolls or foreigners that kept a Rider - and his pillier - busy.

Talking of which . . . Orson frowned. The man on the cart ahead of him appeared to be in some difficulty. Seabirds swarmed about his head, flapping and pecking, whilst others wheeled above, occasionally plummeting into the mêlée. The man had a sack over his head, but already blood stained the hessian.

Orson found himself running, and drawing his sword as he ran. He clambered on to the cart's tailboard amidst all the beating, powerful wings, and started slashing with the precision acquired during hundreds of hours on the schooling ground. Sometimes the blade passed within an inch of the little man's head but, for the likes of Orson, an inch was a huge margin of error. For the likes of Cantiger, who risked a peek, it was no margin at all. Indeed, this plainly murderous, smock-faced young man who towered above him was merely further proof, if proof were needed, that the entire planet was unjustly dedicated to hurting him.

Thanks to the young hooligan's poor aim, however, it had to be admitted that the number of big white squawking birds was declining and the number of joints - wings, legs and so on - on the floor of the cart rapidly growing.

"There now," the young man called cheerfully. "Are you carrying fish?"

For a moment, Cantiger thought that this must be code.

Quick as ever to adapt to circumstance, he said, "No. My dad's lugger went down with the loss of all soles. And, it seems . . ." he added for good measure, "halibut." Then light filtered into his brain. "Oh. The birds, you mean? No, they just attacked me for no reason that I know."

"Does this sort of thing happen to you a lot, then?" Orson beamed.

"Quite a bit, actually," Cantiger admitted. He bent to pick up his pointy hat and crammed it on to his head. His gaze fixed on something behind Orson. "Um, excuse me . . . ?"

"Yep?"

"Well, I don't like to trouble you, but you seem to be quite handy with that sword, and . . ."

Orson turned to follow the direction of Cantiger's terrified gaze. "Oh," he said, "trolls. Hang on."

Cantiger ducked down. He hung on.

"There," said Orson, broadly grinning. "They're strong, but they have postural problems. All that time spent under bridges in the damp. Slows them up."

"Oh," said Cantiger. "Yes. Would."

"Sorry about your father's boat, by the way. So why are all these creatures attacking you?"

"I really don't know," said Cantiger sadly. "Buildings do it, too, actually. I try to be a quiet, studious magician – get a bit of base metal, turn it into gold, that sort of thing, you know – and everything goes round attacking me. Stools do it, women, men, walls . . . Talking of which . . ."

The skeleton took a little longer than the trolls, because it was in full armour and wielded a sword. At last, however, with a few bones broken, it adopted the generally accepted position of its kind.

"Strange," said Orson. He sat on the side of the cart as it rocked on its way. "Can you really turn base metal into gold?"

"Oh, yes. I seem to have left the spell somewhere, but it'll turn up. Should I give you some money?"

"What? Why?"

"All this helping you've been doing. I mean, I've got some. I thought maybe . . ."

"No, no. Got plenty of money. Good to get a bit of exercise, to be honest Getting soft. All this eating, drinking and carousing."

Cantiger sighed. Bruce and Bertelot had abandoned him with the declared intention of eating, drinking and carousing, and Cantiger had seen a fair bit of all of these being done in the streets and squares. The Ochtie girls had enlightened him to a considerable degree as to the nature of nestling turtle-dove thingies. The problem was that, whilst Cantiger could buy food and drink, he had no friends, which seemed to be a prerequisite for a carouse, and his opening lines to strangers[29] had not proved successful. All the taverns in the town, furthermore, were booked solid, and Cantiger had no idea where he would spend the night.

"I really hate to trouble you . . ." he said.

Orson raised his eyebrows. "Again?" he said. "Ah." And then, as he kicked the huge dogs' bodies from the cart, "Why do they always foam like that, I wonder? Tell you what. Why don't you come back to the Golden Cow? You can do some tricks at the entertainment tonight, and my friends will really like these adventures that seem to happen to you."

"Nice of them," said Cantiger. "And if nothing attacks me, they could always do it themselves."

"Well, OK." Orson shrugged. "If you'd rather face all these enemies on your own . . ." He vaulted lightly over the side of the cart. "I'll see you."

"No!" Cantiger leaned back on the reins. This young man might be useful to him – might even organize a bit of carousing for him. "No. No, that's really kind. Thank you. Can I give you a lift?"

Kes glared sourly at the great sarsen stone where it stood on the lawn outside the Abbey. "It just doesn't seem very – well, very democratic, if you ask me," he said.

"Dem—" his father scowled. "Course it's demithingy. Lot more demithingy than primowhatchemecallit. Look at you!" He suited the action to the word, and shuddered. "Firstborn fruit of

[29]He had so far tried, "Hello, I've got twenty pounds in my pocket," which, though true at the time, was not so two minutes later, and, to a likely-looking damosel, "I've had terrible problems with worms lately. How about you?"

my loins, at least within the bounds of holy matrimony, and you cop the lot. Riderhood, castle, estates, villeins . . . You don't get much more of a closed shop than firstborn fruits of loins. Strange system, really. Works sometimes. Me, for instance. Sometimes – well, there we are and we must put up with it and that's all there is to it and there's an end on it."

He sighed and slowly shook his head as he perused his heir. It was a depressing subject. He returned to a study of the crowds that milled about the stone.

Kes appeared oblivious to any disappointment implicit in his sire's analysis of primogeniture. "No, but removing stones from lawns to become king. I mean, where's the relevance? Honestly, Papa, how often does the average king have to remove stones out of lawns? It's not the sort of thing you do. Ruling, smiting, carousing, bit of dubbing, all stuff that people like you and I sort of do naturally. Born to it. Raised to it. But landscape gardening? Smacks of the circus, if you ask me. Some villein conjuror'll do it, probably."

"That's why it's demiwhosit, surely?" objected Buller. "And anyhow, the general view is that the gods put it there by way of a marvel or augury or whatnot."

"Yes . . ." Kes mused. "Yes, I've been thinking about that too."

"What?" growled Buller

"The gods," twanged Kes. "I mean, good chaps, top of the range in their way, sense of style, all that, but who appointed them is what I want to know? Do they ever come down and prove themselves in single combat? Not that I've noticed. Or stand for election? No way. Just, 'I'm demiurge and supreme Ruler of the Universe so yah boo'. Cheek. I'm thinking of standing for God. Be jolly good at it."

"I need a drink," groaned Buller, as so often after a conversation with his elder son. He pulled himself wearily to his feet and lumbered down the terraced seats erected around the marvel, lately sprung up in the centre of Greatwen to the outrage of the planning chappies. He sidestepped through the throng. "No. On reflection, I need twelve drinks."

"Steady, Papa, I say!" bleated Kes as he followed, jumping and weaving through the people. "Remember your arteries!"

This remark puzzled Buller. There were many things that he

needed to remember: to wear a sword, for example, and to carry gold when in Greatwen, the date of his birthday and the name of that new austringer. He had no idea, however, why he should remember his arteries, which, to the best of his recollection, he had never forgotten. For a moment, he considered asking Kes for enlightenment, but then he thought better of it. He ground his teeth and puffed out his grizzled moustaches as he rejoined his men-at-arms. They formed about him. "The Golden Cow," he ordered, "and quickly, if you please."

The men-at-arms set off at the trot with Buller at their midst. This was, admittedly, a primitive form of transport, and far from Buller's favourite, but the sight of twelve liveried men, bellowing, "Make way for Boss Buller! Ware the party Delamere Maudite! Beep beep!", the front rank with swords held stiff-armed before them, did wonders in heavy traffic. And the traffic in Greatwen at the time was heavy indeed.

Boss Buller did not argue with his elder son. He had learned that to be futile. He simply despaired of him in silence.

This was not because, as was sometimes asserted, the boy was a congenital bloody idiot. Kes was not stupid. He merely happened to be one of those people, so his nurse said, who had slipped into the wrong epoch. It happened, apparently, in every generation. "Think of it like a huge baby-farm," said this weird old bearded Brownie woman, who generally seemed to know about such things. "There are all the little cootchy darlings yet unborn, just waiting for the allotted time to come slither-withery out into the nasty gary-glary day. So one's labelled, like: 2nd June, 1822, human, son of Jethro and Makepeace Placket, say.

"And, sure enough, Jethro and Makepeace do the bold thing that makes lovely squirmy babies, and they go and fetch the appropriate child and put him in his mummy's yummy tum-tum. More's the pity, oh, ever so early on, they made a mistake or two, like dropping stitches, you know? There was a rush on, and they couldn't find the right one for the right mummy and daddy, see? So they skimpied down the line to find another icku yummy-bobs to take 'is place, thinking as it was so far off no one'd notice, so a spirit meant for 1822 got squittered into 540, say, to fill the gap, and either got burned as a witch or became a useful sleep-inducer. Then they tried to get it right again, so they slipped a boy labelled 1070 or something into the nineteenth century to take our little Placket's place, and Logris won a Test Match or a few damosels got a very nice surprise.

"They've been trying to sort it out for ever so long now. I'm told they've even used snorty smelly animals to stand in for missing humans on occasion. I'm sure I've met the odd human camel or spaniel or pig in this very castle. That is what has happened to our K. If he had been born in 1950, say, he would be perfectly normal. In our time, he's just the teensiest bit out of the ordinary."

Boss Buller had believed in progress until this had been explained to him. He now realized, with a sinking heart, that, if the world was ever going to accept the likes of Kes as "perfectly normal", he might as well vote Conservative.

The Golden Cow was Boss Buller's property, as, indeed, were the three acres of dwellings to the south and west of Golden Cow Square. The inn took its name and emblem from Boss Buller's coat of arms, "a cow rampant or or or and argent on field gules", and that same emblem hung above the door through which the men-at-arms now decanted him. Impelled by the force of their progress, he staggered forward over the reed-strewn floor until brought up short by a long oak bench that struck his kneecap, and a long oak table that, demonstrating a species solidarity rarely found in woodwork, followed up to the groin.

Buller sagged but did not topple. He was of the sort that, proverbially, they do not make any more. He merely said, "Bugger."

Buller was aware, however – none more so – that there are means whereby the woes of the world can be dispelled and pain soothed even without the application of leeches. "Brandy!" he roared, and then, after a moment's reflection, added, "And wine, and mead, and ale! Oh, and sack!"

Assured by the bustle in the taproom that these matters were being afforded immediate and sufficient attention, he straddled the bench and considered, for a moment, his arteries. Perfectly normal arteries. Had always gone wherever he had gone. Full of blood (Buller and his chums had never heard of William Harvey, but had no illusions regarding the circulation of the blood), generally good things. Why on earth should he remember them?

Again he gave up these deep thoughts and instead studied the other people in the inn. Greatweners, he had long since concluded, were a soft and decidedly eccentric bunch, given to preening and prinking around in impractical garb.

A woman, to Buller's mind, should wear as little as possible until she attained thirty, and should then, so far as possible, cover herself from throat to foot in linen or hessian.

As for men, they had no place wearing anything that had not formerly graced a beast. Buller wore a goatskin jerkin over a dogskin smock, breeches of tanned and bleached polecat and boots – admittedly a trifle snazzy, but this *was* Greatwen – of the privy parts of cameleopard. Sensible, hardy, practical garments.

Glancing around him now, however, he saw samite and satin, lace and frothy frills. The men all brayed like asses and the women yapped like brachets and tittered like rivulets. Buller thought them halfwitted.

"How're you doing, sir?"

Buller started from his deep thoughts at the familiar voice. "Ah, Orson!" he beamed. "Splendid. Awful place, this Greatwen. Still, no, no. I'm fine. Sit down, my boy. Been looking at this marvel whatnot, suddenly sprouted up out of nowhere. Stone. Lawn. Whoso removeth me becometh king. Rather jolly, really. Novelty."

Orson straddled the bench beside his mentor, facing the door. "It's a marvel altogether," he said. "That's the thing about Greatwen, so I find. Marvels at every corner. If I met one damosel promised me a trip to heaven today, I met a hundred, and then there was the man challenged me to find the lady . . ."

"Oh, God," moaned Boss Buller, "how much did you lose?"

"I won," said Orson simply. "I thrust my ballock-knife through the card, fastened it to the table, just to be sure, and said, "That's the one." Your man got strangely testy, but I had him bang to rights. Easy money. I did it twelve times, then some varlets approached me with truncheons, so I struck off their heads altogether."

"Splendid," said Boss Buller, who approved of his foster-son's sense of justice. At this moment, a woman appeared at Buller's shoulder with a laden tray. He allowed her to lay down the tray, said, "Gramercy, wench," and encircled her waist with his mighty, goat-clad arm. "Most obleeged. Go on, my boy, go on!" urged Boss Buller, tipping brandy into his ale. "What else have you seen today?"

"Figures of men wrought in wax," said Orson. "And a great hall in which I saw the stars at night, though it were day. Oh, and a lady who had given birth to an elver, and people who drank water, oh, and a magician who gets attacked by buildings and things. He's just tying up his pony."

"Magician, eh? Splendid. Rabbits, hats, things like that?"

"Base metal into gold."

"Hm. Don't suppose he can do the other way round?"

"I don't think so."

"They seldom can," said Buller sadly. "Got more than enough gold. I want armour and bell-metal. That new bell at Dispater's church goes splidge-splodge. Ding-dong's better to my mind."

"Ah, here he is . . ." Orson stood and waved. "Hi! Cantiger! Over here!"

A few of the drinkers in the tavern turned to see the new arrival, and, because he was privileged to be known to Orson, drew back out of his path. Cantiger smirked. You can't blame him. Someone was calling him by name without intending to hit, kick or abuse him when he arrived.

It didn't last, of course. Sometime later Kes at last strode into the tavern, looking flushed and tetchy. "Papa," he said briskly, then, "Ah, Orson, what are you doing sitting around chatting to villeins?"

"K, this is a magician called Cantiger," said Orson. "Things attack him."

Kes's eyes flickered over Cantiger. "Hardly surprising," he said. "He shouldn't go around looking like that. Small, I mean, and pink, and gormless. 'Course things attack him. Anyhow, you should be working, not lounging around in bars."

"Working at what?" asked Orson.

"I don't know. Getting my sword sharp, polishing my shield,

tarring hooves, things pilliers do."

"I've done them all," said Orson simply.

"Well – do them all again," said Kes. "It looks silly, having your pillier sitting around swilling. And talking of which, Papa, you should darned well remember your arteries."

"Don't worry, my boy," bellowed Buller, who was now, with a large quantity of alcohol inside him and the bartending wench on his knee, in high spirits. "Haven't forgotten them once. Never go anywhere without them. And leave poor Orson alone. We're having fun."

Kes went a little pinker. He puffed. He looked from his father to Orson. Then he raised his gauntleted fist and brought it hard down on Cantiger's head.

"Small and pink," he fumed as he strode away. "What on earth does he expect?"

"Poor Madame Bovary," read Snugsnuffler to the party of Lamere Maudite that night,

> *Poor Madame Bovary*
> *Ruled by her ovaries;*
> *One simple instance of naughty leg-over re-*
> *Sulted in shame and in over-expense,*
> *Over-reaction and want of good sense.*
> *Oh, what a shame that one roll in the clover re-*
> *Duced dearest Emma to such a pushover re-*
> *Sulting at last in a glum overview,*
> *And overingestion of strychnine.*
> *Adieu.*

He bowed. Applause pattered.

"Very moving," said Buller.

"Thought-provoking," agreed Brastias.

"Happy bit, bit of rumpy, sad bit. Just what's needed in a great work of literature. Leaves you wanting more. Oy, Snugsnuffler! Give us another!"

"Er . . ." Snugsnuffler laid down his drink and pulled himself unsteadily to his feet once more. "I got three odes," he said, and hiccoughed.

"Yeah. Why not? Love a good ode. Not too long, though."

"No, no. Distilled from an ancient text, these are. Very good odes. Hang on." Snugsnuffler adopted a declaiming position, and fell over. He scrambled to his feet again. "Here we go," he announced hopefully. "Right. Ode to a Nightingale:

You sing and sing, tweet tweet chink chink!
Dear God but I could use a drink!
Life's a pain and death seems sweet
But you just go chink chink tweet tweet!

"Ode on a Greesh'n Nurn," he announced portentously. He wriggled as he tried to resist the joke, but it barged up like vomit. "Whassa a Grecian Urn? 'Bout two drachmas a day. Ha ha. Oh. Yes. Well.

I've got wrinkles; this old pot
And its embellishments have not.
Truth is beauty, beauty truth;
It's such a pain to lose one's youth.

And fin'ly, laze 'n' gelmen, *To Melancholy:*

Don't take tonics; melancholy
Really can be rather jolly;
My best verses all come to me
(See above) when I feel gloomy."

Snugsnuffler sank slowly to the stage. Once more the assembled Riders and their ladies applauded politely. A band of musicians stepped over Snugsnuffler's recumbent body and struck aggressive poses with their mandolins. A quick timbrel break, and the familiar, romping, soulful recorder solo streaked and purled through the *obbligato* avenue of mandolin foliage and hard, unrelenting faggot trunks. As it were.

"Raucous rubbish,"Buller sighed." I don't know . . ."

"Such a good idea of yours, Buller," said a visiting lady, "the miniature library. Space-saving. No more dirty great books, and everything quick and exciting."

"Thank you, my dear," said Buller. "Yes, it's coming on nicely." He turned to the lady's daughter who sat beside him. "Are you interested in literature, Geneva?" he shouted.

Geneva shrugged. "It's all right," she drawled.

"Ah, you're too young. Probably prefer dancing, eh?"

"It's all right," she sighed.

"Would you like to dance?" hazarded Orson.

Her lips twitched. "Why do pilliers actually need tongues, Daddy?" she leaned across Orson to ask King Leo. She smelled of vanilla.

"Ask your mother," said Leo, apparently absently.

"Now, what about that magician chappy of yours, Orson?" called Buller. "Must have a trick or two up his sleeve . . ."

Orson had by now consumed his fill of wine, though "fill" was very relative, and inwardly he thought that there was still potential. "Yes!" he cried. "Cantiger! You going to do some magic after this number?"

Cantiger had been enjoying the evening up till now. Several Riders seemed to have accepted him as a *bona fide* sorcerer. Drinks had been pressed on him, though they needed no pressing. He had even encountered a woman who had recently had trouble with worms and, although it soon became plain that these were not quite the same as Cantiger's worm, had held forth on the subject in quite interesting detail. Better still, no animals, birds, Riders or roofs had attacked him for at least two hours.

Always underlying his new-found happiness, however, had been the awareness that this moment had to come and that he would be expected to sing for his supper. He had spent the afternoon riffling through Iseult's papers, but discovered that, whilst he had a recipe – and a remedy – for cheese straws and veruccas, he had no spells that would rank as showbiz. There was a spell "to render invisible" but it took two hours at Gas Mark 4 and required camel particles.

Then there was X-Calibre, but Cantiger had yet to work out precisely how it worked or in which direction it should be pointed, and he did not want to jeopardize his popularity by putting a hole in one of his hosts or hostesses. As for the fleas, if he had understood Marina properly, they had the power to alter people's emotions but not, he thought, to make people roar with laughter and gasp in awe at a man standing on the stage doing nothing.

"Um, could I have a word, young sir?" said Cantiger.

"Course you could! Many as you want!" answered Orson, who was feeling generous.

"No, sir. In private."

Orson frowned. "Private" was not a word much in use at the time. Still, sorcerers were meant to be mysterious, so he excused himself and followed Cantiger to a quiet corner of the tavern. "What is it?" he asked.

"Listen, that's not – I mean, sorry if you got the wrong end of the stick – but I don't do that sort of magic, sir. Mine's more sort of mystical, like, and slower. I mean, if you want to be invisible, fine, only it takes two hours at Gas Mark 4 sort of thing, and we need a camel first. That sort of thing."

"A camel?"

"Yeah, well, particles of a camel. They come pre-packed at Saracen shops."

"Oh. Shame."

"I mean, if you wanted someone made very wood for love, no problem. I'm your man."

"Wood?"

"Yeah."

"That sounds rude," mused Orson. "And uncomfortable."

"No, not wood wood. Wood crazy. Wood mad."

"Wood-mad for love? Is that useful? In love, I mean?"

"No, sir. You don't get it . . ."

"Not much, no . . ." admitted Orson.

"No, wood is sorcerer-speak for mad, crazy . . ."

Orson thought. When he spoke, it was slowly. "You mean . . ." He cast a quick glance at Geneva where she sat considering her face in a little glass. "You mean, you could take a girl, say, and make her crazy for love for someone?"

"Doddle, sir. But it takes time, see. It's not the sort of thing the punters want to see. Standing stones I'm good at, and making people top themselves . . ."

"Useful." Orson nodded. "Hang on. Did you say 'standing stones'?"

"Er, yeees . . ."

"What do you do with them?"

"Remove them, I think."

"But if you can remove standing stones, you could be king!"

"Oh, dear." Cantiger shuddered. "Oh, yeah. That would be just typical of my luck. Wandering around, not hurting anyone. Oy, you, just come and be king, would you? That way every Rider in the land gets to have a pop at you. Great."

Orson was excited. "No, but haven't you heard? There's a by-our-lady big stone on a lawn outside Greatwen Abbey, and it says that whoever removes it can be king. It's destined! You can't argue with destiny!"

Cantiger looked surprised. "Yes, I can," he said, "always have." Orson had got him on his favourite subject "What we need, I reckon, is a lot more people. Get a lot of people, you get a whole lot less destiny. I mean, if there are only two marriageable girls in the county and they're both your cousins and one of them smells, you're going to fall for the other one and everyone says it's destiny. Same thing with you guys. Riders. Only six Riders in the area, all brothers, right? What's the odds one of them's going to kill another by mistake? Ooh, it was all tragic destiny. Garbage. It was the law of averages. If I hadn't argued with destiny, I'd have been dead a hundred times over. Destiny doesn't like me."

"Well, perhaps you're destined to come here and meet us and show us how to do it. I mean. Kes could be overlord . . ."

"That pompous ninny, begging your pardon, sir? This nation needs a king like him like . . . like a puffin needs a pianola."

"What's a pianola?" asked Orson.

"I'm not sure, sir, but I know they're not good for puffins. No, this nation needs the impossible, a king who's good at fighting but doesn't like war, a practical man with no illusions who is also inspired and inspiring, a man who could use a good magician, a man with absolutely no imagination but sympathy for the downtrodden like me, a . . ."

"Well," said Orson, "how about me?"

Together the two men examined the stone in the darkness. It was the biggest standing stone – the biggest *single* stone, indeed – that Cantiger had ever seen, and he had no idea how such a thing could be moved. He whispered, however, "I think that I can do it."

"You can?"

"You're sure, if you're made king, you'll give me a tower and a bodyguard and lampreys and partridges and the job of counsellor-in-chief by appointment to His Majesty with access to the royal ear?"

"Can't see why not." Orson shrugged. He glanced nervously at the stone's guards to ensure that they were out of earshot.

"And an income of . . . what did we say?"

"I think you said a hundred thousand pounds."

"Yeah. I did. I just wanted to hear it again. OK. Let's give it a whirl. Tomorrow afternoon, when everyone's at this Blitz thing . . ."

"But I've got to be there . . ."

"Invent an excuse. Diarrhoea is a good one. Social letdown for a Rider, that. Don't win much worship if your pillier . . ."

"No. OK. Then what?"

"Well, if it works, we say to everyone, 'Here's the rightful King of all Logris,' and everyone cheers."

"And if it doesn't work?"

"We say nothing at all and no one ever writes a single book about us, let alone one of the greatest canons of myth and legend in the world, and we creep down history's page to the obscurity of a footnote."[30]

Marina did not ride discreetly, politely or cautiously. Compared to her, Jonas Crabapple was a sluggard. She rode breakneck, headlong and without the slightest reck. She urged her horses to wild, flat-eared, staring, glaring, gleaming, frothing panic. And that was just when she went shopping in Dunheved. Tonight the froth flew from them like spume in a gale and their hooves sparked like Zippos at a windy marine's funeral. I mean a marine's windy funeral. Or better, perhaps, a marine's funeral in a high wind.

That night saw her party arrive at Choppenmead in Withershire. Her black cloak thudded in the wind and flared as

[30]If that.

she dismounted and strode into the Angel Inn. Garnish followed, dragging her feet in her exhaustion. "Eleven rooms and dinner for thirty-six, please, landlord," Marina ordered. She swung round to the green-haired girl who now shimmered in. "Chloris, get humming. I want to talk to Iseult."

"I'm sorry, ma'am," said the portly landlord, "but my rooms are occupied and this is a traditional family tavern, and we have a strict dress code. Ladies must wear gowns with no silly masks, if you don't mind, and as for green hair ∴.."

Marina gazed into his eyes.

"There's rules and regulations . . ." he said softly.

Marina kept gazing.

"All right, I did, but that's natural, and it was a long time ago . . . Yeah, well, we're none of us saints . . . I might have, what's it to you? Please don't look! I never meant to . . . Oh, Lugh! So small, so revolting, so despicable, so . . . I didn't want . . . Oh, loathly! Loathly! The laundry bills! The yuk! The waaaaaaa!"

He bawled now like an infant. Marina turned away her mirror eyes. "Silence," she said, "and change your breeks before you prepare our dinner."

"Yes'm . . ." The man walked gap-legged and bent towards the door. He was very old now, and he shuddered. "Nothing . . ." he whimpered. ". . . Oh, Lugh, I am less than nothing!"

"All I did was show him the truth," said Marina. She shook her head, bemused. She pulled off her gauntlets, slammed them on the bar, then vaulted over to collect bottles. "There was a time when people paid for that. 'Mazing."

Now turn we again to Orson and Cantiger where they stood in Orson's bedroom in the Golden Cow. "So you're saying that this Thing puts holes in armour?" asked Orson.

"And in whatever's inside." Cantiger nodded. "I think it's to do with the bits . . . here . . . that you can take out. The only trouble is, there are only five of them left. There were six before, but now there are only five. I don't want to waste them."

"Very wise. No, by my reckoning, the thingy moves this whatsit, which hits this whatchemecallit, which probably drives the whosit, which comes out here."

"Ah, well, you obviously have the technical mind." Cantiger shook his head. "Still, it works. And if you're going to be overlord, you're going to need all the help you can get." He walked to the window and gazed out over the city. There was raucous singing from below. "It's getting late. I've got to sort out the fl–, the spells, for tomorrow."

"What do you reckon the trick is, Cantiger?"

"What?"

"For overlordship?"

"National Elf," said Cantiger vaguely.

"What?"

"Everyone to have a free Elf, I think," said Cantiger, picking up drifting soundbites from the aether. "Government of the rulers, by the rulers, for the rulers. Liberty, holidays and maternity. Free love for magicians and Riders (and kings), by-our-lady expensive love for everyone else, because otherwise they breed. Death for those who use glottal stops,[31] eschew offal, wear beards or bell-bottoms, except for people called Gene. Um, pea-ea-eace all over this land. Yay yay yay yay. High taxes on people on big horses, tiny taxes for people on ponies, no ponies for people in taxis. The unemployed . . ."

"There aren't any."

"No, but there might be."

"OK."

". . . to be given five turnips and a free insult weekly, just to make them feel wanted. Be nice to people, especially the weak, or else. Blessed are the merciful, for they shall obtain mercy, but kick the crap out of bullies. That sort of thing."

"Sounds good to me." Orson nodded. He sat on the truckle bed and leaned back, his head on his clasped hands. "I'm not sure about the Elf bit, but . . ."

"That's negotiable," admitted Cantiger. "Strong and just. That's the main thing."

"Equality?"

Cantiger scowled. "What on earth's that? Nah. Fairness. That's all that matters. Anyhow, there's time enough to discuss

[31]Never, alas, implemented

all this stuff when we've got you there. I've got a lot of work to do tonight."

"Work away, magician." Orson swung his long legs up on to the bed and crossed his ankles. "Can you really make Geneva wood for love of me?"

"Huh." Cantiger grunted. He had seen Little Miss Toffee-nose and did not think much of her. "You get to be overlord, she'll be wood all right."

Orson cocked his head to consider his new friend. Then he bethought himself that there were more agreeable things to consider, such as Geneva being wood and him being king. Both, of course, were unattainable really, but the fantasy looked a great deal better than the too too solid Cantiger. With a happy smile, Orson closed his eyes. The scenery was suddenly lovely.

Left now to his own devices, Cantiger reached into his sack. He pulled all the solid articles one by one and very carefully out on to the washstand, tapping them carefully at the mouth of the sack so that any detritus had to drop back in. At last, satisfied that all that remained within was salad, sandwich crumbs, fungus and fleas, he bunched up the neck of the sack, put his mouth to it and, in his most magisterial and, he hoped, magical tones, announced, "The weight must go. The stone must sink. We need air and freedom. When Orson – that's him over there – speaks the words 'Stone, begone!', let the friendly earth yield and engulf it. Please. I beg it and command it with every fibre of my being. I will it with all the might of magic. I invoke the support of every god and demon and the spirits of all the dead creatures that make the soil. This boy could make people stop hurting other people. He could be good for all of us.

"'I know I don't know what I am doing. I know that that Marina probably had all the right words, and that I should be speaking in Latin or something, but you are Logrian creatures as I am a Logrian creature, and you, and Lugh, and I, really really want the best for Logris, and there's been enough nastiness, enough stupidity, enough pompous farts lording it over everyone because they can, and please, please help now, because we all only get one chance, and I think this is worth a try.

"I mean, OK, he's thick, but he's honest, he's strong, he likes nature, and I may be pretty bad at this business, and cowardly and greedy and all that, but I think life could be better.

"I don't know. I seem to have lost track here. I mean I want rats to have a chance, so long as they're happy to be rats and look after their own, and me to have a chance, and the young innocent idiot to have a chance. Please help me. Please, please, please . . ."

He stopped, to find himself sagging on the washstand with tears in his eyes.

Exhausted, vile, venal, lustful and loathsome, he had meant to say, "Look, you pesky little things, I need money and lots of it, and damosels and treasure and a fan club, so move this stone or else." Instead, as if by magic, he had just spoken his first-ever real spell. He had hungered. He had longed with all his body and soul for something not entirely selfish.[32]

Whether the fleas agreed, only time would tell.

Well, and me.

If you're lucky.

Marina nudged Garnish at six in the morning. They arose and dressed quickly, shivering and shifting from foot to foot on the icy floor. Outside in the darkness, there was already clattering and tinkling as ostlers saddled the horses. Inside, everyone was strangely quiet as they went about their business. Riders whispered and bustled to and fro. The landlord had received his orders the previous night. He was silent as he served breakfast to the two girls at the table beneath the window. (Eggs, bacon, black pudding, sausages, kidneys, sweetbreads, grilled tomatoes and field mushrooms in Marina's case – well, not in her case, because that would have made a frightful mess of the sponge bag and the smalls, but . . . A bowl of bran, an apple, three mice and a crescent pastry with honey in Garnish's, since you ask.)

The day was just tentatively rubbing at night's tarnish as Marina strode to the front door and showed Garnish out into the stable yard. It was snowing again. Snowflakes swirled and bobbed like midges on the darkness and snagged on eyelashes.

[32]A small thing, but his own . . .

The horses were led out. Marina mounted astride again, Garnish side-saddle. The Riders materialized from nowhere and formed up around them.

"Right," said Marina, and her clear, melodious voice came as a shock amidst all the muffled sounds. "We must be in Greatwen by tonight. There will be a change of horses and a gallon of ale at Glossing on Thuinne. Otherwise, we stop for nothing and no one. Has everyone been?"

"Yes'm," came a quiet chorus from the Riders.

"Good. Let's go."

The people of Choppenmead were rudely awoken that morning by irresponsible traffic with no respect for speed limits in built-up areas, and the landlord of the Angel was left wondering how to explain to his wife (who was on holiday with her Aunt Omlet[33] in Little Logris) that he hadn't quite liked to present two young ladies with a bill for half the value of his property.

Orson awoke early. He had work to do.

He stepped over the slumbering carcass of that funny little magician, who snored into his sack. The illusions of the previous night were banished now. King, indeed. Overlord, him? Nonsense. The Great Lance needed oiling, the sword must be honed, the shield polished, the plumed crest brushed out, the saddle and bridle soaped and boned, the horse fed, watered and

---

[33] A note here about Logrian names at the time. Most inherited names were lost at the time of the Great Hiding and the White Sickness, and there were now few specialist skills such as "Baker" or "Fletcher" to give their names to families. Riders tended to have duly awe-inspiring and thus provocative names, but, amongst the villeins, it had become the custom to name the infant after whatever the mother was thinking about at the time of the birth. This was salutary in that no one was ever, ever given a name with undesirable sexual connotations. Singalette – from the sticks of herbs which Logrians smoked – and Stifdrinc were typical names of the period (Geneva was more fortunate than those girl-children named "Heavy" or "Rum'n'black"). Two generations earlier, it was the very sounds that the mother made at the time of the birth that made up the child's name, but there were so many "Ngs" and "Comeonyoulittlebastards" that this practice soon fell into disuse. One boy was even called "Cantisticka@=**£ingpumpkinupmy£**%=@ingnostril nextime?" He was quite badly teased at school and later shortened his name to "Nextime?" He became extraordinarily successful socially.

lightly exercised just to get his back down.

The Blitz would officially open at half-past nine, when the Riders would process past the great pavilion, saluting with lowered lances the aged Princess Persimmon who, as the senior lady present, was standing in for the monarch. Then the Riders would declare for one side or other – Kes, Buller and Brastias would be fighting for Lynch – and then the various sides would be rude to one another and tell one another what they were going to do with one another's entrails. This was traditional. Then battle would be joined to the uttermost or to death, whichever came first.

There would then be a break for lunch.

Following lunch and a little nap, the Blitz would resume.

There were two varieties of Blitz. One, List-Blitz, was a sort of knockout competition in which individual Riders would take on other individuals and fight until one of the two was yielded, incapacitated or dead. These individual jousts could continue for weeks until one supreme champion had won the day.

Battle-Blitz was a more haphazard affair, in that any one unfortunate Rider might find himself up against three or four of the enemy at the same time. Basically, Battle-Blitz was like battle, only without villeins or men-at-arms, and with a bit of mercy chucked in where begged for nicely.

Each side charged at the other. Individual fights broke out on all sides. If a Rider yielded himself to another, he was out, and his conqueror rode back into the fray to win himself more worship. At the end, sometimes after one day, sometimes after as many as seven, either only one Rider would still be fit and horsed or, if there was more than one remaining on the same side, public opinion was consulted as to who had won the field, the degree and the prize.

Public opinion was seldom divided. Not with a fully armed Rider eyeing the voters down a sharp, proven and blood-smeared lance.

The prize was usually a cup or a suit of armour. Sometimes it was a lady's hand. Sometimes it was even more of her.

Today it was a kingdom.

* * *

When Orson on his palfrey arrived at the Blitz-field that morning, he was aware of four hundred tents and pavilions and great array and marvellous great ordinance. Everywhere Riders and their pilliers busied themselves with harness, horses and hot-dogs.

It was a brilliant scene. Brightly coloured pennants fluttered above the pavilions, and the same colours were painted on the shields at each Rider's door. The greatest Riders even had their browbands, nosebands and even sometimes their reins and saddlecloths embroidered in their livery, and a few (regarded as "flash" by the old guard) extended their colours to their villeins' uniforms.

It was, predictably, these last who did most of the work. Orson and his fellow pilliers merely supervised, and compared views with their expert artisan employees.

So the grinder, who knew almost as much about blades as did Orson, demonstrated the gleaming cutting-edges of broad-swords, short-swords and battleaxes, squinted down his handi-work and encouraged Orson to do the same so that the young master could approve and admire the already long-agreed angle of bevel. And the saddler, who knew almost as much about tack as did Orson, demonstrated the rigidity of the saddle-tree, the pliability of the hammered rawhide leathers, the tension of the home-woven girths. And the ostler and the farrier, who knew almost as much about diet as Orson (and, to be frank, a deal more about legs), merely approved the young master's thoroughness.

Orson trotted the courser (not Demeter, who had developed a convenient limp) twice up and down the tumulus, then cantered him a brisk mile on the road back to Greatwen, then, crouched over his bobbing neck, rode him a steady upsides wallop back again. At the last, he slowed the animal to a walk and allowed him to cool.

He thought of the fair Geneva.

Damosels were Orson's weak spot.

Oh, he got on famously with the giggling villein girls back home. He tugged their hair, played jokes on them and tussled with them, and derived peculiar enjoyment fom those tussles. They seemed to like close-fighting more than boys, to which he had no objections, and, because they were villeins and he destined to remain a pillier, their romps, which, more often than not ensued after one had said, "La, sir! Don't you love to watch the antics of the tufted dung-beetles at close-quarters?" or, "Ooh, I seem to have lost my reticule in this long, surprisingly warm grass, sir," always seemed to be innocent and strangely inconclusive.

And then there was Cressy, whom he – well, "love" didn't come into it, of course. He just felt at home with her . . .

He dispelled thoughts of those mocking brown eyes. He saw them, and could hear her cackle, more clearly even than he could see and hear those about him. That was something different. A one-off. Special, of course, but she could not be in his life nor he in hers . . .

But then there was the other sort of girl, like Geneva, with whom any sort of tussle was quite unthinkable, and for whom love made you sick and daffy and suicidal and blissful and – well, wood. Orson seemed strangely susceptible to such woodness. Geneva was far from the first unattainable object of his awe and slavish adoration. His poems, starting with,

"Alisoun, you make me swoon,
"Your eyes, they gleam like frogspawn;
"They make me feel all warm inside,
"Like when a nice new dogs's born!"

proceeding to the more accomplished:

"O, Heloise, you're such a tease,
"I worship you quite madly.
"I love your elbows and your knees;
"And want to kiss you badly"

did not meet with anything like the enthusiasm with which they were penned. So Orson had resorted to Snugsnuffler's services to celebrate the next lodestar to swim into his ken, which, since the lovesome damosel in question was called Rosinante, and he had already started, *The sweetest things are Rosinante's . . .*, was probably just as well.

Unfortunately, Snugsnuffler, from provident habit, wrote "©

Snugsnuffler" at the bottom, and he and Rosinante mysteriously vanished from circulation for the next week. She emerged staggering strangely and complaining of a hangover, he with a smug grin on his bearded face and a volume of new poems which had since been banned throughout Logris and consigned to a Hunnish monastery.

Ah, well, Orson concluded as he dismounted on that lovely, clear blue morning, he would sooner be a courtly, anguished lover than brutish and cynical, like most of the older Riders, who, for some unaccountable reason, did not seem to experience similar passions themselves. If only they knew, he thought, how much agony they were missing out on.

Orson had faith in the ideal damosel.

It was to be his undoing.

Chapter Six

Now beginneth the first day jousting, reads the thrilling account of that day on the back page of a packed *Logrian Star,* and at that day Boss Brastias made him ready; and there came against him King Persil. Then it befell that Boss Brastias and King Persil met together with spears, and King Persil had such a buffet that he fell over his horse's croup. Then came there in a knight of King Persil to revenge his lord, and Boss Brastias smote him down, horse and man, to the earth. So there came a Rider that hight Arouse,[34] and Boss Bruce Sans Pitie, and an hundred Riders with them of Ochtia and the Northern Isles, and the King of Northgales and King Skinner were with them, and all these were against them of Logris. And then there began great battle, and many Riders were cast under horses' feet. And ever Boss Brastias did best, for he first began, and ever he held on.

Blood brast from ears

Ger, Warhawk's brother, smote ever at the face of Boss Brastias; and at the last, Boss Brastias hurtled down Ger, horse and man. Then by adventure, Boss Winston Maisonette, that good knight of blackest countenance, met with Boss Housewolf. And either smote other with great spears, that both their horses and Riders fell to the earth. But Housewolf had such a fall that he had almost broken his neck, for the blood brast out at nose, mouth and his ears, but at last he recovered by good surgeons.

Squab with noodles

And then they blew unto lodging, and unarmed them, and ate squab with noodles, roast peacock with mushy peas, farmed worms' tongues and treacle tart, coffee, mints and cheese. And then they took the field again, and Woborn of Loonis came into the range, and there met with him Warhawk of the Northern

---

[34]His mother had been thinking of hawking, actually.

Isles, and he with him, with great spears. And then they came so
hard together that their spears all to shivered, but Woborn smote
him so hard that he bare him backward over his horse, but yet he
lost not his stirrups. Then they drew their swords and lashed
together many sad strokes, that many worshipful Riders left
their business to behold them . . .

EVEN THE FINEST of journalists, however, cannot
convey what it felt like to be there and to witness
these deeds of valour as they occurred.

Orson watched engrossed. He cheered Brastias. He groaned
when Kes came a cropper, rapidly bested by Warhawk who,
he later claimed, had just been lucky to hit him with the point
of his lance. "I sneezed just as we met," he told anyone interested. "Otherwise he'd be cat's meat." Orson just nodded
sympathetically, staunched the blood with bandages and saw
the courser bedded down, then returned to watching the fray.

When Woborn came on to the field, Orson was entranced.
He had heard, of course, of this young Rider – no older than
Orson himself but already possessed of a formidable reputation. Now Orson could see why. The young Loonian was
agile, enormously strong and apparently tireless. Tall and
broad-shouldered, and clad in black armour that looked
perilously lightweight, all edged with gold, he met with three
Riders and downed them all before his lance shattered. He
then drew his sword and smote four more of the enemy
Riders to the ground.

By now he and his iron-grey courser were warwood. Orson
knew the signs. The horse snorted and bored and tossed its
head and tore chunks out of anything within reach of its
stained teeth. Sweat darkened its pelt, and its eyes were wild.
As for Woborn, he seemed to have forgotten that self-preser-
vation is generally considered provident in battle. With his
right hand he hacked and he hewed, he slashed and he
foyned. With his left, he punched and he tugged. His shield
was slung over his shoulder, but he seldom held it in his hand,
and he guided the horse with his legs alone.

His horsemanship was perhaps the most remarkable thing
about him. He could lean at an impossible angle to strike a

blow, and once, when a spear was aimed at him, he slid down the horse's side at the gallop and vanished wholly from view, only to resume his seat and smite off the head of the impertinent Rider who had, without worship and most unRiderly, matched lance with sword. He wheeled the horse to slash at another assailant, then saw King Nentres where he dressed his shield and harness and couched his spear and made to wallop at him, and Woborn ran unto him and smote him down with so great force that he made his horse to avoid his saddle.

And all this while, as he fought, Woborn sang in a resonant, lusty voice – the *Battle Hymn of Loonis*, the Warrior's Song, "Almighty Cernunnos, thou feedest the ravens" and so on, interspersing the words with "Ha!" and "There!" and "Yes!" as he dealt yet another blow.

Orson marvelled. His comments were knowledgeable. "Oh, well foyned!" he shouted. "Smighty might, I mean . . ." and "Yes! Kill the fat pig!"

When Warhawk, with a roar, engaged Woborn, Orson knew that he was witnessing one of the great matches. Here was might against prowess, weight against agility – not that Warhawk wanted speed nor that Woborn's blows were not devastating. It was just that each showed up the other's deficiencies which, in lesser Riders, must have been deemed virtues. Warhawk appeared just slightly cumbersome against his younger opponent, whilst you felt that, should the bigger man ever score a direct hit (and not glance off the helm or the shoulder as happened so often with Woborn), no human frame could withstand it. For three hours now they had traded blows, foyning and tracing as they were wood wild boars, and never once did Woborn give the bigger Rider the space or the leisure to smite as he would.

All thoughts of Cantiger and that nonsense about being king were forgotten in the excitement of the day's sport. Suddenly, however, it all came flooding back.

The first time, Orson gulped and said, "Whoops. Excuse me . . ." and scurried, bent double and with his knees together, to a tree behind the pavilion. He squatted, and the subsequent noise caused six rooks living in the branches high above to caw in alarm and leave home for a while.

Orson's relief, however, was considerable. He returned to the pavilion looking insouciant. He told himself that he was only imagining that everyone turned to glance at him, then moved a step or two away from him. It couldn't have been *that* loud.

"Now, what's been happening?" he said blithely. "Oh, good. Oh, well done Woborn! By my head, he is a passing good Rider. Is Brastias still up? Oh, great. Feeling better, Kes? Oh Lord . . ." this as something whimpering wriggled very fast down his intestines. "Excuse me."

The rooks had circled a bit, and were settling down in their nests again, assuring themselves that, whatever it had been, it was not likely to happen again, when it did, most stridently and explosively, and at great length.

This time, when Orson returned to the pavilion, there could be no doubt that people glanced at him and moved away from him. Orson felt obliged to explain. "Mushy peas," he said, and smiled.

Kes was playing host to a group of young bucks. Their mouths were working like hasty caterpillars. Their cheeks were reddening and, in one case, turning purple. Strange little squeaks and sniffs emerged from them. One was spluttering in a goblet. Kes wriggled in embarrassment He frowned at Orson. "What on earth's the matter, pillier?"

"Oh, nothing, nothing," said Orson airily. "Just a bit of an upset tummy. All over now. Nothing to worry about. Nothing at all. You know. Mushy peas. Squab. These things pass. Oh, my God. Excuse me."

He almost ran to the flap at the back of the pavilion this time. One of the young Riders could hold the laughter in no longer. It burst from him like a tittering rivulet, followed by a giant honk.

Even as Orson smelled the slightly less than entirely fresh air, Boss Buller who had done well this afternoon by dint of experience and wiliness, but had, at the last, been knocked from his horse by Boss Bruce, limped up the ramp to the pavilion with Magsin Toodux, a great and statuesque lady with substantial lands, who wore a corslet of leather, leather chaps and little else save a sword.

The moving things in Orson's stomach squeaked. He groaned. As a pillier, it was his duty to stand back to allow the Rider and the lady to pass through.

". . . Not sure that it's entirely sporting and dignified, but I'll grant that it's effective," Buller mused.

"Well, that's all that counts," said Magsin. "I mean, we'll have to see when Lynch enters the range, but, as things stand, it has to be between Woborn and Brastias and maybe Warhawk, and I'd say that young Woborn should carry the day . . ."

Orson shifted from foot to foot. He hugged his stomach and grimaced. Buller and Lady Magsin stood in the very doorway. "Yes. Strange that," said Buller, his eyes flickering lecherously over Magsin's legs, "so Lugh me help, meseemeth yonder is the best jouster that ever I saw. Don't expect great Riders from Hornwoggle and Loonis, but that boy has the makings of a true champion. All well, Orson?" Orson nodded and gulped. "Good, good. My boy, Orson. You know Lady Magsin, don't you? 'Course you do. Well, Magsin, my dear, let's have some of that Deedong blonk I promised you, and perhaps tonight we could have a little . . ." he now eyed her majestic cleavage ". . . a little tête-à-tête over dinner. Haven't seen you for ages . . ."

At last the two of them moved into the pavilion and Orson was free to fling himself down the ramp and into the shelter of the trees once more. Sweat beading his brow, he fumbled with his belt.

But it was too late.

Laughter rattled in the pavilion. The rooks left home for good. Several Riders later claimed to have been put off their stroke by an unearthly racket from the woods and demanded a rematch when they got out of hospital.

Buller's master-at-arms had instructed Orson again and again. "The blow matters," he had said, "but it's the follow-through that really counts."

The same held true, he found, with mushy peas.

* * *

125

Mortified and disconsolate, Orson rode back to Greatwen. Everyone save Kes, who had been incandescent with rage and embarrassment, had agreed that it really wasn't his fault, but that was small consolation. Before the flower of chivalry, the loftiest and loveliest of ladies, at his first big social engagement, he had noisily and shamefully . . .

Youth takes itself seriously, and Orson was convinced that his misfortune would be the subject of ribald jokes at every table in the land tonight, and that people would speak of it whenever his name came up in conversation. Villeins and varlets would snigger behind doors as he passed and blow innocent raspberries just within earshot for years to come. No damosel would consider marrying him. He wondered whether a silent order of monks would take him in, or whether the story would reach them too. In mime. Did "silent" in that context simply mean "no words"? Did it also preclude rude noises? Or should he merely kill himself right now and have done with it?

He might have considered this last option really quite seriously had he not considered what would be carved on his tombstone. Tombstones recorded your notable achievements, didn't they? And there could be no doubting Orson's most notable achievement in his short life. *Hic iacet Orsonus Delamere Maudite, crepitator,* it would say, and small boys for generations afterwards would gather to snigger and to retell the tale.

Magsin had been sweet about it. She said that it was always happening to her. "Lugh, yes! Pebbledash the garderobe? I should say so. Specially after a good night's carouse."

Villeins did not wear breeks, only shifts or habits, and all the Riders needed theirs, but Magsin had fetched a small skirt in blue and red plaid from her pavilion, and it was with this as the only covering for his nethers that he rode back, ruing his fate and cursing the day that he was born.

The streets of Greatwen were empty, which suited Orson fine. He considered riding down to the docks and running away to sea on a pirate ship, but the river was clogged with ice floes and no self-respecting pirate would be setting sail until spring. No. There was nothing for it but to return to the

Golden Cow, retire to his room and remain there until this whole hateful adventure in Greatwen was over.

"Ah, good," said a voice at his heel. He looked down to see that funny little magician guy walking along beside him. "Well done. Use the diarrhoea trick, did you?"

"I didn't need to," said Orson glumly. "I *had* diarrhoea and my life is ruined."

"Oh, good!" said Cantiger, surprised. "So that worked, did it?"

"What do you mean, 'that worked'?"

"Well, I didn't want you forgetting or changing your mind or anything. Got a lot invested in this project. So . . ."

Orson gaped. "You mean, you made me ill? You mean that, thanks to you, I've just been shamed and sent home in a skirt in front of everyone in Logris? You mean that that is all your doing?"

Cantiger considered whether this was indeed what he meant. Then he nodded. "Yup," he said. "At least, I think so."

Orson saw the light

He realized that he had been blind.

He had not understood why everyone and everything wanted to attack Cantiger. Now he could see the reasons with startling clarity. It was indeed the natural, right and proper thing to do. In not attacking Cantiger, he had been guilty of a crime against nature for which he himself should be punished. Attacking Cantiger, abusing him, torturing him and killing him were civic duties that should by rights occupy every sane person's every waking hour.

Orson decided to start the process with the abusing, then the torturing, then the killing, then a bit more abusing at leisure. "You filthy little runt!" he squealed.

"Yes." Cantiger nodded. "But filth is only skin-deep, and you should have seen my brother."

"What?"

"Tiny."

Orson struggled to find the right obscene, gross and grotesque words to describe Cantiger. He knew that they were near at hand, but they were hiding. Perhaps, on reflection, he should get the killing, which he knew how to do, done first, then work on the abusing when he had more time. His hand was on the hilt of his short-sword when suddenly his stomach did that thing again. He had to dismount very quickly.

"Oh, dear," said Cantiger a moment later. "Nasty."

"Nasty?" Orson panted. "You bet it's nasty. You give me the worst gut-rot I've had in my life . . . How long will this last?"

"I don't actually know," admitted Cantiger. "It's a flea. I'm sure if you had a bath . . ."

"A flea?" shrieked Orson from his undignified position in the gutter. "You mean . . ."

"Yes, yes. It's the very latest sort of magic. Pulverizing pelicanosis, I call it. Talking of which . . . Oh, dear, oh, dear. Very nasty . . . Talking of which, I've got it all set up."

"You have what set up?"

"The moles and mice and earthworms and so on. At least, I think I have. We'll just have to go there and find out."

"I haven't a clue what you're talking about." Orson made use of the snow and tentatively stood. "But I am going nowhere. I am going to murder you, only murder is far too grand a word for it. You can't murder a disease, can you? Eradicate, exterminate . . . All good words."

"Oh, no. You can't do that," said Cantiger.

"I can't?"

"No, no. Because if I'm dead, you can't give me £100,000 a year – or, at least, you can, but I can't receive it, sort of thing, so I doubt whether that would really be giving, and you promised."

"That was before you made me the laughing stock of the nation," Orson spoke through gritted teeth. "And anyhow, I'm not going to be king. That's all moonshine. Particularly after this afternoon."

"*Nil pudor in sudore*, I always say," Cantiger consoled. "Don't you?"

"No," said Orson.

"And moonshine is powerful stuff. Why aren't you going to be king? It'll be fun. That little Geneva would like it . . . "

"She'll never look at me again."

"She never did."

"True."

"But she will if you're king . . ."

"But you can't make me king."

"I gave you the trots, didn't I?"

"Mmyees," said Orson slowly.

"There. Same thing."

Orson puzzled over this extraordinary assertion. He didn't, in the end, seem to have an answer for it. "So you're saying," he said at last, "that you can move this stone?"

"I am saying that I have set things up so that, with a bit of luck, and with you really wanting to do it, I think that you can move it"

Orson sighed. Then he looked up to the heavens. "I must be mad," he muttered, then, "OK, let's do it."

"Hum, Chloris, hum!" shouted Marina over her shoulder as her party rode a wallop through Cockmead-on-Thuinne.

"What? Here?" The green-haired girl opened her green eyes wide. "At the wallop?"

"Just do it!"

"OK, but it won't be a very good connection!"

"Do it!" Marina's hair wrapped about her face, then was pulled back by the wind as she turned to face forward again.

Chloris set up her humming, but the movement of the horse beneath her made the sound jolt and jerk. It was barely audible above the clatter of hooves and the panting of horses and Riders. "Dame Iseult!" called Marina. "Dame Iseult! Can you hear me?"

The humming momentarily became a squeak as the girl ducked beneath a low branch overhanging the road. "Dame Iseult!" Marina shouted. "Are you there? What news?"

She listened for a while, then turned to Garnish who rode at her side. "She's there, but she keeps breaking up! Cantiger what? On live? He can't be! Please what? Fleas? My fleas? Something about a young man . . . Lugh, the reception's terrible! Going to the stone? My stone? He can't! He must be stopped! Filled rolls? Killed trolls! Who? Dung . . . Oh, *young* man! Moles? But that's my technique! Stopping on the roadside for a what? I don't need to know that, Dame Iseult. No, you're breaking up again! He must not be allowed to move that stone, do you hear? He must be stopped, whatever it takes. No, not favourite steaks, what – ever – it – takes. Yes, plague's fine! Just get rid of him! All right," she snapped back at the green-haired girl. "Stop humming!"

Again she turned to Garnish. "That loathsome little swine Cantiger! He's found a young man to stand for him! He's planning to move the stone! With my fleas! My magic! Oh, Lugh! Come on, come on, come on!"

The stone stood forlornly in the middle of the lawn, forgotten now by everyone. The guards were trying to win worship at the Blitz. Even Hector Potter and his wife were inside, consoling one another in their grief and desolation. The sward itself, usually so perfectly presented, was now covered with snow, and Orson noticed a sprig or two of longer rye grass jutting up from its smooth surface. Hector Potter had lost the will to tend his life's work.

"Big," said Orson decisively as he strolled around the sarsen again. "Big and very, very heavy."

"Yep, but you're not trying to lift it. You're just going to try to get the earth to swallow it again."

"So what do I do?"

"You stand there. You close your eyes. You think of the future of this land unless someone decent becomes king pretty soon, and you say, 'Stone, begone!' three times."

"And that's it?"

"Far as I know." Cantiger shrugged.

"You don't actually know much about this, do you?"

"Er, no," Cantiger admitted, "but magic's always pretty much a hit-and-miss affair, you know. Give it a try."

"OK. Lugh, I feel a bit of a prat. OK. Right. Hold on. Stand here. Think of Logris and what it could be like, what it will be like if it carries on like this. Right. Stone, begone! Stone, begone! Stone, begone. Please . . ."

"No, no, no!" Cantiger jumped up and down. "You have to be precise! 'Stone, begone', not 'Please begone'."

"Well, I just thought – I mean, manners cost nothing."

"No, no! Try it again, but with no fancy stuff. Stone—"

There was a long sigh from the snow-covered earth. The stone creaked and groaned. Then there was crunching, and scuttling, and rattling. The stone lurched for a moment, then trembled violently, then righted itself, then slowly, still trembling, sank into the earth as though into thick liquid.

The two men watched in amazement. They had talked of magic, but Cantiger did not really believe in it, and Orson, though he did, had never believed that Cantiger was its master. At last, only the topmost part of the great sarsen stood proud of the sward. It perceptibly shook itself from side to side as though working its way in, then, again with a sigh, slid back into its mother earth.

There was silence. Snowflakes started to fall again from the bruise-grey sky, large snowflakes that seemed to search conscientiously for the right spot before landing. Orson found that he had caught hold of the little magician and was clasping him to him. He said, "Sorry" and released him, then, in awe, "Lugh almighty!"

Cantiger stood staring at the place where the stone had been. He muttered, "Shit!"

And Orson said, "If that's a spell, I don't think it's very funny."

"Glory glory!" came a bleat from above. "Hallelugha! Wonder of wonders! Ooh, it's you! My sward! My sward is back again!"

Orson grinned up at Potter's beaming face. "That's right, Mr Potter."

"Ooh! Your Majesty!" screamed Potter. "The king! Whoso whatsits is rightwise . . . Oh, that I should live to see the day! And right here, on my sward! Just a minute whilst I get some shoes on, then my lady wife, if that's all right with you, sir, and I will come and reverence you!"

"That would be very nice," said Orson. "I've never really been reverenced."

"Hmm, I bet it's nice," said Cantiger.

Windows were opening all about the square as villeins heard the commotion. Faces emerged in doorways. The word "king", though spoken in hushed tones, rang from building to building.

"Ohdearohdearohdear," said Cantiger. "Here we go . . ."

The Riders' return to the capital was less jaunty than had been their progress to the Blitz Range that morning. The pennants, the shields, the gorgeous apparel and the panoply of war were all there, but many a shield was dented, many a suit of armour twisted and incomplete, many a garment streaked with mud or blood. The horses dragged their feet and hung their heads. Several Riders had bandages about their heads. Several had limbs truncated. Some lay pale-faced on litters, staring up at the sky. Of these, some did not blink when snowflakes landed on their eyes.

In general, however, the mood, if weary, was upbeat. Most Riders did not want to be king and were quite relieved to have been beaten without loss of worship. Of those who did have regal ambitions, most had acquitted themselves well enough and would fight another day, and those who wouldn't did not care any more. Young Riders like Kes had, for the most part, had a brief first taste of top grade Battle Blitz and were euphoric simply at having survived it. They hailed one another cheerily and drank as they rode. The serious warlords rode grim, battle-scarred and menacing. They did not drink, any more than they fought, frivolously. They would carouse seriously when once their horses were bedded down and their kit consigned to the armourers, who would see no sleep tonight.

The bookmakers, in six luxury carts, counted their takings at the rear of the mile-long procession.

At or near its middle, King Leo sat slumped in his saddle, weighed down by gloom and fatigue.

It was not the fighting that had so depressed him, but the certain knowledge throughout the day that it would be followed by the harangue that now battered at him far worse than any warrior's sword. "I mean, we're only talking about the throne here," snapped Arachne, his wife, unnecessarily and not for the first time. She was a gaunt, nervous-looking woman some ten years Leo's junior, with bulging, flashing, cabochon eyes to match the giant stones on her fingers, and constantly working lips, red as a gash in her leathern face. "I mean, this is the chance of a lifetime, and what do you do? Mess around jousting with no-hopers! You should have gone for that ridiculous young man Woborn. All those tricks. Absurd. Or Winston Maisonette, or the King of Northgales or one of the big fellows, but no. Oh, no. Well, let me tell you, if you throw away this opportunity, I will never forgive you. Never. I am obviously born to be Queen, and Mortmain will make a wonderful king. So regal already, the lamb. And what about poor Geneva here? Is she going to remain a mere princess like every other tuppenny-halfpenny princess, all because her father couldn't be bothered to fight for her welfare? I mean, twenty-two thousand acres! How much of that does she get? Six? And how is she meant to live on the income from six thousand acres and one measly city, pray? She was not born to slum it, and nor was I. What on earth is the point of trying to save your own precious life if we're going to starve and you let us all down in the process? I mean . . ."

What she meant was brief and self-evident. What she *said*, however, was long and frequently obscure, with references to the day, for example, when Leo had omitted to kill Boss Buller when he might have done so because he quite liked him, and the day when Leo had omitted to gralloch a hart intended for Mother's Night dinner, in consequence of which it went off and exploded, and to the amount of money that Leo had spent over the years on his collection of budgerigars . . .

Then, of course, there were the inevitable, interminable comparisons between Leo and his younger brother, the late Cobdragon. Many would say that Leo had done well for himself. He had inherited a smallish demesne and increased it a hundredfold. He had never, however, had the hunger or the vigour of his younger brother.

Cobdragon had always been a wild child, and had early on initiated a feud by overcoming several Riders on the fringes of Leo's territories and claiming them as his own. Leo had been inclined to shrug this off as youthful high spirits and impetuousness. He had always been fond of old Cobber. Arachne, however, had insisted on revenge. Cobdragon had been "that thief", "that vermin", and Leo had been nagged into burning the interloper's villages and storming his castles. Of course, now that Cobdragon was acknowledged as the greatest warlord of recent years and was also now conveniently dead, Arachne never ceased to chide Leo with not matching up to the "magnificent achievements" of his brother.

We could take up a whole book with what Arachne said, but what she meant was, "I want to be queen if it kills you."

To be honest, King Leo might have had pretensions to the crown of all Logris twenty years ago, but he was tired now. Years of being henpecked and harangued by Arachne had worn down his once-proud spirit, and he knew well enough that any overlord must fight many sad battles if he was to maintain the peace.

Leo had fought long and hard to win such lands as he had. His children had been reared in the lap of luxury, indulged in everything by their mother, and the result was that young Geneva, who rode on the other side of her mother, was a spoilt brat and Mortmain, his son, a thoroughly nasty, vengeful, effete bit of work who spent most of his time drinking in low taverns with young actor chappies. Mortmain said that war and the arts of war were "brutish and pointless", though where he thought the gold for his fancy clothes and fancy friends came from, King Leo would very much have liked to know.

The idea of Mortmain as heir apparent to the throne of Logris – with a mother like Arachne behind him – turned Leo's stomach.

He had fought today, therefore, with his usual courage and skill, but with circumspection. There were always young Riders full of vainglory and more enthusiasm than technique whom an old warrior like Leo could take down a peg without danger and without inflicting too much damage. He had met with twelve of them today, and had known before each encounter just what was going to happen because he had first studied his opponent's style and noted his weaknesses. He had kept worship, yet risked little.

To be frank, he would welcome a decent overlord and

would willingly yield him to him if it meant peace in the land, and decent laws whereby he could dispose of his wife without incurring the wrath of her sister, Elaine of the Northern Isles, and her vile brothers Warhawk, Ger, Housewolf and Garech – as gruesome, taciturn, clannish and treacherous a quartet of thugs as ever emerged from those dark, desolate lands.

At last Geneva interrupted her mother's tirade. "Mummy, darling," she drawled. "Do stop being dreary. There are other days, and anyhow, something's happening. Who is that?"

"It's Cador of Hornwoggle . . ." said Leo. He frowned at the gathering of Riders and pilliers earnestly talking up ahead. "Looks like there's something afoot." He snatched at this chance to escape Arachne and kicked his horse into a trot.

He returned three minutes later at a canter. "Looks like we may have a king!" he shouted, only briefly reining in. "Lad's removed the stone twice and put it back again twice already. I've got to find Buller!"

"Why Boss Buller?" asked Geneva.

"Because it's his ward!" bellowed Leo. "That boy who's been mooning over you!"

"The *pillier!*" shrilled Geneva, outraged.

"Yeah, well, madam," Leo snarled. "Your dad was a pillier once. And your mother had a lot to do with pilliers before I was offered the lands to take her away and make her respectable. Oh, and your brother's father was a pillier and all. So put that in your fancy filigree pipe and choke on it."

He rode off happily, pursued by shrill squeals of "Leo! How dare you?" and "Mummy! Is this true?"

He had been wanting to do that for years. A new era was on its way.

And not before time.

The snow had stopped now, and the sun had emerged, a fluffy white thing in a dirty white sky at first, which darkened as it sank and as the mists faded until now, deep gold, it pulsed and wavered in a bright blue sky.

The Riders queued to take their turns on the sward. The smaller and lighter of them tried their own versions of magic, which failed to move the stone an inch. The bigger and stockier tried weightlifting. Their faces went purple and deep runnels appeared in their necks and their veins throbbed visibly, but still the stone would not budge. The crowd urged on their efforts and rewarded their failures with jeers and catcalls.

"Everyone is free to try!" hollered Cantiger into the crowded tiers of seats. "Men or women. Come try your luck! Your very own chance to have a delightful, well-appointed kingdom with extensive woodland, coastal frontage on every side, mountains, rivers, livestock, plentiful sporting facilities and power of life and death over two million inhabitants. Roll up, roll up for the chance of a lifetime! Let's be having you! Oh, bad luck, sir! Nice try! There can only be one king or queen and Supreme Ruler and we think we've got him, but everyone should have a go! That's it, sir – oh, I am sorry, madam – put your back into it! Oh, dear. Shame. Medics! Another one. Now, sir. You look a brawny fellow! Show us what you can do . . ."

Suddenly he was aware of two concerned faces looking up at him. He lowered his voice as he jumped down from the chair. "Oh, hi, Boss Buller. You've heard the news, then?"

"Yes," Buller growled. He was out of breath. "What in umber's going on?"

"Orson, sir." Cantiger shrugged. "Just came along here, said, 'Stone, begone!' and it went."

"Orson?" said Kes, who was brilliant red but essayed a dismissive laugh. "This is some sort of sick joke! He's my pillier! He shouldn't even have tried to move it!"

"Nonetheless, he did, sir, which, according to the legend on the stone, is the right of every freeborn Logrian. And then he commanded the stone to return and it did. Just like that 'Mazing. Bewildering. A miracle, I calls it."

"An absurd trick is what I call it," snorted Kes. "If you think I'm going to bend the knee to Orson . . ."

"Sh, now. It hasn't come to that," said Buller sternly. "Where is the boy?"

"He's a trifle indisposed," said Cantiger.

"He was more than a trifle indisposed at the Blitz," said Kes. "I mean, that's what I mean! Anyone who can thingy like that just can't be king!"

"So you won't want to have a try yourself, sir?"

"Well . . ." Kes eyed the stone warily, then frowned. "I don't thingy! Are you saying I thingy? If you're saying I thingy, I'll damned well . . ."

"Of course you do, you pompous fool!" barked Buller, "and so will the king, whoever he may be, or else he's not human and we don't want him."

Cantiger approved of this sentiment. He drew closer to Buller "'Scuse me, Boss," he said out of the corner of his mouth. "Could we have a quiet word?"

"Of course, of course. K, my boy, go and get in the queue and have a go. Yes, now, whatsyourname, what was it?"

"Well, sir, if you approve of Orson being king, and if you think the country can do with someone honest and straightforward like that keeping the peace, and if you would like to have a close relative and friend of yours and Kes's as monarch, and if everything works out . . ."

"Yes?" prompted Buller.

Cantiger glanced quickly over his shoulders, then beckoned Buller to stoop. "You might just think it worthwhile to recall how I might have brought Orson to you as a baby sixteen years back . . ."

"You? No, it was that lovely little thing Bessy, dead now, of course. Shouldn't have done it, really, but she had such lovely big—"

" . . . And I said to you, 'This is King Cobdragon's little boy,' don't you remember?" he prompted.

"—brown eyes . . ." Buller snapped from his reverie. "Cobdragon? Good feller, but no—"

". . . got in wedlock, you will remember, before his wife died . . ."

"Ah." Comprehension glimmered above the horizon. "Succession, you mean. Biggest kingdom in Logris, hereditary alliances, sort of thing . . . ?"

"Those are factors," agreed Cantiger.

"And remind me, you devious little rat. Just why did Cobdragon not want to rear his own son?"

"Because I had seen in a vision that he would be killed by one of his own offspring, and naturally he didn't suspect dear sweet innocent little Marina . . ."

"Ha! That woman's a devil, by all accounts. Wouldn't surprise me in the slightest if she did the old boy in . . ."

"He died of a bloody flux earlier this year while sitting on the garderobe. A man-at-arms with a bow was found stabbed to death on the ground floor of the garderobe."

"Ouch."

"Exactly."

"Darned clever of you to foresee that all those years ago."

"Ah, well," said Cantiger modestly. "It's what we do."

"Yes," Buller sighed. His eyes had a faraway look. "Yes, now that you mention it, I do seem to remember. Dark, rainy night as I recall. Little bundle. Cobber trusted no one like he trusted good old Buller. That's what you said. Fine example to the boy. Couldn't wish for better than to grow up like good old Buller. Head screwed on, you said, valiant, just, noble, lusty . . ."

"I knew you'd remember," said Cantiger with satisfaction.

"Oh, yes. Clear as day. Absolutely. Ah, it's K's turn." Buller turned to the stone before the Abbey. "He's not a bad guy, really," he assured Cantiger softly. "Just thinks that might is right and hasn't got much of his own."

"Except his position," said Cantiger sourly.

"Yes. Do him good to find a bit of meek-inheriting-the-earth stuff," Buller thought aloud as his son grew pucer and pucer and at last collapsed in the muddy, trampled snow. "Don't want too much of that sort of thing. The meek are usually smug gits. Just enough to keep life interesting and remind us that all things must pass sort of thing . . . Surprises. Turn-ups for the book. That's what's needed. Make life interesting . . . King Orson, eh? Well, why not? Young, strong, honest, not too bright . . ."

"You know," said Cantiger, "I think that King Cobdragon made a very wise choice."

"What?" Buller awoke again. "Oh, Cobber. Yes. Little bundle. Rainy night. Stormy. Remember it as if it were yesterday."

* * *

Orson felt drained. He also felt distinctly frightened. If he had not had an upset stomach before, he would certainly have one now.

When this little Cantiger guy had turned up and proposed that Orson should become king, he had thought of it as a delightful fantasy, a bit of fun. Now he was looking at the very alarming prospect of demanding fealty from the greatest Riders in the world, men who gave fealty only when subdued by force and offered no alternative save death.

He was a boy – and he suddenly felt very, very young.

But the die was cast The world knew that he had moved the great stone, and, if he were to refuse to try at least to do it again, he would not only lose such little worship as he possessed, but would almost certainly lose his head into the bargain. Riders did not like whippersnappers demanding fealty, then saying, "Sorry. Didn't mean it really. Just my little joke." It riled them.

He had pledged that he would be back at the stone at five o'clock, when the sun sank below the top of the Abbey tower. From the window of his room in the Golden Cow, he could see that he had just ten minutes or so left. He had washed thoroughly under the standing pipe in the courtyard, scratching every suspect area in search of the missing flea. Every flea that he had found, and he had found several, he had handled as gently as possible, explaining that he really was very sorry, but, if they would not mind terribly, he would be grateful if they would go elsewhere.

He did not want fleas to turn against him now.

He had dressed as well as he could in a pair of Kes's pale kid-suede breeks, a fine new pair of riding boots that he had received for Mother's Night, and a loose shirt of white cotton with a broad white collar. He would wear no armour, only his light sword at his hip. Armour would merely have been provocative and presumptuous. Riderly Riders were not supposed to attack men disarmed.

He pulled himself to his feet and strolled across to his bed. He pulled back the counterpane and delicately withdrew the black Thing with the mysterious, meaningless writing on it. "It knocks you over, but you should see what it does to the other guy," Cantiger had told him. Orson did not know whether he should believe him. Somehow everything that Cantiger said sounded uncertain and insincere, yet everything that he had pledged had so far come true, much, it seemed, to his own surprise.

He looked around the little room at his familiar possessions – the clothes, the arms, the fanzine picture of Lynch smiting a dragon, the purse-nets, the box said to have been carved out of unicorn horn, the swords, the gauntlets, the rose wrought in gold, the few paltry possessions accumulated in a short life. He had never aspired to greatness, but he rather fancied that, whether by greatness or by death, that life was about to be brought to an end.

He sighed and, shaking his head in bemusement at the oddity of life, shambled from the room and down the stairs to the snowy square.

Twilight thickened. The shadows of the Abbey and of the stone had lengthened until they spanned the sward, the banked seats and, at the last, the entire square before they were subsumed into the great shadow of night. Torches were lit, and braziers on which chestnuts popped. Hector Potter would not allow a fire on his sward, but instead a huge bonfire crackled on the rougher turf at the centre of the square. As always when there was a bonfire, there was whooping and ululation, and there were children who had to leap through the swirling flush of sparks, and someone was selling burgers.

The bookmakers had set up their stalls, delighted at this unexpected source of revenue. They were offering 2-1 on Orson removing the stone, 7-2 against his failing to do so, and a wide variety of long odds against other Riders doing the trick. Kes was 1300-1. One bookmaker even had Princess Marina of Hennamucus at 5-4 and she had not even put in an appearance yet, but there is always one bookie who has read the book before it has been written.

The Riders and their ladies were now in a place covered with cloth of gold like an hall, for to behold who did best, and thereon to give judgment. This pavilion had a special fenced-off viewing area to the right of the stone. They did not trust burgers. Not since the White Sickness.

Here an entire gleaming, glistening aurochs slowly turned above the flames, and six suckling pigs who really should have given up suckling and gone to college by now, and all you had to do was pull out your knife and a trencher of bread, spear the trencher and hold it beneath the roasting beasts to toast and to absorb some of the dripping fat, then slice glutinous chunks of meat, sprinkle the whole with liquamen, and lo! A toasted sandwich fit for heroes.

Here in the viewing area people had no wish to do things with a bonfire. They just watched it, and, as intelligent people do by fires or the sea, thought. And the conversation of the ladies was of the "Darling, isn't it too wonderful and exciting?", twittering and drawling sort, because everyone was rather nervous. Many of the Riders, however, though they smiled faintly and vaguely acknowledged such overtures, drew rapidly aside and stared at the fire with cold eyes, and kept their own counsel.

Such was the scene when Orson arrived. He did not think, of course, to venture into the Riders' enclosure. He was merely a pillier. He looked around for Cantiger, bought a burger and a glass of ale, and watched the Ochtie girls dancing around the fire to the music of lutes and fiddles and bladder-pipes.

"Kings, Queens, Riders, Ladies and Gentlemen!" called a booming voice. It battered at the walls of the houses about the square. The music dwindled and died. One bladder-pipe let out a last wild squeak that made the villeins laugh. "We come now to the high point of our evening. As you know, we have been summoned here to find a king of kings, an overlord, on the explicit instructions of Lugh himself. And this here stone has appeared out of nowhere, with the magical words, 'Whoso removeth this stone from this patch of grass is rightwise king or queen od – sod it - of - Logris', and you can't get much clearer than that, now, can you?"

The crowd mumbled in approving response. Everyone was drifting now like breeze-blown litter towards the sward. Orson went with the crowd.

"Well, many have tried to perform this apparently impossible feat, but so far no one has achieved it."

"Oh, yes, they have!" cried one man.

"Yeah, I saw it!"

"Yes, yes," shouted the man up by the stone, whom at present, Orson could not see. "But it's still here, isn't it? I've heard the rumours, as have all of you, but the fact is, remove means remove like permanently, doesn't it? And this here stone has not been removed on account it's still here, and you can't argue with that, now, can you?"

Again the crowd mumbled and seethed, their voices doubtful this time.

"So tonight, the Premier League Riders, the best and bravest warriors, the Champion hewers, smiters, hurlers, gougers, pillagers, quaffers and carousers, and one or two of their bold ladies, are going to have a crack at it. So, put your hands together, please, for Sir Bruce Sans Pitie – yea – yea – yea!!!"[35]

The mob applauded politely. By standing on tiptoe, Orson could see above the heads of the villeins a broad, stocky Rider with curly black hair, curly black eyebrows and a voluminous beard. He spat on his hands as he stepped forward from the enclosure and looked up at the stone. The applause became a patter, like that of dripping cement. Then there was silence.

Sir Bruce prodded the stone with a forefinger like a saveloy. He walked around it. He shook his head. He gave a crooked grin, revealing teeth that you would not want to encounter on the top of a wall. "Nah," he said. "Tomfoolery. Move yon bugger, 'e'll squash un. Blow that for a game of corbies and engines."[36]

The crowd gave a collective disappointed sigh of "Ah!" as Bruce stepped back into the Riders' Enclosure.

[35]It was his voice that put in these exclamation marks, all on its own. You don't get many people who can speak exclamation marks. Thanks be to Lugh.

[36]A common expression in Logris at the time which, like "Sort of like" and "Cheap at half the price" and "Chance would be a fine thing" had the merit of complete incomprehensibility. Hawker suggests that it originated in an obsolete game called "Corbies and Engines", in which a man with a flat bat would stand in front of a cactus whilst a specially designed engine projected dead crows (corbies) at him, attempting to hit his cactus, but this just seems too *obvious*.

"Well, each to his own, say I," said the man with the booming voice who, Orson now saw, wore a red tailcoat and a shiny black hat like a funnel. "And, next on the list, a rare candidate from the fairer sex, and very nice too. Always like a good joke. Welcome, please, the gwhorrgeous, pouting, curvaceous – bet she could cling on to a greasy flagpole in a Force Eight gale, eh? – Lady – Magsin – Toodux!!!"

Down in the enclosure, Magsin removed her cloak and shook out her mane of auburn hair. She wore nothing now but a sort of swimsuit of embossed crimson velvet and a torque bracelet of gold, cunningly wrought in the shape of a garden hose. She stepped forward, fists raised and clasped above her head to acknowledge the applause and the whistles of the crowd. She brought the fists down hard on the toastmaster's top hat. There was another flicker of movement as her long right leg arose to slam into his groin. He said "!!!!!!!" All of him subsided except his eyes, which headed in the opposite direction.

The crowd loved that. There was whooping and cheering and great laughing and japing. She gravely accepted this tribute, then lay down on her back at the foot of the stone. She raised her feet and shuffled forward until her bum was against the stone's base, the soles of her feet against its surface and her knees against her breasts.

All right, it was disrespectful of the toastmaster to surmise as to the tenaciousness of a lady's thighs, and you really cannot have that sort of thing in a well-ordered society, but such is gross nature that not a single male watcher, save possibly a small saddleback pig which had unwisely strolled on to the square, did not think, "Phworr" and "Grrrr" and "A hurricane wouldn't dislodge that one once she got a grip," and "Do you think I could be reincarnated as a greasy flagpole?"

Buller, I am afraid to relate, actually said them.

Then she pushed.

Her back arched. Those legs tensed. The calf muscles gleamed, slick and hard as mussel shells. The thighs rippled, and several people at the front of the crowd dropped their food and had to fall on their hands and knees in order to retrieve it.

It was the first time that anyone had tried this technique. It was a noble attempt. It gave innocent pleasure to many people. But it failed.

Others tried. Winston Maisonette strove manfully. Brastias declined the honour. Lynch merely assessed the weight of the stone and announced, "If anyone's going to do this, he will do it easily. I'm not going to make a fool of myself trying, and I'm not cut out for kingship." Woborn, though he had taken the prize for the day's Blitz and so was cheered to the echo, announced, "As does my Lord Lynch, so do I," prodded the stone and walked off.

King Leo put on a great show of attempting to lift the thing, then laughed uproariously, made a rude gesture at Arachne and leaped over the ribbon bordering the enclosure. Warhawk, who was booed, had a go with a rope, as did his brothers, who, when they had failed, sneered and snarled and spat at the villeins. Hammer tried a rope and a team of horses, but was disqualified, and sulked. Boris and Ran, two Deedong Riders of enormous might and worship who were visiting for the Blitz, gave the thing a try, though they were obviously not rightwise born Kings of Logris on account of being Deedongs.

Cordell of Gales, one of the best Riders in the world, had a go with a giant hammer, but the hammer bounced off and hit a fletcher in the crowd, who subsequently thought that he was a pug dog and snorted and whiffled and lived in a dresser. Steadfast, Ulfius and Dreadnought followed Lynch's example, whilst Boss Primrose[37] attacked the stone with a chisel. King Skinner tried to dig it up with an ingenious maroon folding knife with a special attachment for just this sort of thing, whilst Hector Potter beat him about the head with a shoe. The Dean of Greatwen tried a trick involving fire and vinegar, but that did not work at all well, and was very boring for the spectators, and Buller was too busy having a tête-à-tête with Magsin even to bother to try.

Orson was feeling ambivalent. People were getting bored and drifting away to the taverns now. No one was bothering to fuel

---

[37]His mother loved him, and thought that no Rider would attack another called Primrose. She was wrong.

the bonfire any more. The night was wearing on, and everyone seemed to have forgotten about him. In many ways, that was an enormous relief. He would go back to familiar lands, familiar practices and familiar people, and, aside from an occasional allusion to mushy peas, the whole episode would be forgotten.

On the other hand, he felt that he really might be quite good at being king, and he thought how Geneva would look up to him if he were, and he knew that this was certainly the only chance that he was going to get. If he did nothing now, he would probably regret it for the rest of his life . . .

"Well, that about wraps it up for this evening's entertainment," the toastmaster was saying. He had a headache and a sore groin and not a single exclamation mark in his voice. "But be at the Blitz-Range tomorrow sharp at eleven for some truly sizzling, blood-soaked action. And remember, be nice to one another. Life, after all, is just a pot of poppies, and doesn't add up to a whole hill of turnips, and we still have the stars, and what I say is, tomorrow's just another day. Will be. And so is yesterday. Was. And today isn't. So, as you stroll down life's broad, strait, bendy, straight, obstacle-strewn highway, just remember . . ."

"Hold!" cried a mighty voice.

The toastmaster's jaw dropped. He looked about him with not just one wild surmise but at least four. "Who said that?" he gasped. "And hold what?"

"I," said the mighty voice, which seemed to come from the Abbey, "I who will be heeded. There is one here who shall be king. Marvel ye nothing thereof, for he is bred of a king's lions, er, I mean loins, and brother to a queen, though he knows it not, and he shall prove the mightiest and sagest of all kings of this land. Call forward Orson Delamere Maudite. Call him forward, I say!"

"?" murmured Orson.[38]

Some of the villeins had fallen to their knees. Some, for some strange reason, had covered their heads with table napkins or towels. Others were grinning at this unexpected turn of events. "Orson, did he say?"

[38]A lot more people can do this than "!!!"

"Who's Orson?"

"I don't know. Let's see him."

"He's the one did it this afternoon, they say."

"Yeah, in the woods. Dramatic, by all accounts . . ."

"Nah, not that! Moved the stone. He moved the stone!"

"Did he? I only heard about the thing in the woods."

"Mushy peas, they say. Is that how he moved it, then?"

"No, I don't think so. I think the stone came later."

"We want Orson!"

The toastmaster was still goggling and trembling, uncertain, as it seemed, what status a disembodied voice possessed. Of a sudden, however, he found that two Riders had stepped forward and usurped his mastery of ceremonies. "I know Orson," declared Lynch, the flower of chivalry. "He is a fine young man. Orson? Are you here?"

"Over here!" Orson raised a hand. The people in front of him turned and drew aside to make way for him. He stepped forward slowly, nervously, glancing from side to side, the black Thing hanging loosely from his right hand.

"This is just trickery!" called the other Rider. "This is just some sort of hocus pocus conjuring trick! Someone will move the stone one day, and then she – I mean . . ."

"Silence!" roared the mighty voice. "Bring Orson to the stone . . ."

"Just some sort of silly stunt," cried the other Rider breathlessly. "She will be here soon, and you'll see that this is all a mistake. Just wait . . ."

"Get off!" roared the crowd, which was enjoying this bit, and fancied the idea of someone other than an established Rider beating the odds. "Who do you think you are?"

"His name is Sadok!" boomed the MV. "He seeks to steal the crown for the sorceress Marina!"

"Boo!" bawled the crowd and "We don't want no sorceresses!" and "We want Orson! We want Orson!"

Orson found himself patted and pushed forward into the circle of torchlight about the stone. His cheeks were flushed, his brow slick with sweat despite the cold. Lynch embraced him. He said, "Don't worry. Just give it a go."

Orson nodded and gulped. He murmured, "Would you just

mind standing back a bit, please?"

"Sure. Back! Back!" Lynch shouted. "Give him room to breathe!"

Orson looked at the Riders' enclosure. Buller was there, proudly preening. Magsin caught Orson's eye and made a little clapping gesture. Kes looked frankly furious.

"Look, this is ridiculous," said Sadok. "Most irregular. I think we should wait until tomorrow at least . . ."

"Shut up," said Lynch. Then, with uplifted hands, "Everyone! Silence!"

The crowd fell silent. One big gust of wind made the flames from the torches flare sideways, puddering. Then they stood upright again, and sinuously danced.

Orson kneeled beneath the stone. He bent until his nose was mere inches above the turf. "Stone, begone!" he said softly, "Stone, begone! Stone, begone!" Then, "Please, please, please, stone, for the last time . . ."

Someone coughed. Otherwise there was total silence save for the swishing of the wind in the buildings all around.

Orson waited. And prayed.

"When's he going to start?" whispered someone.

"When you're ready, Orson," said Lynch softly.

Orson felt the movement in the grass beneath his calves. It seemed to churn and tremble and seethe. Stones crunched and scraped against one another. There was a creaking, a groaning. The shaking grew more and more violent, causing Orson's teeth to chatter. He lowered a hand to the turf as though to prevent himself too from being consumed by the earth. Then, in the moth's-wing torchlight, he saw the ground at the foot of the stone actually billowing, rising and falling like silk on a breeze. At the last, it sank into shadow and remained in shadow.

The stone dropped with a sudden thud. The crowd gasped as one.[39]

The stone tilted to one side. It sank further, in a series of little groaning, crunching stages. The crowd was murmuring now, like a high-voltage cable. One or two shouts arose. One woman screamed. Lynch breathed, "Yes!"

[39]As one what? As one does? As one crowd? As one beach-ball? You say these things, all casual like, and they prove monsters, banishing sleep . . .

This time, the stone's final descent was accomplished all at once, like a great ship sinking. One minute, there were three or four feet of rock. The next, it was gone, all gone, and the soil settled over the wound in the ground.

The rumbling in the earth continued for some time. That fateful stone still had a long way to go.

The crowd saw all of this. But, for a good ten seconds after the stone had vanished, they said nothing. Then, as the realization of what they had witnessed and what it meant truly sank in, they burst out as if to a conductor's cue in cheers and clapping and squealing and thudding. Timbrals tinkled. Horns blew. Cymbals clashed. Even the bell of the Abbey mysteriously broke into a clamour of peals.

Orson remained where he was. Amidst all the noise, he did not hear the ring of steel on steel. Amidst all the blur of movement and colour, he did not see the blade raised to strike.

It was a voice – Kes's voice – "Orson! Look out!" – that rang through the air and checked the jubilation. Orson ducked and rolled. The blade hissed, nearly thudded into the turf but, at the last minute, swung round and upward again. Orson caught a glimpse of the savage rictus on Sadok's face as once more the blade descended. He thrust up the black Thing to parry.

He would never know if he recalled Cantiger's instructions at that moment or whether it was pure reflex or chance that made him pull the wiggly bit.

What he did know, in a fuzzy sort of way, was that there was a flash. Sadok's expression changed to one of terminal astonishment. There was a sound louder than anyone there present had ever heard, a sound that slammed at eardrums and walls and shook windows and ran rattling through the streets of Greatwen. But, long before that happened, Orson had seen Sadok toppling towards him and had rolled again. The man lay still, face down, by his side.

"Dear Lugh!" Lynch breathed. "What in the name of Rosmerta was that?"

"Er, it's called X something," said Orson, pulling himself to his feet. "It's a magical sort of sword thingy. Look, it's got a sort of whatsit here and these little hard things here and . . . ermm . . ."

He looked about him. Lynch was doing something down on the floor. So was Buller. So, with his father's hand firmly on his shoulder, was Kes. So was Woborn, of all people, and Magsin and . . .

Orson began to kneel himself. This had happened to him before in church. Then it suddenly struck him that that was what everyone was doing: kneeling.

And to him.

"Um . . . I think . . ." said Orson, wondering what a new king should say to his people. He knew that he should speak some memorable words. They should be inspiring words, spoken confidently but without vainglory, they should speak eloquently of justice for all and a bright new future under his sovereignty. Something about a National Elf, perhaps . . .

Inspiration visited him. ". . . I think we should all have a bit of a party," he announced. "And the drinks are on me."

He had struck exactly the right note.

Chapter Seven

CANTIGER sidled up to the King-elect mere moments later. At first, the men-at-arms who had formed about the sward tried to bar his progress, but Orson heard the shrill "Waaghs" and "Who-do-you-think-you-ares" and ordered that he be let through. Smugly smirking, he fell to his knees at Orson's feet on the once-more-level sward.

"Where have you been?" Orson asked out of the corner of his grinning mouth.

"In the Abbey." Cantiger winked up at him. "Amazing, the effect you can get with a megaphone in the nave. Then I had to ring the bell, all that. Theatre, you see. Essential."

"Oh," Orson nodded. He extended a regal hand to raise Cantiger to his feet "So what the umber do I do now?"

"Well, absolutely nothing tonight. Make the most of the feelgood factor."

"What's one of those?"

"The fact that everyone's pissed."

"Oh."

"Then tomorrow we get down to business. First thing's to get crowned. That way, you get the army on your side and you can give anyone who opposes you the chop, legal-like. We'll set the date for a coronation for, say, a month from today and, of course, when that happens, all the other Kings and Riders must swear fealty to you. At least that way, we'll know who's going to make trouble. Openly, at least. Then you'll have to get a wife and an heir, pronto. You're going to be busy."

"Oh, I'll cope. What was all that about son of a king and all that?" Orson asked as he waved to the jubilant crowd.

"Yeah, well, I'll tell you about all that tomorrow. Sixteen years ago, I delivered this little foundling to Boss Buller . . ."

"Sixteen years?" Orson bowed low to some curtsying ladies as he walked back to the pavilion. "But sixteen years ago, you'd have been ten or twelve, max."

"Cantiger."

"What?"

"I said 'Cantiger'," said Cantiger

"Why?"

"Because that's my name." Cantiger was bullish.

Orson frowned. "Yes, I know that. My name's Orson, but I don't go round saying it for no reason."

"No, but you called me . . . Oh, forget it. No, but we develop young, us Cantigers." Cantiger was still frowning as they re-entered the pavilion. The Riders and ladies stood back with bows and curtsies to create a passageway to the stage where tonight's cabaret should have been. "No, that's not right . . ." Cantiger considered. He took a goblet of fizzy Deedong blonk from the proffered silver tray. He gulped. Suddenly he snapped his fingers. "No. Got it Thing is, we great wizards live backwards. That's it. I get younger every year, see? That's how I can prognostellwhat'sgoingtohappen."

"Are you sure about that?"

"Yeah. Yeah, that's what it is. I was forty . . . um . . . two when I brought this little foundling . . ."

"Orson, my boy!" Buller leaped up the steps to enfold Orson in an embrace that smelled strongly of polecat and cider-brandy. "Never knew you had it in you! Great trick, that, with the stone. And as for that black thingy! Couldn't have a look, could I?"

"Of course." Orson smiled fondly at his erstwhile putative parent. "Just don't touch the wiggly bit."

"Extraordinary," said Buller as he studied the implement. He leaned close to Orson and murmured, "Look, Orson, K's taking this pretty badly. Bit of a shock, you know. Heir to an ordinary little Ridership, and suddenly your little brother's king and all that. Difficult. Is there some sort of job he could do? Something that sounds important but doesn't need brains?" He stepped back and spoke louder. "Amazing! So it's this wiggly bit that does the business, is it?"

"Hello, Orson . . ." Kes appeared at his father's shoulder. "Done well for yourself, I'd say. High King, eh?"

Orson blinked affectionately at the man he had always thought of as his brother. It was strange, he thought, how acceptable, even endearing, faults in people could be when they were transparent. K was transparent as a chalk stream. "Thanks for what you did back there, K," Orson said. He took his brother's hand. "With that Sadok, I mean."

Kes shrugged. "Well, can't have people killing the king, can you? That sort of thing catches on, in no time – well, you won't have a king, will you? Stands to reason. I'd pass a law about that if I were you. Anyone found killing the king will be in seriously big trouble."

"That's a very good idea." Orson nodded. "I'll tell you what. I hereby confer on you, Boss Kes Delamere Maudite, er . . ." He looked about him and grabbed something from a passing tray: ". . . the Squirrel-and-Mushroom Vol-au-Vent of Honour for saving the High King's Life, and appoint you Hereditary Captain of the King's Bodyguard and Lord Chief Justice of all Logris with special responsibilities for the rights of damosels and villeins. How about that?"

Kes looked at the Order that had been placed in his hand. A strange magic had been done. A moment ago, this had been a canapé. Now it was a national treasure and a family heirloom.

"And that is quite enough appointing for one night," murmured Cantiger. He grasped Orson's wrist and steered him away to a quiet spot. "Now listen," he said firmly, "that was all very nice and well done, but just you remember. Everyone's going to want everything from you, and if you just give it away to the first people who ask, you're going to make enemies fast. People have got to earn their advancement. Except me, of course," he added hastily.

"Oh, all right," Orson sighed. He could see that Cantiger was going to be a frightful killjoy. He caught sight of a flash of gold hair, a golden arm, a dress of molten sapphire. "Hey! Geneva!" he called. "I want a word with you!"

"And that's another thing . . ." bleated Cantiger to no one in particular.

* * *

"It's gone!" Marina gasped. She stared briefly, then her head swivelled this way and that. She was panting. "It's gone! What are all these villeins doing? Out of my way, villein pigs!" She lashed at the celebrating people who obstructed her path to the site of the stone. "How dare you drink blonk like Riders, and in a public place? This is anarchy!"

"No, it ain't," answered one rocking, bleary-eyed man with a gleaming nose. "It's on King Orson's say-so, so you just watch out, or 'e'll chop you down with X whatsit, like 'e did that Sadok bloke."

"Sadok?" Marina yapped. "Sadok's dead?"

"Dead as a dollop of dung. Which is what 'e was any road. Trying to argue with Lugh, indeed. And trying to kill our King Orson. Disgusting, I call it."

"Who *is* this King Orson?" demanded Marina of the assembled villeins about the table, where huge barrels of ale and blonk lay dripping. "You!" she pointed with her whip at a fat woman who looked marginally more sober than the rest of the gathering. "Tell me now, before I turn you into a carthorse."

"'E's the new King," the woman replied, with a huge shrug that caused her bosom to arise momentarily above her putative waistline. "Did that thing in the wood. Then comes 'ere and removed the stone. No arguing with that, now. An' I'm not afraid of you, missis, 'cos you do somefing nasty to me, Orson'll use X fingy on you. That'll larn yer. By the way, your friend's 'ead's gone a bit dodgy."

The villeins all nodded at one another and mumbled sagely.

"Impertinent slag!" snarled Marina. Then, under her breath to Garnish and Ondslake who rode at her either side, "This is a disaster. It's that Cantiger. I know it is. Come on."

"What are you going to do?" asked Garnish.

"Gauge the situation. There will be a lot of Riders who are not going to like this. Some nobody coming out of the woodwork and claiming overlordship. We need to know how much support he has. If his claim is strong, I have a failback plan . . ."

Garnish looked suspiciously at her friend. Snake's heads are not normally expressive, but there was genuine concern in those amber eyes. "Oh, Marina, you wouldn't . . ."

"Only if it was absolutely necessary, darling. And it wouldn't be for long."

"It's too terrible even to think of."

"Nothing is too terrible," said Marina as she dismounted. "Not for the throne."

Marina strode to the pavilion's entrance. Her followers hobbled after her. No sooner had she crossed the threshold, however, than Woborn stepped forward. "I'm sorry," he said. "Only Premier Riders or their immed— " He stopped. He stared at the grimy face and the leaf-cluttered hair of the woman in front of him. "Um . . . Marina?"

"Hi, Woborn," said Marina, scanning the burbling crowd. "You left rather suddenly last time I saw you."

"Er – oh, yes," said the frank-faced young man, who had been one of the many suitors invited by Cobdragon to woo his daughter. "Sudden, um, prior engagement. Made before. Prior. Very. Damosel. Terribly distressed. Forgotten. Fleas – I mean, please forgive me. Fleas well, are they?"

"Fine, fine."

"Good. Interesting business, I should think, flea-keeping."

"Oh, it is. Now, what's this I hear about a new king?"

"Oh, yes." Woborn's face lit up. "Isn't it great? Orson. Young guy. Nice, I thought. And you should have seen the way he killed your Sadok. Brilliant. Used a thing called X-Calibre. Never saw anything like it. Royal blood, too, so they say."

"Oh?" Marina's eyes were narrowed to mere observation slits.

"Yeah. I don't know exactly how, but Buller and Professor Cantiger are giving a press-conference in the morning when all will be made—"

"*Professor* Cantiger?" Now Marina was shaking like a docking ferry.

"Yes, well, that's not his real title. We were told it. His Excellency the Panjandrum and Plenipotentiary-in-Ordinary, Counsellor-in-Chief to his Royal Logrian Majesty, Possessor of the Royal Ear, Lord High Chancellor and Minister for Blonk Production with Portfolio for the Care of Fallen Damosels, the Egregious – I think it was Egregious – and Serene Professor Cantiger. I think that was it, or most of it. Funny little chap, but King Orson says he's indispensable, so I suppose he must be. Why? Do you know him?"

"That little—" Marina was still shaking, and her gauntleted right hand closed and opened on the pommel of her ballock-knife. She reflected that now was perhaps not the time to give a character sketch of this luminary. She practised deep breathing and finally managed, "Yes. I know him. So, what sort of support has this so-called King got?"

"Well, having seen what he did to the stone, and to Sadok, most of us are behind him. Lynch, Leo, Brastias, Winston, Skinner, me . . . I don't think the guys from the Northern Isles are likely to accept any overlord of any sort, so there may be trouble there, but the villeins are going to like him. No, I'd say he has a pretty good power-base, especially with this X-Calibre thing . . ."

"Would you, indeed?" hummed Marina. "So, where is this paragon?"

"Umm . . ." Woborn stood on tiptoe and searched the crowd. "No . . . Oh, there he is! Over there, talking to Lynch and the Professor and that pretty little girl of Leo's. Do you want me to introduce you?"

"What a good idea," cooed Marina. "How delightful. Too kind."

Cobdragon would have beamed his approval. All that expensive education had not, after all, been wasted.

His Marina had turned out a proper little lady.

"Well, I'm prepared to accept the evidence of my own eyes," said Lynch. "I couldn't have moved that stone an inch, Jen. It was always going to be a surprise . . . "

"Yes, well, if you're king, you're king," sighed Geneva to Orson, "and there's nothing anyone can do about it, I suppose, but really! It does seem the most extraordinary business. Are you sure you're really of royal blood?"

"Um . . ." said Orson.

"Yes, he's quite sure," put in Cantiger. "It will all be explained tomorrow. Your Majesty, I really think . . ."

"Will you go away?" Orson muttered. "Can't you see I'm wooing?"

155

"Well, don't."

"I'll darned well woo when I want to, thank you."

"Because we really can't have kings just popping up out of the woodwork if they're not really royal." Geneva was addressing Lynch again. "I mean, only this afternoon, he was just a pillier doing the strangest things in the woods, so I hear. Very unroyal behaviour."

"Oh, I don't know . . ." said Lynch.

"I thought you said she'd be all over me . . ." Orson whispered urgently to Cantiger.

"Well, she's talking to you, isn't she?"

"Great." Orson tutted.

"Well, what do you expect? She's just been proved catastrophically wrong. She's consistently insulted the rightful king. Her sort don't apologize."

"She's wonderful."

"She's a walking disaster."

"She's dignified."

"Snotty, more like."

"Will you go away?"

"No."

"Well," said Orson loudly, "no one was more surprised than I when I realized I was the chosen one. Still, we have to accept these things . . ."

"Oh, look," said Geneva, "there's Marina. She's filthy. Cooeee!"

"Ohdearohdearohdear," said Cantiger as he saw Marina striding towards him with a bright smile on her face. He retreated behind Orson and thought that he should have bought some camel particles before starting this whole business.

"Hi, Marina," said Geneva brightly. "Lynch, do you know my cousin, Queen Marina LaMaya?"

"I know her by repute," said Lynch coldly. He afforded Marina a curt little bow.

Marina paid no attention to either of them. She had dropped to one knee before Orson. She took his hand and kissed it. "Your Majesty," she said, "may I be amongst the first to pledge my service, love and loyalty, my Riders, men-at-arms and villeins entirely to your cause?"

"Oh," Geneva frowned. "Well, I suppose . . . Your Majesty, this is Queen Marina LaMaya of Hennamucus."

"*Snake!*" hissed a voice at Orson's back.

"Oh," said Orson, who had just discovered that he quite liked having his hand kissed. "Thank you, Marina. And I am sorry."

"*Sorry!*"

"Sorry, Your Majesty?" Marina stood very close to Orson. She recalled her Eyelash-Fluttering classes and gave a demonstration of the art that would have had her tutor moaning at opportunities missed. With natural proficiency like that, she could have reached degree standard.

"Yes," Orson explained. "The god who spoke to us from the Abbey said that you wanted the crown, but that I should have it. Can't think why, but there we are."

"Me? Want the crown?" Marina purred. "Silly." She stroked his forearm. "It's obvious that the country needs a big, strong man on the throne, not a poor, frail creature like me."

Cantiger popped his head out at that. He said, "Pah!"

Marina recalled Withering Scorn and gave him a blast. He ducked back behind Orson but felt the icy coldness on his ear as it passed mere inches away. "This is the woman who tried to have me killed," he squeaked. "She tried to have you killed, too, Your Majesty! Sadok was her man!"

"Yes, Your Majesty," Marina's voice throbbed. "I hear that poor Sadok had another of his fits. Always happening, I'm afraid. The number of times I've had to kill him when he was about to kill me. I can't tell you. So boring, and I do apologize. As for trying to kill you, dear Professor Cantiger, you quite misunderstood. It is a tradition of Hennamucus that every magician be put to the test. It pushes back the thresholds of technology, you see. So we set them trials. Yours was simply to escape durance vile and summary execution. As you so cleverly did."

"Well, that's true," said Orson. "You must have done, otherwise you wouldn't be here. No denying that."

"Oh, he did, Your Majesty, he did. He conjured a giant worm that ate three poor innocent damosels."

"Cantiger!" Orson was appalled. "You didn't!"

Cantiger considered this. There are occasions when it is advantageous to be thought nice, but they are few. "Well, they shouldn't have got in the way," he said, again daring to confront Marina. "And you, madam, should not have abused the mighty Cantiger. My wrath fell on you and all your household. And serve you right." He took refuge behind Orson again, only to remember an important omission. He stuck his head out again and said, "Ha!"

Marina ignored him. "Anyhow, all that is past . . . " She moved in still closer to Orson. He could feel her breath on his lips. "Now begins a new era of peace and prosperity and love, sweet, sweet love. That's the only thing that there's just too little of."

Orson gulped. There was a strange tickling sensation at the back of his throat, and all sorts of strange sensations elsewhere. He seemed to be engulfed in eyes and lips. It was like viewing a kaleidoscope in which the swirling pieces were giant star sapphires and rubies, gleaming slivers of rhodocrosite and tiny pearls. And then the sapphires became cool pools into which he yearned to plunge, and the rubies and rhodocrosite became crimson coverlets over pale pink silk sheets and he was tired beyond measure, and the pearls drew back to reveal sweet darkness.

He was vaguely aware that someone was tugging at him and saying "Ohdearohdearohdear" again and again, but he was used to that. Why couldn't people just leave him alone to swim and to sleep? He needed so badly to swim and to sleep . . .

Geneva had watched her cousin's work with a keen critical eye, and it had suddenly become clear to her that Orson was, after all, the most handsome, desirable and kingly of men.

This was no magic. It was merely the normal response of a young lady accustomed to getting her own way. She might have done Disdain on Orson (and Geneva had in fact won a first in Disdain from Kynke Kennadonne), but at least he had been hers to do Disdain on. Now that some other woman was moving in on her adoring slave, he was transformed into Geneva's adorable king.

"Your Majesty," she said, barging Marina to one side and taking Orson's hand, "I really must take you to see the fish."

"Fish?" snarled Marina.

"Um . . . What?" Orson blinked. "Fish? What fish? Sorry?"

"The—" Geneva checked, then spoke very fast. "The fish on the plate. No, in the river. The fish on a plate in the river. I mean, the dish. It's absolutely essential that a new king should see the dish. Traditional."

"Oh, all right." Orson shrugged and grinned happily. Geneva, whom he worshipped, was actually smiling at him and holding his hand, so he did not much care whether he was to view a fish or a dish. "Now." He turned to Cantiger and that strange Marina woman. "You two kiss and make up. I don't want these petty squabbles going on."

He suffered himself to be led off by the now doting Geneva.

"There, Professor," said Marina grimly as she advanced on the quaking Cantiger, "we have received a royal command."

Garnish and Ondslake had been observing this scene from the entrance. When Marina picked up Cantiger and planted a kiss on his blubbery lips, they gave their views succinctly.

"Bogging Ada," said Ondslake.

"Eek!" said Garnish.

As for Cantiger, he had long dreamed of his first kiss, had regarded it, indeed, much as, we are assured, the hart when heated in the chase regards cooling streams, and had panted accordingly. Now, when it came, he felt much as would the hart on finding the streams dammed and stagnant and smelling strongly of processed caviar – processed, that is, by a badger's intestines. He said "Waagh", of course, before it, "Yuk!" after it and "Pt! Pt! Pt!" when Marina had dropped him unceremoniously on the floor and stalked back to her friends.

The king, it goes without saying, could not sleep in the Golden Cow. Security had to be considered, and status. There was also the feeling that such royal particularity in the matter of lodgings might be regarded as personal endorsement, which would never do.

Tradition had it that the Tower of Greatwen was where High Kings had resided in the distant past. Thither, therefore, were sent men-at-arms and bedders and temporary ladies of the bedchamber to prepare the royal household's apartments.

The Tower had been looted and stripped during years of neglect, and the great rooms were bare save of graffiti.[40] The Archbishop, however, sent up some hangings lately discovered in the Abbey crypt depicting Lugh getting Mil on a thistle, Lugh getting Cernunnos on a goat and Lugh getting Queasy on an unnamed contortionist human, together with several framed colourful ancient scripts, including the famed *"It's the real thing"* of Swinesdown.

Skinner, who lived in the area when he was not questing, sent up beds and bedding. Aromatic reeds were sprinkled on the floor, gallons of ale, blonk, liquamen, ketchup and olive oil transported to the cellars, together with three barrels of oysters, two sides of bacon, forty carp, several ducks, a great deal of butter and a carrot[41] for the royal breakfast. Within hours, they had a palace fit for a king.

Now a procession formed. It was headed by six very drunk heralds bearing and blowing long horns. Then came Kes at the head of Brastias's men-at-arms, then twelve Riders in Lynch's service, all armed at all points. Behind these came His E the P and P-in-O, C-in-C to his RLM, PRE, LHC, etc., Cantiger, looking morose, Snugsnuffler, now comatose, with two bearers, and the royal nanny, then two hundred Riders in civvies, all huzzaing, then six dancing girls, waving large hankies and demonstrating PhD wiggling, then Buller and Magsin, Lynch and Woborn, Leo, Arachne, Brastias, then some more dancing girls, then Orson, who had drunk quite a lot of fizzy Deedong blonk and been kissed goodnight by Geneva, and therefore suffered him to be bustled into place

---

[40]Of these, some, especially those in the prison quarters, were thought to be ancient. "Put not your bust in chintzes", for example, was thought to have been written by a lady awaiting execution under the draconian Bikinis Act of which mention is made in one of our few surviving histories of the days of the Weirds, whilst "Fain would I rhyme yet fear I to scrawl," to which someone has wittily appended the legend, "Sentenced to death for defacing this wall" was almost certainly penned by "a bicycle manufacturer", whatever that may mean, with an unpronounceable name, of whom mention has been found in ancient fragments of newsprint. "There but for a brace of cod go I" has baffled innumerable scholars.

[41]Even kings had their eccentric moments.

and duly processed with a vague but contented grin.

Behind Orson came the men-at-arms of Lamere Maudite, all puffed up and looking lordly, then the archbishop, with a representative group of Snotbuckets, then the saddleback pig, which really did not seem to understand its position in society or its commonly perceived purpose, and anon a further twenty Riders, again armed at all points.

It is these last who concern us. Or rather, it was the Rider in the bronze armour with the green plume on his helm and the leopard sitting on a sheaf of straw on his shield at the very rear of the column who should concern us very much indeed.

The breastplate was full in shape, and so gave no indication as to the contours of its contents.

Its contents were in fact surprisingly shapely. Its contents were warm. It was not the wearer, however, who had generated this warmth, but a Rider named Shoehorn who lay sprawled and unnoticed in the straw behind Buller's pavilion. A lot of people were lying sprawled about the town tonight, but they were still generating warmth. Shoehorn was getting colder and colder. But at least he did not have to worry about a hangover tomorrow morning.

Pulvicovectoral telekinesis is an effective discipline, but its critics point to the difficulty in gauging the timespan that must elapse before its effects are seen and felt.

Many are the factors, aside from windage and elevation, that must be taken into account. First, of course, the subject's temperamental predispositions come into play. It is easy to persuade a comedian to commit suicide, but – such is the cruelty of fate – it may take days to persuade an estate agent to take a similar step.

Then there is the little matter of cleanliness. If, like Cantiger, you believe bathing to be dangerous and rude, you probably carry a thriving colony of fleas about your person. These, which have for some time grazed happily in your lusher and plusher regions, untroubled by thoughts more complex than "Three times over the limit, yum," "This beats chicken" and "Oy, that's my tuft! Bog off!" are suddenly afflicted with a thought.

And we are not here talking a random, passing, stray thought plucked from the aether like an errant dandelion seed grabbed by a bullfinch, but a thought trained, a thought with a mission, a thought at peak fitness. This sort of thought goes about its business with the unseemly vigour of a scoutmaster in a hippy commune, and soon has that slovenly resident rabble knocked into shape. You then have a whole host of intent, highly telepathic fleas with but a single thought.

That is power.

We have already noted that Cantiger, on what should have been the happiest night of his life, was looking morose as the procession made its torchlit way to the Tower of Greatwen. By the time that he reached the Tower and was shown to his lavish room (there was lavish room there, but very little to fill it) he was experiencing the compelling, unanswerable, illogical logic of the deeply depressed.

Healthy people know full well that no joke survives the person enjoying it. Cantiger did not even believe in jokes any more, save the one, great, vengeful joke of his own death. His mother would regret having fed him filthy milk instead of cream, preferably laced with brandy, and his sister would feel really, really sorry that she had treated him like dirt, even though, on reflection, he was, and Iseult . . . Well, he would haunt Iseult and moan at her and chide her for being nasty, even though he deserved nothing better. In fact, he would haunt every woman for not showing him turtle doves that turned out not to be turtle doves but rather nice-looking sort of blancmange things with pointy bits on top, and every man for being coarse and rough and not female, and that would serve *them* right.

"Ha!" he thought, and jumped.

He fingered the silk hangings about his bed. He sighed. What, after all, was the wealth of this world, what trinkets and chattels, gold and jewels? Burdens, encumbrances all . . .

Oy! cried a familiar voice inside his head, *I'd like a bit of encumbering for a change, as - it - happens!*

Cantiger groaned. "Shut up," he breathed, "I'm just getting into this . . ."

He slumped on the bed with its embossed golden coverlet, fringed with gold leaf. "What is position, what power," he asked himself, "save a means to inspire insincere fawning and the simulacrum of passion from lissom young damosels?"

Simulacrum's fine . . . said the voice, *Yeah. I'll take simulacrum, partickerly with lissom—*

Cantiger ignored the interruption. "Where are the snows of yesteryear?" he asked himself, *a propos* of nothing much.

Turned into the slush of yesterday and the wine of today, said the voice. *Let's get at it!*

"And of what use are fine wines?" Cantiger thudded. "They serve, like crude ales, only to produce urine and oblivion."

Yeah, but we can have some right fun meantime!

"And what is fun but futile gadding?"

All for a bit of gadding. How do you gad, anyhow?

"And what is pleasure save more oblivion? Why not take the wholesale deal and get oblivion, not in doses, but by the bathful?"

'Cos if I'm already oblivious I can't enjoy getting there, can I? You got to work at oblivion . . .

"Ah, woe is me . . ."

Well, you may be woe, mate, but I'm looking at girls and booze and lampreys and partridges and wealth beyond the dreams of avarice for the rest of our mortal, and I'm pretty chirpy about it.

"What is life but . . ." He considered, then squinted. "A bowl of cherries?"

Cherries are nice . . .

"2b or not 2b, that is the question . . ."

Is it? Well, 2b is the answer, then. 2c is nice, 2i is good, 2f, even 2p, but you can't do anything if you choose 2d.

"What are you talking about?"

I'm not sure. Come on. Let's party!

"It's all so pointless!" Cantiger squeaked, and sobbed.

No, it's not, I saw some . . .

"Variety of vanities, all is vanity!" Cantiger covered his face with his hands. "All flesh is grass . . ."

No, it's not! Flesh is flesh, grass is grass! You're getting confused here. If all flesh is grass, you could have a lot of fun having a roll in the hay on your own and vegetarians should give up the lentils and have a nice, juicy—

"The world is too much with us, late and soon!" howled Cantiger.

Late and *soon? Whass that mean? Late and soon? You're gibbering, man!*

"Hopopopopopoiote!" Cantiger's body was punched by massive sobs as he sank his face in the pillow.

You what? Look, this is getting depressing . . .

"Let the day perish wherein I was born, and the night in which it was said, 'There is a man child concei-ei-eived!'"

That's not what she said. She said, "Is that it, then?" and he said . . .

"Is that it, then?" screamed Cantiger, recognizing these as the most tragic words of all.

Oh, Lugh, you've done it now, said the voice dully. *You're right. It's all pretty darned futile, isn't it?*

"Totally, totally . . ."

Haven't got a hanky, have you?

"Let's go and find a battlement from which to precipitate ourselves."

Good idea. Bound to be one handy.

"You think precipitation is better than hemlock, say?"

Oh yeah. More dramatic. Show 'em . . .

"What I thought." Cantiger stood, wiped his nose on his sleeve and sniffed deeply. "It's the only logical thing to do, isn't it?"

Absolutely. QED.

So Cantiger, at last an integrated personality, with many a sniff and a shake of his head as he congratulated himself on perceiving the obvious, shuffled from the room, relieved to have come to one conclusion and intent upon coming to another as soon as possible.

No such doubts or qualms afflicted Orson, who had had a bath this afternoon and regarded his giant, high-vaulted room with pleasure. He bounced on the carved four-poster. He strolled out on to the balcony to study the river way below. He helped himself to an apricot from the fruit bowl and ate the chocolate that had been left on his pillow.

[42]The royal household did not get paid better than any other, but the rude poor have always inexplicably envied the refined poor, and there was always the possibility of a deal with the Press.

All around him, people bustled. The royal household had not yet been appointed, but everyone was anxious to be part of it,[42] so everyone was doing everything all at once. Six women, for example, had elbowed one another as they battled for the privilege of removing Orson's boots and putting on his slippers. Six men had stood menacingly over him with combs and scissors until instructed by Kes to go away. "Poisoned combs," he said. "Oh, yes. Well-known trick."

Kes had examined the undersides of tables and chairs for hidden— well, he was not exactly sure what. Chewing gum, possibly. He thought that grubs came into it somewhere.

Men-at-arms stood sentry all around the room, attempting to look formidable and indispensable. Orson's pillow had been plumped so often that it had burst. Several men with nothing better to do were busy peeling grapes. Riders clattered about shouting, "By the right . . . !" and "Chop, chop!" to everyone and no one, whilst, in the corridor outside, knaves and scullions fought for the right to lie outside Orson's door. The Press would buy a lot of drinks for a Royal Draught Excluder. Several girls had said, "When you're ready to be disrobed, sire?" and done something peculiar with their eyes and hips. Orson supposed that this must be the secret signal of the Guild of Disrobers.

Orson was tired, and all this bustle at last irritated him. He beckoned to Kes. "K," he sighed, "what I'd really like . . ."

"Your wish is my command, sah!" barked Kes.

". . . If it's possible . . ."

"All is possible on the command of the rightful monarch, sah!"

". . . And I don't know how these things are meant to be arranged . . ."

"Arrangements are at the explicit behest of the monarch, sah!"

"Aromatherapy, sire?"

"Do a nice line in massage, me, Your Majesty. My mum says . . ."

Orson raised his voice above the wheedling clamour. "K, what I really want . . ."

"His Majesty will want for nothing whilst I breathe, sah!"

". . . Is for you to stop being noisily deferential and for everyone to leave me alone!" Orson yelled.

Everyone in the room came to a standstill and turned towards him. Mouths hung open, arrested in mid-word. Orson's words continued to circle about the vaults of the room for some seconds after they were spoken. Then a woman gave a little yelp. A man cleared his throat. A few brave souls whispered, "Um, good night, Your Majesty," and started skulking towards the door.

"Look, I'm sorry, but I have had an umber of a long day and I'm very, very tired," Orson explained. "Tomorrow we can make appointments and so on. For now, I want to sleep. If you will quietly organize whatever guards you think necessary, K, I would be most grateful. I am as capable of undressing myself and brushing my own teeth as I was last night."

"Of course," said Kes softly. He gulped. "Right. You have heard His Majesty's command. Everybody out. You, you and you are to stand guard outside the door. You will be relieved every three hours. All other men-at-arms of Lamere Maudite are to take up positions around the Tower. I will personally awake His Majesty tomorrow morning at seven o'clock and none other may enter his chamber until summoned. Is that clear?"

There was a sussuration of "yessirs".

"Good."

The people cleared the room quickly and quietly. Then it was Kes's turn. His cheeks were very crimson. "I'm sorry about that, Your Majesty," he said. "Takes some getting used to, all this."

"Of course it does, K." Orson grinned. "How d'ye think I feel? Oh, and K . . ." He laid a hand on his brother's shoulder.

"Sire?" Kes momentarily raised his gaze from a study of the flagstoned floor, then dropped it at once.

"It may be 'sire' and 'Your Majesty' and so on in public, but I'm Orson, same as ever, when it's just the two of us. I have a feeling it could be quite lonely, this job. Don't want to make it worse than it has to be."

"No. OK. Thanks, Orson." Kes at last met his brother's gaze, and smiled.

Orson punched Kes's arm. "I'm going to need you with me if this is to work, K."

"I'll be with you."

"You never know. It might be fun."

"You never know. Good night, then, Orson."

"Night, K." Orson threw himself back on the great bed. "Good night, good night."

The door creaked shut. The latch clanked. Footfalls receded, echoing. Orson was alone.

He was tired and tipsy and it had been, by almost any standards, an eventful day, but that was not the only reason that he now craved solitude. Over the past few minutes, he had been afflicted by curious, inexplicable yearnings of the sort best experienced *à deux*, tolerable *à un*, but unbearable in any save the most accommodating crowd.

The image that provoked these sensations was not, surprisingly, that of Geneva, but rather that of that older woman, Marina Lawhatsit. He recalled the look in those pale eyes, the plushness and pinkness of those lips, the leanness and length of those limbs, the intensity of that gaze which had swirled him in a sort of pleasurable if alarming vortex, and he very much wished to be caught up again in such a maelstrom.

He knew, or thought that he knew, that she was bad – or, at least, far from the pure icy ideal of his fantasies – but then, as with most young men, his fantasies lurched alarmingly from the celestial to the terrestrial. Some of them, indeed, were so terrestrial as to be positively muddy, but he had a sort of consoling – a positively psychic – intuition that Marina would not be averse to a bit of dirt.

As it were.

He was at first ashamed of such thoughts. But so vivid now were his visions that he found, not for the first time, that shame was ephemeral. He lay back, all thoughts of kingship, all apprehensions of battle and rebellion, all sense of presumption banished. Nothing now concerned him, nothing now mattered save Marina, who not only could read his most disgusting and disgraceful thoughts but actually seemed to approve of them.

That was one hell of a trick.

So how would it go? He would summon her. He would ask her to support him in his new role. He would tell her something like, "Uncomfortable lies the head of the king (or queen, of course – because I really fancy feminalists)."

Yes. That had a ring to it.

And then . . . And then? Then she would once more lay a warm hand on his forearm, once more tell him that the Orsonian Age would be one of love, once again gaze deep into his eyes or, rather, enable his gaze to plunge deep, deep into her eyes, and something vague and delicious would happen, like bathing in fresh, warm livers . . .

Fresh livers?

He sat up.

Bathing in livers?

I mean, yuk.

What was happening to him? He had no desire to wallow in offal. He really hadn't. Maybe this was the affliction of kings that made them automatically murderous exploitative swine. He was not going to be a king like that. Not he. He was going to concern himself with deprived children and National Elves and Justice for All and . . .

Mind, fresh, warm livers wouldn't be that bad . . .

He lay back again.

Of course, travesty was always strangely attractive. The thought of Marina in her fissure-fingering suede breeches was appealing, for all that she was ancient – at least twenty – and wicked. For some reason, consideration of such sub-equatorial regions persuaded him that he would quite like to eat an olive direct from her more northerly mouth.

That was another totally disgusting thought, but this time Orson did not even bother to sit up . . .

Disgusting was OK really, he concluded.

There was a clanking, a scraping of metal on stone.

Orson sat up fast.

He managed to say "Wha— ?" before a slender warm hand covered his mouth.

He saw gin-clear grey eyes gazing twinkling into his.

"I think we feel the same, Your Majesty," said the armoured Rider seated on his bed. "Let's talk very, very quietly, shall we?"

Orson nodded, and smiled beneath the hand.

* * *

"It has got to be the highest rampart, hasn't it?" puffed Cantiger as he rowed himself up the spiral staircase.

Oh, yeah. No point in messing. Make 'em use a spatula, not a spoon. Swine. Got to go down in history and legend.

"Oh, we'll go down, all right. Be quite interesting flying, too."

Well, plummeting, actually. Not – well, not quite – the same thing. I suppose we might have time for a "Whee!"

"Don't you think we should do that first . . . ?"

"I'm impressed," said Orson as he strolled out on to the balcony with Marina tucked neatly into his arm as though, he thought, designed for it. "You actually did all that just to be with me?"

"Love is like that," said Marina. "I love my king. I love you, Orson, king or no."

"You must do." Orson shook his head in amazement. "Borrowing this armour, waiting all that time on the balcony, risking discovery . . ."

"That's me, my love. Impulsive, modest but determined . . ."

"Why me?"

"Ah, how can I tell you? From the moment I saw you, I just knew . . ." She raised a hand to the nape of his neck and pulled him to her.

"Oh, so did I," he gasped.

His nose hit her visor, which clunked shut. Marina raised the visor to find Orson hopping on one leg, clutching his nose and chanting, "Owowowowow!"

She removed the helm. Once again she reached for him and drew him to her. "Orson," she purred. "My king . . ."

Their spoken dialogue now ceased.

As a chronicler, I am saddened and embarrassed by my fellows' idleness when it comes to kissing. Trivial dialogue is recorded in detail, but, when it comes to the all-important osculation, "They kissed" is the standard form. Does that suffice? Did the great lovers of history sacrifice armies, fortunes and kingdoms because he said, "Gosh, you look nice," or she, "Nice day for the time of year"? Of course not. Yet these peripherals are faithfully chronicled while for some obscure reason, the kisses that engender such passions and that soon come to constitute 90 per cent of lovers' dialogue are passed over with two mere monosyllables. Well, you will not find me neglecting my duty in such shameful fashion.

Marina now did "Mmmmmslurpshluckshluckshillashilla shluckshluckshhhhhhlubbaslickclickomygod."

During the second "shluckshluck", she drew her tiny stiletto knife.

"I think we ought to do that again," she panted.

"What? That Mmmmmslurpshluckshluckshillashillashluck shluckshhh thing?" asked Orson in a voice deeper than usual.

"Well . . ." Marina winced. "Something like that." She reached up again. "I was thinking more in terms of 'Shlurpshlurpmmmmyesclickclickpleasegurdlegurdlegaspshloc-shlock'."

"Sounds good to me."

"Let's try it, at least."

"Oh, absolutely. Um, you wouldn't mind . . ."

"Hmmm?"

"It's probably rude to ask, but could you remove that breastplate? I mean, I have to bend double to get to you, and it's freezing cold."

"Of course, my dear. Would you help me with the straps?" She spun around. Orson undid the thongs with practised hands.

"There," sighed Marina as she allowed the straps to slide down her arms and the armour to clang on the floor. She turned again. "That's better."

It was indeed better. The black leather cuirass was not soft but it did at least yield a little. They had got as far as 'yesclick' when Marina, finding both her arms clasped firmly to her sides, gasped, "Hold on. Let's get more comfortable."

She bent to untie the poleyns and greaves from her leggings. They clattered and rolled on the flags. She went to unfasten the cuisses, but Orson said, "No. No, please. Leave them on."

"Ooh." Marina giggled slowly, like a drain. She came into his arms again. They did "Shlurpshlurpmmmmyesclickclickplease gurdlegurdlegaspshlockshlock," but still Marina had a problem. The knife blade was short, and she had to be confident of puncturing a vital organ with the first blow. Otherwise she might suffer the embarrassment of the guard being called and the nuisance of having her head cut off. Unfortunately, she held the blade in her left hand, and was not confident of penetrating the liver at an angle.

"That was great," breathed Orson.

"Thanks. I learned that at St Anne's."

"Wonderful thing, education," said Orson. His voice now sounded like timpani rumbling. "Do you ever think about fresh, warm liver?"

"What!" Marina started and paled. Did this boy know something? Was he playing with her? She studied his frank smock face. Impossible. "Er, no," she said, bemused, but not neglecting to transfer the stiletto from her left hand to her right behind her back. "Frankly, no," she admitted. "Not often."

"Just wondered."

"Do you?"

"What?"

"Think about liver. Because if you do, I'm more than willing to do it with you."

"What?"

"Think about liver. I mean, I think a man and a woman should share their interests and hobbies, so if it's a thing you do a lot . . ."

"Oh, no. It's not. I don't. Never, really. It just came over me."

"Happens."

"So what do we do now?"

"Well, I liked that putting our mouths together and making that noise business."

"So did I. Shall we do it again?"

"Let's. If you put that arm here . . . and the other one there . . . That's it . . . And now . . . Shlickswiggleslurp . . ."

Orson straightened suddenly. The blade that had been poised to probe his liver tinkled on the veranda's floor. "What was that?" he demanded.

"Oh, nothing. My ring." Marina pounced on the glinting thing and snatched it up, her back turned to Orson. "Did it scratch you? How dare it? I'll throw it away. There . . ."

Orson was paying no attention. He was peering over the parapet. "Something fell right past us, just inches away. It went Ohdearohdearohdearsplash!"

He put two and two together. "Cantiger!" he shouted down

171

at the dark river, which was now churning and thrashing. "Is that you?"

"Urk!" gasped a familiar voice. "Gog Fwim!"

"What? What are you doing down there?"

"Glowning!"

"What? I can't hear?"

Cantiger bubbled a bit, then, with a supreme effort, pulled himself from the water sufficiently to squeal, "I can't swim!"

"Oh," said Orson.

"Oh, leave him," Marina spat disdainfully.

Orson was stripping off his shirt. "Oh, no," he said, reflecting that, as eventful days went, this one was a dilly. "If he sinks, he'll drown, and I've seen that happen to kittens. They were all dead afterwards. Can't have that."

"Why not?"

Orson did not hear her. He was standing now, bare-chested and barefoot, on the parapet. "Wait for me here. We can try some more of that nice slurping stuff," he said, and plunged.

"I can't wait, Your Majesty," Marina murmured drily as she saw him vanish. The water sloshed in the moonlight and the silver rings spread way below.

She sighed, and went off in search of another weapon.

The water of the river Thuinne is a sort of lumpy soup made daily to an age-old recipe. As with a stockpot, you start with the previous day's broth. To this add a quantity of dead cats and a few ex-enemies for protein, vegetable peelings for fibre and the entire city's sewage output for thickness and fragrance. Gastronomes are agreed that the only ingredient which it is absolute heresy to include in Thuinne-water is fish.

There are those who consider such a concoction unhygienic. Orson, on first spitting it out, was of that opinion. On the other hand, being guaranteed to kill almost any living creature save maggots, it was a first-class pesticide. Any flea on Cantiger and Orson that had survived the plunge and the shock of hitting the water had now had the precious candle of life most definitively snuffed by immersion in the Thuinne.

In consequence, Cantiger suddenly discovered that he was after all very eager indeed to remain on live, whilst Orson's views on liver and girls reverted to normal, to whit: liver was for eating, with onions. Girls were not. Girls were for worshipping from afar.

He had time, but not much, to reflect on this as he dragged a wriggling, coughing Cantiger to the river bank, deposited him spluttering there and ran up to the great gate of the tower to summon the guard.

The guard took some persuading that the mud-soaked young man before them was in fact the heroic young king of the previous evening. But Kes, who was still hanging around organizing people, soon made his way to the gate, said, "Phworr, Ors— Your Majesty, you don't half pen-and-ink," and ordered baths drawn.[43]

"So what's this all about?" demanded Kes when finally Orson and Cantiger lay in steaming hip baths smelling strongly of roses.

Orson might have changed his views about girls, but he felt embarrassed now by his earlier antics and anyhow suspected that Marina might get into trouble for hiding in his room. He did not mention her, therefore, but simply said, "I was looking out over the river when suddenly Cantiger plummeted past."

Kes turned to Cantiger. "What did you do that for?" he demanded.

"I couldn't stop myself," Cantiger explained with a shrug. "Once you start plummeting, it's hard to stop."

"Yes, but why did you start? Most irregular, people plummeting all over the place. Dangerous, too. If everyone started plummeting, where would we be?"

"Good point," agreed Orson. "Maybe we should have a law about that."

"I think so. The Plummeting Act . . ."

"I was depressed," explained Cantiger.

"That's no excuse," said Kes. "I often get depressed, but I don't plummet. Have you ever seen me plummeting, Orson?"

[43]This caused some confusion in the guardroom, where baths were little known. "Drawn", however, was understood. By the time Y.O.Y. Chitterlings, the renowned cartoonist, had been summoned and sent away again after a few preliminary sketches, it was really quite late.

Orson considered. "Once, when you fell off the hayrick, you remember?"

"Ah, but I wasn't depressed, was I? And I fell. Nothing wrong with plummeting when you fall. Natural. What we're trying to get to the bottom of is why you were dashing about the place plummeting left, right and centre when you should have been safe in bed."

"I wanted to die."

"Well, that's easily arranged. No need to go plummeting here, there and everywhere. And outside the king's bedroom. Lots of people die and fall no further than the floor. That's all that's needed, you know. Seen it done, often."

"Why did you want to die, Cantiger?" enquired Orson.

"I don't know . . ." Cantiger paused and frowned. "Oh, yes, I do. I was bewitched, that's why. That Marina, when she mauled me this evening. She's got fleas that do that to people. She was trying to kill me. She's always trying to kill me."

"Well, she must be frightfully inept," grumbled Kes. "Why on earth hasn't she succeeded yet?"

"I'm sure you're maligning her," said Orson. "She's naughty, but not that bad."

"Yes, you can't go around slandering perfectly respectable queens like that. You jumped, didn't you?"

"Well, of course I jumped!"

"That's all we need to know. Don't know why we've had to beat about the bush like this. You jumped, therefore you plummeted. Simple. No need to drag anyone else in or ramble on about depression. Irrelevant drivel. Jump off a parapet, that's what will happen, almost invariably. Plummeting. Well, I don't want any more of it around here, do you understand?"

It was a pensive and wary Orson who returned to his chamber as the sun rose. He found Marina lying in his bed, apparently asleep. He cautiously pulled back the bed-clothes for fear that there might be weapons hidden about her person.

The breath escaped from him in a sort of involuntary whistle.

There were no weapons about her person.

There was nothing about her person at all.

"Sorry," he whispered, once more mysteriously persuaded that she was after all sweet and vulnerable.

He was very tired, and the bed was very large. Carefully, therefore, for fear of disturbing her, he slipped beneath the coverlet at the far side of the bed, and almost immediately fell deeply asleep.

Marina too now slept deeply. She had been aware of the bedclothes being lifted from her naked body, and she had smiled to herself as she heard Orson's gasp and apology.

She had abandoned her initial plan to assassinate this ridiculous young man, not least because Kes had been thorough about his work and she had found nothing more lethal than a banana in the room. There were, however, more ways than one to skin a cat. If Orson must be king, why, then, he would need a queen, and there would be plenty of opportunities to be rid of a burdensome husband later. He would surely appreciate her domestic skills when she rustled up a deathcap-mushroom omelette for an intimate *diner à deux*.

She did like the appreciation of her menfolk, however short-lived. It always seemed to be short-lived. But then, so did they, poor dears.

A small smile touched her lips as she slept. She did not usually like being awoken in the morning, but just now she could not wait.

Every royal Court has its conventions, its rituals of Pomp and Circumstance. In certain Courts, ceremony attaches to the monarch's least scratch, and every royal suppuration and shed body-hair is bottled and enshrined. Emperor Yi Ha of Gwinko, it is said, cannot eat a mouthful without a fanfare of grifflehorns, a tattoo of dherbas and the instant prostration of the monks of the High Citadel on pain of the removal of one or more nostrils, whilst his every breaking of wind is transliterated into pictograms, illuminated and issued as a royal proclamation that must be obeyed by every subject.

Kes, however, had no established model from which to draw. He was aware that royalty demanded ritual but he had to invent it as he went along. The Royal Reveille, or *levee*, was his first such challenge. After a great deal of thought and the crumpling of many sheets of paper, he came up with the following order of precedence:

Two heralds with trumpets.
Two scullions with crumpets.
The bearer of the royal pitcher of hot water.
The bearer of the royal teabag.
The Archbishop of Greatwen.
Two acolytes.
The bearer of the censer.
The bearer of the royal sausage.
The bearer of the royal egg.
Boss Kes Delamere Maudite.
Two dancing girls left over from last night, just in case.
His Excellency the Panjandrum and
Plenipotentiary-in-Ordinary, Counsellor-in-Chief
to his Royal Logrian Majesty,
Possessor of the Royal – oh damn it –
that pink-and-white plummeting feller.
Boss Brastias
The bearer of the royal kipper.
Mother Uncumber of the Holy Kidney of Lugh.
The bearer of the royal kidney.
The bearer of the royal black pudding.
The royal physician (temp.).
The bearer of the royal senna.
A saddleback piglet.
Y.O.Y. Chitterling (to record the historic occasion).
A gnome, aka "the press".
Boss Buller Delamere Maudite.
Demeter, the royal courser.
A page.
Another page.
The rest of the ancient text by Richard Francis.
Ablutionists, with bath and loofahs.
Abolitionists, with banners.
Pipers.
A large saddleback sow.[44]

---

[44]Who had never really made it on her own account, but had no intention of letting her son be spoiled by his success and only wanted 40 per cent of his earnings.

Mr Hector Potter, Keeper of the Sacred Sward.
Mrs Potter With Your Permission, Sir.
Various Brown-noses (*remember to pay*)
Minstrels.

He lined these up in the kitchen, appraised them, and, satisfied, took his own place in the historic procession.

Someone at the head shouted, "By the right, queeeek: March!"

They marched. All except for the piglet, which wove between the legs of those ahead until it tripped up the bearer of the egg.

They reached the door of the royal bedchamber.

The guards pushed the door inward.

The procession did what processions do best.

The trumpets blazed.

The Court took up positions about the bed.

"Your Majesty!" announced Kes. "We have the honour to wh—? Er. Oh. How . . . ? Oh, what . . . ? I mean who . . . I mean, good morning."

Marina raised her tousled head from Orson's chest. She sat up and grinned. The pages grinned back and frankly stared at things that they had not seen since infancy. Mother Uncumber fainted noisily. Cantiger said, "You!" and ducked behind Buller The bearer of the royal teabag said, "Phworr!" and was subsequently dismissed. Y.O.Y. Chitterling and the Press scribbled frantically and with glee. Buller said, "Chip off the old block, eh?" Brastias contented himself with a raised eyebrow. The bearer of the royal pitcher said, "Disgusting!" and ran from the room. The piglet jumped on to the bed.

Orson awoke and gazed about him, blinking and bewildered.

Kes struggled to regain his composure. "I'm . . . I'm afraid we only brought one sausage," he said.

"Oh, His Majesty won't mind that, will you, my sweet?" Marina cooed.

Orson looked as frankly confused as everyone else. His eyes skittered from Marina to the assembly, then to the pig, then back to Marina. "Er, no, no. One sausage is fine . . ." he said absently.

"So, erm . . ." the archbishop intoned loftily. "I take it that I will shortly be posting the banns?"

"The what?"

"The banns," said Buller. "Things they post when you get married. Don't know why."

"Married?" Orson stared.

"Well, yes. Done thing, isn't it? Spend the night with a girl of royal blood, same bed . . .

"Of course it was terribly naughty of us not to wait," purred Marina. "But Orson was just so passionate that I couldn't resist. Impetuous boy."

"But . . . I didn't . . . I mean, she was asleep!" protested Orson. "We didn't actually do anything . . ."

"Oh, Your Majesty, darling, it's sweet of you to try to preserve my reputation." Marina tapped his nose with her forefinger, and giggled. "But you needn't worry. When we are married, all this will be forgotten."

"But I don't want to be married!" Orson at last contrived to sit up. "We didn't do anything and you know it!"

"Oh!" Marina gave a little choking gasp. Tears welled in her lovely eyes. "How can you say that? How can you be so cruel? How can you use a poor maiden so? We did . . . we did mmmmmslurpshluckshluckshillashillashluckshluckshhhhhhlub balubbaslickclickomygod, didn't we?"

The archbishop clapped his hands over the ears of the page closest to him. Mother Uncumber, who had just dragged herself upright, fainted again.

"Well, yes," admitted Orson.

The tears were now streaming down Marina's cheeks. "Have you forgotten shlurpshlurpmmmmyesclickclickpleasegurdle gurdlegaspsglockshlock? Did it all mean nothing to you? Was that all it was? Just a quick, careless shlurpshlurpmmmmyesclick clickpleasegurdlegurdlegaspsglockshlock and then move on?"

"No!" Orson wailed. "It was very nice . . ."

"Very nice?" Marina whimpered. "Ah, he cuts me to the heart."

"I must say, it all sounds marriageable stuff to me," said Buller. "How d'ye say it goes? Shlurp—?"

"Definitely marriageable," pronounced Kes.

"But that was just a bit of fun! I was in a funny sort of mood, so I thought 'Why not?'"

The archbishop groaned. There was a murmur of "Swine!" Marina clucked and keened.

"That's unRiderly said, my boy," rumbled Buller. "True, of course, and quite understandable, but it wins you no worship to go round actually saying it. No. I'm afraid that you've made a grave mistake, but there really is no alternative to marrying the girl. She is a queen, after all."

Orson regarded the disapproving eyes all about him. His right hand absently fondled the piglet. "But . . . but . . . I . . . I was bewitched!"

"Ah, yes, we've all said that before, but it's no excuse, I'm afraid. Bewitching's what girls do. I remember a girl . . ."

"But . . ."

"Excuse me," said Cantiger loudly. He stepped forward. Marina stopped whimpering for a bare second to open one baleful eye. "I fear that we have a problem here. His Majesty cannot possibly marry Queen Marina, however much he may wish to."

"I can't?" Orson turned to his improbable saviour with hope in his eyes.

"Nope."

"Oh?" demanded the archbishop. "And why not, pray?"

"In the first place because, if we are to believe Queen Marina's evidence, they must both be executed . . ."

"Exec—" Orson's hope and gratitude, which had flared at Cantiger's first words, now dwindled as fast. He considered. As so often when execution is discussed as an alternative, he suddenly saw the attractions of married life.

Cantiger had won Marina's attention too. She had sat up straight again, though this time clasping the coverlet to her, and her tearful eyes glared at him with undisguised hatred.

"Boss Buller was going to make an announcement this morning . . ."

"I was? Was I? Oh, yes. Yes, I was." Comprehension dawned on Buller's amiable face. "Oh," he beamed. "I see! Yes, indeed I was!"

"In the circumstances, I feel that perhaps you should make that statement here and now . . . ?"

"Absolutely. Word to the wise. I say. Canny little feller, aren't you? Yes." Buller struck a pose. He cleared his throat. He looked about his expectant audience. "It was a dark and stormy night, some sixteen years ago . . . *if* I may have your attention . . ." he glowered at the piglet, which was apparently truffling under the bedclothes. It stopped and backed sheepishly out into the air. It sat, blinking innocent, long-lashed eyes at Buller.

"Thank *you*," said Buller with heavy irony. "Indeed, it was a dark and stormy – even tempestuous – night when this Cantiger chappy came to me with a little bundle. 'Here,' he said, 'is a boy-child, the son of King Cobdragon . . .'"

Marina gasped. Buller frowned at her and continued.

". . . and His Majesty asks that you bring him up as your own and instil in him some of those remarkable qualities that make you one of the most respected Riders in Logris. I fear, he said, for the little mite, for Cantiger here has warned me that there is treachery afoot, and I would have him reared by one whom I can trust, one whose principles I honour, whose character I revere, a man whose courage is legendary and wisdom renowned . . ."

"Lies!" shrieked Marina. "Lies! He used to call you 'That pompous old warthog'."

"Manly badinage, my dear." Buller shook his head, unruffled, and smiled. "Mere banter. Good old Cobber."

"So now you understand why these two young lovers can never marry and why Orson is rightful born king," said Cantiger smoothly. "He is of royal blood, and he is Queen Marina's brother. Touching, really, that these two siblings should meet, all unaware, and feel drawn to one another."

"Aaaah," said the dancing girls.

"Aaaah," said the bearer of the kipper, and dropped the kipper.

"Aaaah, indeed," said Buller. "Unfortunately, however, if they have done what Queen Marina alleges that they have done, this sweet little friendship can't last long. The law is quite clear, I think. Death by . . . What was it? Beheading? Being ripped apart by carthorses?"

"Stung to death by bees, I thought," put in Brastias.

"You're sure? Wasn't boiled in cheese fondue?" volunteered Buller.

"Could have been. Or eaten by pigs?"

"Or both, perhaps. And wasn't there something about a cactus up the jacksie?"

Brastias mused. "That might have been for shouting 'Celery' in the streets, you know. I'm not sure it wasn't the four gallons of dried rice, followed by the old hosepipe."

"Ah, I remember that one." Buller shook his head nostalgically. "Have to clear a space half a mile around for that one. Bits, you see," he explained to anyone unfamiliar with the process. "Lots of flying bits." He paused to consider further. "Are you sure it wasn't castor oil?"

"Oh, I can't remember," said Brastias, exasperated. "It was nasty, I know that."

"Oh, very, very nasty."

Marina's glare had flickered this way and that during this double act. At first she had glared defiantly. Now she sat sulkily staring down at her hands. Her cheeks were flushed.

"All right," she snarled, but nonetheless mumbled, "Nothing happened."

"Sorry, my dear?" Brastias cocked his head and raised a hand to his ear. "Didn't catch that."

"Nothing happened."

"Old war wound . . ." Buller pointed to his ear. He winced. "A little louder?"

"*No–thing hap–pened!*" Marina shrieked.

The archbishop sighed and beamed. The Press tore pages from his notebook, spat and threw them on the floor. Buller strode across the room to clap Orson on the shoulder. Cantiger smirked. Marina yelped as the piglet, its attention no longer required, burrowed under the bedclothes again and sympathetically nudged some sensitive part with its wet nose.

"So I don't have to be married?" Orson sought assurance.

"Oh, no, my boy."

"Or even executed?"

"Nope. All clear."

"Phew," Orson sighed, and smiled. "Now, did someone say something about a sausage?"

Chapter Eight

IF THIS WERE a fairy tale or some fanciful nonsense bred of a feverish imagination, the reader would here expect the words THE END to appear. We have seen magic, suffering, bloodshed, monsters, ambition thwarted, ambition attained. What, then, could more eloquently speak of enduring happiness and of satisfactory solutions than the homely yet deeply suggestive "sausage"?

All passion is spent before the sausage is brought on.

Had King Lear, of whom we read in Snugsnuffler's rendering of the ancient (now lost) drama,[45] come in from the storm, patted Cordelia on the head and said, "Now, did someone say something about a sausage?" the audience would at once know that now was the time to sneak out and claim a window seat in the tavern in the certain knowledge that all unpleasantness was resolved.

Madame Bovary, of whom we have already read, must surely have been saved had she returned home and uttered these simple words to her husband.

There is about sausage something domestic, reassuring, yet, at the same time, packed with promise and potential. Who knows what joys the knife may reveal as it cleaves the golden-fried intestine? Whatever the contents, we know that they will somehow be sausage-like, and so satisfactory. The sausage may thus be seen as a symbol for a bright, if uncertain future, suppurating in the juices of joy in the frying pan of fate.[46]

---

[45]See Appendix 1.

[46]Owing to the shortage of parchment, I cannot afford to erase. I would like to take the opportunity, however, to apologize for this metaphor, which happened late at night when I was not looking, and particularly to all readers named Joy.

For this reason, in not one of our great works of literature[47] dealing with towering passion and bitter feuds will we find the word "sausage" in the body of the text. Never once do the heroes of legend, embroiled in battles with demonic forces, speak that potent word.

We can have no doubt that, after his fourteen years' travel and adventure, it was amongst the first words spoken by Wandering Stupor on his return to the land of his fathers. I mean, if you had been wandering away from home for fourteen years, it would be, wouldn't it? Hello, darling. Hi, kids. My, you've grown. Anyone got a sausage?

A logical sequence.

The poet does not actually record the fact, but it is all part and parcel with the happy ending.

Would that we were thus romancing. But this, alas, is harsh reality. Orson spoke that word, but this was not to mark the end of his troubles nor those of this troubled nation.

Orson had friends, it is true, but none gain advancement without incurring resentment and acquiring enemies.

Of Marina, Iseult and Garnish we know. Their hatred for Orson and for Cantiger would never abate, but rather grow until they threatened to engulf the entire kingdom. Marina and Garnish now returned to Hornwoggle to plan their next move.

As for Warhawk and Bros., they had watched the process on the sward with sneers and jeers. "If he thinks we are going to give him truage and behave like fodge-pockers all for a bit of landscape gardening," snarled Warhawk's subtitle, "he can think again. We'll correlate him."[48]

"Bowdlerize him!" supplied Housewolf.

"Coppice him, and that damned magician!" said Garech.

"We'll go home and rebuild that old wall."

"Adrian's?"

"Yeah. Sounds like a hairdresser – I hate hairdressers—" said Housewolf. "Built a nice wall, mind . . ."

"And if this Orson kid so much as sends a vassal across our borders . . ."

[47]Until now.
[48]The subtitle-writer had had a long – or, rather, a short – night.

183

"We'll tesselate him."

"Exactly."

"Castellate his scoobies."

"You got it."

Warhawk considered the state of affairs for a minute with a stern frown that looked, in the hot and wavering firelight, like an oil spurt at sunset.

At last, he came to a decision. "I think," something deep in his belly spoke, "that we must call a conclave of the Kings."

The brothers gasped.

The Kings of North Logris hated one another and were perpetually at war with each other. Each remembered an occasion when another had massacred his clan, usually by inviting them to dinner and then falling upon them and slaughtering them when they were in their cups.[49] Each had abducted his wives from amongst other kings' daughters. Each had vowed to kill the kings and cull their kiths and kins.[50]

They hated one another, but they hated outsiders very much more, and, once in a generation, if that, they met to see off a perceived threat to their collective autonomy.

They had to be disarmed before they were admitted. Sometimes they had to strapped to trees or rocks to prevent them from attacking one another.

A conclave of North Logrian Kings was a scary thing for its members.

For those whom they met to discuss, it was petrifying.

The brothers rode northward that night.

Orson was kept busy in those first three weeks. There were committees and councils, conclaves and courts. The years of anarchy had seen many lands about Greatwen unjustly seized by force of arms, and the courtyard was crowded every morning with complainants suing for justice. Sometimes deeds were produced and justice easily administered. More often, Cantiger,

---

[49]Traditionalists to the last, they continued to accept dinner invitations and to get into their cups, as it were. Also, they could not quite work out how someone sitting beside them could fall upon them.

[50]They then tried "She sets seashells on the seashore".

Kay and Orson and the saddleback pigling[51] had to get into a huddle and make decisions on a scientific basis, such as, "He looks a decent sort of guy," or "Never heard a more blatant load of crap," or, "She may be exaggerating a bit, but she's nice and I'd rather have her owning the land than that creep". If there was still dubiety, the men then turned to the pigling, who either made a noise that sounded like a North Logrian king's word for "waking up to feel a sharp-toothed dog panting at your nethers" or another that sounded like the Ochtie word for cheese. That was the casting vote.

Then, of course, they had to recruit an army to enforce these judgments and magistrates to enforce the law in the regions and clerks to record the royal decisions, and meanwhile the preparations for the coronation were being made and furnishings ordered and moved into the Tower. Orson staggered exhausted to bed most nights. Cantiger staggered to bed most nights because he spent his evenings making up for lost time and savouring every variety of food and drink yet devised.

It was just one week before the coronation when Orson finally considered personal matters of moment and invited Geneva up to the now fully furnished Tower for supper.

They made stammering and embarrassed small talk about the plague of brackrats in the boglands and such whilst supper was served. Orson had a pillier now, a fresh-faced, fair-haired son of King Skinner, by name Brown Willy, and two pages called One and Two for convenience's sake. Not until they had retired were the two young people able to discuss more personal matters.

Geneva had heard, of course, the tale of Marina's bid for the throne. She was smug in triumphant disapproval.

"So she tried to entrap your poor majesty." She sipped at a tiny glass of golden liquid. She flicked back an abundance of matching golden hair that splayed and flew like floss and settled slowly on the glittering white fabric at her back. "Ah, well,

[51]This beast, like most intelligent beasts, had no idea of his own social status but was acutely aware of that of his superiors. In later years, each was to wonder just who had adopted whom. The pig had acquired the ancient name of 'Bollard'. Nobody knew why. It just seemed to suit him.

that's Marina for you. She always was a plotter and conniver. Frightfully devious, even at school. Was she totally bare?"

"Yes." Orson nodded.

"Frightfully rude, that sort of thing. I mean, bare! Shameless. Mind you, she always was. It must have been beastly for you."

"Oh, no," Orson assured her. "It was all right, really."

"You *are* brave. I should have hated it So common, nudity, I always think."

"Is it?" asked Orson. "Oh, well . . ."

"Well of course it is. Even villeins can do it. If Lugh had intended us to be bare, why did he create silkworms?" She nodded as she appraised her own logic. "You'll have made an enemy there, I'm afraid."

"Oh, dear. I really didn't want to."

"Of course you didn't." She stood and sauntered towards him, one leg circling the other. Her long purple gown swished and sighed. "It's just that people are so, so ambitious. They are never content with what they've got. You'll need people who really really care for you to protect you and soothe you and keep you safe from them." She laid a hand on his shoulder. "You tell me if anyone gets in your bed bare again. Disgraceful behaviour. With a king, too."

"Thank you, Geneva. I will." He looked up at her and covered her hand with his own: "Have you . . . Have you ever done mmmmslurpshluckshluckshillashillashluckshluckshhhhhhlubba lubbaslickclickomygod?"

"Oh, *that* boring stuff! I got the exam, of course, but really! What *is* the point? Talk about time wasted! I'm surprised Marina could remember it. She didn't try shlurpshlurpmmmmyesclickpleasegurdlegurdlegaspshlockshlock, did she?"

"Umm, well . . ."

"She did!" Geneva squealed and giggled. "I bet she did 'gargle' on the second 'gurdle'. She used to get into frightful trouble for that at school."

"It was nice, though . . ."

"Oh, well, if you like that sort of thing . . ." She sank on to the settle beside him. "Here, try this . . ."

The nuns of St. Anne's[52] Academy have been criticized in their time for excessive strictness, but that rigour and thoroughness paid dividends for those students who applied themselves. Nothing could have prepared Orson for the sheer virtuosity of the shhsplodgeglugflickerflickermmmslurp snickerdribble now executed by Geneva. It was a masterpiece of economy, discretion and style, reminiscent, certainly of the work of the Flatlands school, but distinguished by flourishes that were Geneva's alone and the products at once of intensive training and natural flair.

"There," said Geneva. "That was my matriculation piece."

"It's wonderful," gasped Orson. "I think . . ."

"Mmm?"

". . . I think I'm in love with you, Geneva."

"Of course you are!" She smiled sweetly. "Heavens, I know I would be."

Now turn we to the castle of Boss Buller Delamere Maudite, the which had lain unguarded this long time save by the skeleton garrison that Buller had left there. He had reasoned that, with all Riders of worship up at Greatwen, the countryside would still be relatively safe. His men-at-arms and archers, though few, were highly trained and more than competent to deal with the outlaws and small bands of mercenaries who sallied forth from their forest hideouts to attack travellers and to fall upon farmsteads and undefended settlements.

He had also, knowing his own prowess and that of Kes, thought to be away for only a few days. Orson's sudden elevation and all the attendant excitements and duties had already kept Buller and his men-at-arms away from home for over a month.

The villeins under his protection were not unduly alarmed. They too had confidence in their men-at-arms, who had seen off or hunted down many a pack of vagabond varlets, and they were accustomed to Buller's long absences on campaigns in the past.

[52]St. Anne's Academy was, in fact, founded by a very peculiar man named Stanley Bluebell. He inserted the full stop and the capital "A" as a mark of refinement.

They had grown careless, perhaps. Whilst the snow lay on the ground, they had had to live on smoked and dried meats, eggs steeped in waterglass and pickles – all delicious in times of plenty but wearisome day in, day out. It was natural, therefore, that, so soon as green showed in the meadows, the brooks started to purl, and the chickens and sheep were at last driven out into the meadow, Cressy and some few of her friends should beg to ride out with them. In hope of finding chickweed, hairy bittercress or wintercress for a salad or a soup, they said. That, at least, was their excuse.

In fact, in Cressy's case at least, she had simply been cooped up too long and wanted to feel the fresh air on her face and to smell the coming of spring.

Her mother, of course, chided her with time-wasting and gallivanting, but she was one of those mothers who expressed her love by such chiding. Cressy just smiled and went blithely on her way. The captain-at-arms told her to stay close to the three men whom he was sending out to guard the shepherds, and of course she said she would.

But Cressy had been haunted by strange hankerings of late. It was not just that she fretted against the restrictions of winter. She fretted too against the endless turmoil and bustle of the castle. She yearned for privacy and silence.

Cressy had always been regarded as something of an oddball in those days when people lived with the gregariousness of seagulls but without their abilities to drift and to soar. Her limp had not alienated her from others of her age, for she was in general a mild-mannered girl with a ready smile, and had successfully turned derision back on those who essayed it. She could not share, however, the other girls' passion for frippery, nor the boys' for war, and often her contemporaries claimed that, whilst her smile remained present, her mind was far away.

And, though she would never admit such a thing, she missed Orson. He was perhaps the only one who, with his education and sensitivity, could communicate with her in silence and respect her variable moods. You couldn't really have moods in such a community where everyone had to work together for survival, but Cressy, however she tried to hide it, was afflicted by pensiveness, and so by mood swings. This was fine in summer, when she could ride out into the country under Orson's protection and muse to her heart's content. For the past month, however, she had been surrounded by her fellow humans and, in the only and temporary solitude afforded by darkness (though she shared her room with her parents, younger sister and two younger brothers), she found herself aching for something, and crying, without quite knowing why.

The world into which she had been born seemed to offer no bourn for such as she. Her leg and her natural temperament had made her a reader, and so too much of a thinker to be content with a villein's workaday lot, yet too lowborn to live amongst Riders and their ladies, whom, anyhow, she considered often to be frivolous and silly. She might, perhaps, have married well had it not been for that leg – and then, although she would like one day to have children, she was unsure that she wanted to share her life with, and sacrifice her autonomy to, a working man.

Had you asked her what she wished from life, her answer would have been a shrug, because the true answer would have been simply nonsensical. It would have had something to do with a cottage somewhere, where she could live alone with children, books and animals, and where dear friends could visit from time to time . . .

But he who lived alone died soon. She who lived alone merely died that much sooner. Books were priceless. The shrug made a whole lot more sense than that sort of hallucinatory vision.

Whilst her friends, then, browsed on the fringes of the woods and traded jokes with the shepherds, Cressy let her palfrey wander away from them and once more saunter down the streamside as with Orson all those months ago. No one noticed her go. They were all too busy spotting as if for the first time the birds and the deer and the badgers that most of them had not seen for six weeks or more. She heard their cries and laughter above the chatter of the stream. They grew fainter and fainter as she rode down the valley, cherishing the silence that embraced her like a mother.

Down by the roaring waterfall, she could hear no other sound. She smiled at the dippers where they bobbed their tails and hopped from rock to rock. She was startled to see an early

Brimstone lurching in its flight mere inches from her knee. She saw a green log beneath the water waver into the sunlight to flash bright silver. That made her happy and unhappy all at once. No one thrilled with unalloyed pleasure any longer to the sight of a salmon – even a healthy springer like this. No one ate salmon any more. It was in this noblest and most persistent of piscine aristocrats that the White Sickness had first manifested itself.

For just a moment, Cressy closed her eyes and let the sounds and the sensations wash over her. It was like sinking into a deep warm bath after the unceasing clatter and hubbub of the castle . . .

The hand over her mouth was plush and leathern and stank of earth. The whiskers against her cheek were hard and wiry. The breath on her face was hot and rasping. It smelled of truffles and dung.

"Keep it quiet, missy," said the clogged voice in her ear as she wriggled and struggled to free her arms from the tight grip of the man behind her. She did not understand how he could have jumped up behind her without her hearing or feeling anything. "I 'ave a keen blade that 'ates fresh air. I'm 'olding it back, see? 'Olding it back wiv all my might, 'cos I don't want you to get hurt, my dear little woodlouse."

The man stepped back, but Cressy could still feel the point of the blade cold at the small of her back. She gulped. She said, "Please . . ." Her head turned, and now, with a gasp, she realized how the man had approached her. He was astride the palfrey. But he was not sitting on it but standing, both feet on the ground, and bent double to talk in her ear.

The White Sickness had given rise to many oddities. Most – the humans with fish-scales or quills, one of whom was stuffed and mounted in the munitions room, the two-headed pigs, the talking falcons, the hermaphrodites, anthropophagi and so on, all well-attested – had never reached breeding age and so died out within a generation. Some few, however, bred true. This was particularly true of those afflicted humans who were hunted and so retreated into the wilderness where they bred amongst themselves.

Of such were the true giants. Hounded into the forests and

the marshes, they became solitary and vengeful. They learned to hunt animals and people by stealth.

Some bore arms, and were even reputed to have mastered aurochs as riding animals. Unsurprisingly, they hated ordinary humans.

All this Cressy knew, and she had in her time expressed some sympathy for the poor brutes whose original crime had been no more than to have the misfortune to be born in the wrong place at the wrong time.

Looking now at the huge bewhiskered man who stood over her, snot swinging from his giant hairy nostrils, saliva bubbling at his leering lips, the point of his blood-streaked sword at her spine, she suddenly found that sympathy to be wholly misplaced.

Giants had some difficulty in finding clothes to fit. This one was no exception. The coarsely stitched hides that barely covered his body included pig, roe-deer and badger. Had Cressy had any difficulty in identifying these, the lolling heads still attached to them must surely have given the game away.

"You come along with me." He tried to wheedle but simply sounded menacing. "I'm not going to eat you, my little black beetle. You can be my servant. My seventh. My seventh little helper."

"Please put away that sword," begged Cressy. "It makes me nervous."

"What we'll do . . ." he drooled, unhearing, ". . . we'll go deep into the forest to the Morass de Foys and, soon as we're out of earshot and out of sight, you can have your little scream. We'll take your little pony along of us. Cook up nice, he will."

"Y-yes," Cressy breathed. "All right . . ."

"There's my sweet," he rasped. "You an' I are going to get on just fine. I can see that . . ."

He leaned forward once more to caress her face with his black-nailed, black-creased fingers. His face loomed towards hers. The whites of his eyes were startlingly convex and webbed with ochre.

Cressy fell from her horse.

It was all that she could think to do, and it was, in fact, a good move. The giant could move swiftly and silently and could duck beneath branches with far more agility than his race was generally credited with. What he could not so readily do, however, was to stoop in a confined space to grab something at his toes. Cressy slid smoothly from the saddle to the ground, he rolled beneath the palfrey, drew her legs up beneath her and sprinted towards the light.

Of course it was futile. She was fit, but that short, heavy leg lumbered her and made it difficult to judge the height of briars. She stumbled and sprawled, picked herself up again and staggered on. As for the giant, his initial reactions might have been slow, but he covered ground fast. He made no cry, which was almost more alarming. All that she heard was his rattling, rasping breath, which sounded like water clogged with gravel being pumped.

A hand snaked about her ankle. She yelped and leaped, bounced off a rough tree trunk, tripped on another looping briar and was out in the open. Only then did she think to scream for help to the brightly coloured specks at the top of the hillside. The screams were frail things that shuddered as she ran, but heads turned and arms pointed, and answering yells drifted down to her. A badger's teeth rattled as its dead head hit her hip, a dead deer's nose slid over her shoulder and nudged at her cheek, and again vile hairy arms and vile breath enveloped her.

Again she struggled and kicked, but his grip was hard and angry now. She found herself tilted to the horizontal and borne fast back into the darkness of the woods. The giant was careless or inept at judging distances. A sapling struck her forehead a glancing but hard blow. A bramble clawed at her face, bit and ripped. She managed to extricate an arm and to cover her face. An oak trunk loomed. She closed her eyes at the last moment, felt her arm jolted and her teeth slammed together as it hit, then saw the ground drop away. The giant slithered down a steep hill of ferns and leaves towards a dew-pond. His footfalls clashed and, as they neared the bog, sucked and slurped, and all the time the man's breathing, now hastily gulped and gasped, provided an accompaniment to the dreadful ride.

Other sounds now reached her as the giant heaved his bulk up the hill towards the cover of the trees. Hooves rolled. Dog's feet pattered and one hound gave pealing tongue. Suddenly there was a snarl. Air whooshed. There were twin thuds, one after the other, and Cressy was blinded by familiar warm black and white fur. The alaunts were upon them.

She heard the giant grunt as he wrenched or struck at the great dogs. She heard the waffling worrying, then a sharp canine yelp. Blood trickled down the pied fur and on to the giant's forearm. He had loosened his grip to wrestle with the dogs. Cressy raised her head, bared her own teeth and sank them deep into the thick hairy arm.

At last, the giant roared. Cressy felt her weight lifted, her legs arising. Her arms flailed. A massive shove sent her flying. Her back slammed into something hard and she knew in a split second that her head must jerk back and hit whatever it was, too.

It did so.

She saw a vast sheet of spangled scarlet, then a wave thundered in and swept all colour away.

Orson stood before a mirror as tailors kneeled with pins in their mouths and fondled the deep red velvet of his cloak. "Ooh, lovely," said one. "Haven't seen schmutter like that since I don't know when."

"Lovely cut to the pantaloons."

"Thanks, dearie. Clusters are so in this year."

"Do you think the ermine trim is dee tropp?"

"Oh, no. Love an ermine trim, I do. Regal, I always say."

Mmm. Now, if Your Majesty would just cock that leg. That's it. Ooh, super. Just right . . ."

Orson scanned the parchment in his hands. "Busy sort of week," he observed.

Behind him, his equally improvised Privy Council did a lot of nodding where they sat in a circle. "And that's just the ceremony," said Cantiger. "Coronation, royal military procession, three days' Blitz and feasting, passing of twenty-seven charters and laws, meetings with ambassadors, declarations of allegiance and fealty from every Rider, executions of such Riders as refuse . . ."

"Do they really have to be executed?"

"Nah, it's just traditional. No one's actually going to refuse to kneel to you if they know they'll get topped. It makes a good show, that's all. The ones who really hate you will either be faking and waiting their chance or will be back in their homelands by now, raising rebel armies."

The Council nodded some more and said rhubarb. Aside from Cantiger, Kes, Buller, Brastias, Lynch, Woborn and the Archbishop, there was a smattering of those ice-axe-faced or chubby and enthusiastic personages who, unwanted, affix themselves to committees as burrs to tweed. Put a committee down for a few seconds unattended, anywhere in history, and you will find it infested with such people, who were born, it seems, with clipboards tucked into their nappies in order to record motions.[53]

"'What's this?" Orson pointed at the bottom of the parchment and read, "Get married. Get an heir?"

"Oooh, an ickoo babby yum yum," said Orson's old nurse, who had co-opted herself on to the Council willy-nilly.

Cantiger ignored this contribution. "Ah, yes. Marriage, heirs. That's matters of state, that is. Bit of a priority, but you don't need to worry about it. Leave all that to us."

Orson turned, surprised. "What, all of it? To all of you?"

"If you'd just stay still, Your Majesty . . ."

"Oh, yeah, absolutely." Cantiger was nodding gravely. It was surprising how quickly he had managed "gravely" after his elevation. He was growing a grave beard now and wore a grave frown. He had commandeered a great tower as his school of magic and had twelve sorcerer's apprentices working day and night on spells and philtres, and several comely female sorcerer's apprentices who had a vague idea that they were there to learn how to make crockery. "Find a suitable queen. No problem. It's essential we get an heir before anyone kills you. Stability, that's the main thing."

"Er, sorry?" Orson gulped. "But is that part of the job description? Getting killed, I mean? I don't see it on this timetable."

"No, well, naturally we don't *want* it to happen," said Cantiger. "But 'king' is one of those jobs like 'bibulous

---

[53]As already stated, I have a limited supply of parchment, so cannot amend work already done. But why does this sort of sentence always happen to me?

steeplejack' or 'our racing correspondent' that somehow doesn't inspire actuaries to slash premiums. People like to kill kings . . ."

"Of the past forty-four kings of Logris recorded in the chronicles, twenty-two were poisoned in suspicious circumstances, seven stabbed in the back, three suffocated by their wives (one accidentally), four killed in battle, one executed by a falling tree, one frozen to death in a locked ice-house . . ." pronounced a chubby young man with a quiver full of pens, and pins stuck in neat ranks in his collar. This was the new Statistician-in-Ordinary.[54] He spoke with unseemly keenness. "One fell off a bikykle – whatever that may be – and a lofty turret in suspicious circumstances, one drowned in the bath in suspicious circumstances, one died of a red-hot poker up the jacksie in suspicious circumstances, three were shot in the eye in suspicious circumstances when out hunting and only three died in bed. Oh, those were the ones that suffocated."

"Ow."

"Well, I'm sorry, Your Majesty, but if you will jump like that, you're bound to get pricked . . ."

"Yes. Occupational hazard," Cantiger sighed. "Sometimes it's republicans. More often it's your ardent monarchists. It's just, they happen to think the labels got swapped in the maternity ward and they should be king. Then you've got your dispossessed, your why's-everyone-having-a-better-time-than-mes and your straight, extra-nut-rich fruitcakes. A crown's like catnip to all of them. You may have noticed that you can't so much as lick your fingers without someone tasting them first . . . ?"

"Us used to suck us thumbly, didn't us, Orsy?"

"Um, yes, nursey. I met a Rider with a lobster the other day. Might get on with you." Orson turned back to Cantiger. "Yes, I've been meaning to talk to you about that. It's a pain. The emissary of the Tzchipitas brought me a box of unique handcrafted chocolate truffles yesterday. Flavoured with the rarest essences and dusted with moondust and gold, they said.

---

[54]Later promoted to Statistician-in-Extra Ordinary and, at the last, elevated to the rank of Statistician-in-Staggeringly Dull.

By the time the taster had tried them, all I got was the wrappers."

"Yes, well, chockies is bad for us toofy-pegs," mumbled nursey.

"That's being king for you," said Brastias "Your security is that of the state and all that. My loyalty was such that I tried a few of them, too."

"So did I," said Woborn proudly. "Delicious."

"Absolutely scrummy. Anyhow, when we've got an heir, we can probably relax things a little. The odd hazelnut whirl, perhaps . . ."

"What's all this 'we' stuff?" Orson demanded mildly. "I mean, 'when *we*'ve got an heir'? Don't I have anything to do with it, or does someone have to test the queen as well?"

"Oh, no, no. Oh, dear me, no." The archbishop shook his head. "At least, I don't think so . . . ?" He looked around the other members of the Council. "I mean, if anyone asked me, I should regard it as my duty, of course . . ."

"No, that will not be necessary, thanks, bish," said Cantiger. "No, we choose a queen for you, Your Maj—"

"Whoa, there!" Orson held up a halting hand as the tailors removed his cloak. He strolled into the centre of the circle. He squatted. "Don't I get a say? I mean, what about true love, two minds with but a single thought, two hearts that beat as one, all that?"

"Lovey dovey billy-cooey, ickoo birds in their nests should agree or have us little bonces smashed together . . ."

"There is no provision or precedent for coronary synchronization . . ." twanged an ice-pick woman with flashing glasses who had somehow found herself appointed Under-Secretary for Constitutional Procedure and Waterworks.

"Oh, you can have as much of that sort of thing as you like after we've found you a wife," said Brastias. "If you felt like that about your wife, you'd be *exhausted* in no time."

"Yeah, well, I'm sorry, but I'm not happy about this," said Orson. "I want to choose my own wife, thank you."

"I don't think that that is a very good idea," said Buller gravely. "I mean, look what nearly happened with that Queen Marina. Very susceptible at your age. When you get to my age, it's different. You look at a young lady and you calmly assess things . . ."

"What sort of things?" asked Orson.

"Well . . . relevant considerations . . . Her legs, for one thing. And her personality, of course. Strangest thing. Always found that you can see more of a girl's personality from behind. And her hair, and her smile, and if all these are right and suitable . . ."

"Yes."

"Well, you say, 'Wayhey' and 'How's about it?', and she says, 'All right', and you go down to that little potting shed that no one knows about down by the pigpen."

There was silence. Certain members of the Council studied the ceiling, others their feet. Throats were cleared. "Erm, that's not quite the sort of politic approach that we were talking about, Buller," said Brastias. "We are talking about the stability of the kingdom, assured by a provident union."

"Not the same thing?" Buller puffed at his moustaches.

"Not quite."

"Oh. Right."

"I would like to record my profound offence at the inference of these observations, Boss Buller," said the Under-Secretary for Constitutional Procedure and Waterworks.

"Would you?" Buller looked surprised. "Offence, eh? Goodness gracious. Suppose you'll want to have ado with me, then? Last chap took offence, I remember – oh, ten years ago, it must have been – we spent four hours tracing and foyning and smote one another many sad strokes. Great stuff. Rased off his head, of course. What was his name . . . ?"

"'Er, kindly strike my offence from the record," said the Under-Secretary hastily.

"Anyhow, I intend to do my own wooing, thank you very much," announced Orson. "I intend to marry the woman I love."

"Wrong way round, surely?" suggested Kes.

"No, I think it's worth trying." Orson frowned. "It might work, you know . . ."

"Well, it might," agreed Brastias. "Highly unconventional, but . . . Has Your Majesty made his selection?"

"Well, yes, actually." Orson's mouth twitched and curled into

a little smirk of embarrassment "Princess Geneva has agreed to
. . . bmwf."

"To what?"

"To mreme."

"To do *what*?"

"Speak up, Orsy, dear. If I've told us once, I've told us a
hundy times. Nice clear Logrian, please."

"To marry me," said Orson crossly. "And that's that." He
looked around him. "Couldn't we have a table in here? It would
make life easier."

"Oh, my Lugh." Cantiger was clutching his brow. "That
Geneva . . . ?"

"Nice girl," mused Lynch.

"Very appropriate. Very proper," said Buller.

"Proper!" Cantiger groaned. "Proper poison . . ."

"What was that, Cantiger?" asked Orson with one eyebrow
raised.

Cantiger recognized Orson's tone and that raised eyebrow
from his youth. He had encountered both a lot, somehow. "Oh,
nothing, sire. Nothing. Many congratulations. Might as well
make it a joint coronation and wedding, then. OK with you,
bish?"

"I see no problem . . ."

"You don't? Oh."

"We have tried to get a table," said the Statistician-in-
Ordinary. "There are no trees big enough."

"Yeah, but if we took several laths and cut them to shape,
surely we could make a nice long thin table. I've always wanted
a nice long thin table."

"That's a thought," admitted the Statistician. "Yes. I'll look
into it."

"Splendid," said Orson. He surveyed the Council for any
further signs of dissent. He was really getting into this kingship
business. After all, what was the point of being king if you had to
do what you were told all the time? When it came to minor things
like tables and wives, he would jolly well make his own decisions,
thank you very much, and if Cantiger wanted his hundred
thousand a year, he would have to learn who was boss, sharpish.

* * *

Now turn we again. Being kissed by Arachne was rather like being dabbed with a wet chamois leather, but Geneva was used to it. She assured herself that the ordeal would soon pass.

"At least *someone* has done something constructive!" her mother purred. "I always knew that you were born to be queen, one way or the other, and that Orson seems a charming boy. Simple, but charming. A lummox, but charming. And royal. That's the main thing, isn't it? Queen of all Logris! Too, too exciting. Well done! Now, you'll want to appoint dear Mortmain regent whenever dear Orson is out of the country, of course. And I wouldn't be in too much of a hurry to have babies. Better to enjoy yourselves for a few years, and dear Mortmain will be there should anything happen, which Lugh forbid, of course. Now, what should we do about a wedding-present? What do you give a Supreme Ruler?"

"I've heard he wants a table," droned Geneva. "A long, thin one."

"Excellent. Your father can go and get one. Leo!" she shrieked. "Leo! Come here!"

"Bog off!" came back the reply from the newly emancipated King Leo, who was outside playing bowls with his men.

Geneva's lips twitched in amusement. Arachne's dug a pit in her cheek. To her mind, husbands were members of staff whose function was to serve, flatter and provide money. And Arachne did not keep impertinent staff.

"Your daughter is to be married!" Arachne bawled.

There was a moment's silence. Had she announced, "Your son is about to be disembowelled," Leo would have continued with his game. He was a fond father to Geneva, however, for all that he despaired of her high-falutin' ways. The silk of the pavilion's door flapped inward. Then so did King Leo.

"What did you say?" he demanded.

"Your daughter . . ." started Arachne.

"Daddy, darling, King Orson has asked me to marry him, and I have said yes.

"Nonsense. Far too young. Ridiculous. Little girl. Silly."

"Daddy, I am seventeen."

"Exactly. Far too young. Damned impertinent puppy, asking you to marry him. I mean, I like the chap. But really . . ."

"Oh, do stop being so tiresome, Leo," snapped Arachne. "Your daughter is going to be queen of Logris, for heaven's sake. You can't sniff at that."

"Oh, yes, I can," said Leo, and did so. His face then worked as he battled with his feelings. At last he sighed and shook his head sadly. "Well, I suppose if that's what you really want, my dear . . . I mean, he is a good sort."

"And we need a table," ordered Arachne. "As a wedding present. A long thin one, you said, Geneva?"

"That's what I was told."

"And the wedding's going to be in a week's time at the Coronation. So off you go and find a cabinetmaker, and be sure you have it here in time for lunch on Saturday."

"But . . ." Leo glanced helplessly from one woman to the other. He wished to defy the one as much as he wanted to indulge the other. "Oh, bugger," he sighed. "How long's long?"

"Oh, to seat a hundred and fifty or so, I should think." Arachne's fingers flashed as she waved away such trivia. "And make sure that it's in nonrenewable-resource tropical hardwood of quite fantastic rarity, carved with acanthus leaves, scallop shells, Pekingese snouts, aubergines . . . Conventional but stylish should be the tone. Carbuncles, do you think, Geneva, dearest?"

"Nice."

"It'll cost a by-our-lady fortune!"

"Has anyone mentioned you paying for the wedding? Or the reception? Your daughter is about to become your queen. Your son . . ."

"My *what*?"

". . . Oh, if there's one thing I can't stand it's nit-picking! Mortmain is going to be Chief Counsellor and Regent, I think you said, Geneva?"

"Something like that . . ." said Geneva vaguely.

"And I am going to be Queen Mother – and *you* are complaining about the price of a table? Lugh, you are pathetic."

"Well, presumably there'll be a dress . . . ?"

"Of course there'll be a dress. Ivory silk, I thought, fringed with ostrich-feathers and studded with pearls, dog-skin panties, of course . . ."

"Lugh! The fortune I've spent on dog-skin panties . . ."

". . . And calf's-caul net stockings . . ."

"They're half a serf a pair . . ."

". . . And slippers of dolphin-skin, studded with diamonds . . ."

"The price of dolphin-skin!"

"And antique ice-cream wafers in her hair . . ."

"Profligate, profligate . . . My dear old father . . ."

"Is dead."

". . . He never bought an antique ice-cream wafer in his life. Life's too short, he always said. And it was. He died. Just like that, out loud."

"And of course we'll need reticules, floral essences, soaps, palfreys, silken saddlecloths embroidered with 'G' and the crown, hatpins, miniature poodles, an outfit for each day of the Blitz, shoes, handmaidens, a bridal bouquet, bright copper kettles and warm woollen mittens . . . um . . . Oh . . . anyhow, things like that, but leave all that difficult stuff to me. You only have to worry about the table. Come on. Off you go . . ."

"Oh, dear," Leo sighed. But went.

"He's giving land back to people!"[55] Warhawk informed the hastily convened Conclave that had assembled in a grove in the Forest of Kincoghran. This was not a dappled sylvan glade but a custom-built meeting place of tree stumps, gnarled roots and briars in which stood a circle of rough stones. Each of the kings sat within this circle by his clanstone. Each had eleven arrows aimed at his heart, for, behind the stones, each had a select body of twelve men-at-arms to discourage treachery.

"He's encouraging people to complain if they get injured or imprisoned or killed!" Warhawk was incredulous. "He's inviting people to dinner and not falling upon them and murdering them in their cups! Has he no respect for tradition? No sense of justice? This beardless boy telling us how to run our countries! Well, I don't know about you filthy horrible ugly bastards, but I'll not bend the knee to no poncy so-called king. I've ordered the wall-built-by-that-hairdresser-guy built up again

---

[55]Well, he didn't actually. He said, "Gon's burgle bastards flockering margie pox integer stunk!"

and outposts set up all along it. This sort of revolutionary stuff must be nipped in the bud. They're all down there celebrating and calling one another 'fair Rider' in that poncy way. I vote we assemble our armies and take them by surprise."

"Ye are filth nicht fit to scrape from my least concubine's tichts, but ye are richt," growled another bearded giant, known as the King with the Hundred Knichts. "Haven't had a proper massacree in months. Those Greatwenners can't take it, you know. Don't eat enough oats, ye see, and wear ticht troosers. Saps the manhood, that sort of mullarkey."

"Mind, that Lynch feller was impressive," mused Housewolf. "And yon Woborn is a fancy wee fellow."

"Oh, I'm not saying it's going to be easy," admitted Warhawk. "It's the principle of the thing that counts, though. Possession is nine tenths of the law, and I possess whatever I've taken, therefore it should be nine tenths mine by law and the other tenth should be paid annually to me in rent and taxes. Way we've done things for hundreds of years. I didn't ficht all those fichts just to have the land taken away from me and given back to people I've beaten in fair ficht."

"Well, hardly *fair*," corrected Garech.

"Well, quite pretty, some of them. That stroke when I smote off three heads at once in Greendale. I call that fair."

"I don't think you've quite got the gist of their version of 'fair', Warhawk," Garech persisted. "It's not fair as in 'fair damosel'. You see, those three men were unarmed and on foot, and you were armed at all points and mounted, so . . ."

"Yes?"

Garech looked at his brother's stern but bemused face. "Oh, it doesn't matter," he sighed.

Warhawk shrugged his mighty shoulders. "Anyway, the point is, their lands became mine on account of they don't need them any more on account of their being dead. I mean, there's no point in dead people having lands, is there? Course not."

There was a mumble of agreement from all around the tree house. This was stark logic being served up to them.

"So, are we all agreed? We're not putting up with all this giving lands to dead people and bending the knee to whippersnappers on account of he moved some girt big rock. Rock-moving's useful in its place, but it's not kingly. How many men can you bring, Brandegoris, you filthy murderous donkey dropping?"[56]

Brandegoris struggled against his bonds. "Five thousand armed men on horseback, excrement-head."

"You, Clariance, that smell like a dead badger?"

Clariance spat. "If that filthy son of a very sick sow with very dubious morals can bring five thousand, so can I."

"Urience, cowardly cur's crotch unwashed for six and a half years?"

"Ha. See your five thousand and raise you one, you pustule on the buttocks of a woman of very few morals."

"Cradelmas, skunk vomit?"

"I'd like to rip your liver out, suppuration from a scrofular duck's groin, but will bring six thousand."

"Carados, may your bowels wither and your nose turn into the rotten pumpkin that it so closely resembles?"

Carados was apopleptic with rage. "Garderobe ordure! Dirty drawers worn for sixty-two years by a fat, bearded hag. Son of a man with the sexual predilections of a goose! Camel scrotum! Pig's bottom!" he shrilled. "*I* will bring six thousand!"

And so it was at length agreed. Two nights hence, they would meet on Goregargle plain, by the Dubhglas. Each of the ten kings would bring five or six thousand men and horses.

None of them would obey orders from anyone. Northern Logrians did not have armies. They had hordes. If you gave a North Logrian an order, he invariably said "Poo".

"Good." Warhawk almost smiled. He adored a good horde. "Go back to your kingdoms and prepare for rapine!"

A messenger's lot was a variable one. The bearer of glad tidings might find himself showered with gold and plied with good food and drink, whilst the bearer of bad might find himself dead or imprisoned just because the recipient Rider was cross and had to take it out on someone.

The greatest problem in the messenger business was resolving just what constituted good and what bad tidings.

---

[56]I can only here give expurgated approximations of the appellations used, at once for reasons of decency and because no language, not even Schweizerdeutsch, equals the guttural obscenity of North Logrian.

Many a messenger had discovered too late that he should not have indulged in what-hos and japery on announcing, say, that a Rider's wife had gone on a visit to her mother, only to have it revealed that her mother had been dead for ten years past. Many again had made passing great dole at, say, the announcement of a great-aunt's demise, only to find the supposedly bereaved Rider dancing and singing and cracking open the blonk.

In general nowadays, therefore, messengers compromised. A grovel did no harm, especially when there was a stout piece of furniture between groveller and Rider. The news was stated briskly, with a duck after each final consonant, but otherwise without comment. It was then customary to duck a few times more.

The general consensus amongst messengers was that old Boss Buller was one of the easiest, if not one of the more lavish customers. He did not shower you with wealth beyond the dreams of avarice,[57] but then, neither did he fling javelins at you to show you that he was displeased. He was an equable sort, not a man to demonstrate excitement or displeasure until it was time to draw his sword in fair fight.

He was plainly unhappy with the news from his castle – three fine dogs and two men-at-arms killed, the captain-at-arms minus two fingers and that funny, nice little Cressida Whatsit captured by the giants. He felt guilty about it. Back in November, he had received reports about a group of the brutes in the Morass de Foys, and had made a mental note to hunt them down as soon as spring came. Yet here he had been, fair wallowing in the fleshpots of Greatwen, whilst giants played fast and loose with his people.

He growled, then, at the messenger, and told him to request tea and a bed in the servants' quarters, before he even thought to hit anything. He walked to the window and very lightly hit the mullion with a loosely clenched, gauntleted fist. He was angry, angry with himself, angry with this ridiculous city. He knew his rightful place, and it was back amongst his people on his lands.

[57]Few did. It is hard to get beyond the dreams of avarice. They extend an awful long way.

But then, he told himself, he had an obligation to be here too for Orson's sake. The boy needed his help and advice, and there was no guarantee that the coronation would pass off without trouble. If, as appeared likely, some of the Riders refused to accept their new king's claim to the throne, Orson was going to need every Rider of prowess and stout man-of-arms as could be found to fight for him and make good that claim . . .

Buller was torn. He must recover the Cressy girl, but when and how? Giants were a Rider's responsibility. Men-at-arms might be sent against their equals, but they did not have the requisite skills for dealing with armed creatures three times their size and more, and any Rider who sent his troops against such foes must lose much worship. On the other hand, Buller, Brastias and K were all needed here in Greatwen . . .

Buller strode to the door. "Hoy, you!" he called to the guard who stood at ease there. "Would you trot down to the parade ground for me and fetch Boss Kes, an it please you?"

The guard nodded and set off at the trot. Buller resumed his anguished meditations at the window. A few minutes later, K clattered in through the door. His face was damp and crimson. "Hello, Papa," he said loudly and briskly. "Sorry. Can't be long. Honestly, some of those Sotis seem to think that marching is a branch of dancing. No idea. Now, what was it?"

"Problems," said Buller briefly, "at home."

He succinctly summarized the messenger's account of the giant's attack.

"Head in the clouds as usual, I suppose," muttered Kes, thinking of Cressy. "Ah, well, we've got bigger fish to fry now . . ."

"Mmmyes," said Buller softly. "If there is anything bigger in the long run than looking after your own. Still." He pulled himself upright and gazed for a second at the ceiling. "It's made up my mind. I want twenty of our men sent down there at once to strengthen the garrison . . ."

"But they'll miss the coronation!" Kes objected. "They've been rehearsing . . ."

"I am aware of that," Buller said drily. "But a soldier best serves his king who best serves his master. I myself will ride back there so soon as the coronation is done. This is not my place, nor these my people."

"But you are the king's foster-father! You cannot go back to just being a rustic squire. We must move with the times, move onward . . ."

"Must we, indeed?" Buller smiled sadly at his son. "Well, just you remember, my boy. If there is to be peace in this land, it is going to be thanks to us rustic squires, and if we want to be able to keep the peace, we must serve our people and die for them if we must. You move with the times as you will, K, but remember: the most important things are those that do not change, and service is one of the most important. Do as I bid you. Gramercy." He turned on his heel and resumed his study, as it seemed, of the city.

But his eyes were on the green fields and forests beyond the city walls, and his gaze was misted with tears.

Chapter Nine

"SUCH A DAINTY little damosel," crooned a woman's voice. They were the first words that Cressy heard as she bobbed up into consciousness. "So clever, the way it's all put together so small. What will they think of next?"

Cressy's first thought on awaking had been to keep her eyes closed and find out as much as she could whilst feigning unconsciousness. She had no desire to open her eyes anyhow. Someone was playing a funeral dirge, very close to her ear, on a giant muffled drum. With each beat of the drum, pain shot like an arrow from the back of her neck to her eyes. She was aware, too, of cuts and scratches that felt cold on her face and arms, and of a bruise at the back of her head that had set up a rhythm section all its own.

This first plan, however, proved impossible of fulfilment, because giant dry fingers that tingled alarmingly were prodding and fumbling at her body. She had to see their owner if only the better to bite them.

Her eyelids seemed glued together, but she prised them apart.

She looked up into a face of surpassing ugliness. Its size was just one factor that would have secured the prize in any competition. The ruddy lumps at the brow and in the cheeks, the towering square brow, the bristling eyebrows, the tiny piggy eyes, the squashed snout, the mouth that looked like two huge rose-hips surmounted by a smear and the chin that simply wasn't there at all, having been engulfed by the neck – any one of these would have dispirited rivals. Together, they cleared the field.

And atop all these – gilding, as it were, the lily – were the moles. These were like a normal woman's paps, only almost pitch black, and from them there sprouted – or spouted – tufts of thick black curls.

Cressy screamed, rolled over, and was about to cover her head with her pillow when she saw that her pillow was the distended belly of an entire dead beaver that lay gaping across the bed.

She leaped up. The floor, which seemed similarly strewn with dead animals or animal skins, their heads in varying stages of decomposition, rocked up towards her, then spun about her. She held out her arms for balance, but to no avail. She fell to her knees and slumped forward.

The hands were on her again and the smells of fish and dung and truffles on the giants' gurgling breath were wreathing about her face. Four hands lifted her back on to the bed.

"Such a wriggly little missy!" declared the female.

"Arr," said a voice that she recognized as her captor's. "Gave us an 'ard time day afore yesterday an' all. Bit me, too. Should work well, a fighter like that."

"Bit of a waste to put it to work, Gumble," the female mused. "Shame really . . . Can you imagine the braised snowhills we'd get out of that? With wild garlic and Slippery Jack? All silky and tender . . . Ooh, makes me drool just to look at 'er . . ."

Cressy lay there, trembling. She did not know whether to open her eyes again or whether to continue to feign unconsciousness. She suspected that neither would make the slightest difference to these creatures.

"When we done with 'er, Ugmay, all right, maybe . . ." mumbled Gumble sulkily. "And Midgic . . . Then we'll see. But she's young yet, and we can feed 'er up."

Cressy opened her eyes very suddenly, and Gumble fell as suddenly silent.

"Hello, Father, dear," Cressy smiled. "Hello, Mother. Sorry. Was I sleeping? Must be the late night at the ball. What a to-do! Now, Mother dearest, I am famished! Any chance of some . . ." she considered the horrors that might be served her. She played safe. ". . . Cheese?" she said at last. "And apples?"

The two giants exchanged rapid glances. "Ah," said Ugmay, "There's a little bogeycurd! Course we can find an apple for the little dote. Can't we, Gumble?"

"Yeah." Gumble frowned. "Thing is, dear, we're not . . ."

"Oh, thank you so much, Mother," gushed Cressy. "You are a darling!"

"But she's not . . ." objected Gumble. He was silenced by a fierce glance from Ugmay.

"You just go and find the cheese and apples and then get off to your work," she ordered. "I'll take the little honeypot to meet the others."

Gumble stood with a scowl and shuffled away.

Cressy had leisure now to look about her. She and the giantess were in a room of sorts, or rather a cubicle within a giant hall. The cubicle was made of withy hurdles through which living ivy had been woven. It was perhaps ten feet high. Way above it, however – some sixty feet at least – was a great domed ceiling of tree branches, again interwoven so that light filtered through as through netting. Cressy could already guess at the nature of this massive hall. The outer walls, she was sure, would be of tree trunks interspersed with holly bushes and briars. The passer-by, then, would see only an impenetrable copse, never guessing at the open space within.

Ugmay, with much clucking and cooing, led her from the cubicle into the main body of this great hall. Cressy's head was still aching. Even had it not been, she would have been bewildered by the number of people and the amount of activity in here.

And yet, for all the lively bustle, death was everywhere. Dead animals hung from hooks in the tree-trunk columns. Animal skins again strewed the floors.

Glaring or snarling heads of foxes, horses, bears, deer, goats, moufflon, dogs and badgers had been pinned as trophies to the trees, and Cressy started and closed her eyes for a second as she passed two trees devoted entirely to grinning human heads, the skin shrinking and withering or falling in dry flaps from the skulls, the beards and the hair wispy as smoke.

For all that it was day, and the seeping light from the ceiling bright, the hall was dark about its perimeters, and the flames of tallow torches bowed and danced. In their light, she saw giant women and children hard at work, skinning; disembowelling or jointing beasts and birds on a long table made of one great pine tree, simply sliced down its centre and propped, flat side up, on the convex side of its erstwhile other half. Amongst the giants were men and women of Cressy's size. There was no light in their eyes, no curiosity as they saw the new arrival in her robe of saffron hessian. They worked on, arms slicked to the elbows with blood, working, burrowing and kneading flesh.

The phrase 'production line' was unknown to Cressy, and has only recently been unearthed in a newspaper found in the sensational Houndsditch Hoard where its meaning is precisely explained. This, however, was what she was witnessing. The carcasses were skinned at one end of the table and the pelts thrown to the tanning section that scraped off the fat, salted and dried them. The carcasses, meanwhile, had moved on to the gutting crew, who flung unwanted intestines on to a steaming pile in the dust. At the last, the beasts were chopped up and the joints cast into the one of the two great pits in which hot stones made the water seethe and dimple.

The stench turned Cressy's stomach, but she gulped and skipped and expressed her admiration for everything. Villeins did not do advanced Girlish Glee at school, but few graduates of Kynke Kennadonne could have excelled her performance that day. She clapped her hands at the giant hogsheads of birch and sycamore blonk. She admired – she genuinely admired – the fine working of bones and antlers into sword or dagger hilts, dice or ornate figurines, which seemed to be the occupation of the bent and wizened old. (Though, had she known it, these "old" were no more than thirty-five or thirty-six. Giants rarely lived to the age of forty.)

She fought down nausea at the sight of the human children caged in shadow at one end of the hall, begrimed in their own mire so that only the whites of their imploring eyes betrayed their presence. "Them's for Grove Milsday," said Ugmay. "Stuff 'em with pigeons and thyme and blonk, score 'em and salt 'em and paint 'em with a little honey to get the lushmiest spangling crackling, then spit 'em till they'm golden."

"Sounds lovely," said Cressy, and turned away.

She cooed over the romping giant toddlers who were taller and burlier than her. One hurled a toy brick at her. She picked herself up, rubbed her breastbone, blinked back the tears and said, "How sweet."

But, smile and question as she might, she could see no way out of the hall. The walls, as she had thought, were of thick holly. The huge beds of ferns with their animal pillows lay along them. Even the garderobes here were just pits in the ground, barely concealed behind hurdles.

She did more guesswork. Aside from the tallow candles, there was no fire nor trace of a fire in the hall. One of the cooking pits was empty of stones. She supposed, then, that the pits must be used alternately and the stones heated somewhere away from the hall, where smoke could not attract the attention of the curious or vindictive, and somehow carried back here. She supposed, too, that the men must pass their days hunting in the forest and return here with their quarry at night. It would be then that she must keep her eyes peeled for doors or tunnels.

She passed that first day, then, in proving herself a willing worker and a doting daughter, and she waited for the men's return. That was her chief source of hope – and terror.

Night clustered around Greatwen. It swarmed in the corners of the courtyards and the runnels of the Tower. It crept in through the windows, tarnished the mirrors and smoothed the colours of hangings and paintings into earth-coloured homogeneity. Ghosts yawned and rubbed their eyes and gargled a scale or two in preparation for the howling. The lamplighter . . . well, lit the lamps.

Lynch, King Skinner, Cantiger and Orson were halfway through the first course of a light supper[58] when Kes came in, puffing. He slammed his gauntlets down on the sideboard and speared a chicken. "Lugh," he breathed, "I am famished. All that drilling . . . Oy! Who ate my cavy?"

"Whoops," said Cantiger.

Kes glared. "Pink-and-white persons should be very, very careful," he announced. "Especially small pink-and-white

[58]Three 9 lb chickens, stuffed with bread, milk, minced veal, blood pudding, sage, rosemary, onions, garlic, pine kernels, cumin, mace, lemon juice and finely chopped lamb's sweetbreads, all bound with egg and sweet blonk, boiled with a large selection of root vegetables, an ox tongue and a calf's head. With these were served hogweed braised in butter, pickled samphire and an aspic of rabbit, pistachios and ground elder, a delicious cavy apiece, marinated in Geneva and orange juice, barded with bacon and spit-roasted with juniper berries and almonds, and a frumenty flavoured with woodcock trails. For the second course, there was a stewed conger, stuffed with dulse and bejewelled with sea urchins and limpets, with its tail in its mouth, a pie enshrouding twenty-four whitebirds, topped with bread and honey. Then came . . . But you get the picture. Things had improved for our heroes.

persons. Orson, what is the penalty for pinching a cavy?"

"I don't think we've done that yet," confessed Orson. "Capital crime, do you think?"

"Oh, definitely," agreed Lynch with great gravity.

"No question," said Skinner.

"Retrospective, too," suggested Kes, sidestepping along the bench to sit by Skinner. He wrenched a leg from the bird before him and sank his muzzle into the flesh. "Anyone who ever stole a man's roast cavy to be executed."

"I'll enact it at once," said Orson. "Cantiger, have you anything to say in your defence?"

Cantiger glanced nervously from one large man to another. "It was an accident. They stuck together. It was someone else's fault – the cook's. She said you weren't coming. And how was I to know they only had four legs? Always thought they had eight legs. They used to call them gwinny-pigs. Did you know that? Fact. And, um . . ."

"It's amazing." Skinner grinned. "It's totally natural to him. I woke him up the other day when he was snoring in council. He opened his eyes and said, 'It was the other chap I have independent witnesses I come from a broken home would you like some money?'"

Skinner, a lean, long beardless man with high cheekbones, was a born mimic. He captured Cantiger's plump tones to perfection. The other men hooted with laughter, save Lynch, who merely grimly smiled. "I wasn't snoring! I was thinking!" a very red Cantiger protested. "Anyhow, that wasn't me. There's a chap looks just like me . . ."

The laughter rattled. The Riders thumped the table and honked. Kes thrust a bread roll into Cantiger's gaping mouth. "Shut it, conjuror," he said. "It's been a hard enough day without having to listen to your blather."

"Problems?" asked Orson, who, whilst he enjoyed chaffing Cantiger, was nonetheless protective of him.

"You could say. Seven cheerleaders down with favism. Two suffering concussion because the mace-bearer couldn't see the mace. Then, with Papa sending twenty of our men home, which has knocked the heart out of the procession, because they were easily the most disciplined . . ."

"I didn't hear about that . . ."

Kes picked up a stalk of hogweed, tipped his head back and chomped at it like a thrush with a worm. He quaffed and wiped his mouth on his sleeve. "I told him it was crazy just before the coronation, but he got all stuffy and priggish. They've been having giant problems."

"Giants?" Lynch smiled wistfully. He was a good-looking chap, Lynch, with curly brown hair, pale grey eyes and a lopsided smile. But often those eyes, though alert, would glaze over. It was a strange thing. In his thoughts, he was plainly somewhere else, fighting one of his titanic battles or journeying alone through some wild and misty land. But anyone foolish enough to assume that in consequence he was vulnerable would rapidly discover his mistake. His reactions were the fastest that Orson had ever seen. He had seen him catch a swallow in flight. "They can be tricky, giants. Always go for the genytours. That's the thing . . ."

"Buller mentioned that there were a few out in the Morass de Foys," Orson murmured. "What have they been up to?"

"Oh, the usual . . ." Kes reached for the ewer and recharged his goblet. "Kidnapped one of our girls. You remember that Cressy . . . ?"

Orson frowned. Orson stared at the wall. Orson said, "Oh . . ."

I had a twelve-footer last year," said Skinner. "Name of Gildas. Same thing. Grabbing damosels. I slew him easy enough – well, four, five hours, some serious bruises, but you know . . . But his sister! Lugh! Just nine foot seven, but she had fourteen men of gentil birth in her harem, and she fought harder than – well, I have been beaten by Marhaus . . ."

"Sotis Rider . . ." supplied Lynch, ". . . of much much worship, and a marvellous good man of his hands . . ."

". . . But I don't think I was ever so adoubted as when I fought that grisliest of women. She wielded a great iron club . . ."

"Normal," said Lynch.

". . . and she had wicked blades at the tips of her toes . . ."

Orson did not hear. He continued to stare. He was suddenly ware that he had been feeling guilty throughout his sojourn in Greatwen. That guilt had, until now, been general, unfocused –

a sort of general, nagging ache. At night, however, someone had visited him and whispered in his ear, someone with a gruff but caressing voice, someone with dark hair and haunting brown eyes.

Every morning, that visitor had faded to a wraith and been all but forgotten. But the guilt had remained.

Cressy.

Cressy, his friend and critic. Cressy, the strangely beautiful, the strangely ugly, whose face suddenly lit up when he smiled at her or when someone talked nonsense.

He had sent her a card when first he came up to this city. A "having a wonderful", "You can't imagine", "Miss you and the dogs" sort of card. A show-off card. Since then, whilst things had unquestionably happened to Orson, he had devoted hardly a thought to his hobbling villein friend.

But she had visited him at night, and, he now knew, had been demanding his attention all the while.

And she was in the hands of giants.

"Hold on." Orson raised a hand. "Cressy has been taken?"

"Aye." Kes drank again. "Aye, apparently she rode apart from the rest. Some fourteen-foot brute grabbed her. Middle-aged – nineteen, twenty. The men-at-arms tried to rescue her, but they never had a chance. Two killed, and Cap'n Hardpad had two fingers bitten off. Ripped two of our alaunts apart, too, and ate a brachet on the spot."

"Brave dog," said Skinner.

"They do that." Lynch nodded. "Their teeth are as dangerous as their hands or clubs, particularly since they are always infected. A bite from a giant can kill you months later . . . So who was this girl?"

"Dreamy little thing," said Kes. "Read books a lot. Something of the witch in her, I always thought – the way she'd read your thoughts . . ."

"She is my friend," blurted Orson simply.

Lynch suddenly leaned forward, his forearms on the table.

"Your Majesty . . . ?" he started.

"Papa has said that he'll go straight down there after the coronation and sort the whole business out," Kes interrupted. "After the coronation, we can send a whole army down there.

Anyhow, I am simply not prepared to see good Riders abandoning their King."

"They take them," said Skinner, "for just two purposes – to eat them and to use them as slaves."

"Oh, Lugh . . ." breathed Orson.

"Anyhow, these things happen," said Kes impatiently. He pushed his littered plate away from him and sighed. "Now. Conger . . ."

Orson was standing. "Ah, well," he yawned. "Long day, and another one tomorrow. I think I'll head for bed. Please give orders that I am not to be disturbed until limelight."[59]

"Hmm. Think I'll turn in early too," said Lynch. "I feel a bit tired . . ." He stretched and creaked, just in case anyone should misunderstand.

Cantiger's eyes lit up. "Does that mean I can have your conger?"

The broth in the great stone pit seethed and rolled. Huge chunks of meat jostled with one another, rose to the steaming surface and sank with gulping sounds, only to bob up again. The stench of wild garlic was strong.

There was a sense of expectancy among the womenfolk and the children now. Some seemed bright and excited, others nervous, irritable and snappy. Wailing giant babies were hushed and hastily given their stitched cows' udders filled with warmed blood to keep them happy. The great table was scrubbed down until, though liberally stained with blood, it gleamed. The bones had been piled high. The fat scraped from the hides had been burned. It had sizzled and gone up with a great, foul-smelling "Whoomph!" before being swept into a corner to smoulder. Insofar as a vast, teeming cookhouse-cum-shambles-cum-nursery whose only soft furnishings were dead animals could be said to be tidy, the hall was tidy.

Cressy was exhausted by a long day of startling and repellent sensation and by the sheer effort of 1dissembling. She had been sweet and charming to everyone, but particularly to Ugmay and

[59]Roughly eleven o'clock. "Redwoodlight" (i.e. the time at which the sun clears the tree) was noon.

to the older giants, to whom the women seemed to defer. She had danced for them – an ungainly, hobbling dance that they seemed to find charming and funny – until her feet ached. She had scrambled up the old men's limbs with great horns filled with blonk or mead or with quids of the fetid muck that they smoked.

She had even – and she would blush to recall it – kissed the oldest of the giants, a huge, stooped, creature with spindrift white hair, by name Dockspurge, on his pocked and flaky crimson cheek. She had thought Gumble's breathing to be bad, but Dockspurge had to struggle, hands flapping like sails, to muster enough gravelly breath to gasp the words, "Little . . . chitterling . . ." apparently a term of high approval.

The men's arrival, when it came, was sudden. A section of floor, complete with animal hides, suddenly tilted and erupted inward. Two shrivelled giants, smaller by far than their companions, were the first to emerge. Their faces and bodies were white and puckered and streaked with mud. They grinned inanely. Their bulging eyes swivelled this way and that. The eyeballs were blue-grey jelly. They were totally blind.

They scampered to the pit and hastily snatched up meat and crammed it into their mouths.

Behind them, one by one, rising from the ground like trees growing at high speed, came the giants. At times, with the largest of them, Cressy was convinced that the whole creature was in the hall, only to see him rising further and further. The greatest of them, a fat, red-faced brute with six lank streaks of red hair painted across an otherwise bald skull, was a good seventeen feet tall.

They all carried clubs, and they all carried meat. Each on arrival flung down a pile of corpses – deer, oxen, sheep, pigs, fowl, the smaller variety of horse and the fatter variety of child. Cressy saw a unicorn amongst the carrion, and her heart bled. There were dogs there, too, and brackrats, sleek and grey and four feet long, with their jagged orange teeth.

There was no jubilation when the males arrived back home. The women examined their men's kills with quiet cooing sounds. They worked the dead jaws and prodded the dead flesh approvingly, but they and the children were cowed, and kept out of the hunters' way.

As for the men, they uttered no greetings beyond grunts. Their eyes scanned the hall suspiciously. Any perceived transgressions or omissions were punished with cuffs which, with the human women, sent them flying. The women neither wailed nor snivelled. They just picked themselves groggily up and again took their places in the ranks around the pit. Domestic duties done, the males strode immediately to the pit and addressed themselves to feeding.

Watching giants eat is usually a pretty compulsive business. There is the fascinating speculation as to just how far those jaws can spread, the intriguing, "Nah, it'll never fit! It might . . . By-our-lady Nora! That is seriously gross!" There is the fascinating sight of the food actually going down the giant gullet, because giants like to gulp, and the passage of an entire leg of mutton can do significant things to an Adam's apple. There is the equally compelling sight of the food going down the giant chin and chest, to slop and gather, usually on the pig's head, worn at groin level that year.

To a betting man, no less than to a zoologist or a student of abstract expressionism, then, the study of eating giants is fraught with interest. Cressy, however, whilst doing her best to look admiring like the other women – gasping as an entire horse head was swallowed in one, politely applauding a drool measured at fourteen feet – kept her eyes on the area of floor through which the giants had entered the hall. To her horror, she saw the blind tunnelers carrying the day's bones to the hole and flinging them down it. They wrenched the hot rocks from the sides of the pit and scurried across the hall to pile them about the edge of the hole. When all the rocks were lining the hole, the two twisted creatures climbed down and pulled them down on them. A moment later, the flap of turf and hurdle was lowered and it was as though the hole had never been there.

"Use a different tunnel every day," murmured Ugmay, catching the direction of Cressy's glance, "and fill it in every evening. Keeps us safe, see."

Keeps us prisoner, thought Cressy. But she said, "How clever! Um, Mother . . . ?"

"Yes, dinkums?"

"I still got a splitting headache. I'd like Father to tell me a story or something, but I think I really ought to go to bed early. Would that be all right?"

"Of course it would, sheepstone. Don't you worry. You go and lie down on my bed. I'll be with you soon."

Normally such a pledge would have filled Cressy with horror. After today, however, the notion of Ugmay's gross and bulbous body at her side, her hideous face by hers, and her foul breath fanning her hair, was positively reassuring.

Sneaking out of Greatwen Tower with arms and armour sufficient and apt for confronting giants presents problems. Arms and armour clank, and, if poorly tailored, scrape and screech as a Rider walks. The flagged floor and high stone ceilings of the tower enhance and amplify these noises many times, so that even a tiptoeing Rider sounds like a very progressive and lively percussion section.[60]

All this Orson considered when he returned to his chamber. For a moment, then, he considered placing all his armour in a sack, padding to the gates and only then arming himself. This too was a non-starter. First, padding with a sack of metal was no more possible than mime with your tights on fire. Then there was the possibility – nay, the likelihood – that the guards at the gate would recognize him, consider such behaviour suspicious and raise the alarm before he was so much as greaved.

For Orson had no doubt but that Cantiger, Buller and Co would deter him from his mission. They would preach to him of duty. They would point out to him that now the nation's security stood firm or shivered with his shield. And he knew that, in theory at least, they were right.

In practice, however, Cressy came first.

What sort of king would it be, what sort of commander, who did not fight for his own? Orson had trained in the arts of warfare and was more proficient in them than Kes, but, if he were incapable of rescuing his own damosel-in-distress, how could he lead other men in imposing the justice that he sought throughout this kingdom?

[60]Particularly when, as a tiptoeing Rider must, he falls over.

And Cressy was his own. Small, trusting, difficult, tough and troublesome, but his own.

She might have defended herself had she been reared in arms, as had he, but she was denied all such protection, all such right of assertion. She was all alone.

Save for her friends.

Of whom he was first.

For her, he must ride.

He had a sort of idea that kings on occasion donned disguise and went amongst their people. He could not remember where he had heard such a thing, but something told him that others too would regard this as acceptable, if eccentric, conduct. He summoned Brown Willy, therefore, who arrived with One and Two, and, of course, Bollard, who, like Cantiger, was acquiring gravitas, particularly in the area that more sylphlike porcines described as their "waists". Bollard and Cantiger were both of the "Want not, waist not" school.

"Time to disrobe, sire?" asked Brown Willy.

"Erm, no, actually," said Orson. "Or, rather, yes, but then I want to get dressed again, in clothes as ordinary as you can find, and with a big cloak."

"Certainly, sire." Brown Willy started rummaging in the great oak press.

Orson strolled around as he unlaced his shirt. "I want to go out amongst ordinary people and see what they think about things."

"Good idea, Your Majesty." Brown Willy handed Orson leather breeches and a black high-necked sweater of finest goats' wool. "How many men-at-arms will you be requiring?"

"None. And I want no 'sires' or 'Your Majesties' tonight. You can call me . . . What's a good name?"

"I've got a new cousin called Banana Blancmange, Your Majesty," said One, who hadn't, but just fancied the idea of calling his king Banana Blancmange.

"Um, no . . ." Orson considered. "Something simpler . . ."

"How about Leroy, sire?" asked Brown Willy. "That's quite clever really, you see, because it means 'the roy' in Deedong . . ."

"Yes?" Orson frowned. "And?"

"I'm not sure," admitted Brown Willy. "What is a roy?"

"Oh. Well. OK. Leroy it is. And I want you three to bring Demeter and my arms and armour in sacks. And a plain white shield. I'll take the black Thing with the wiggly bit." He slung X-Calibre over his shoulder, pulled his boots back on and stood. "All go out separately. We'll meet outside the Eastern Judas in fifteen minutes, and you are to tell no one, you understand? If anyone asks you where you are going, tell them that I asked you to go out to buy a shoehorn or – a roy or something."

"Aye, sire." The three boys nodded.

"Leroy," corrected Orson with a wagging finger as he opened the door. He moved the finger to his lips to hush them, and padded out into the corridor.

He made his way down the great stairs and along further corridors, ducking into shadow whenever he heard the tramp of armed feet or the hush of leathern slippers. He slid like a shadow past the great gilt throne room and the barrel-vaulted dining hall, in both of which the guards' helmets dully glowed in the moonlight or torchlight. From there, he trotted briskly down the service stairs to the kitchens.

Work had not ceased here. Work here never ceased. There were watches of the guard to be victualled as they came in from work. There were Riders and officials calling for food at all hours. As Orson crept past, he heard the homely kitchen sounds dear and familiar to all. Knives squelched on flesh, ground on bone, rapped on chopping boards. Food burbled on the ranges and hissed on the charcoal fires. Cooks hurled abuse and knives. Under-cooks whined and blubbed. Dogs scratched and yawned.

Along the shadowy cloister, then, and into the great, booming, breathing chapel, and down into the crypt where lay buried the mortal remains of the past Kings and Queens of Logris,[61] and so at last into the secret passage built by the legendary Abbot Klopstok in the age of the Giants.

This debouched, by curious chance, on the site of the ancient nunnery of Morrigan, in what had been the bedchamber of the Abbess Dechtire, virgin and mother of six, and was now the upper chamber of a common lodging house. Several common lodgers stirred as Orson tiptoed between their recumbent and malodorous forms. Some did not stir, but their clothes did.

[61]Their immortal remains were up to their usual tricks all about the Tower.

Downstairs, where once the little sisters of Morrigan had danced the lupa and prostrated themselves before the Rearing Vorbal, mittened vagrants sat about a fire, drinking acorn brew and playing Mavis in the Bushes.

"Evening," said Orson cheerily as he passed amongst them.

They did not look up from their cards. "Panty," said a bearded woman, and played a nasturtium.

"Singlet," said a jowly old man, throwing down a brace of sprouts.

"I think you've got Mavis." Another woman squinted at him. "I'm playing safe." She laid down three legumes and a partially formed brassiere of turnips. "I'm out. Evening, lad."

Orson left them to their game and strolled casually out into the street. He breathed deep of the night air, even though it was the same air that he had been breathing in the Tower. This, however, was the night air of freedom.

He walked about the walls of the Tower to his rendezvous. At the north-easternmost corner, a chunk of shadow detached itself from the wall. It carried a sliver of winking crystal. It thrust this at Orson's throat and said, "Giss yer money."

Another man materialized behind Orson. "Come on, come on . . ." he urged. "Giss yer money, gold, silver, rings, linen . . ."

Orson considered. "No," he said.

The word seemed somehow naked and rather rude on its own, so Orson gave it some company. "I would. I mean, I'd love you to have some of those things. I've got masses. The trouble is, I sort of feel that you wouldn't use them well. If I gave you money, you'd go off and get drunk and bully more people, or, even worse, employ other people to bully them without you running the risk that you now run. Isn't that right?"

"Well, yeah," admitted the man in front of him. "But the point is, we got knives and you 'aven't, so you're meant to say, 'I want to live, so 'ere's the dosh'. We're not debating effics 'ere. I mean, I studied effics at Kynke Kennadonne, as it 'appens. Nothing wrong with a bit of contractual reciprocity in a society, is what I always say. But it's got to work froughout that society, innit? I mean, I'm going to give you the gift of life – precious, you'll agree?"

"Certainly." Orson nodded.

"And in exchange, you're going to give me the gift of money. Vat's only fair, innit? Well, it's not even really fair when you come to fink of it. You see a guy wants only money, gives 'is life to it, like, you say, 'Poor berk! I mean, get a life or what?' don't you? If you've got your 'elf, 'oo gives a monkey's about welf, right? Nah, you got 'elf, and (you're going to keep it, all fanks to me's the way I see it. Me, like you say, I'm going to go off an' get drunk. Tomorrow morning, I'll be all unelfy, and all fanks to you. So you get the better of the deal. I should get some recompense for that, is 'ow I see it."

"You're a philosopher," said Orson in a tone of some surprise. "But suppose I could keep my wealth and my health?"

"Not possible," said the man behind him. "Contr'y to the laws of natural justice. 'Umans 'ave got to share. 'Elf *and* welf is unjust. Also, I gotta blade, what you 'aven't . . . Come on. Pay your dues, mate."

Orson pursed his mouth. He frowned deeply. "You know," he said at last, "I really can't. I am so sorry."

It was then that he moved.

He moved roughly and rudely, snatching the man ahead of him by the privy parts and striking at his neck with the side of his hand, even as his left foot struck backwards at his anterior assailant's groin. Using the unconscious philosopher's body as a battering-ram, he then turned and charged the acolyte, who, doubled up, was struck violently and suddenly on the jaw, and straightened again.

Orson dropped the one man, whilst the other one did it all by himself. Intransitively, as it were.

Riders learned that sort of thing at primary school. And that was in country-dancing classes.

It is a rule universally acknowledged that the quality of a drinking establishment is in inverse proportion to the quantity of interior decoration. Orson and his companions therefore peered into the Dog and Dingleberry – "famed for its brose and gobbets" – and the Scallop and Astrolabe – "childer welcome, no boots or working habiliments" – and, seeing battered armour and obscure agricultural implements on deep red walls, rapidly turned away.

You just had to look at The King's Buttock, however, to know that the ale would be splendid and the company congenial. The walls had been decorated once with a coat of lime-wash, and subsequently with smoke, beer, sebaceous suppurations and other ex- and ac-cretions. The floors were of stone, worn smooth and undulant by feet and heads. The tables were thick and solid and designed for thumping or dancing on. No one was dancing on them as Orson's party entered, but fists and tankards were thumping on them, several women were sitting on them and the poet Snugsnuffler, stuffed to the gills with inspiration, was sleeping on one of them.

An accordionist supplied material for that time-honoured conversation "The accordion: why?" and a man was telling the dubious story of the duke, the actress, the monkey and the mangle. This, the beaming smiles on One's and Two's faces clearly said, was The Life.

The four men squeezed on to a bench in the midst of the company. A pretty blonde girl took Orson's order for ale – black for Orson and Brown Willy, amber for the pages on account of their age. It was generally thought at the time that those under fourteen should drink no more than a quart of strong ale a day. The girl returned with the drinks, and Orson was surprised to see that she was a paid-up member of the Union of Disrobers. The man telling the story came to the famous punchline – "Not without starch it won't, madam!" – and Orson joined in the raucous laughter.

Conversation – 'The accordion: why?' – became general. The general consensus was "No reason it all", but Orson pointed out that it kept cats away and, if played near milk, resulted in cheese far faster than usual. Brown Willy said that it was expressive of the sufferings of all living things and thus good for the soul, and the pages, now on their third pints, said cordionshoundlikechickenshfartinancordionishtshdallbeshot. A lot of people agreed.

Orson excused himself and moved towards the urinal wall at the back of the house. Once there, he turned back to ensure that he was out of sight of his party, nipped through the taproom and clambered through the window. He made his way round to where Demeter stood tethered, the three bulging sacks of armour slung over his back.

It may occasion some surprise that a valuable courser could be left tethered in a public street, but no thief would think to touch a warhorse. The notion that horses are exclusively vegetarian is mistaken. In hot blood a horse will tear – and eat – flesh, and every courser was trained as a foal to kick and strike at enemies. Anyone save Orson or Brown Willy who had thought to grab Demeter's bridle would have found himself, if he could still look, dispersed about the street.

Orson unslung X-Calibre and armed himself. As a former pillier, he was proficient in tying the bands and cantels, even in darkness, and he was armed at all points within five minutes. He heaved himself up on to a mounting block, eased himself into the saddle, straightened, drew in the reins, and was about to click to Demeter when a smaller figure, on a smaller horse, rode silently alongside.

"Sorry, Leroy," said Brown Willy. "You have yet to learn subtlety. Actually, I hope you never will. Where a Rider goes, you know . . ."

"Yes, yes, I know. There goes his pillier." Orson was momentarily irritated. Then he smiled. He had not been looking forward to riding alone through the night. "Thank you," he said. Then, "Not subtle, eh?"

"Transparent as water, sire."

"Oh. All right. I warn you. This could be perilous."

"Goes with the job, sire."

"Stick to 'Leroy' for now. Let's go."

Orson clicked his tongue. Demeter spurted into a clattering wallop. Brown Willy, on his smaller, lighter, but less burdened palfrey, easily kept pace with him, one length behind.

The taproom girl had seen Brown Willy leave, and had watched the two young men through the window. Now, as they walloped off, she turned to One. "Who was that nice young man?" she asked.

One stirred. "'S a king," he burped. "Name of Balarma Bronge."

"Bramana Bralonge," corrected Two.

"Yellow puddin', anyhow," said One, as his head subsided on to the table.

"'S right. King . . . Yellowpuddin' . . ." drooled Two. He, too, sagged. His eyes flickered blearily open for a moment. ". . . And Brown Willy," he pronounced. His fair head joined his brother's.

"Ooh," said the girl, bemused and strangely sad. "Yes, I think I've heard of him . . ."

One and Two did not hear her. They were dead to the world, but the last thought of both was: "This is the life."

Lynch was well ahead of Orson, travelling at a steady hack canter through the forests, his gazehounds and lymers alongside him, his pillier two lengths behind. He was a confident man, and rode without gage or helm. He could hear, therefore, the cacophony of the woodland night – the shrieks and howls, the squawking and crashing of beasts and birds, some alarmed at Lynch's passing, some engaged in their own transactions of life and death, some seeking what they might devour.

His king's command did not need to be explicit. It was enough that he had spoken with emotion of this villein girl and that there was an adventure to undertake for Lynch to saddle up and ride.

Lynch is often portrayed as dour and devout, and he was often the one and always the other. But his dedication and single-mindedness were those of a sportsman, and he truly loved the game. His eyes were cold as porcelain when he was in battle, but they twinkled before and in recollection after, and the sight of a blow well struck by another could even bring an involuntary smile of startling brightness to his leathern face. His manners were courtly and impeccable, but damosels complained of an Olympian inaccessibility behind the kindliness and thoughtfulness.

The fact is that Lynch was a solitary at heart, and never happier than, like this, riding alone through his beloved Logris with battle in prospect. When in battle, he discovered a tranquillity and stillness denied him in day-to-day life. When in society, he felt alienated and fretful. His manners only masked his longing to be out once more on range or moor, free and striving for worship.

Lynch knew – none better – the habits of giants. He aimed, therefore, to go to his brother Buller's castle tonight and to ride forth, rested, at first light on the morrow. His best chance of finding the giants' hiding place and hunting them down was to catch them as they emerged in the morning.

An hour's ride behind him, Orson had much the same plan. He only knew about giants from the accounts of other Riders and from his study of the bestiary, but he too knew that giant-cubbing was done in the early hours. He looked forward to a night amongst his friends in the familiar ramshackle bustle of home.

It was not to be.

Lynch it was who, just five miles short of the castle, came upon a river. He looked for bridge or ford, but saw none. He saw instead a long, low boat with pavilions set thereon. The boat was rich and well bisene. Gold glinted on the prow in the moonlight. The fabric of the pavilions was silky, and worked in whorls and arabesques in some metallic thread. Pennants fluttered from their gleaming finials. Drawing closer and peering down into the keel, he saw that it was entirely covered with a thick carpet of white water lilies and madonna lilies that seemed bright pale purple whilst the moon was out, but were plunged back into rustling darkness as the moon slid behind a mantilla of cloud.

"There is some adventure here," Lynch murmured to his pillier. "You retire into the woods and light a fire to ward off animals. I will see what marvels this barque may hold."

The pillier was used to this. He hissed to the dogs and turned with them off the track and into the shadow of the trees.

Lynch dismounted and whispered a word or two in his horse's ear. The horse grunted and wandered off to graze on the river bank.

Lynch's sword hand, as if by reflex, grasped the hilt of his sword, withdrew it only so far as to expose an inch of blade to the moonlight, and let it drop back into its scabbard. He stepped on to the boat

No sooner were his feet on the wood and the flowers rustling about his poleyns than light burst out, and cold, clear female voices in close harmony shivered out across the waters.

Lynch started. Again his hand flew to his sword hilt. All the way along the boat's sides, torches had in a moment been lit, and their flames, crested with orange smoke, throbbed and undulated in the breeze. Within the pavilions, too, light suddenly showed, and the curtain across the doorway buckled. A slim white hand adorned with sparkling diamonds formed the buckle.

Through the door, Lynch saw goblets, metal plates (rare in those days) and a bowl of rare fruit on a table, all surrounded by female bodies in gowns of silk of many colours. Lynch could not see the heads that, he presumed, accompanied these bodies, but the bodies were of the sort that make mere mortal females think, "Of course, she's bound to be a total cow and it's all fake really and she's no better than she ought to be and it'll all end in tears" and make mere mortal men stop thinking altogether.

Lynch said, "Oh, hell. Here we go . . ." But he walked forward nonetheless and ducked beneath the door.

He straightened. And yes. The bodies had heads. And yes. The heads matched the bodies rather well, being full comely and so on. Just in case he should have any prejudices, there was a straight flush – two blondes, one brunette, one black woman with no hair at all, and an auburn redhead.

The brunette who was holding the curtain let it drop. "Welcome, sir," she said with a broad smile.

"Welcome," echoed the others.

The singing continued from somewhere at the stern of the boat. It was very lovely, very soothing.

All the women now busied themselves about Lynch. The blondes removed his armour. The black woman massaged his shoulders. The brunette filled his goblet from a ewer of ice-crystal and gold. The redhead pulled out a chair, flapped out a napkin and smoothed it in his lap. Food was brought – course after course of sweetmeats, and therewithal there was such a savour as all the spicery of the world had been there.

Now, there are two ways in which we can respond to events like this. One is to say, "Wayhey! This is great!" The other is to say, "Hold it. Things don't get this good. There's something very wrong here." It is a curious fact about the sexes that a woman will always say one or the other and act accordingly, whilst a man, being blessed with extraordinary co-ordination, tends to think both simultaneously but to act only on "Wayhey, this is great!"

Lynch was not a ladies' man. He believed that all that stuff debilitated a Rider and that he should keep his mind on the job. Lynch was neither a gastronome nor a tippler. He was content with beef jerky from under his saddle and water from a stream. Lynch cared little for music. No number of sackbutts or serpents could thrill him as could the blast of warhorn or hunting horn.

But he *was* a man, so he ate and drank whilst the women cooed about him and told him that he was the best Rider of the world and the flower of Riders and the most courteous rider that ever bore shield. And at first he murmured, "No, no, honestly," but very soon he found himself agreeing with them. He wasn't in the mood for an argument. And then he felt sleepy, and the lovely women, who had seemed lovelier with every glass of blonk that he took,[62] showed him to a litter all cushioned with deep velvet, and they undressed him and soothed him and asked him if there was anything more, sir, and what time would he like his morning call and did he like kippers? And the music went on and on, and Lynch drifted off as if in his own barque, through swirling mists to a brilliant land where swords and armour glinted always in brilliant sunshine, and damosels were lovely and stayed where they belonged – on the dais, admiring . . .

A few minutes later, Orson rode up to the river and looked for bridge or ford, but saw none. He saw instead a long, low boat with pavilions set thereon . . .

Some women say that men cannot be relied upon, but they can, you know. They can. You cannot rely on the weather because it is unpredictable. Men are as predictable as synchronized watches . . .

---

[62]It was not magic blonk, by the way. It cost 2s. 2d. from the shop down the way. Blonk does this trick to men all unaided. Hence the growth of the villein population of late.

Chapter Ten

THE SUN PEEKED in through the topmost window of Cantiger's tower. It got no response, so it clambered over the sill and on to the floor. Still there was no movement.

The sun expected some respect. It felt neglected. It climbed up on to the bed and touched the sorcerer's shoulder. The sorcerer pulled up the blanket and rolled away. The sun said, "Right. I've had enough of this," and lifted itself higher. Its beams slammed square on the sorcerer's face.

Cantiger groaned. He said, "Sod off!"

The sun paid no attention at all.

Cantiger moaned, "Oh, Lugh!" and pulled the pillow over his face. A moment later, he was forcefully reminded that he had had two helpings of cavy and two of conger, coupled with a deal of blonk last night. He stumbled from his bed and ran for the garderobe.

Whilst he busies himself with matters of no concern to us, let us consider the decor of this room. It tells us much of the man.

It is as well not to look at the tallboy over by the door. It may have been noticed that Cantiger slept with his spectacles on. He claimed that this was so he could see his dreams better. But, in fact, he had installed the basilisk in a cage just inside the door in order to discourage the curious.

And what did he not want the curious to see? The arcana of his craft? The darkest and most potent spells and incantations that, in the wrong hands, would devastate the known world? Nostrums and potions, perhaps, crystal balls and sacred symbols, the which should be entrusted to no hands save his own?

No. None of these.

The basilisk was there to conceal the fact that there *were* none of these.

Downstairs, the apprentices were amassing a large body of

spells and potions. Cantiger could now turn base metal into gold, or cause hounds to fall in love with foxes or summon a grilled tomato from thin air. He could conjure spirits to keep him posted on events throughout the world, he could translate himself in a twinkling from one place to another, were it ever so distant, and he could – temporarily, at least – transform one creature into another or make himself invisible.

Or rather, he couldn't.

He had the spells, and they worked for his bright young students who understood how and why they worked. But somehow, whenever *he* used them, things went wrong. He had tried the grilled tomato spell, and had found himself explaining to a very large, very angry blonde singer why she had been transported from an opera stage halfway across the world to land heavily in Logris with Cantiger's extended hand up her skirt. He had had to call the guard to pull her off him.

He had tried to conjure spirits from the vasty deep to tell him what would win the 3.45, but found himself instead consulting a bottle of genever lately dropped by a disconsolate fisherman off Budleigh Salterton. He had tried to make Margerina the maid and Portmanto the butler fall in love, but had somehow missed. Portmanto wrote several compromising letters to Cadger, the under-bootboy, whilst Margerina nearly killed herself for love of Bollard, the pigling who, she said, never wrote, never told her how he felt about her or complimented her on her hairdo, and just didn't seem to care.

These spells had had to be reversed by the students. Cantiger explained that he had been experimenting with some minor variations. Now he found it easier simply to command them to do spells for him and to grumble that they did not do it as quickly or as stylishly as he would, but that he supposed it was his duty to give them the chance to learn.

In this room there was a large bed expressive more of hope than necessity, a huge wardrobe, already filled to bursting with robes and pointy hats, a fully equipped bar with rare antique bar stools of chrome and a ceiling painted like a starry night sky, and, on the walls, various pictures commissioned by Cantiger himself. There were one or two damosels artistically showing their turtle-doves-which-weren't, a charming study of Loonis, of which Cantiger now claimed to have happy memories, and a picture of "Hackaway" Hasty at play.

Hasty was – and remains for many nostalgic sports fans – a hero, perhaps the greatest headball player of all time. Admittedly, the game was still in its infancy. Boots were, by today's standard, primitive, and there was no offside rule nor limit to the number of players on each side. Otherwise, the rules were much as they are today. The selected – and honoured – man who was to represent the old year was clad all in green and duly decapitated. His head was regarded as bad luck, so boys and men of one village would kick it towards those of another. Hackaway's speed at pouncing on the head before the bloodspurt had abated, his astounding control in dribbling and the formidable force and accuracy of his final kick are spoken of today in hushed tones.

Orson thought that they might try to dispose of the decapitation bit and use, say, a bladder filled with air instead of a head. Cantiger could not see it. It would take half the fun out of it, he argued, and a spherical bladder would bounce and roll far too predictably really to test a player's skill. It would never catch on.

And, of course, he was right.

There was a hammering at the door. Cantiger, emerging from the garderobe and adjusting his long johns, called, "Come in!"

Nothing happened.

A moment later, the hammering resumed.

Cantiger said, "Oh, yes." He shuffled to the tallboy. He flung a cloth over the basilisk's cage and opened the door.

Turquin, his most promising student, a thin nervous boy of thirteen, stood on the threshold. "Hi," he said. "Images coming in of an advancing army with a giant lobster."

"The Northern Kings . . ." Cantiger frowned. "How many?"

"About sixty thousand."

"Where are they?"

"The weather's stormy, so we haven't been able to identify any landmarks. We've sent out pigeons, and we're trying to pinpoint their position on the charts. First reports indicate that they are through that hairdresser's wall and travelling fast."

"They could be here for Coronation Day . . . Right. I'll just get dressed and go and see the King, then we'll plot their progress. We must stop them north of the city. I think we'll need allies." He mused. "Boris and Ran, those Deedong kings?"

"Ran rides a dragon, doesn't he?"

"Does he?"

"So they say. In battle. I'd like to see that."

"Try and set up a hum to his principal sorcerer. What's his name?"

"Maître Soosoopier."

"Right. I'd like to talk to him."

Turquin headed back down the stairs whilst Cantiger returned to his wardrobe. After a little humming and hawing, he selected a robe of bright orange, embroidered with a dragon in gold thread, together with matching slippers and pointy hat. Orson and the army must march today if they were not to meet the enemy in the very streets of Greatwen, crowded with unarmed tourists and other villeins. There were far too many people in the city at present to withstand a siege, and, if they were to scatter about the countryside, they could be mown down by the oncoming horde.

"Oh, dear, oh, dear," muttered Cantiger as he pottered down the stairs and along the corridor towards Orson's rooms. "I wasn't cut out for this sort of thing at all . . ."

The guards outside Orson's door shouldered arms as they saw Cantiger approaching. Cantiger nodded to them, rapped once on the oak panels, and walked in . . .

"Orson!" he called. "We've got a prob—"

Then he looked – and realized that he had not known the half of it.

Lynch awoke to find himself lying on his front on hard turf. He was unarmed. As ever instantly alert, he rolled to his left. Now on his back, he felt a ridge curled around his spine. He put down his left hand to project himself to his feet. His left hand hit nothing. His head jerked to the left for the merest moment. Where a head goes, a body tends to follow. For a second, off balance and flailing, Lynch gazed down a glistening green tube to his doom. With all his enormous strength, he rolled to his right and sprang to his feet without the help of his hands.

Panting slightly, he stared at the trap that had been prepared for him. He had been laid a mere foot from the rim of a well. He glanced down it. He could see the algae-covered walls for some forty feet before they disappeared into darkness. He picked up a stone and flicked it down. Long after it had vanished, it rapped the bricks at the sides before it was gulped by water.

He shivered – but then, in only his shirt and hose, he was cold in the dawn air.

He looked about him. He was in a broad glade of cropped grass the colour of bones. The birds were twittering, but the new grass had not shown. He somehow wondered if, in this strange place, it ever did. The trees surrounding the glade were high as the highest steeples, and so thick and dark that they seemed black in the mist of dawn. Above the well, for some strange reason, someone had constructed a fountain – a vast bowl of malachite surmounted by a smaller one of lapis, surmounted in turn by one smaller still of rhodocrosite, all around an upwardly tapering trunk of black basalt. The fountain produced a mere sad trickle at its top, and water dribbled from bowl to bowl.

Aside from this, there was, apparently planted at random, a single bright pink rose bush, trimmed into a ball atop its single stalk and flowering at a time at which no rose with a sense of propriety should flower. Apparently unrelated to the other two items in the glade was a giant sculpture of a gum tree, all in black iron, whose leaves, each individually delineated, clunked dully together above a simple black iron chair.

Feeling as though this was the sort of thing one ought to do in the circumstances, Lynch walked across to the chair and sat down tentatively.

A hare emerged from the wood-shaw and lolloped, rump high, across the glade, dainty yet inelegant, like a crippled dancer. Lynch nodded. Hares were to be expected in the circumstances.

The hare came up to his feet and spoke. "Lord Lynch of Lynchmere," it said – and its great eyes spoke of terrors beyond human ken. "Yonder stands a hovel, and therein dwells a hag with a tortoise, the which guards a cavern of amethyst in which all earthly pleasaunces and agremens are in abundance."

Lynch nodded again. Pretty standard stuff.

"But she has nothing to do with this," said the hare. "Yonder," the hare cocked its head, "dwells a dwarf with two heads who eats worms and beetles and who guards a great treasure of surpassing worth."

"Ah," said Lynch. "Right."

"Just thought you'd like to know," drawled the hare.

"Thanks," said Lynch.

"And yonder, in the forest, stands a pavilion wherein lies a Rider-errant of great prowess, the which hight Billowmere, and he is wounded full sore through both his thighs with a spear."

"Poor chap," said Lynch.

"And in his cause will you suffer great pain and hardship and find arduous adventure."

"Sounds good," said Lynch. He pointed. "Yonder, you say?"

"No, yonder."

"Oh, *yonder*. Right. Well, thanks."

And Lynch strode off from that strange place with a steely glint in his eye.

It was not the light that awoke Orson, for there was none. It was the sound of men's voices – a dull, dispirited rumble – that brought him bobbing up from his enchanted sleep. ". . . Say as there's some poor idiot's been set up as High King. Nice idea, but I can't see it lasting . . ."

"A little more of this duck with cherries . . . ?"

". . . And crispy fried potatoes."

". . . And cheese on toast."

"I wish you wouldn't do this every day. I'm trying to forget real food."

"I have forgotten real food. Wasn't there a thing called cream?"

"Oh, don't . . ."

"Eggs and bacon . . ."

"No!"

"Did I tell you the one about the hunt terrier and the hole . . . ?"

"Yes," intoned a bass chorus.

"Maybe the new boy will have something new to tell us."

"Oy, you! New boy!"

"Me?" Orson sat up. He was on a hard wooden bench. "Where am I?"

"We've got questions to ask *you* first. What time of day were you taken?"

"Um, night-time. Around midnight."

"Allow an hour either side . . . So it's morning, is it?"

"I'm pretty sure that it is," said Orson.

"And what's this about a High King?"

"Um, yes, they've chosen one. It's me, actually."

"You? Ah. So the project's what you might call a qualified success, then."

"Shortest reign in history, likely."

"More a short, sharp shower."

"A squall."

"At least you've brought us a new joke, lad. Should last us a good month, that one."

"Can *I* ask a question now?"

"Oh. Yes. Sure. Ask away. Our knowledge is not exactly up to date, you'll appreciate, but what we have is yours."

"Where are we?"

"Three guesses. Dark, wet cold? Could it be – a dungeon? Give 'em long enough, they'll get there in the end."

"Yes, but whose dungeon?"

"The deeds are held, I believe, by a Rider that hight Damas, who is not a nice man."

"Nasty, even."

"Treacherous, cowardly, devious, mean . . ."

"Not nice at all."

"He has this habit of imprisoning Riders who pass through his lands. Hence our position."

"He must be a man of much prowess," objected Orson.

"Him? Pah! He couldn't punch a hole in a wet echo!"

"Then how . . . ?"

"Crossbows from behind trees, witchcraft, sleeping draughts, every cowardly means you can think of. And when you think of his younger brother . . ."

"Not nice?" asked Orson.

"Billowmere? Nicest chap you can imagine! Great guy! Look, we'd better put you in the picture . . ."

Orson's faceless fellow prisoners told him the tale with the weariness of men who had heard it, related it and thought upon it many times.

Damas had inherited his castle and lands when he was seventeen and his younger brother, Biilowmere, just fourteen. Billowmere should have come into a full fair manor and a rich, but Damas, with the help of his brutal storm troopers, denied him his inheritance. Biilowmere grew up to be a fine Rider, and much beloved of all people. He, as was right and proper, challenged his brother to a fair trial, man against man, to prove on his body that the livelihood was rightfully his, but Sir Damas refused. He would, he said, find a Rider to fight for him instead.

And so, for the past seven years, Damas had appealed for a champion. But everyone hated him so much that none came forward. He had therefore taken to capturing Riders and imprisoning them, offering to release them only if they would fight and kill Billowmere. There were twenty Riders now in the dungeon. Eighteen others had died of hunger sooner than take up arms against Billowmere for the vile Damas.

All this Orson heard with growing anger and indignation. "And yet," he thought, "I would sooner meet a man in fair fight than rot in this hole. After all, this Billowmere might beat me, but I would die, at least, in the open air, and with worship as a Rider should."

He kept his own counsel, however, and told the silhouettes in the dungeon of the great Blitz and the tale of the stone in the lawn.

Within the hour, bolts were shot and chains rattled. An arch of light appeared in the darkness. For the first time, Orson could see his fellows. All were bearded, some so covered with hair and beard that only their eyes and cheeks were visible. Their bodies were thin and pale, their limbs deeply channelled.

Two large men-at-arms in chain mail, swords drawn, stepped in through the arch. "Right, scum!" barked one. "Back against the wall where I can see you!"

The prisoners jeered, but shuffled backwards as ordered. Two scullions scampered in, bearing bowls of gruel. They laid them down swiftly and as swiftly scampered out again.

"You!" ordered the man-at-arms who could talk – or, rather, bellow. He pointed his sword at Orson. "You come with us."

"Yah!" cried the skeletal prisoners, and, "Great lummox!" and, "You tell that Damas where to put his freedom!" as Orson walked towards the now dazzling daylight.

The men-at-arms grasped his upper arms and frogmarched him along an all-grey corridor whilst one of their colleagues again slammed shut the dungeon door. Orson was pushed up two flights of stairs, through a studded oak door and into a great hall. The hall was lined with carved panels and with men-at-arms, all of them bull-necked and armed to the teeth. At the far end of the hall, beneath a large portrait of himself surrounded by dead game, Damas sat on a dais in a great carved chair.

He was a dark man who himself looked carved. He had a hooked and twisted nose and a beard cut precisely square. He wore heavy embossed robes and quilted velvet slippers. At his feet, a slender girl with cropped green hair sat curled. At his side, another bull-necked man held six huge alaunts on leashes. The dogs growled and snarled at Orson as he was marched to the foot of the dais.

"So, Orson Delamere Maudite, pillier . . ." began Damas. His voice was surprisingly flat and adenoidal.

"Orson de Logris," corrected Orson. "Your king."

"Her her," said Danias. His lips crackled as though he unwrapped each sentence before speaking it. "Yes, yes. We have heard about all that fakery up at Greatwen. Anyhow, it is all academic now, isn't it? You are either going to spend the remainder of your life in my dungeon or you will have to fight to the uttermost with a Rider older than you, stronger than you and of more prowess. You will, in short, have a long life in darkness or a short one in the light."

"There is another alternative," said Orson softly.

"None that I can see. If, by some strange chance, you win, of course I will be only too delighted. But I find that a most improbable eventuality. So: dungeon or death?"

"I really think you should choose death," said the girl with the green hair. She had a voice of unspeakable sweetness and clarity.

Orson frowned at her. He was sure that he had seen her before. "Do I know you?" he asked.

She smiled a beautiful smile – the sort that you could read by at night under the covers, if you could think of nothing better to do with it. "Of course not, your, er . . . majesty."

Damas crackled, "So, have you made your decision?"

"I have," said Orson. "If you will arm me and horse me . . ."

"You shall lack none," quoth the girl.

". . . And if all the Riders in your dungeon will go free should I win . . ."

"I swear it," said Damas.

"I hereby covenant and vow that I shall do battle in your name."

"To the uttermost?" supplied Damas.

Orson shuddered. "To the uttermost."

"This is a disaster!" squeaked Cantiger, jowls juddering as he bustled along the corridor towards his Tower. Kes had never seen anyone actually wringing his hands before but, sure enough, Cantiger seemed to be trying to squeeze the juice from his fingers before the full sail of his belly. "I mean, I know he's young, but there can be no excuse. None! If he gets killed or injured now, that Marina will be back or the Northern Kings will take over, and that's the end of me, I can tell you. It's just so *selfish*!"

"Well, yes," said Kes, "there is that. And, of course, the entire kingdom will be cast into turmoil and bloodshed . . ."

"I mean, Marina hates me. The Northern Kings are already on the march, and I don't even speak North Logrian, so they're hardly likely to keep me on . . ."

"There'll also be murder and massacre and rapine, whatever that is, and unspeakable horrors."

"Yes, yes. But what about *me*?" Cantiger shrilled. "Honestly, can he think of no one but himself? He feels like a night on the town, so it's, 'Oh, to hell with Cantiger what does he matter?' I mean, supposing he behaves disgracefully and the Press gets hold of it? That Press! Horrid person. Always on the lookout for anything untoward! I mean, power should be fun, shouldn't it? I've worked hard for this, and he is risking it all for the sake of a binge. Kings aren't meant to enjoy themselves, except with all the 'Off with his head' business, which is an acquired taste . . ."

"He didn't go out for a night on the town," said Kes, his voice shaking as he trotted upstairs behind Kes.

"So where did he go?"

"He went to save a girl – a villein damosel – who's been taken by a giant."

Cantiger stopped suddenly. Kes got a muzzleful of magician's bum. "Back at Lamere Maudite?" he gasped.

"Yes," Kes spat a bit. "In the Morass de Foys."

"Oh, Lugh, Lugh," Cantiger panted as he hurried on up the stairs. "Giants . . . Villeins . . . Girls . . . Morasses! Foys! Selfishness! Does *no one* think of me? Can't we send the army to fetch him back?"

"He wouldn't thank you," said Kes. "And, from what you tell me, the army is going to he needed elsewhere."

The two men entered Cantiger's lower laboratory. This resembled Dame Iseult's in many ways, only four times as large and with several smaller tables in place of one great one. But again the walls were lined with shelves laden with jars containing unpronounceable vegetable and mineral[63] ingredients. Here too were the machines, intricate and beautiful and wrought to Cantiger's orders, the phials, lenses, crucibles and alembics, the bewildering intricacies of the alchemical and necromantic arts, beyond the comprehension of lowlier mortals.

Yes. All right, all right. Beyond mine.

At one table, two students were extracting the gallbladders from dead mice. The gall thus extracted, mingled with attar of roses, with three grains per peck of *nux vomica*, six of arsenic and a great deal of pigeons' urine, thrice distilled and emulsified with egg yolk, was a sovereign remedy for surfers' ear.

At another, two earnest young men with spectacles had conjured the spirit of Empedocles, which now hovered above them, pumice-encrusted and slightly singed, glimmering, fading and cohering. The young men were taking notes concerning the

---

[63]And seriously disgusting animal . . .

virtues of great burnet for staunching wounds, and the evils of beans.

At another, students were weighing lead taken from the Tower's roof for sale to a scrap merchant. Cantiger had at last worked out how to turn base metal into gold.

And now, for the first time, we come to a part of the narrative that many may find incredible. The skills which the magicians of Cantiger's age possessed are now in large measure lost, to be replaced by the scientific revolution that, in recent years, has seen the development of chicken-sexing, quills with bladders of ink, custard powder and other such marvels.

Believe it or not, Kes and Cantiger now approached a table at which Turquin gazed into a box that showed moving pictures. This was not the multifaceted crystal modelled on a dragonfly's eve with which we are all familiar but a contraption known at the time as a crystal spectrographic receiver, which, by the agency of magnetism and suchlike, actually showed the ghosts of living people. The principle behind this was of course, that living people have spiritual emanations no less[64] than the dead, and this contraption, though unable (of course!) to see the physical reality of people or animals many miles away, was able to show their spirits, which, in the case of the living, was very much the same thing.

Got that?

Well, that's roughly how it worked, according to the Deedong book.

"I've located the Northern horde," Turquin said with a nod at the screen. "The blizzard is over. They're past Cakeborough and travelling fast."

Kes whistled. "Two days' riding. Three at the outside. I'll take the army out to the plain of Heathscull and meet them there."

"Any joy with the hum to the Deedong sorcerer, whatever his name is?" asked Cantiger.

"Maître Soosoopier. Yes. Kevin's got a great hum going. Clear as a bell. Soosoopier is holding for you."

"Holding what?"

[64] . . . Or somewhat more . . .

"I don't know. He just said, 'I'm holding'. I didn't really like to ask."

Cantiger swept over to where a boy sat cross-legged by the wall, humming a deep, throbbing hum.

"Allo!" called Cantiger. "Maître Soooopier? How goes that? What? How goes what? Well, I don't know. That. That's what you people say, isn't it? They tell me you are holding, is that right? What, exactly? No, what exactly are you holding? How was I to know? Just taking a polite interest . . . No, what I was calling about – Kings Boris and Ran, I gather they've been having some problems with the Bordellos? Yes, well, we've got a bit of a problem ourselves at the moment. Northern Kings sweeping down on us like a wolf on a fold. No, I don't know why wolves sweep on folds. Maybe the crumbs get caught in them. They do when I have breakfast in bed. Get caught. In folds. So I suppose if— Do wolves have breakfast in bed? You reckon not? Anyhow, yeah. We need a little help, so if your two kings – I can't wait to see the one with the dragon – felt like lending King Orson a hand, we could come over and drive the Bordellos back for you. What do you reckon?"

Cantiger listened intently for a while, and nodded. "OK. You just have a chinwag with them and get back to me as soon as possible. They'd have to be here in two days. Right, bye – oh, and sorry about the holding business. I really couldn't have guessed . . ."

Cantiger looked down at the humming boy. He said, "Thanks. That's fine."

"Well?" asked Kes.

"Oh, he thinks it's a good wheeze. He'll talk to them."

"Yeah, yeah," said Boss Kes Delamere Maudite, S&MVauV, Hereditary Captain of the King's Guard and Lord Chief Justice of all Logris. "But what was he holding?"

Given the nature of the forest that all but smothered Logris at the time, it must be considered unsurprising that most of the conversations – as opposed to random and violent encounters – took place in glades and groves.

Everyone knows, of course, that glades and groves are magical. A spirit inhabits each, and it must be that spirit which ordains its interior design. For some, like the broad one that Lynch had just left, were cold, stark, and minimalist, whilst others, such as that in which he now sat with his new friend Sir Billowmere, idly biting the heads off sparrows from the stewpot, were positively homely – all dappled with shifting shadow and sunlight and carpeted with soft moss and leaves, with butterflies, wild daffodils and aconites spattering the gloom.

The Rider with whom Lynch shared this dainty breakfast was a slight man with fragile features and melancholy aspect. The skin was pale and powdery, the thin lips pale, the hair swept back in a sandy shock so dry and colourless that it might be thought grey. The moist eyes looked as though they had gazed on desolation, and the mouth had a grim set to it. He had been shaving as he talked. Now he appraised himself in a small hand-held mirror and towelled off the last of the foam.

". . . So here I am, s-s-stuck out in the forest, and it gets c-cold in these parts, I can tell you. A few weeks ago, I went for a w-w-wee w-w-w-w . . ."

". . . Wee?" supplied Lynch.

"Exactly. And I accidentally touched my p-p-person with my gage. It was so cold it s-s-stuck solid. Embarrassing. Had to travel around with this gauntlet dangling from my p-privies. Looked odd, I can tell you. F-f-felt a bit peculiar too. That's why I didn't ride up to G-Greatwen for the b-b-bl-blitz. Not the done thing, is it? Not with your p-person hanging out."

"No, I understand that," said Lynch sympathetically. "Nasty."

"Eventually, a very nice m-m-midwife of my acquaintance freed it with b-b-brandy. I can't tell you how glad I was to get my g-g-gauntlet back."

"And your willy," said Lynch.

"Oh, no. I never lost my w-w-thingy. There it was all the time, d-d-dingle d-d-dangling away. Nuisance."

"Would be," said Lynch gravely. "So was that why this Rider errant managed to overcome you?"

"Oh, he didn't overcome me. Oh, no. No, I won. He really wasn't very good. He had a severe p-p-point-jiggle and a decided swing to the left . . ."

"So many of us do," said Lynch, shaking his head sadly.

"But yes. It was distracting, j-j-jousting with my p-person hanging out attached to a gauntlet. The gauntlet b-b-bounced up and down like anything."[†]

"Terrible handicap."

"D-d-dreadful. So he speared me through both thighs."

"Bad luck. And the worst of it is, you have a nice manor, you say?"

"Lovely. Bedsyde, it's called. Early Morphic, with a modest thousand acres, a few little villages and some charming v-v-v-villeins. Oh, yes. But my brother – I don't know – name of Sir Damas, he won't let me have it."

"You should fight him for it."

"Oh, don't think I haven't tried. Challenged him again and again. He doesn't dare f-fight me. Just keeps trying to get other Riders to do it for him. But they're decent fellers mostly. They won't do it, b-bless 'em. The few that have, I've managed to defeat, but he still doesn't let me have my inheritance."

"He sounds like a varlet and a coward," said Lynch decisively. "Is this a mussel?"

"What? Oh, yes. I picked some up in D-Dumnium last year. It's getting to be quite good, I think . . ."

"Delicious," said Lynch. And indeed, this stockpot – the common food of Riders errant – was far more the sort of fare that Lynch favoured than the gewgaws, kickshaws and spicery of last night. Day after day, it had been brewed up and added to – here a hedgehog, here a squirrel or coney, here a trout or a few sparrows caught in a brick-trap, here a potato or a handful of berries – then sealed and borne on its way. Into this precious amalgam, too, went any leftover blonk, ale, bread and frumenty. After a few months, it became very interesting.

Billowmere limped over to the bank on which Lynch sat "Oh," he said sadly, "poor D-D-Damas. He's not all bad. I mean, he's a m-murderer and a licentious and exploitative and cruel l-l-landlord and he killed our parents, but . . ."

"Yes?" Lynch waited.

"Well, he once told me quite a good joke . . ." said Billowmere weakly. "It was about this chicken that wanted to get to the other side of a t-t-track." He paused for comic effect. "So it went," he concluded.

He waited for Lynch's reaction. Lynch frowned very deeply and ate an ear.

Billowmere sighed. "Yes, well I suppose he's not really very n-nice when you come down to it. He's got all these nasty fellers who never look at a manuscript or a d-d-damosel. It's all, 'Kill him' or 'Put her to the sword' or 'Burn down that hovel!' Even the d-dogs don't play games. They're trained to kill, even the b-b-brachets. Busy, busy, busy. Work, work, work."

"I'd like to meet this brother of yours," said Lynch in a tone of urbane but lethal menace. "So, what do you reckon the adventure is?"

"Adventure?"

"Yes, well, you don't usually get put into an enchanted sleep and laid beside a well in the middle of a forest and directed somewhere by a talking hare unless something at least slightly out of the ordinary is going to happen, do you?"

"S'pose not," agreed Billowmere.

So the two men waited.

Adventures are not always punctual. This one missed its cue by a full five minutes, during which Lynch and Billowmere shuffled and hummed and kicked things. When it came, it took the shape of a horseman. They heard the tinkle of harness, the creaking of leather and the crunching of footfalls, and Lynch said, "About time, too."

The horseman was a mere man-at-arms on an iron-grey cob. He had a bull neck and a puffed-out chest, and you just knew that, had he been on foot, he would have clicked with every stride.

"Oy! You, Billowmere!" he bellowed. "Yer bruvver says . . ."

"You're late," said Lynch.

"Wha'?" said the man-at arms. "Oo are you?"

"That me concerneth," said Lynch smoothly. "But you were well advised to dismount before addressing two Riders, and to kneel and make obeisance, and to beg our pardon for your tardiness. We have wasted five good minutes . . ."

A sneer creased the man's nose. "I dunno. I see an unarmed man telling me what to do," he said in his bulbous voice. "And me, I got a sword and a battleaxe and a dagger and chain mail, and where I come from that means I gives the orders. So less of the lip from you. Now, Billowmere . . ."

The man-at-arms ceased to be a man-at-arms at that moment. Years later, as a devout monk and much consulted beekeeper, he would shudder and make the sign of the ankh and sometimes evacuate his bowels when Lynch was mentioned. Post-Traumatic Stress Disorder was very widespread amongst those who picked fights with the flower of Riders.

This was a flower with thorns.

Because one moment, there the man-at-arms was, all lordly on his horse. And the next, he was on the ground, with his horse's weight crushing his legs and stomach and the stranger squatting above him holding a sword-point to his neck.

The man on the ground recognized the sword. He had seen it only a moment back, hanging at his side.

The horse got up, which accounted for a few more of the man-at-arm's ribs. It headed homeward at the gallop. It too was at a loss to explain how its legs had been swept from under it. Years later, pulling a milk cart on the streets of Ambleside, it would cause quite a serious traffic accident involving the deaths of two dwarves, a hangman and a contortionist who had killed her animal-impersonator husband, because the word "lynch", though in an entirely different context, was spoken.

"Now," said Lynch, apparently unaffected by the exercise. "You see, sir. Arms do not the gentleman make, nor give authority for more than a moment. Give your message in a manner befitting your status which is, by my assessment, somewhat lowlier than that of a tufted dung-beetle, but, I will allow, loftier than that of the common bluebottle maggot."

The man gulped. This was unwise. His Adam's apple felt the tip of a sword that he had lovingly honed to the sharpness of an edge of paper. "Yes, Boss," he gasped. "Sorry, Boss."

"And apologize to your rightful master, Boss Billowmere . . . ?"

"Yeah, I'm very sorry, your Bossness."

"Oh, that's quite all right," said the amiable Billowmere.

"I am, um, commanded to tell you that Boss Damas 'as found a good knight that is ready to do battle at all points with you and to prove upon your body that your claim upon the manor which 'ight Bedsyde and all lands and messuages pertaining thereto be false and unfounded, if you don't mind, Boss. And therefore 'e bids you make you ready and to be in the field within the hour."

"Oh, b-bugger," sighed Billowmere. "He would do this when I am sore wounded. Ah, well, tell him that I will be there."

Lynch stood back. "There," he said. "You have your answer. Now, run along, lad, and please remember that it takes more than steel to command respect."

"Yes, sir. Yes, boss. As you say, sir." The transformed man-at-arms scrambled to his feet and backed out of the glade. A moment later, he turned and ran.

"And now," said Lynch to Billowmere, "if you would care to give me your armour?"

"What?"

"Your armour, man, and your sword and lance. Come along, come along . . ."

"B-b-but this isn't your battle," objected Billowmere. "I can't ask you to risk your life for me . . ."

"You're not asking me, and this is my battle. The hare said so. I'm not going to argue with a talking hare, for Lugh's sake. And you're in no fit state to defend your claim. Come on."

And so it was that Billowmere reluctantly disarmed him and armed Lord Lynch, and so it was that Lynch rode to the field beneath the castle of Sir Damas, there to do battle to the uttermost with his friend and king.

Now stood the kingdom in the greatest jeopardy that ever it had known, for neither Rider might know the other. Orson wore armour all of white, whilst Lynch, in armour of burnished steel, bore the shield of Boss Billowmere, on which was blazoned the figure of a tortoise rampant.

A light breeze scurried about that strip of green where Orson sat waiting upon a great brown courser. The breeze sprayed and tugged at the white-feathered plume on his helm. It swooped to ruffle the grass. It fingered the green hair of the girl who sat by Damas's side on the dais, and it swayed the damask hangings behind the chairs. It had no effect on the men-at-arms who stood, bullet-headed and stiff as steel, staring expressionless out on the beautiful scene.

246

"I love an afternoon's sport," Damas drawled, and stretched. "So healthy, I always think."

"Not, however, for the participants." The girl grinned.

"Um, no. There is that. And look, there's my dear brother, hobbling, poor dear, and all unarmed. I think that, when the main event is over, my men-at-arms might put on a little sideshow. How say you, Cap'n?"

"It could be arranged, boss," said the moustachioed soldier at his shoulder. "Target practice for the bowmen, do you think?"

"Excellent notion," said Damas gleefully.

"Mind if I set up a hum?" asked the green-haired girl. "My mistress will want to know what's going on."

"Oh, you must, you must!" Damas drawled. "It was her brilliant idea, after all. Hum away. I shall supply a commentary . . ."

As Lynch fewtered his spear on Billowmere's dancing white courser, the girl's hum, low and faint at first, arose to that familiar ringing whine that meant a clear connection. "It's a lovely day here," said Damas. "The sun is scudding across a blue sky and the small fluffy clouds shining down on us like sheep. And we are in for a feast of sport, a contest such as fans dream of. Here in the white is the brightest young talent to enter the list for man a long year, 'King' Orson Delamere Maudite, and here in the grey the flower of Riders, the best man of his hands in all Logris, the Deedong superstar, Lynch of Lynchmere.[65] And they have – yes, they have chosen the great spears, and I think I can promise that there will be no late sideswipes here. Point or nowt with these lads.

"And yes, they are dressing to one another. The crowd is

[65]There is often confusion about Lynch's origins. Lynchmere was indeed a Deedong settlement, though on the mainland of Logris. Nowadays, we are inclined to limit kingdoms to land masses. In those days, there were kingdoms that spanned the ocean. King Boggis of Derrida, for example, a Sotis chieftain, ruled over a kingdom that stretched deep into geographical Ochtia. Kings Ran and Boris, both Deedong, lived only fifty miles from Greatwen, the capital of Logris. Lynch's mother was a Logrian, his father a Deedong. He grew up bilingual and, in fact, had far more to do with Logrian matters than Deedong. He had many Deedong traits. He liked garlic and goose livers and had very little sense of humour. On the other hand, he did not run away from battle and he bathed several times a year.

hushed. Lynch spurs his white horse, Orson his brown, and they are off, the wind in the coursers' manes and the Riders' plumes. Faster, faster, closer, closer they draw at the wallop, lances steady as . . . cakes . . . and they thrust – and strike . . . Now! Yes! A direct hit by both men to the other's shield, and both horses and men are down! What a blow! What a collision! And lightly each man avoids his horse, and yes, the swords are out, and glittering in the bright spring sunlight like . . . trumpets! Lynch swings the sword! He smites! Orson reels, but the blade slips from the helm like, er, silk, er, from a shoe. He feints, and foynes to Lynch's belly, then scythes at his ankles. Lynch leaps and backs away! He parries the next blow and closes in, blade held high . . . Oh, this is thrilling stuff!"

"Is there nothing we can do?" whined Cantiger, who watched this scene of carnage on his Incredible Viewing machine.

"Oh, yes!" Turquin clenched his fist and struck at the air. "Well smitten, sir! Whoops! Ooh, that must have hurt! Sorry, what?"

"I was, er, thinking of a spell whereby I might be translated to the scene of the fight in the form of, say, an eagle, or on a flying carpet or something. I seem to have lost the spells just at this moment, but . . ."

Flying carpets we can do, of course – the old 'Tapis, try . . .' spell with Jerusalem-artichoke essence for extra altitude, but they're tricky, carpets. They never seem to know which side is up, and it can be embarrassing if they change their minds on the matter at six hundred feet. Not much to hold on to. Eagle? Sure, you can do that. Anyone your grade can do it, and probably sustain it even that far. My record is three and a half minutes as a bumble-bee before my concentration wavered and I reverted, and even then I broke my nose on landing. Oh, well played, Lynch! Look at that blood!"

"Oh, Lugh." Cantiger groaned. "Oh, Rosmerta! Think of something else. They have got to be told what they are doing . . ."

"I think they know that . . ."

"Yeah, but who they're doing it to, and what it's going to mean to me if they kill one another!"

"Well, the easiest way . . . Nah, you'll have thought of that."

"Probably," agreed Cantiger hastily, "but I'm always pleased to see how you're getting on. Initiative is nine tenths of good wizardry, I always say."

"Do you?" The boy frowned. "Last week you said obedience was."

"Yeah, well, initiative *and* obedience. In equal measure. That's the thing. Now, then, you were saying . . . ?"

"Well, they've got an open hum down there, haven't they? And Damas is doing all the talking with Marina only once in a while saying 'Yay!' or 'Yeeha!' So, if we were to transfer her line to us, Damas would never know the difference, until . . ."

"Exactly!" gasped Cantiger, who had not a clue what the boy was talking about. "Yes, do one of those!" He caught another glimpse of the screen and breathed, "Ohdearohdear," then, "Well, get on with it, then! A hundred pounds if you can get it sorted in time! Come on! Come on! Now!"

In a great cavern below Hennamucus, coloured orange with manganese and furnished with encrusted spikes, a creature heard Cantiger's cry. His eyes snapped open.

For the past month, the laidly worm had had no intimation of its progenitor's distress. Cantiger, indeed, had been living much the same life as his creation – feeding, sleeping and frightening people into doing his will, and thoroughly enjoying life. Both, if asked for minor cavils, would have cited the tendency of damosels to run away from them as a bit of a nuisance, but the worm always caught them whilst Cantiger was rather frightened of doing so, and was perfectly happy so long as the food and blonk were plentiful and everyone remembered to call him "Your Excellency".

People did not call the worm "Your Excellency", but a good "Aaaargh" does wonders for the ego as well.

Now, however, Cantiger was distressed, and the worm, who had never been attached to anyone else save in a very literal and visceral sense, knew once more that his place was by his onlie begetter's side.

His gleaming, roseate head emerged from the cliff face.

The tide was in.

The worm uncoiled its enormous length, slithered down the slab of black rock, slipped very smoothly into the churning surf and wriggled out into the ocean . . .

Now the two men traded blows. It was stylish, for both were well-trained. But it was anything but beautiful. The weight of the swords and the force of gravity alone meant that these blows caused damage, for neither man seemed to have the strength to raise his shield. It was a slugging match, which must, presumably, have ended only when one man could take no more or when one lucky blow clove a brainpan.

The spectators were all saying "Oooh" and "Ahh" in a sympathetic way, but not so sympathetic that anyone might feel tempted to stop the fun.

The acoustics within a helm, too, particularly when you were panting and grunting and running with sweat and hearing the echoes of the last blow to your head, were not good. Neither Lynch nor Orson, therefore, heard the familiar voice now called, "Ohdearohdearohdear! Oy! Oooh, do stop it! This is just really aggravating and silly! Exactly who is going to look after me when you two have finished slicing one another to rashers, I'd like to know? Oh, nooo! Stop it, please! Has no one ever heard of proximity talks?"

Damas heard it. His head swivelled. He frowned. The captain-at-arms heard it. He grimaced. His hand darted to the pommel of his sword.

Damas reasoned. Then he understood.

"Stop the—" he started.

But the voice returned, squealing now. "Ooer! No! Stop pushing! Wha—?"

Another voice broke in, the cracked but strident voice of a boy. "Lynch, you are killing the king! Orson, you are fighting Lynch! Lynch, you . . ."

"Stop the hum!" screamed Damas. "Someone's crossed the . . . broken into the . . . Oh, I don't understand these damned newfangled things! Just stop it!"

The spectators turned to watch the source of the disturbance. The girl with green hair said, "Sorry. Phew! Lugh, but that's high magic. They must have a listening centre. Barging in on a private hum? What I say is, what about civil liberties?"

"Never heard of them," said Damas briskly. He was standing now, and gesturing to the two men on the sward. "Come along, now. That's right. Fight, smite and all that. Don't worry about the disembodied voice. Happens all the time. Wind. That's what does it. Come along. Chop chop!"

But Lynch was leaning on his sword and considering his opponent. His opponent was considering right back.

The height was right. The posture was characteristic. The skill with arms . . .

"Orson?" he gasped. "Your Majesty?"

"Lynch? Oh, Lugh . . . What are you doing here?"

The two men staggered towards one another and embraced. Rather noisily.

The spectators were silent. One booed, but rapidly fell silent.

"We are sworn to fight to our uttermost this day," Lynch said. "And I am nearly come to it."

"And I." Orson nodded. "The earth spins fast. Witchcraft brought us here. That female with the green hair. She was with Marina's party in Greatwen . . ."

"Was she indeed?" Lynch growled. "They have tried to murder us . . ."

"And we were at once victims and weapons."

The two men nodded to one another. They turned towards the dais. Very slowly they advanced upon it.

"Ah, no, no, no!" teased Damas, and wagged a knobbly finger. "You can't do that! You are sworn! Don't you remember? Oh, yes. Can't go breaking the rules of chivalry, now, can we? No, no, no. That would never do. Er, Cap'n . . . ?"

"Boss?"

Damas's gnarled fingers flickered. "Um, form up around us, if you please, and order the archers to fire and all that. Sell your life dearly, there's a good chap."

The captain considered the two Riders approaching him. "That's Lynch, is it?" he said.

"It doesn't matter who he is, for the Dagda's sake. Start selling."

"The half was not told me," breathed the captain, awed. "And the other chap? That's the new king, is it?"

"Oh, Balor take you, man! They've been fighting for hours. They'll be child's play."

"Yeah, well, I'm out of nappies, me, and I don't like offending kings. Dangerous pastime. As for that Lynch . . ."

Orson and Lynch were climbing the steps now. The spectators drew back. Some even bent a knee in cautious salute.

"Loose the alaunts!" Damas shrieked. "Archers, fire! Kill the traitors!"

Two archers, from force of habit, actually did fire. The arrows clunked on Orson's helm and bounced off into the crowd.

"Anyone for a free crash course in metaphysics?" demanded Lynch of the men-at-arms. "No study, no speculation, no late nights. Short cut to the underworld, all questions answered, diploma in seconds?" He scanned the men, surprised. "No? Sure? Well, don't say I didn't offer. You. Damas, isn't it? Seeing as you are not prostrate before your sovereign, I can only assume that you wish to have ado with us. Captain, a sword for Boss Damas, if you would be so kind."

"Certainly, Boss," said the captain. He drew his sword and thrust the hilt at Damas's stomach. "Honoured to be of service, Boss. Splendid fight, that, Boss. A drink, perhaps, Boss? Polish your codpiece, Boss?"

"No, thanks. Take the sword, Damas."

"I don't want a sword," said Damas tetchily. His eyes swivelled this way and that, looking for assistance or escape. "Nasty things. Cut people."

"Very well, you may fight me without one. You are, after all, a murderer, and therefore have forfeited all rights." Lynch hefted his own blade. "Stand back, Your Majesty. The blood makes a terrible mess. Gets into everything."

"No, hold on, Lynch." Orson raised a commanding hand. He removed his helm and turned to address the crowd, which gasped to see how sorely be-bled was his young head. "Boss

Damas has proved himself a dishonourable coward, a bully and a murderer, and not at all nice," he announced. "I therefore decree that he shall be stripped of all his lands and all his clothes saving only a strip of cloth to cover his nethers, and that he shall ride on an ass rather than a courser, and that he shall live henceforth on this, his brother's land, and venture beyond its borders on pain only of a very unpleasant death involving pigs in some unspecified way."

"Oy," protested Damas. "You can't do that! What about 'Might is right' and all that?"

"Oh, might is right, is it?" Lynch raised his eyebrows in some surprise. His sword swooshed and snickered. Damas's eyes widened. His hands grasped at his dropping garments in vain. He was left wearing a collar and nothing else. Lynch's sword-point was pressed to his chest just hard enough to draw a dribble of blood. "I think we have just found you in the wrong, then, don't you?"

"And you, Boss Billowmere." Orson pointed. "I am told that you are a Rider of much worship and well-beloved of your people. Appoint, therefore, trustworthy people to care for these lands and to enforce the law, stand down all save the best men-at-arms, then come and join me as a Rider of my long thin table which I'm hoping to have built as soon as I can get round to it."

"Certainly, sire," said Sir Billowmere.

"Please release the Riders held prisoner, return to them their coursers, armour and harness and any property taken from them, and give them some sparkly treasure to make them feel better. Now, where is that girl?"

"Girl, sire?" said the captain.

"Green hair," said Lynch. "Big eyes. Hums a lot. Works for His Majesty's sister. Queen Marina . . ."

"Oh, her!" The captain frowned as his eyes sought her. "Odd, I thought. Green hair, indeed. She was here a moment ago . . . Just vanished . . ."

"Doesn't surprise me," said Orson. "Never fear. My dear sister shall pay dearly for this. Now, Damas, find that scrap of cloth as a matter of urgent priority, then show your new lord where you have hidden my arms, my pillier, my courser and those of my lord Lynch. If they aren't here within ten minutes, I'll have to order your abbreviation."

Damas tried to snarl disdainfully. But, divested of his robes, he was also divested of his dignity and resembled nothing so much as a scrawny monkey with sore gums.

"And now," said Lynch, "His Majesty and I have other business to do today."

The people ran off, and several persons who, mere minutes before, had wanted to see either – or, preferably, both – men disembowelled, now solicitously escorted them, cooing of their courage, back towards the castle.

Chapter Eleven

A GREYISH, UNDULANT, wedge-shaped rock with a patch of moss at its centre suddenly opened up to become an "L"-shaped rock with moss at its topmost point. This mossy summit swivelled, and twin shards of mica in the stone glinted in the sunlight. The rock shivered. The mica became concave. The long base of the "L" shape was sundered. The rock shivered again, as though shaking off calcification, and suddenly, where there had been a knobbly column, there were a shapely torso and slender arms.

The girl – for girl she now undoubtedly was – at last shook her head. Stone receded as flesh bubbled forth. She stretched luxuriantly, extending her long fingers and twisting her wrists. She bent one leg and sprang to her feet. She glanced over her shoulder, dropped to her hunkers and muttered a few words.

She screwed up her lovely face, and withered. It was like . . . it was like the sound of a Deedong horn sucked back into the bell of the instrument. It was like a gale suddenly shut out with a strong door but continuing to whistle and worry outside. She passed three-quarters of the way down the gullet of the space that she had occupied.

It is not a good explanation. But it will have to suffice.

Then she hung her short furry forelegs out to dry, hunched her magnificent quarters, and plunged forward into the shelter of the long wet grass.

Her ears were laid back upon her head, her tail black because all but slotted between her buttocks. A male of her species approached her through the grass at the diagonal, smiling on one side of his face. She reared up and struck him so hard with her right paw to his jaw that he fell stonied on to his back. She sped to one hedge, jinked through a smeuse and skittered across a field to a thick and ancient hedgerow by a lane.

Lynch had not noticed, or, if he had, had dismissed as stray vegetation the green tuft at the centre of this morning's messenger's head.

Aside from that, only the wild eyes and the lovely legs gave any indication of her former shape.

She was a very useful person to have on the staff.

The hare did not emerge from the hedgerow. A patient watcher, however, would, a few minutes later, have seen a handsome young girl stepping out on to the road. In her hand was a curious long thin black Thing with a circular bit at its centre and a wiggly bit that she was very, very careful not to touch.

"A hundred pounds?" Cantiger gaped. "You expect me to give you a hundred pounds? After you pushed me and interrupted me? I mean, that was well out of order, that was. Pushing me. I've given that up. Being pushed and that. I used to do it, I admit, but I said, 'No. It's not good for my health,' so I stopped it, just like that. No cutting down. No 'Maybe just one quick shove or kick after breakfast'. Nope. Self-discipline. That's my middle name. It's my turn to do the pushing. I can't have apprentices shoving me around. Bad for discipline."

"But if I hadn't spoken, she'd have stopped humming!" protested Turquin, blinking through his fishbowl spectacles.

"No, no. I had the situation well in hand," Cantiger told the boy. "I suppose you've never heard of translateral telemorphic defibrillation?"

"Er, no . . ."

I thought not. Or Bassinet's Principle of Porric Oscillation? Hmm?"

"Porric means 'to do with leeks', doesn't it?"

"I did not say 'porric'. I said 'Pyrrhic'. Pyrrhic Oscillation. Heard of it, have we? Mastered it, perhaps, after hours? Had a little chat with old Urgowyukisthatit Bassinet, maybe?"

"Ha! Exactly!" Cantiger was smug. "You see? Just the teensiest bit out of our depth, I think? Oh, yes. Shoving me, indeed." Cantiger grumbled. "Here am I with half a mind to dismiss you for gross thingy, and there's you asking for a hundred pounds. Ridiculous. No. You've got a lot of making up to do, boy. If you want to stay on as my apprentice, I suggest that you apply yourself to working out how we stop the king getting killed by giants. I've got to get out there and talk some sense to him."

"No problem." Turquin shrugged. "Be there by tomorrow midday . . ."

"No! By tonight!" Cantiger clenched his fists, bent his elbows and jumped several times. "You don't understand! The king and Lord Lynch are totally loop— " He took a deep breath. "I mean, totally sane and very suitable to represent the interests of the people of Logris, but their sanity is of a peculiar variety. When struck violently about the head and body, they experience a desperate need to strike and be struck again. There's no such thing as one smite for the likes of them. They take it one day at a time, but they have lapses, you see . . ."

"Tonight . . ." Turquin stuck out a tongue-tip to consider. ". . . No. It's too far, unless you have a flying carpet, or a dragon, of course."

"Of course . . ."

"There is a school that relies on wind," said the boy, with the casualness of youth.

"We're back on the artichokes, then?" said Cantiger, with the casualness of expertise.

"No. Not self-propulsion. Turn yourself into a mote or a thistle-seed, sort of thing, and go where the wind takes you. But it's terribly risky and imprecise, and it's easy to get eaten *en route* . . ."

"That won't do anyhow. The wind is southerly. I want to go north-west."

"Exactly. I have heard of wizards in Tai-pin who are working on becoming light . . ."

"Diet?"

"What?"

"Well, if my mother couldn't fit into a robe, she would diet."

Turquin narrowed his eyes. "Cunning," he concluded. "What colour?"

Cantiger winced. "Turquin," he said, "had your parents ever heard of continence?"

"Certainly. Hosea, Upper Stasis, Lower Stasis . . ."

"Put a sock in it!" Cantiger squealed. He exhaled violently. "Becoming light, you said?"

"That's right. Dematerializng and travelling along light beams. Of course, you'd need to be very high up and have a very bright light to go fifty miles. Also, no one has ever yet rematerialized. Otherwise, it's quite a good idea."

"Otherwise . . ." echoed Cantiger

"The only other thing . . . No . . . Silly . . . No, I can't think of anything."

"What were you going to say?"

"No. Honestly." Turquin blushed and waved a hand. "It's nothing."

"What's nothing?"

"Well . . . Polly and I . . ."

"Yes?"

"It's only at the experimental stage . . ."

"What is?"

"And we never thought of it actually carrying anyone . . ."

Cantiger took a deep breath. "If, within three seconds, you do not tell me what you are gibbering on about, I will turn you into a chestnut and stuff you up a guinea fowl."

"Um, why a guinea fowl?" asked Turquin, whose mind was of an enquiring and literal variety.

Cantiger made a noise like something very heavy being moved across bare boards.

Turquin moved to the other side of the table. "Of course, our research costs have been considerable," he bleated.

"Research costs?" Cantiger struggled with the words. They fought right back. He stared at Turquin. Turquin stared right back. The boy even grinned.

Cantiger did not know what the youth of today was coming to. As one who had always said "Yes, sir" when given an order, and had sometimes even pretended to obey it for as long as he was watched, he had assumed that, now that he was in authority and had real live letters after his name to prove it, people would be similarly acquiescent. If the younger generation did not even respect letters after a name, the future looked murky.

"Yeah, well, there's the cost of the cow, and the elastic . . . Two hundred should do it . . ."

"T-t-t-tu . . ."

Cantiger's stammer came and went. When someone said,

"Who wants . . . ?" there wasn't a trace of it.

"Who's buying?" brought it on something chronic.

Two hundred pounds. In advance. The thought of each one of those precious pounds – worth a pound at least, stabbed at Cantiger like a gorse needle. So did gorse needles.

When – no, if – he got back, he was going to disembowel that little swine Turquin, *and* sack him, *and* rip his teeth and fingernails out *and* – ohdearohdear – make him eat his eyeballs, *and* – ow! Bugger! – take back every one of those two hundred pounds *and* fine him a thousand more to be worked off at five pounds a year. Oh, Lugh, please, no . . . ! Whoops!

Cantiger had dreamed of flight.[66] In those dreams, he had soared and swooped, skimming above the ground like a swallow, hovering and wheeling like a falcon. In those dreams, flight had been fun.

But then, in his most fanciful dreams he had not had a black-and-white cow above his head or, sometimes ahead of him at the same level, tugging his arms from their sockets. Nor had he been dropped to ground level whenever a particularly offensive bush or tree appeared, only to be jerked sixty feet up in the air whenever the ground was clear. In his dreams, he had not been dragged wailing through lakes and holly bushes and swung against tree trunks. Above all, perhaps, in his dreams the cow that was not there had not been farting.

This one was. Almost constantly.

"It struck us, you see, that, if we could concentrate the gases from the sewers, and seal in a skin, it would make a rather original kite," Turquin had explained. "We tried it with a Cairn terrier first, and it worked a treat. Since then, we've flown pigs and an old lady whom no one seemed to want, and last week we experimented with this cow.

"We take out all the meat and bones, you see, except the legs that give stability, stitch the orifices up tight and pump it full of gas. We were thinking that it might be rather a picturesque

---

[66]That's flight as in "airborne volition". The other variety was altogether too familiar to warrant dreams. For Cantiger, it would be like dreaming of sleeping.

sport. We could release them and have a race, sort of thing. But we had the cow tethered to a big table, and we had to sit on the table to hold it down, so it will certainly take your weight, and there's this harness we rigged up . . ."

"Yes, but the wind is, as I did observe, blowing from due south," Cantiger had told him tetchily.

"Aha! Yeah! That's the ingenious bit!" Turquin said proudly. "We put a valve in, you see, and separated the gas into two separate compartments. One keeps the thing afloat. The other releases carefully controlled jets that alter direction. There's easily enough to get you fifty miles. You should be there in an hour, tops."

It had all sounded so logical, so eminently *sensible*!

So, earlier this afternoon – about *five years* earlier this afternoon, by his calculations – Cantiger had suffered himself to be strapped into a criss-cross harness that passed over his shoulders and between his legs. He had wound the twin reins about his wrists. Turquin had said, "Ready?"

Cantiger had considered. He had said, "No, actually! On sober reflection . . ."

He was unaware that he was uttering a Quotation. These were the selfsame words that many of Logris's heroes had spoken just before becoming heroes. Flashgit the Great had spoken them just seconds before he sacrificed his life in establishing the world record for ski-jumping after a carouse on a snow-covered Mount Nice. Boss Cob of Borrowdale spoke them immediately after his better-known "Do your worst, cravens!" speech to the massed giants of Glenfford. The celebrated actress Dame Irae Darling, clutching the Order of Service in her dainty white hand, had spoken them on the parapet of Greatwen Cathedral, after her famous declaration "An artist must sacrifice everything for her art. If that's what the stage directions say, that's what I shall do."

People remembered the earlier bits, but somehow forgot "No, actually! On sober reflection . . ."

They always chose not to hear that bit.

So had Turquin. He had bent. A knife had flickered. There might have been a glimmer of a grin behind the boy's flopping hair. Cantiger had had time to shout "No! Oh, shiii. . ."

He vocalized the "t" three hundred feet above the Tower.

That part, then, had been exhilarating in a "Wouldn't have missed it for the world, but wouldn't dream of taking the opportunity to experience it from someone else" sort of way. Cantiger got a good view of the city below, and the city below got a good view of Cantiger's nethers in their long johns. The cow went right on rising, and soon both views were extinguished by cloud, which Cantiger discovered not to be lovely fluffy warm stuff but cold, dark and very wet.

"Figures," he said philosophically. He liked the universe to be constant. It was somehow consoling.

Now came the technical bit.

He turned the cow above him in his chosen direction and, with the index finger of his right hand, pulled the thread that opened the valve.

"Carefully controlled jets", Turquin had called them.

That was like the charioteer who comes in ashen-faced and with wet breeches and tells you that he had the brutes under control all along.

The cow's tail straightened in the blast. There was a noise like ripping canvas. Cantiger was jagged in the groin so that his eyes watered.

When he could see again, the cow was directly ahead of him, slewing and tumbling and corkscrewing. At the outer edge of each yaw and circle thus described, Cantiger was swung at prodigious speed. The G-forces tugged at his cheeks and pushed the lips back from his teeth. At the same time, a foul odour engulfed him.

To add to his problems, he was spiralling downwards.

He had not seen much when first the cow crepitated, at once because of the cloud and because everything swung past him in a high-speed diorama blur. Now he recognized that half of that blur was green. A few moments later, two-thirds of the blur was green, and some of it had leaves on it.

A roosting buzzard roused and squawked in alarm as Cantiger's slipper narrowly missed its head.

It was at that moment that Cantiger recalled Turquin's advice.

Almost everything about him had tautened when the cow had started careering about the skies. (We will not concern ourselves with those parts that loosened, save to observe that his upper lip was anything but stiff as a great "Waaghaaghaagh!" emerged from him and swirled so fast that he ran into the third "aagh" even as he squealed the fifth.) Amongst those things that had tautened, however, was the finger that had opened the valve. Now, although reluctant to relax his grip on anything, he let go.

His flight became almost stable.

The only problem was that too much gas had now been expended. The cow, somewhat shrunken at its rear end, proceeded at a height of roughly thirty feet. Since the leashes were just twenty feet long, these were not the sort of Club-class conditions that you expected for two hundred smackers.

Every so often, something genuinely nasty loomed ahead – a minaret, for example, or a Rider, lance uplifted. Then, with a shudder and a squeak, Cantiger tilted the cow, rump downward, and opened the valve once more. The resultant upsurge might have saved Cantiger's life. The resultant expulsion of gas really quite seriously threatened it and made him wonder why he wanted it saved. The world had always been a hostile place. At the moment, it was giving him a Glaswegian[67] Kiss every five seconds.

Cantiger believed that the world should be kept in a zoo. It was wild and unfriendly. It was a thing to be visited and looked at, and you'd say, "Great old world, eh?" or think to yourself, "What a wonderful world". But it should be kept caged.

The problem was . . .

No, that was wrong. It was not *the* problem. When you are being dragged across the countryside by a large inflated black-and-white farting cow, it is invidious and unfair to pick out just one of the several problems confronting you and to give it special status.

One of the problems, then, was that, because of the diabolical twin gas-bladder arrangement and the stiff breeze, there was no stopping this unorthodox conveyance or prospect of bringing it to land. It was moving far too fast to unfasten the harness without leaving a nasty smear on the landscape, and, whilst its buoyancy was slowly diminishing, the cow, at its front end at least, was still

[67]We have looked about the world for "Glaswege" but can find no trace of it, even in ancient maps.

decidedly buoyant. It might occasionally drop so far that Cantiger could actually scamper a few paces on the grass, but then a gust of wind would take it and it would rocket upward again.

The only consolation . . .

No, that was wrong, too. There are *no* consolations when being dragged across the countryside by a large inflated black-and-white farting cow. The only thing, then, that Cantiger could point to as a success *if* he survived this experience and after, say, four years of intensive therapy, was that, thanks to judicious use of the brute's – well, engine – both cow and magician had maintained a roughly north-westerly course.

At the moment, this seemed somewhat irrelevant, in that he looked set to become a low-flying astronomical feature in perpetual orbit about the planet.

Some curious scanner of the skies on Mars, perhaps, would gaze through his glass and summon his colleagues to see Earth's new satellite and say, "Funny, the illusions you get looking through these things. I saw one the other day that reminded me of a toothbrush, and, just for a second, there . . ."

The emanations of distress now clamoured in the laidly worm's brain. He idled off Bottom-on-Sea, making the physiological adjustments necessary before moving from salt to fresh water. He was impatient to continue his journey and the delay, coupled with the urgency of the impulses in his head, made him angry.

He raised his great pink head from the water.

There, on the muddy strand, were two damosels – of sorts. They were, he recognized, of the succulent variety, and they wore horizontal-candy-striped robes, one pink and white, one lime-green and white.

These robes were of a variety that the worm had never seen before. He had seen damosels' legs, of course, but only when the damosels in question were ready to eat. In their pre-preparation state, when upright, they had a retractable plumage that was only barely palatable.

These damosels were just asking to be eaten.

They were *advertising!*

Every fold, every bulge in those exposed upper-arms and thighs spoke – nay, screamed – of tender flesh and thick juicy fat.

Large hoops dangled from their earlobes, and the damosels teetered at an impossible angle as though walking downhill.

The worm drew closer. His fangs showed orange-edged. He licked his lips with a lashing tongue the length of a giraffe's neck. His breath was hot and fluffy.

The worm gulped once, twice . . .

He knew how to treat a girl – none better – but he was in a hurry just now, and, with specimens that succulent, chewing was really superfluous.

Restored now, he wriggled back into the water and turned upstream. His great pink tail lashed. Cantiger called.

The statement that "They don't make 'em like they used to" usually evokes yawns and groans from the youthful, who are persuaded that they not only make 'em much as they ever did, but better. In the case of warriors, however, the old style and techniques of manufacture – and possibly the raw materials – were plainly very different.

I can honestly state that I know almost no one today who can eat a spicy enchanted dinner, sleep an enchanted sleep, be bashed about in full armour for a while and still set off that same evening to do battle with a rout of giants.

Howbeitsoever, Orson and Lynch rode towards the Morass de Foys as the sun sank beneath the trees that same day.

In truth, they make neither men nor forests like they used to. There are two sorts of forest – the primary variety and the secondary. Primary is virgin and, funnily enough, much more readily passable than secondary because the trees rule. Trees do not like undergrowth fussing around at their feet, so they cast a canopy of shade that keeps briars and brambles and bracken stunted and sparse.

Briars and brambles and bracken all start with the same thing. Br. But they really start flexing their muscles and wrestling and doing very cryptic crosswords and setting insoluble puzzles in secondary forest, which was once managed or cultivated by man. Now the trees have to struggle and the undergrowth thrives, and nature gets her own back.

Even sparrows found it hard to flutter through the lower levels of the forest that had reclaimed the roads, fields and even towns of the Age of the Weirds. Sometimes you would happen upon great blocks of lichen-covered stone and realize that, although nothing more was visible but mounds of briars and vines and holly, you were standing in the midst of a once-great Weird town or city.

To some extent, then, finding your way was easy. You had no choice but to follow the track. Unfortunately, animals had no choice either, and you never knew, unless armed like Orson and Lynch, whether you were about to encounter dinner or be it. Canned food had not caught on with the wild fauna of Logris.

Now, if a modern traveller had come to a fork or a crossroads or a stellar grove in such a bosky maze, he would have had a problem. Lynch and Orson did not, because at any moment they could tell you where north, south, east or west were. The sun told them by day, the stars by night. When the sky was blanketed by cloud, they knew that moss grows heaviest on the north side of trees and lichen on the south side of rocks.

Then there were messages left by previous travellers. It was amazing how much information could be conveyed by a bent stick, a chalked drawing of twin half-melons on a tree trunk and a small pile of sheep droppings.

Sometimes there were contradictory signs. One Rider might give it as his opinion that, whilst the daughter of the miller up ahead was charming and accommodating, the food was filthy. But another might make a large pile of droppings, indicating disagreement, pinning a shrew's tail to the tree trunk and awarding the miller's kitchen three forks and an exclamation mark made with a cactus cunningly suspended above a potato.

So Orson and Lynch followed the trail without consultation or recourse to map, until they came, just as the sun turned red, to the Morass de Foys.

The Morass could not make up its mind whether it was swamp or forest, so it contrived to be a bit of both. The forest extended in spits into the gleaming, gulping mud, and the odd pioneering sort of tree had even tried to set up house in the marsh, only to list to one side and grow, if at all, twisted and stunted, with only a few pale shoots indicating life.

Things plopped sporadically.

Lynch appraised this scene with a practised eye. He nodded

towards the high mound at the centre of the Morass. "The stronghold will be up there," he said. "What do you reckon? Do we try to pick them off as they return or follow them in and kill them in their shambles?"

"I bow to your experience," said Orson. "I must say, I shudder at the thought of encountering such an enemy underground."

Lynch nodded. "And I," he said. "I would sooner fight in the open air and die, if I must," he looked up at a scribble of returning rooks circling around the crowns of the trees, "to sounds such as these, scents like these. And yet . . ."

"We must be sure of all of them."

"Aye. We must find their tunnel's entrance before nightfall. They seldom leave them open for more than a boiled comfit."[68]

"Well, we know that it'll be upwind of their lair and on highish solid ground, not swampy. I think our best chance will be to split up and hunt out a giant. Start on the fringes of the mound and work inwards. As soon as one of us finds one, we drop behind and mark his position and the direction he's taking."

"You pilliers, keep the dogs leashed," ordered Lynch, "and your bows to hand. There are no rules to gianting. The aim is simply to exterminate them. Don't attack one unless you have to. An arrow will annoy, but it'd be a lucky shot that would kill one, and they move faster than you would believe. If you see one, lie low and give us a treecreeper call. All clear?"

The two pilliers nodded.

"Right. As soon as we are across the causeway, hide the lances and spread out about three hundred yards apart. I'll take the left flank. Your Majesty, if you would take the right?"

Orson nodded, and did as he was bidden.

"Phew!" said Cantiger, and wiped his brow.

People have, of course, been coupling precisely that word, if word it be, with precisely that gesture for generations. But seldom when perched at the top of a tree so high that they cannot see the ground.

When, however, you have spent a long time being dragged

[68] 2 singaletties equalled 1 boiled comfit. 2 boiled comfits equalled 1 song. 2 songs equalled 1 singa. 2 singas equalled roughly 1 hour.

across the countryside by a flatulent cowhide balloon, your perspective on these things changes.

Yes, being at the top of a tree so high that you could not see the ground had its disadvantages, but at least trees tend to stand still and almost never break wind.

Well, they *do*. Break wind, I mean. I mean, people plant trees as windbreaks, presumably in hope that they will . . .

Anyway, the point is that Cantiger was relieved. Getting down from the tree was a problem which would doubtless have to be addressed, but he had at least got down from the cow.

The tree had happened very suddenly.

It was by no means the first tree that Cantiger had encountered. In fact, he had learned more about dendrology today than he had ever wanted to know, having passed over and through and seen and felt and, on occasion, tasted almost every species of tree that grew in Logris. He had grasped at some of them, only to have them wrenched from his hands by the buoyant bovine as it sped on its way. Others he had fended off with a forearm raised across his face.

This, a giant that towered over others in the forest, just happened to be the first one which he had hit bang in the centre, and at a point where he could wrap his arms and legs about its trunk.

The cow had pulled, but Cantiger was not, was *absolutely* not going to let go.

The tree had swayed. Cantiger had held on.

Each time the tree had swayed backward, he had struggled to extricate himself from the harness.

He had sworn a lot – really savoury, succulent swear words of the sort that have to be spat, not spoken, and that give a man strength – and at last he had wrenched the accursed leather straps free.

"And sodding stay out!" he roared inconsequentially as he released the shrunken cow.

Now freed of its drogue, it bobbed higher and higher and drifted on above the forest towards the North Star, which had just pricked a pinhole in the rosy satin of the sky.

Now Cantiger was at liberty to consider his other problems.

He yearned for "terror firmer", as he called it. He was halfway back there.

Once reach terror firmer and he could consider his next problems. Like where the hell am I, and what was that which just went whifflegrr?

Problems beset Cantiger like casualties did an Accident and Emergency unit on a Saturday night in Greatwen. He triaged them, and hoped that most of them would die before he got round to them. It was the only way to get through a day.

Orson was frankly nervous as he rode up the mound. He had seen giants' heads mounted on trophy walls but had never had ado with a live specimen. He knew that they were brilliant natural woodsmen and hunters who could creep up on their quarry unseen and unheard.

He knew the theory of fighting them, and knew too that, with the customary combination of the great spear, dogs and arrows, a good Rider could expect to kill a giant eight times out of ten. But that was when the Rider was doing the hunting, and hunting, furthermore, an individual specimen. Here they were in pursuit of an entire rout, and he might find himself, in these darkling woods through which he now slowly rode, the quarry, not the hunter.

If he was caught and held by one of the brutes, he had but little faith in his power to free himself.

There was something very strange about this woodland, and it took Orson a minute or two to work out what it was.

It was silent.

Woods were not meant to be silent.

At any one time, you would expect to hear birds twittering or chiming, clucking or cawing, small animals pattering, larger ones padding or crashing through the foliage, grunting or panting, whining or snorting or screaming.

Of course, it did not all happen at once, nor near at hand. It was just a sort of ambient rustle of life, and it was not here. But for the distant "chip-chip-chip" of an alarmed redshank down in the Morass, there was no other sound.

Even the cow floating high overhead did not low. It did make the odd distant spluttering sound . . .

Orson guided his horse only with his knees, and Demeter wove an intricate path between shrubs and brambles.

Often, Orson had to bend forwards or backwards under low branches until he lay flat on the courser's back. When the obstruction had passed, he sat up fast, glancing from side to side, one hand on his sword, the other holding X-Calibre.

"Teeteetee tit tit doooee!"

Orson rode on for another six paces, eyes flickering about the gloaming in search of sudden movement.

"Teeteetee tit tit doooee!"

Suddenly Orson recognized the treecreeper's call. He slung X-Calibre and reined in. He turned Demeter and once more rode downhill before taking a narrow badger-track to his right.

"Teeteetee tit tit doooee!"

The call came from up at his right.

He urged Demeter between two pink-flowered camellias that shuddered and shed diamonds, and so on up on a winding way over the zig-zagging terraces.

These had once – subsequent excavations were to show – been gardens, and there were all sorts of very choice blooms asserting themselves really quite impressively amidst the undergrowth.

Orson was accustomed to having his foot gripped by brambles. When, therefore, he felt something grasping his right ankle, he pulled his foot away and kicked on.

The thing, whatever it was, grasped again.

Orson's hand slapped on the sword-pommel. The blade sang against the scabbard.

"Quiet!" said Brown Willy, emerging from a purple-flowering ponticon.

"Quiet!" was not polite or deferential, but it showed good sense. People who say, "Sh!" or "Psst!" tend to get heard, and hurt.

"It's up ahead of us," said a rhododendron in heavy yellow bud. Orson had not realized how deep was the dusk. Lynch's head was barely discernible from the glaucous leaves. "A twelve-foot brute with no hair. It's carrying four red deer, yet it made less sound than the breeze."

Lynch's pillier, disguised as a very interesting rose bush holding six alaunts and two great spears, whispered, "I saw one too. Only for a second. He was very tired."

"How do you know that?" asked Orson.

"I'm only guessing, but he kept saying, 'Gor, I am tired! Gor, I am tired!' I thought that was indicative. And he was carrying a carthorse . . . Oh, and there was a farting cow up there."

"All right," said Lynch, who had the sense not to whisper. "We follow them. Pilliers first, bows at the ready, but stay under cover. Fire as soon as His Majesty gives the signal, and keep firing. Release the dogs as soon as the creatures turn on us or as soon as we attack. We'll do the rest. Keep firing whenever you get a chance, but don't hurt the hounds."

The pilliers nodded and swallowed large lumps of nothing.

"Spears," said Lynch.

The spears were handed up.

"Ready, Your Majesty?"

Orson nodded. He did not feel at all ready, nor majestic.

"As quietly as we can . . ."

The pilliers took diagonal courses away from the two Riders. The Riders followed at the apex of the triangle thus created, side by side. "Remember, Your Majesty. Go for the genytours. Giants invariably bend over when their genytours are cut off. Then you've got them."

"Right," said Orson, and licked his lips.

"Still!" breathed Lynch, and grabbed Orson's upper arm. He pointed over the bushes at something.

At first, peering through the trees, Orson could only see more trees and rocks silhouetted against the sunset, trees and rocks dark amidst the bushes, but suddenly, not a hundred yards away, some of the trees moved. As his eyes adjusted to the twilight, he made out twelve giants of varying sizes.

They did not move much. They simply shifted from foot to foot and scratched or shifted their burdens like shoppers waiting for a conveyance.

"Too many," hummed Lynch.

"No," said Orson. "They line up to go down the tunnel, don't they?"

"Usually, yes."

Orson nodded. He very slowly dismounted and handed Demeter's reins to Lynch. He unslung X-Calibre.

He had studied this implement in the privacy of his chamber, and had, he thought, worked out the mechanics whereby it worked, if not the magic that gave it power. Even if he had got it wrong, he reasoned, the sound that it made would do much to panic the giants.

And now, gazing down its length, he saw slabs of turf rising, gouts of earth spurting into the air as the tunnelers arrived at their destination.

The silhouetted figures with their swinging burdens moved towards the hole. They jostled one another with their elbows. One or two punches were thrown.

At last they formed a disorderly, ramshackle queue. The first of the giants began to lower himself into the ground. Orson braced himself, and pulled the wiggly thing.

Nothing happened.

"Damn!" breathed Orson. He would have to get Cantiger to look at the thing when . . . if . . .

He climbed back into the saddle and shrugged apologetically at Lynch.

There was a shout from up ahead. A giant had turned and was pointing. The sound of his cry rattled through the tree trunks. No birds flapped or screeched. The shout echoed, rang and sank into silence like a rock into a still lake.

But by then Orson had his spear fewtered, and he and Lynch were charging.

A hedge loomed. The two Riders sat into their coursers. The horses leaped and were over. Dogs streaked across the forest floor. Somewhere, arrows struck flesh with that unmistakeable "phch!".

And the Riders were in amongst the screaming, barking giants.

The giant immediately in front of Orson let drop the animals over his shoulder and swung his club, too late. Orson thrust forward with his legs, and the great spear's point bored into the giant's stomach. The club flew through the air as the giant went down with a gargle. Orson twisted the spear free with a practised movement, and ducked as another club swung in a giant haymaker at his head. Again he lunged with the spear. A giant with an arrow in one eye and an alaunt firmly attached to one ear found himself propelled backwards until his back slammed against a tree, and the spear, at last finding some resistance, was at liberty to split his breastbone and jerk through his body.

Orson dropped the spear and drew his sword. He wheeled Demeter round on his hocks, and two giants were upon him. The sword slashed off a grasping hand and, in the same movement, thrust at the other giant's genytours.

Lynch was right. Giants *did* bend over when their genytours were removed. Suddenly a giant bearded face with a gaping mouth and very surprised eyes was inches from Orson's. Orson drew Demeter back almost in a rear to buy himself room. He swung the blade. The giant's head jerked upward momentarily, then dropped off for good.

The handless giant was stumbling away, a great jet of blood spurting from him. Orson spurred Demeter after him and smote downward just once, cleaving him from his pate to his breastbone. Thus perished Gumble.

Orson swung Demeter round again.

He saw Lynch hard-pressed. He held his shield above his head whilst blows rained down upon him from four clubs.

He had gone a trifle too far with his policy of cutting off genytours, and had not managed to kill all those whom he had thus offended.

And those yet on live seemed decidedly offended.

The biggest of them all roared as he raised his club, roared as he brought it down on Lynch's buckled and misshapen shield.

He was very annoyed to have lost his genytours. He might have been annoyed, too, to find a substantial section of his entrails trailing on the forest floor.

Orson yelled "Yah!" as he urged Demeter towards Lynch.

He did not know why he yelled "Yah!" It just seemed the sort of thing you should do in the circumstances.

He swung his sword at the knees of one of Lynch's assailants, who fell over Lynch's courser and slid to the ground where alaunts waffled at his throat. Orson turned to the biggest of the giants. He foyned at the brute's stomach, but his sword was swept sideways by a giant arm.

Suddenly he felt himself grabbed and crushed and lifted from the saddle. He flailed with his sword, but the giant grunted and wrapped his arms about Orson's, crushing them to his sides. The sword dropped from Orson's hand.

He kicked, and tried to raise his toes to keep his feet in the stirrups, but he was jerked free of the saddle and lifted still higher. He was gazing down the cavernous gullet of the roaring giant. The stink was overpowering. Then the maws, fringed with red hair, closed at Orson's throat.

Orson saw a bloodshot eye through the visor. He felt the teeth working at the gap between helm and the breastplate.

The giant drew back his head with another roar and wrenched off the helm. In that second of relative freedom, Orson fumbled for and grasped his dagger.

The giant's red-bearded head again bent towards him, teeth bared.

Orson struck at the throat. Blood gushed.

The giant howled and raised a hand to the wound.

Orson struck again, this time to the eye. The giant howled and sank to the ground, bearing Orson with him. He snapped at Orson's head, but Orson raised his arm and felt the upper teeth scraping on his buckler. The lower teeth, however, ground at the mail and, for all that they could not gain purchase in the flesh, bit almost to the bone.

Then the giant was rolling, still roaring, and Orson was borne turning over and over down the hill in his embrace.

The giant's weight forced the breath from Orson's body like a punch, then Orson was on top, then again his head slammed to earth and the vast body was on top of him again. Six times they rolled before at last, with a teeth-clunking jolt, their accelerating progress was arrested by an oak tree that had been there two hundred years and had no intention of moving to make way for anyone today.

The giant lay atop Orson.

And he was still breathing.

Very slowly the giant raised his trunk. His great leathern fingers wrapped about Orson's throat. And squeezed.

Orson kicked and writhed, but the hands gripped like iron. Black spots like scraps of burned paper swirled before Orson's eyes, then redness in a rising tide. His limbs twitched and jerked uncontrollably.

Then a forehead hit his, and there was a great deal of wetness. The fingers stiffened and released their hold.

Orson rolled away from the tree, hawking and retching and gasping tritones. It was some minutes before his vision cleared and even then he had to wipe blood and tears from his eyes.

He saw the giant's severed head staring upwards where it had rolled to a crotch between tree roots. Brown Willy crouched by the body, carefully wiping Orson's second-best sword on the grass.

"I am sorry, Leroy," he said. "You don't mind, do you? I didn't want to butt in or anything . . ."

Orson pulled himself unsteadily to his feet. He frowned. "Well . . ." he mused. He held out a hand. "Give me the sword . . . No. Stay where you are . . ."

"I was only trying to help, sire . . ."

"I'm going to need a new pillier," said Orson.

"Urk . . ." said Brown Willy. His eyes never left the point of the sword circled before his face. "I mean, I just thought . . . I won't do it again . . ."

He closed his eyes as the blade slid past his ears, the blade that he had honed now inches from his throat.

Orson smiled. He hit his pillier with the flat of the sword on both shoulders. "Up you get, Boss Brown Willy," he said.

Brown Willy's eyes snapped open. He said, as people are bound to in these circumstances, "You mean . . . ?"[69]

"I mean that you are now a Rider of the long, thin table that I'm going to get built," said Orson. "And you'll get extensive and desirable lands somewhere or other yet to be arranged."

Brown Willy looked down at himself to check that this wasn't happening to another self.

No. This was the one he had woken up with this morning. He looked up again.

He beamed.

He said, "All right!"

* * *

[69]This means, "I know exactly what you mean, but I do so like to hear it."

So at last the three Riders made their way down the tunnel to the giants' stronghold. Orson was welcomed incredulously by Cressy.

First she refused to believe that he was Orson.

Last time that she had seen him, he had been a pillier. Now here he was in white armour embossed with gold.

Last time she had seen him, too, his hair had been fairish and his face had been pinkish. Now his hair was matted maroon and his face streaked with blood. When at last she was persuaded that he was not only Orson but now King Orson, she said, quite truthfully, that he looked disgusting and Lugh save the poor kingdom.

Lynch was for killing the giantesses and their children there and then. But Orson, looking with some awe about the giant hall, had a notion. "We could take them in chains to Greatwen," he said, "and reconstruct this behind bars, call it 'Giant Life' or 'Giant World', and charge people lots of money to come in. These giantesses could cook children – dead ones, of course – and do all the disgusting things they do, and the giant children could be fed blood-bladders or live brackrats every hour. It would be an educational and exciting day out for all the family."

"It's a thought," acknowledged Brown Willy. "I can't see it exactly . . ."

"But will they play ball?" asked Lynch suspiciously.

Orson frowned. "I don't know. *Do* giants play ball?"

"No, I mean, what if they just sit there and sulk?"

"Well," said Orson to the giants. "If we don't kill you, will you continue to be repulsive?"

"Depends," said Ugmay. "Will there be ginger biscuits?"

Orson mused. "After closing time, yes."

"And China tea?"

"After closing time."

"And . . ." she glanced at her fellows, ". . . mustard?"

Orson shrugged. "As much as you like."

"What about um . . . well . . . dob-gurdling?"

"What?"

"Dob-gurdling. You know . . ." Ugmay executed an explicit and energetic mime with her hips.

"Oh. Um, no. Absolutely not. Never."

"Wow. All that, just for being repulsive?"

"Yup."

Again Ugmay glanced at the other giantesses. They all nodded enthusiastically. Several punched the air. She turned back to Orson. "Right!" she said and grinned. "You got repulsive."

Chapter Twelve

O THUNDER IN THE skies ever rumbled so deeply or so resonantly as that made by the hooves of the great horde as it galloped through the gloaming. Travellers heard it coming a mile off and crouched in ditches or behind trees as the sound swelled and swelled until, at the last, the thunder was joined by wild cries of "Garn!" and "Yeehoch!" and the creak of saddles as silhouette after silhouette streaked by, the horses with their heads bobbing and their tails streaming, the men thrusting with both hands at their mounts' ears.

One silhouette was larger and more striking than the rest. It affords an insight into Ger and his devotion to Sparky, his pet lobster.

As with so many pets – the savage dobermann of the cerebrally challenged weakling, the whippet of the globular – Sparky reflected Ger's aspirations.

Armour was frequently customized, of course, and there was a whole series of standard lion, dragon and wolf masks, ornately wrought, that the best armourers could mould and work in their sleep.

They had had to pay a little more attention to Ger's apparel.

They had had to carve the beak and extrude the savage, whip-like wire antennae and, most taxing of all, they had had to carve the great claw gauntlets.

These extended some five feet on either side of their wearer. The finger claws were equipped with suction pads painted with resin to which flesh or armour stuck firm. The inside edges of the thumb-claws were honed to razor sharpness. They were operated by wires within the mechanism, but there were apertures beneath the armour that allowed Ger, when once he had caught his victim or when an opponent ducked beneath the claws to come in close, to draw his sword and foyne.

Call it vanity,[70] but Ger, who demonstrated no other vanity about his person, had caused his armourers to work this unusual carapace in deep gunmetal blue, mottled with gold and lapis lazuli. Nor did the tail, as it were, end at his, but extended in layered scales over his horse's 'quarters and swept down behind its heels, to end in a sweeping, once more finely honed, fan-shaped ploughshare which, as it swung from side to side, menaced any pursuer with radical chiropody.

This last feature was very useful when pursuers were hostile. When, as now, however, they were theoretically on the same side, Ger was something of a by-our-lady nuisance. Hordes like to hurtle. They like to do things in swathes. When riding behind Ger, however, it was necessary to rein in some-what sharpish if your mount, and journey, were not to be abruptly truncated.

They were within fifty miles of Greatwen now. They would stop tonight at Vampscaster, at the source of the Thuinne.

Tomorrow, they would come to the very purlieus of Greatwen.

The next day, they would pillage.

And rampage.

And slash and bash.

And so on.

That was the bit they really looked forward to: the so on. It was the same with dinner. You had blathered gobbets and broody craw and chuck agley and gurdled oats and so on. The so on came in barrels and skirts. In North Logris and Ochtia, you judged a host and hostess by their so on, even if they fell on you and massacred you in the midst of it.

North Logris was the only place where you said, "We're going to get slaughtered tonight" – and often meant it.

At first, Cantiger had sat still. After all, he had reasoned, he was safer up here than down there. Up here there were no wild beasts that went whifflegrr or Riders who went grrwhiffle.

He was vaguely aware that hunger might soon prove a factor, but he had read in the library of those ancients of old – stylists,

[70]And if you do, you'll be the first.

he thought they were called – who sat on pillars for years, and if ancient stylists of old could do it, so could he.

It was actually quite nice up here. No one shouted at him or attacked him or asked him for anything. The sun was going down. It was all very tranquil – unnaturally tranquil.

Down there, shrieks and squeals indicated that nature was behaving much as usual.

He could live up here quite happily. Everyone could have their wars and scream and bleed and die and he would know nothing about it. He would be above it all.

He felt really quite spiritual.

Admittedly, it was getting quite cold. *And* he needed a garderobe. But there: you couldn't be spiritual without a little discomfort. You had to overcome the demands of the flesh. That was the thing. That was what the ancients of old must have done.

In the distance, a river twinkled in the rosy sunset.

It made him think of the pink blonk that he had had with dinner last night, but that made him think of hunger – and garderobes – again. He must focus the mind on higher things. The sun, for example. You couldn't get much higher than the sun.

Now, what was there to think about it? The sun was hot. He was cold. It arose in the morning and sank at night. Sank . . . into a deep feather bed. Without it – and water, of course, though he wasn't going to think about water on account of the call of nature – there could be no life. No lush green grass to fatten calves or to put lovely golden fat on sheep, no plankton to feed luscious, honey-coloured oysters, no . . .

He began the long climb down.

It took just nine minutes (just one and a half singaletties) to convert Cantiger from a high-minded spiritual being into a very hungry person yearning for a loo.

He could only conclude that the flesh of the ancients of old had been less demanding, and that nature in those days had not called quite so loudly or urgently.

Very soon afterwards he concluded that things had equally dramatically changed since whoever invented the Logrian language had coined the phrase "climb down".

You could not climb down a tree. You slithered, scrabbled, slid and, when branches broke, said "Ohdearohdear!" and plummeted down them. Your nails got broken, your fingers and shins got scraped, your head got hit and you acquired a complex headgear of leaves and flakes of bark, together with a thriving colony of insects in every crevice.

You, in fact, did very little.

Gravity did the doing. You merely tried to stop it doing so too uninhibitedly, whilst squirrels and screeching birds, who should by rights have been on your side, instead did everything possible to assist it.

By dint of the above methods, Cantiger could see a winding lane through the forest some forty feet below.

That was encouraging.

He scrambled down another few branches.

There was the unmistakable clanking of armour.

That was – allowing for the possibility of another Sir Bruce, of course – positively cheering. "Oy!" he shouted, unwisely. "Hang on, there! Wait for me! Just coming . . ."

There was a face looking directly at him through the branches, close at hand. "Hang on!" he called again. "I'm on my—"

He turned back to the face. It was large and exceptionally ugly, with sprouting moles.

That was alarming.

Worse still was that it was now looking down at him, and he was still ten feet above the path.

"Ohdearohdear!" yelped Cantiger, and got down the rest of the tree without having to worry about any technicalities at all.

"What do you think you were *doing*? Who do you think you *are*?" demanded Cantiger as they rode on through the dusk. He rode piggyback on Ugmay's shoulders. "Hitting one another, hunting dangerous giants . . . I mean, I know you people *like* hitting one another and so on, but you're the *king*, for Lugh's sake!"

"You just asked two questions, then answered them," said Lynch.

"Shut up!" snapped Cantiger. "You . . . you . . . you *man*! I saw you. You were hitting the king! With your sword! That's treason, that is! Capital crime! You're in big trouble, I can tell you. Oh, yes."

"No, he's not," said Orson.

Cantiger shook his head. "Look, I don't think you got it. You are a king. Kings got to do what they're told. If this panel-beating moron wants to go off hewing and smiting and getting killed, that's his affair. But there are people who depend on you. You're meant to eat and drink and lie in feather beds and pass laws. And wave. Lots of waving."

"Hardly sport," observed Orson.

"You want sport? Fine. Take up competitive cat-shaving – that's popular, I understand – or tiddlywinks or something. You want excitement? Read a book, or go fishing or count your treasure. That's exciting, I can tell you. Count mine for five minutes, I have to lie down and be palpated, and you've got a hundred times more. One look at your treasure and I'd come over all unnecessary. There's excitement for you. Plenty of wholesome things a king can do, but no more of this fighting!"

"Um . . . who is this person?" demanded Cressy, who rode behind Orson on Demeter.

"Orson's mascot." Lynch grinned. "A magician called Cantiger. Nice of you to be so concerned, Cantiger. Your devotion is touching."

"It's nothing to do with devotion," snapped Cantiger. "If His Majesty croaks, where am I? Eh? Oh, yes. Don't think of that, do you, as you set off, all swagger and swank and clank? Oh, no. Just 'I feel like a bit of fighting and bleeding today. Cantiger doesn't matter. So what if I die? I mean, Cantiger's only given the best month of his life to the service of His Majesty. Doesn't matter if he ends up in the gutter or being torn limb from limb by that Marina. Doesn't matter that he has to conjure high magic and fly here on a magic . . . um . . . carpet at considerable personal risk in order to save your lives and warn you that the Northern Horde is on its way . . .'"

"The Northern Horde?" All three riders reined in and turned their heads.

"Oh, suddenly interested now, are we?" said Cantiger

smugly. "Oh, yes. Always the same. Never a thought for me until I've got something you want. Swank and clank . . ."

"You, giantess!" barked Lynch. "How far and high can you throw a magician?"

Ugmay plucked Cantiger from her shoulders and weighed him in her hands. He wriggled. "No! No! Please! I just got out of those brambles!"

"Well, tell us, very clearly and concisely, about this Northern Horde," said Orson.

Cantiger told them.

Lynch and Orson listened, grim-faced. When Cantiger had finished, Lynch rode back to where Ugmay stood dangling the magician. "Put him on the horse behind me," he ordered. "And you giants, I charge you on pain of death that you present yourselves at Greatwen Tower so soon as you can get there." He swung his courser around. "There will be no sleep for us tonight!"

"I was afraid of that," moaned Cantiger. "Now, you will go nice and steady, won't you? Ohdeeeaeaaarymeee!"

King Leo dismounted at his pavilion. His horse was flecked with foam. His face and his armour were spattered with mud. He muttered and growled. "By-our-lady table, for Lugh's sake! By-our-lady coronation! By-our-lady weddings! Have to wear full armour, I suppose. Sweltering day, riding all night. I don't know . . ."

Arachne was at the door before he had a chance to pull off his gauntlets. Her face was covered with mud, her hair curled about varnished and dried callistemon heads. She could not be seen like that in public, so she peeked through a crack in the hides. "Well?" she demanded. "Where is it?"

"It's coming." He shoved past her and helped himself to a deep draught of ale. He gulped it eagerly and explosively sighed. "They can hardly come as fast as me with a dirty great thing like that, can they? Damn' thing takes up three wains side by side."

"You didn't just abandon them, did you?" she screeched. "It'll get stolen, or scratched!"

"Don't be an ass, woman. Of course I didn't abandon them. They're right behind me. Lugh! The time it took to get it through the gates! I told them it should go feet first, but would they listen? Oh, no. All I can say is, Geneva had better not change her mind. The thing cost a fortune, and there's no refund . . ."

Arachne was at the crack again, peering keenly out. "Of course she won't change her mind," she muttered. "Ah. There they are. Seem to have attracted a fair crowd . . ." She then uttered words which caused Leo's shoulders to hunch and his head to sink. "Hang on . . ."

The great table was nigh invisible for the men-at-arms who stood guard on the drays and the motley crowd of spectators, dogs and geese that it seemed to have attracted. As it grew nearer, and the crowd filled Arachne's view, it was still harder for her to confirm her terrible suspicion. Only at the last, when the drays drew up outside the pavilion and the men-at-arms jumped down, were her worst fears realized.

"But it's round!" she shrieked. "I don't believe this! I said a long, thin table, and you've gone and bought a by-our-lady round one!"

"Yeah, well," Leo shrugged. "You should have seen the price of the long thin ones . . ."

"Skinflint! Idiot!" she hissed. "How are they meant to talk at this one? They'll have to shout! You'll need slings to pass the salt! Are you mad?"

"Well, it was a special discount, wasn't it?" Leo said truculently. "On account it's got a tiny fault. I mean, you'd barely notice it. I like a fault or two in my furniture. Makes it more individual, if you know—"

"A fault!" Arachne yapped. She rushed over to him and dashed the goblet from his hand. She grasped his upper arms and shook them. Her mud-covered face was a grotesque mask, slashed in two by the broad yellow rictus of her mouth. "We are talking a kingdom here, and you are buying seconds! I do not believe this! I just do not believe it! What is this 'tiny fault'?"

"Just one of the seats," Leo mumbled. "One of the seats is a bit dicey, that's all! I mean, you can sit on it, apparently. Well, someone can. If he is of most worship and has no fellow. For everyone else, it's just a bit . . . well, perilous. I mean, if anyone sits in it, he's sort of . . . destroyed. But, I mean, come on! One hundred and forty-nine seats and one perilous, and I got fifteen per cent off! That's a bargain, isn't it? And it's got lovely Pekingese snouts and pomegranates and everything . . ."

"RRRRRAH!" roared Arachne, and struck him on the head with the nearest thing to hand, which happened to be a roast chicken.

Leo said, "Ow." He walked to the tent-flap and summoned six men-at-arms.

When they were all inside the tent and standing to attention, he addressed his wife. "As you are doubtless aware, Arachne, your brothers have invaded this kingdom. Your loyalties must therefore be in doubt . . ."

Arachne dropped a startled giblet.

". . . No doubt you will tell me that your loyalties are to your Lord, your daughter and your King. No doubt you would fling yourself from the topmost balustrade of Greatwen Tower sooner than have it supposed that you might favour your brutish brothers . . . ?"

He spoke hopefully. She, however, feeling that an answer was required, and watching the drawn swords of the men-at-arms, said, "Um, no . . . I wouldn't go that far, but . . . You are going to fight against Warhawk?"

". . . But your own safety must be considered. The people of Logris might question your loyalty. They might seek to enforce it. I have therefore decided to place you under close arrest for your own protection, my precious—"

"Close arrest?" Arachne hissed. She heard herself and suddenly purred. "Silly nonsense and rumour, my dearest," she crooned. "My loyalty? Who can question my absolute devotion to you and to darling Orson?"

"There are such people, I fear. Particularly since you have just wantonly tried to murder me with a poisoned roast chicken . . . It could be coincidental, but you must admit . . ."

Arachne's jaw dropped. "A poisoned chicken?" she croaked. "The Seneschal ate a leg. He's fine!"

Leo shook his head. "Selective poison," he said. "Getting commoner and commoner these days. I'm feeling sick already. No. Sorry, sweetheart. The evidence is against you. Pinel, pick up that giblet and that carcass if you will. They're evidence. No.

It hurts me to do this, but, for the duration of hostilities, sweetie pie, it's chokey for you. And I, like any decent man of spirit, am off to kill as many of your family as possible. Any objections?"

The men-at-arms glared at Arachne. They had hated her for a long time.

"Um," said Arachne. Her eyes were venomous behind the mask of mud. A question like "Any objections?" to one such as Arachne invited an epic response. She took a deep breath.

"Because," said Leo, "any objection will be taken as proof of rebellious dissent and sympathy for the rebels. Now. We are all ears . . ."

Arachne shook. Her fingers formed fists and splayed, formed fists and splayed as she considered the options, which seemed to have boiled down to two. "Er," said Arachne, gazing at the sword-points that seemed to be one of them. She licked her lips and croaked, "Um." And then, "No."

Heathscull was one of those places that have always been battlefields and, presumably, always will be. You could smell the pain undergone there, the frustration and boredom – always major components of battle. Some even claimed to be able to smell the food that had been eaten there. Or perhaps that was the warriors who had fallen and rotted there. It was hard to tell. Either way, there still hung about the place a vague whiff of rancid fat, stale sweat, beer, onions and putrefied Samsonite.

Like most battlefields, it was a plain, but it boasted a few prominences and bushy-topped trees to ensure that generals got a good view[71] and could give cogent orders. "Head two hundred yards south-by-south-east and fire at the fellers in the plumes until they've had enough" somehow does not have the resonance of "Up, guards, and eat 'em!" or "Storm the guns in the Valley of Death, enfilade Downy Bottom and hold the Heights of Whimper to the last man."

There was a river with steep banks running down the centre of the plain. This was needed so that it could run red with blood. The plain was enclosed by further high hills into which deserters could desert, and was entered at either end through valleys that

[71]Generals generally favour the dress circle. You can get confused down in the stalls.

narrowed to ravines that could have been designed for ambushes.

Of course, the Northern Horde could have bypassed Heathscull and stormed Greatwen, encountering almost no significant resistance. They would never have considered such a strategy.

Take a Northern Horde to a crossroads with signs indicating, "Accommodating damosels with few morals and clothes", "Large quantities of free intoxicating liquid and red meat" and "battle", and they would head for the battle first, then come back to the crossroads.

It was a mind-set. You always had a good fight before you did the other things. Looting and pillaging before battle would feel all wrong, like having the gurdled oats and the so on before the blathered gobbets.

In anticipation of their arrival, Kes, Brastias, Skinner and Buller went about doing the things that leaders are meant to do before a battle. They sucked their fingers and held them up to determine which way the wind was blowing.

It was blowing in the same direction as that big orange sock on a stick was blowing. But you never knew.

They marched amongst the pavilions saying, "Keep your pecker up," which, on reflection, was very strange advice, and "Good show" whenever they saw anyone sharpening or polishing, grooming or doing press-ups.

This was also a strange thing to say, because no one ever queued in the rain to see *Man Polishing Saddle* or yelled "Encore!" at *Man Taking Stone Out of Nag's Hoof with full Chorus Line*.

These were just things you said to demonstrate that you were an officer.

You could rely on a chap who was concerned about your pecker's elevation and who equated a press-up with a good night out.

There was no standing army in Logris. This was only in part because quite a few of them had been ingesting *courage hollandaise*, as the Deedong expression goes, in the form of Wheal Maither Tinners' Old Odd XXXX Winter Brew and were now having a little lie-down. It was also due to the fact that everyone had been too busy forming feuding factions.

Aside, therefore, from the six thousand men who had flocked to the new king's banner[72] and the fourteen thousand sworn to the service of Brastias, Buller, Lynch and Skinner, the remainder turned up in dribs and drabs.

Woborn arrived with his two hundred men, his father Melody with four thousand, Sir Bruce with his brother, and six thousand of Hammer's troop without their commander, who was hedging his bets.

Magsin came with her personal guard of one hundred exceptionally handsome and tanned Riders, all decked out in cream-coloured, gold-edged armour that set off her hair something lovely.

Leo had brought nine thousand men. Lucas the Butler had brought two thousand and a plate of cucumber sandwiches. Gwimiart de Bloi, Melot and Morris de la Roche, Griflet Ulfius and many Riders Errant just brought themselves.

And six Riders rode in, followed by two thousand embarrassed men-at-arms, all of whom had labels attached to gold thread round their necks. These labels had pictures of daffodils and a teddy-bear on them, and the message: "For darling Orson, with pots of pash from your adoring sister, Marina."

Now Kes and Buller did something else that generals have always done. They climbed up a grassy knoll and, with narrowed eyes, scanned the lie of the land.

"Good sort of lie, this land," said Buller.

"Oh, lovely lie," Kes agreed. "Sort of bump over there, I see."

"Yes. It's on the maps. Death's Redoubt, it's called."

"Bit of a slope over there, too."

"Yup. Devil's Decline."

"Oh. So I suppose they'll come in at that end – the northern end – and, well, charge us sort of thing."

"That's the usual strategy. And we'll charge right back. Sounds about right."

"Meet in the middle, I'll be bound."

"Seems likely."

[72] Well, they'd flocked, like most armies, to his three square meals and beer ration, which just happened to have a banner above them.

"I've never done this sort of thing before," said Kes. "Noisy, I imagine?"

"Very. Screams and so on."

Kes shuddered. "Are they any good, these barbarians?"

"Some of them. Most of them just rely on being wood. It works, too. Slightly alarming, seeing hundreds of men charging at you, all screaming and totally unafraid. It's a bit like going through a threshing machine. You just have to stay cool or go wood yourself, of course."

"Which do you do?"

"Me?" Buller smiled. "I always went wood myself. You're probably safer staying cool, but it's more fun to go berserk, and you don't notice that you are being killed until afterwards, when you're too dead to mind. Greatest painkiller in the world, being warwood."

"I hope I'm going to be good at this," said Kes doubtfully.

"Oh, you'll manage." Buller was affectionate. He recognized his son's doubts. "You've been trained. You're well armed. You're on a good courser. Just do your best. It's fun because it's got to be, like the other thing. And death isn't all it's cracked up to be. I've seen a lot of it. At least in battle you don't see it coming for long. Live too long and it's horrid."

A cold wind sawed across the battlefield. A few bare bushy-topped trees bobbed and bowed. Kes pointed at the bruise-covered, newly turned clouds that looked like newly turned clods. "There's a storm coming in," he said.

"Yes," Buller sighed. "I always feel as if the gods have a sense of occasion. Probably a fallacy . . ."

"Pretty pathetic," said Kes.

"Oh, I don't think it's that bad . . ."

"You know," said Kes, "I wish Orson was here."

"And that little Cantiger fellow . . ."

Kes started. "Oh, no," he said, and gulped. "I mean, there are going to be thousands of people trying to hit us already. If he were here, we'd have rocks and thunderbolts and probably ravening mice and rabid butterflies having a go as well. We've got enough problems without Cantiger. In fact," he observed, surprised, "everyone's got enough problems without Cantiger."

* * *

Cantiger thought wistfully back to the good old days, like this afternoon, when travelling had been easy. Back then, all you had to do was harness yourself to a nice black-and-white cow, and off you went. All right, the cow did . . . crepitate . . . a bit, and the flight path was a little erratic, but every mode of transport, even the most cutting-edge, if that was the expression, had its little inconveniences. This primitive walloping business was just . . .

Cantiger struggled to find a word to express the full horror of what he was undergoing . . .

"Unacceptable" sprang to mind.

The way the ground was moving. *That* was unacceptable. It was particularly unacceptable when Lynch leaned forward and it suddenly lurched *downward*, and the pummelling of hooves momentarily stopped, and suddenly everything tilted forward, and the horse thing grunted and Cantiger's forehead slammed into the back of Lynch's cuirass, and then Lynch was shouting unacceptable things like "Garn!" and the ground started racing again.

The distance of the ground was totally unacceptable. It was far too close. At least with your average gas-filled cow, for much of the journey at least, "ground" was a vague sort of concept, sufficiently far off for you not to have to worry about it. On these horse things, you could see every rut and every rock as it sped past, and every rut had a treacherous expression, and every rock looked hard.

On the other hand – and he did not know quite how it did this – the ground was too far away. Had it been, say, six inches away, there would somehow have been far less to worry about . . .

He corrected that thought. Eight times tonight he had seen the ground from a distance of six inches, and, had he had time to worry before that distance shrank, usually by six inches, sometimes by six and a bit, he would have had plenty to worry about, like was he going to break his neck this time, and where precisely was that rock going to hit him?

The answers to these questions had proved to be, respectively, "Unfortunately not" and "Just about everywhere".

And the extraordinary, the totally unfair thing was that,

instead of leaving him lying there on the forest floor to recuperate, staring at the stars in the night sky or those behind his eyelids, Lynch and Orson and Brown Willy and even this girl with a name like salad sneered and jeered and sighed as though he had *chosen* to fall off, suffering multiple contusions, and Lynch had picked him up and dumped him back in the saddle, grumbling things like, "For Lugh's sake, hold on, can't you, man?"

Well, what did the brute think he had been trying to do? Did he really think that Cantiger had decided, *Here's an idea. Why don't I find out what it feels like to hit the ground at enormous speed?*

It was typical of the sheer stupidity of these Riders that Lynch seemed unaware – or was unwilling to admit, more like – that he was actually responsible for Cantiger's falling. He kept kicking the horse thing and urging it on, didn't he? So the horse thing, obviously, moved. If he had kept it still, Cantiger would have had no problem holding on, and they could have avoided all these annoying delays.

Logic seemed to play no part in Riders' education.

Another unacceptable element of this breakneck journey was the weather. The storm clouds had mustered, one atop another, like giant boxing gloves raised in a mass salute, and had growled across the sky, blotting out the moon and stars.

When at last the darkness was nigh total, there was a great trundling, grumbling sound. Lightning jerked and flickered through the clouds. The sky barked. And the rain came. Not slowly, not easing its way in, not subtly sweeping in as dropped and drifting veils, but suddenly, all at once, and with force.

Suddenly, the night sizzled. Streams gurgled. Raindrops smacked on eyelids and cheeks, snagged on eyelashes and slithered down collars and, somehow, up cuffs. Suddenly hair became thick liquid and clothes glue. Constant waterfalls purled down the backs of ears. Clouds of steam arose from the horse things' rumps. Their manes were lank, their ears spangled. Their hooves chipped sprays of diamonds.

Within five seconds of the first rain failing, Cantiger had discovered that you could actually be wetter than underwater. Underwater, you were the driest thing around. In a storm like this, there were points of reference called "air" whereby you could determine just how wet you were.

Oh, for a crepitating cow, thought Cantiger, as at last the horse things clattered on to the cobbles of Greatwen. One knew where one was with a crepitating cow.

The streets were not empty. The streets of Greatwen never were. Half the city's population might be out at Heathscull, looking forward to a good show with rich pickings. The sensible people, and, indeed, the sensible rats, might be safe at home, out of the teeming rain. But there were a lot of people – and a lot of rats – who did not match this description. Cantiger was moving too fast to study specifics, but he was aware of glitters in the shadows that were not due to the rain. Each of those glitters spoke of a hunger. Each spoke of a universe distinct from Cantiger's.

And every one of them should be arrested and sentenced to something nasty for non-specific but fundamentally obvious reasons, like being on terror firmer.

The familiar shape of the Tower, the familiar glitter of the Thuinne drew nearer. For all the storm, dawn was here. The sky was still gloomy and menacing, the rain still falling, but night was past.

Hope arose in Cantiger.

Bed was just one of the attractive things in prospect. A good meal, a massage and clean dry clothes were among the others. Then, when he was fully restored to the powers and the dignity befitting a great wizard, he would go to his laboratory and get Turquin to make spells to turn Turquin into a . . . turnip, say, and to afflict this Lynch brute with boils and locusts and dandruff and piles and things.

Oh, yes. There was a lot to look forward to.

Lynch was dismounting before the horses had even careered to a halt before the gates.

Cantiger fell off.

The captain of guards later said that the sound of Cantiger's head on the cobbles was just like that of a half-full drinking-horn struck forcibly with a coconut. It would stay with him, he said, for a long time.

"Come on." Lynch was lifting him again. "No time for that

sort of thing. Work to do. Plenty of time for throwing yourself off horses later. We need to know where everyone is. Buck up, man. Up to the laboratory."

Guards saluted. Gates opened. Orson and Brown Willy led the way into the great keep, up to the throne room and on towards Cantiger's Tower. Lynch, lumbered by a groaning, shuffling Cantiger, moved more slowly. Cressy walked with him.

Cressy looked about her at the hangings, the high windows and the red-carpeted dais with its two great gilt thrones. "Wow," she said, impressed despite herself. "Who's the second one for?"

"The queen," said Lynch. "Didn't you know? Orson's marrying Princess Geneva at the coronation."

"Marrying?" Cressy frowned. "Poor girl. Pretty, is she?"

"Very," Lynch told her. "Haughty but lovely."

"Errrgh," said Cantiger.

"Whoops." Cressy shook her head. "Orson's not the man to deal with haught. Strange. As soon as he gets some clout, he goes and enslaves himself again. I'll be interested to meet this beautiful princess. Love at first sight, was it?"

Lynch pursed his lips. "On Orson's part, yes. It took her a little longer."

"Like as soon as Orson became king, you mean?"

"It doubtless added to his attractions," said Lynch urbanely. "But she is a sweet and lovable damosel underneath it all."

"Underneath what all? I thought she was lovely."

Lynch frowned. "Well, yes. She just seems a little cold, that's all. It makes her . . . fascinating."

"Ungggh," said Cantiger.

"That's it. Nearly there." Lynch pulled the limp magician up the winding stairs. "Come along. Time you did something useful instead of gadding around the countryside amusing yourself on mats and jumping off horses. We need to know where the Horde is, how many men we have . . ."

"And what's wrong with my long black Thing with the wiggly bit," said Orson, who was already standing in the great laboratory. "It doesn't seem to work any more."

"It was plain that there had been no sleep for the sorcerer's apprentices that night. Mugs stained with coffee – as many as twelve to a table – and page after crumpled page bore testimony to their labours. They looked up, hollow-eyed, as the king and his Riders strode in.

Turquin wheeled from the watching-box. "Ah, Your Majesty," he twanged. "I beg to report that the Horde is currently sixteen miles north of Heathscull plain, where Bosses Kes and Buller currently have twenty-four thousand men under arms . . ." He took a sheet of paper from one of the girls. ". . . Twenty-six thousand men under arms, and the auspices and auguries for victory are ambivalent. Three cumolonimbus clouds the shape of horses were spotted yesterday, which is good, but there are unconfirmed reports of a cirrus that looked like cottage cheese, which is bad. The chicken's entrails curled seven times and the colour was good, but the liver was in a terrible state. Kings Boris and Ran are on their way to assist you, but will not be here until midafternoon. Gale-force winds, thunder and heavy precipitation are predicted throughout the day."

"Well done," said Orson, impressed. "At least someone has been working here whilst you've been flying about on carpets enjoying yourself, Cantiger. Give this boy two hundred pounds and the Order of the Suspender."

"Oh, thank you, sire!" said Turquin with an ingratiating smile.

"Gurk?" said Cantiger.

"Oh, hello, Your Excellency Master Cantiger." Turquin was almost pitying. "Yes, I do hope you enjoyed your flight on the crepitating cow."

The Riders and Cressy turned to Cantiger in astonishment. "The *what*?"

"Nothing . . . Nonsense . . ."

"Oh, didn't His Excellency tell you?" said Turquin. "Yes, he went for a little flight yesterday harnessed to this ingenious contraption . . ."

"That's quite enough of this taradiddle . . ." said Cantiger.

". . . A cow filled with gas that could only be steered . . ."

"Yes, yes. Time to get down to some . . ."

" . . . By making it break wind. So clever."

The Riders stared at Cantiger. You could see that each of

them was, in his own way, picturing this phenomenon. It was Cressy who first giggled and, having started, could not stop. Brown Willy covered his mouth with his hand, but still the laughter burst spluttering from him. Even Orson and Lynch, preoccupied as they were by matters of moment, could not resist the potency of the vision and permitted themselves mystified smiles.

"Make that three hundred pounds," said Orson. "Don't worry, Cantiger, I'm sure it'll go down in legend as a carpet. No one'll believe the other version. Now, we must get to the battlefield. Examine X-Calibre for me, will you? Something's wrong with it. As soon as you've mended it or restored its magic, bring it to Heathscull."

"OK," said Cantiger. "I'll have it sent."

"You?" Orson shook his head. "Oh, no. I'll need you in the battle."

"B-b-b . . . Oh, no. No no no." Cantiger too was shaking his head, so fast that his jowls flapped. "Love to see it and all that, but I've got important things to do here . . ."

"It seems to me that this young man has everything well in hand," said Orson smoothly. He slapped Cantiger on the back. Cantiger lay on the nearest table for a while. "You're my chief adviser, aren't you? You can't advise me from here. Cressy, you stay here. Find a bedroom, get dry, order a meal or whatever. Treat the place like your own."

"Sorry, Orson." Cressy's dark eyes were defiant. "If you lose this battle, I don't want to be found lounging around your castle. And if you win, I don't want to miss it. I'm coming with you."

"No place for a young girl, a battlefield," said Lynch, who was a bit like that.

"Lynch," Orson sighed, "spare your breath. Arguing with Cressy is like jousting with the Abbey. Someone find her a good horse, some boy's armour, a light sword and a bow that she can draw."

Lynch was shocked. "She'll never actually *fight*?"

Orson shook his head in affectionate despair. "Some people are just not born to be spectators. Cressy is one of them. Come on. We've got insuperable odds to contend with."

"Oh, good," said Lynch.

Cantiger gawped at him. Heroes' brains, he thought, were subtly different from his, like a gnat is subtly different from an elephant. "I really think . . ." said Cantiger.

"Excellent," said Orson. "Just the thing in advisers. Come along."

Cantiger shot a glance dipped in curare at Turquin. Turquin grinned and bowed a lavish bow.

Cantiger ordered his emotions. Hurting Turquin Very Much Indeed could wait. Not Getting Hurt Very Much Indeed never loitered. Not Getting Hurt always breasted the tape first. "Oh, Lugh, oh, Amu, oh, dear, oh, bugger," he muttered as he was jostled down the stairs, "oh, sod it, oh, Lord, oh, why?"

He came over very religious and philosophical when it came to Not Getting Hurt. It was a sacred subject.

They did not hear the Horde approaching until they saw it, because the thunder was still purring and occasionally growling or barking. They knew that the Horde was on its way, because various scouts had come cantering in from the hills to tell them so, and Kes, Brastias and Buller had ordered the troops drawn up in ranks. But there was no dust, no gradually swelling thunder of hooves.

It was like a dam bursting. One moment, there were just scrub and grass. The next, the Horde flooded in, a giant, ever-swelling deluge.

Several soldiers would later recall seeing a solitary man standing at the centre of the plain, waving orange paddles at the approaching Horde in a vain bid to check its progress. Others dismissed this as hallucination induced by terror, but everyone agreed that the man with the paddles, whether he was there or not, vanished beneath the hooves of the whooping, yelling horsemen.

Kes stood tall in the saddle before the massed troops, his helm thrown back, his sword held high. The wind fluttered his hair. "Come on, my lads!" he cried. "For Orson, Lugh and Logris! Whoops."

His horse, with a proper sense of what was fitting, had

reared. Standing tall in the saddle of a rearing horse is difficult. Kes's head tilted backward. His arms flailed. The horse squealed and toppled backward.

Brastias and Buller watched Kes struggle free of the wriggling horse and bring it once more to its feet. "Ow," said Brastias. Then, turning to the troops, "Kill the buggers! Charge!"

The Logrian army charged.

The interesting thing about battle with lances is that a good man with a lance can do considerable damage to the opposition before he is even in the thick of the press. Woborn, for example, charged Housespider. He struck him full on the breastplate and bore him back over his horse's crupper. Housespider landed with a crash and tripped the horse behind him, whose rider found that Woborn's charge had lost none of its power nor his spear its sharpness. A major pile-up ensued, through which Woborn picked his way, his spear now balanced across his thighs, wielding his sword to considerable effect amongst the fallen.

Nearby, Buller, who had also successfully felled a few Northerners with his spear before flinging it away, was smiting and hewing whilst bellowing, "Send me a red bill, would you? Ha! What do you mean, 'More than your job's worth'? How dare you utter glottal stops at me, you bastard? This beer tastes of mouse-piss, you swine! No, sir, I will not conjugate *amo*!" The list of his grievances seemed interminable, but he paid them back with interest.

Brastias's approach was different. His sword and dagger were wielded like precision instruments, and their blades flickered like light off running water.

Leo was less fortunate. Though he had no need to conjure images to inspire his ire – he was fighting against his *in-laws* – he was unhorsed at the first charge by King Clariance. He did passing well on foot, felling horses to right and to left, though he was oftsides foul defoyled under horse-feet.

But then the lobster came.

Ger, of course, knew his brother-in-law's arms and spurred towards him, his sweeping lobster tail and hooked claws clearing a swathe about him as he went. He chortled as he raised his claymore and brought it down hard on Leo's shield, forcing him reeling to his knees. Another blow struck his helm. Leo's men-at-arms stabbed futilely up at Ger's ornate and now bloody carapace, but Ger merely wheeled his horse and the razor-sharp tail sent them leaping back.

Leo sagged limply in the mud. Ger leaned down. His great right claw encircled Leo's waist and raised him from the ground. Leo opened his eyes to peer directly into the face of the giant beaked amphibian. He knew, in so far as he still knew anything, what must happen now. Every Rider knew how the lobster-Rider killed the victims in his embrace. Stiff stilettos thin as wire probed the vulnerable joints of the armour. If you were lucky, the first one killed you.

There was a jolt. The giant lobster roared "Wha?" before crashing to earth. His grip loosened, and Leo, borne with him, had the presence of mind to wriggle and jerk himself free and to roll as he hit the ground, or the vast weight of Ger and his armour must have crushed him. He pulled himself groggily to his feet to see Woborn above him, spear held high, one hand clutching the rein of Ger's horse.

"Gramercy!" gasped Leo as he grasped the pommel and the rein and mounted.

Woborn nodded once and trotted off to interfere in some other section of the battle, and Leo, having smitten Ger a few times out of family feeling, retreated behind the lines to gather his breath and his wits.

He was able now to see how the battle was proceeding, a luxury denied to those in the thick of it.

It was not, from the point of view of Orson's party, going well.

It had done what battles generally did after the first mad clash. It had broken up into lots of little battles.

Ulfius and Brastias and their followers were sweeping all before them. Kes and Griflet were in the thick of it, cleaving a channel through the Horde.

Best of all, however, was Lucas the Butler, who was wielding sword, spear and port bottle to devastating effect, and roaring, "If sir will excuse me . . ." as he smote.

These heroics were taking their toll, and the archers had decimated the Horde, but still the Northerners came on. There were just too many of them. When Lucas had fought his way through the entire Horde, there was nothing for it but to turn about and fight back again. But even then he would merely have carved two thin strips of devastation through the oncoming enemy. For now, the pikemen and Riders were holding the Northerners back from the pavilions, but soon, like a tide, the Northerners must seep and worry and work their way through the defences.

Leo was a worried man as he once more donned his helm, remounted and rode back into the fray.

"Oy!" screamed Ger from a hundred yards away. "Let me through! Yon bugger's got my tail!"

And so began one of the minor affrays that were to go down in the legend of this battle. Survivors would recall how they had checked in their own fighting to watch the enraged forepart of a lobster, now remounted, in frenzied and single-minded pursuit of its tail. Sometimes it all got confused, and the tail pursued the lobster, and Leo and Ger dealt one another many sad strokes that day. Long after the battle itself was over, the two men and their horses were engaged in a legendary game of catch-as-catch-can, now commemorated by a great statue on that site.

"There are too many of them," said Polly, one of Cantiger's apprentices, resting her head on her folded hands to see the action on the watching machine. "Ooo. Ow. I could feel that from here. That Warhawk is seriously awesome! Look at that! That head must have flown a good forty feet!"

"Yeah, well, it's midday," said Turquin absently. "He's pretty much insuperable then . . ."

"We'll soon find out Lynch is fighting his way towards him right now. Our lot have picked up a bit since Orson and Lynch arrived. That Cressy's doing great. Lugh, she can ride. Oh, I wish I could be there . . ."

"Oh, no . . ." breathed Turquin. "This is terrible . . ."

"What?"

"Oh, Lugh." He hit his forehead repeatedly with the heel of his hand. "Think, think, think!"

"What is it? What's the problem?"

"This!" Turquin raised X-Calibre from the table and flung it at the wall.

"What are you *doing*?" squeaked Polly. "That's X-Calibre!"

"No, it's not!" Turquin said glumly. "That's a crude replica, an ignorant fake! I've looked at X-Calibre. It may be powered by magic, but it's a mechanical device! This thing doesn't work. It could never work! Which means that the real X-Calibre was taken and copied by that Damas! Or that Chloris creature, who works for . . ."

"Oh, my Lugh. Queen Marina . . ."

". . . Who wants the crown." Turquin considered for a moment longer, then drew himself to his full, not very considerable height. His glasses flashed. "You just got your wish, Polly. Take the best horse left in the stables and ride like . . . well, not lightning, because lightning doesn't ride. The wind? No. Some winds are very slow, and the same objection arises. Ride like a Crabapple[73] on the days when they actually intend to win, unlike last week when Mungo hooked that brute and lost me five pounds . . ."

He was talking to no one. Polly was long gone.

"Damn it!" Orson strode into the royal pavilion and flung down helm and gages. "Damn it, damn it, damn it! It's like fighting bracken! You cut it down here and it sprouts again there! They're wild, these people! They're crazy! You kill them and kill them, and they just get up and fight again!"

"I know," sighed Lynch. "My arm aches with smiting. I've never bagged so many, but still they come on."

"How about Warhawk? I saw you having ado with him . . ."

"Aye. As mighty a man of arms as ever I met with. I had to break off when I saw Safere unhorsed. I think I have his measure, but it is a fierce strong assail."

"When will Boris and Ran get here?" Orson demanded. "And where is Cantiger?"

[73]Mungo and Jonas Crabapple, twin dwarves of Wetherbourne in Bayshire, were the best-known jockeys of the day, famous for the miraculous changes that they wrought in their mounts. Previously very lassitudinous horses suddenly discovered a fierce desire to win, whilst previously fast ones developed a terror of getting their noses cold so soon as a Crabapple was in the saddle. "Crooked as a Crabapple", a phrase that survives to this day, originated with the famous "twisted twins".

There was a creak from behind the two men. They spun on their heels. Their hands slapped on their sword-hilts. The lid of a giant carved wooden chest bobbed upward.

"Stand back, Your Majesty!" barked Lynch. "It's mine!" His sword sang.

"Oh, do stop being *chivalrous*!" snapped Cantiger, kneeling in the chest. "It's just so primitive! Why can't you just look out for yourself? This *is* the modern era, you know."

"So was the last one," sneered Lynch.

"What are you doing in there, Cantiger?" asked Orson.

"Um. Oh, er, looking for something." Cantiger climbed from the chest with timorous dignity. "I was looking for something . . . The spell for turning base metal into gold. I left it somewhere, and can't quite . . . locate it. I looked in here, just on the off chance, and . . . overbalanced. Could happen to anyone."

"Why are you wearing a strip of criss-cross-patterned wool over your shoulder?" asked Lynch. "And a skirt, and a sign on your back saying, 'Me mam was called Mac'?"

"Well, she was. Whole village used to rush round in a rainstorm. 'Nothing keeps out the rain like good old Mac,' they'd say."

"What?"

"Um . . . the spell for changing base metal into gold. I had it, but I can't find it. Anyhow, battle going well? Jolly good. Let me know when it's over. I'm particularly good at the old ululation, and I think I'd be quite handy at looting enemy corpses. Never had a chance, but I'm always willing to try new things if they help. Service. That's my watchword. Right, now, where was I . . ." He ducked down in the chest once more.

Orson looked quizzically at Lynch. He sighed. "Cantiger," he said sternly, "the battle is not going well. There are too many of them. At any moment, this pavilion could be flooded with Northerners . . ."

"Oo," said Cantiger, reaching up to lower the lid, "er, sorry. I'm really very busy. You just carry on . . ."

"We need your advice, Cantiger."

"My advice? Um, tactical withdrawal, probably. Rapid and very long-distance tactical withdrawal. Regrouping. Retirement into private life. Spend more time with the family . . ." His skittering eyes briefly fastened on something behind Orson and Lynch. "Er. Oh, Lugh . . ."

This last was whimpered, and was followed by a whimper from the magician's stomach as he contracted fast and drew the lid of the chest down with a bang.

Orson turned to see who or what had occasioned this tactical withdrawal.

A Rider stood in the doorway of the pavilion, dressed all in steel. A yellow gift tag dangled from around his throat. Normally this, with its depiction of a teddy bear and several daffodils, would have evoked interest from Orson and Lynch. Instead, their eyes were drawn to the long thin black thing that the Rider held in his hands. It had a sort of circular bit halfway along it, and the Rider's ungaunleted right forefinger rested against a curved wiggly bit.

"Ah, good," said Orson, extending a hand. "Is it working now?"

"You're about to find out," said the Rider. He flung back his helm. The face beneath was swarthy and handsome. A smug smile wriggled across a field of black stubble.

"His Majesty asked you a question," said Lynch. "Ondslake, isn't it?"

"It is," said Ondslake with a little bow.

"So answer it, churl, and hand over the royal weapon."

"The royal weapon?" Ondslake sneered. "A magic implement conjured from deep in the earth by a mistress-magician and pilfered by a petty fraud and crook? Pilfered, like the crown . . ." He crouched. "No! Stand back, Lynch, or I pull the wiggly bit!"

Lynch hesitated. Even he could not cross the pavilion quickly enough to disarm Ondslake before he unleashed the magic fire from X-Calibre. He stepped in front of his king.

"Oh, very heroic," jeered Ondslake. "But X-Calibre's bolts will not be stopped by one human body, be it ever so mighty. It will simply strike through you and kill Orson as though you were not there, and, by her deep arts, the rightful owner of the weapon has uncovered twelve more of the little shiny bits in which the magic resides, so there are plenty left to drill holes in that chest over there and so bring an end to this charade."

The chest squeaked.

"And then the Northerners will rule . . ." said Orson.

"No, no. Chaos will rule again, and only one person has the power to draw power from chaos. We nearly did it last time, and would have succeeded had it not been for that dirty little Cantiger, who has as much magic in him as does a fishcake . . ."

"A fishcake?"

"Yes."

"Oh."

"I think you will find," said Orson, stepping out from behind Lynch, "that none save the rightful king can use X-Calibre without destroying himself. Still, if you are happy to take that risk . . ."

"Rightful king, ha!" barked Ondslake.

He pushed the wiggly bit.

The resultant noise was such that the clamour outside actually stopped for a moment as the warriors paused in their hewing to consider the phenomenon. X-Calibre sprang from Ondslake's hands, and Ondslake himself staggered backward and sat with violence against the silken wall.

"Ooh," he said, and looked down at his stomach. "It hit me!"

"I did warn you," said Orson. He bent and picked up X-Calibre. He was careful to hold it, as had Ondslake, with the thick end to the fore.

"So you *are* the rightful . . ." gasped Ondslake. He frowned as he tried to puzzle it out. Then his head lolled to one side and his body slumped and slid.

The lid of Cantiger's chest arose a few inches. Two eyes flickered from side to side.

They saw Lynch on his knees. "Forgive me, Your Majesty," he was saying, and bowed. "I confess that I had doubts, but I have seen it with my own eyes."

Orson was magnanimous, "Don't worry about it," he said. "Doubts are natural. Get up, and let's— Dear Lugh! What's that noise?"

The lid of the chest jerked shut again.

"That noise" was a great, full-throated, gargling, puddering roar that grew louder and louder as it neared until at last the two men within the pavilion had to shout to be heard. Lynch had stood and drawn his sword. "It is some great beast!" he bellowed. "I will fight it!"

He flung back the pavilion door. "Oh, yes!" he called, and punched the air with his fist. "It's Ran! It's Ran with his dragon, and Boris! The Deedong Kings are here! We're in business again!"

Warhawk had seldom paused in his smiting all day. Now, like many of his troops, he took a break and eyed the enemy camp suspiciously. First there had been that bang, and now there was this terrifying roaring.

He knew both sounds. He had heard the bang at the sward, and he had heard the roaring of Ran's dragon some years ago when he and his brothers had decided that the Deedongs really did not need cattle or money as much as did they. Ran had disagreed really quite vehemently, and the brothers had had to retire to their northern fastnesses with several punctures.

"Now Lugh defend us from death and horrible maims!" he shouted to King Carados.[74] "For I see well we be in great peril of death, for I see yonder a king, one of the most worshipfullest men and one of the best Riders of the world, is inclined unto his fellowship!"

"What is he?" asked King Agwisance, casually impaling a man at his heel.

"Oy! He was one of mine!" objected Warhawk.

"Whoops," said Agwisance. "Beg pardon."

"It is King Ran of the Deedongs," said Warhawk. "He rides on a dragon."

"This," said Carados, "I must see."

A moment later, he did. Faster than any courser came the great black dragon, fire and smoke belching from its rear end,[75] and astride it the mighty King Ran, a man of the mildest and most gracious of manners in peace, but a terror in war. Behind

---

[74]He didn't, of course. I have again rendered his words into modern English.
[75]People also have the oddest ideas about dragons. If they breathed jets of flame at their victims, they would never find mates, even in Bottom-on-Sea, their food would taste disgusting and they would go backwards just when they most needed to go forwards.

him, King Boris stood astride the saddle, his broadsword swirling above his and his comrade's head.

Where the dragon had come from, none save the kings knew. There were few now left. Their skeletons were found sometimes, ranging in size from that of a large dog to monsters like this, tall as a palfrey at the front and long as a tiger.

The kings were said to keep the dragon in a secret cave protected by trolls and by powerful magic. Here it slept in silence until need arose, and then Ran gave it to drink of the fantastically rare and precious fire-spirit, and the beast stirred into roaring life and emerged to terrify all who saw it or heard it.

It was not just its speed that rendered it superior in battle to any horse. Its very roar made horses rear and squeal and plunge and panic. Even now it clove a path through the Horde – a path littered with fallen Riders and lined with sitting, rearing or fleeing horses. Lynch, Orson and Woborn, following, dealt summarily with the fallen. Only a man-at-arms on foot could check the dragon in its course, and then only at the cost of his life. If Ran's spear or Boris's sword missed him, the dragon hit with the force of a charging aurochs, sending the man flying and spinning through the air to land like a stringless puppet.

I am sure that you would resent an enemy who wrought such devastation on your troops, but then you probably do not come from the desolate lands north of Wyfor. The Northerners watched the two kings' progress with undisguised admiration. Here were men of *worship*. Some of the more reckless – and the Horde in general had about as much reck as air-freshener about it – actually vied with one another to be knocked down by them.

Their grandchildren would really have something to brag about when the deadly duel of the albums began.

And now the Deedong troops swept into the field. As they advanced, they cried out things about "glory" and "honour" and "fatherland" and "death". To those who understood their barbarous tongue, it rapidly became clear that, of these, "death" was the favourite. "Death" was preferable to dishonour or ingloriousness. "Death" was preferable to everything, in fact, except sex and tripe.

Death was welcome, provided that it did not turn up just now, when they had other things to do, like composing warlike odes.

They were fine whilst they followed Ran, Boris, Lynch, Orson and Woborn. They hewed and smote with the best of them. When, however, the Riders and the Deedongs were briefly separated, the Deedongs suddenly remembered that "living", a word that did not feature in their rhetoric, was also quite nice, and turned about, screaming, "Mayday! Oh, Skewer!"

In the course of their precipitate retreat, they came up against the scavengers of the Northern Horde, so they turned about again and advanced, the better, as they would say, to retreat.

Your average Deedong aspires to the perfect retreat, shrouded in philosophical propositions and festooned with glory.

And then something pink and very, very big arose from the waters of the brook at the centre of the plain, and even Warhawk breathed, "Gurdle honk mastic!" and reined back.

The worm turned towards Orson's pavilion, registered, in its clouded way, that others were headed towards it with hostile intent, clambered from the tiny stream and lashed its tail . . . It reared up, tall as a church tower, and now swung around to face the Horde. With a sound like a blast of fire confined and released, it bared its great fangs. And went to work.

The worm was usually motivated by hunger. Today, however, it was anger that moved it, and anyhow, most of the people here had unappetizing prickly sticky-out bits and quite a few were in tin cans. It did not bother much, therefore, with the time-consuming business of consuming. Instead, it used an instinctively learned technique of quite startling efficiency. It raised its giant body from the ground, fixed its beady little eyes on some unfortunate minding his own business at the very back of the Horde, and lunged for him.

Its body slammed down on to the ground, crushing everything and everyone beneath it. The worm then chomped a bit, spat a bit, writhed a bit – and each lash of that sickle tail cut the legs out from under horses and men alike – before rearing up, spotting another person who particularly annoyed it, this time over to the left, and repeating the process.

Orson's troops had, as advised by Cantiger, made a tactical withdrawal all by themselves, and now stood uncertainly about the pavilions watching this.

Every one of them was of the opinion, founded, unjustly if accurately, on appearances alone, that their new, giant, pink ally was unlikely to possess a giant intellect. It was coincidence only, they told themselves, that at present the worm was devastating the Northern Horde. At any moment, it might turn its attentions to them. Not one of them, therefore, rested his weight on the balls of his feet, ready to surge forward in such an event. Some even watched affairs over their shoulders whilst kneeling in a position suspiciously akin to that adopted by athletes at the start of a race.

The Deedong kings, Lynch, Kes, Leo (still with his lobster tail), Lucas the Butler (now handing around goblets of tonic blonk and dainty cheese puffs), Woborn, Magsin, Buller and Cressy, now unrecognizable behind a mask of mud, had gathered about Orson to watch the sport.

"Now that," said Woborn to Orson, "is a laidly worm. And when I say laidly, I mean really *laidly*!"

"What's laidly?" called Orson above the growl of the Deedong dragon and the ever more distant screams of the Horde.

"I don't know," admitted Woborn. "Sort of spoon-like, I suppose."

"Can't see much resemblance myself," Buller frowned.

"No, no!" shouted Boris. "Is how you say uggy!"

"Ly!" supplied Lynch. "Ugly with an extra 'ly'."

"Whaffor?" demanded Buller.

"Dunno," Lynch admitted. "Worms always have one. Anyhow, enough of the idle chat and persiflage. Pillier! The great spear, if you please!"

"What do you want that for?" asked Orson as the pillier rode up with the towering lance.

"Well," Lynch shrugged. "Sythen I am come so nigh this grisliest miscreature, I must prove its might or I depart from it or else I shall be shamed and win me disworship an I now depart from it. And therefore," he continued as he fewtered the spear, "have ye no doubt I shall have ado with yonder laidly worm to the uttermost for either I will win worship worshipfully, or die knightly in the field!" He gathered up the reins and said, "Gramercy for the cheese puff, by the way," before lowering his visor with a clang.

"Um . . ." said Buller.

"Oy!" called Magsin.

"Stop the berk!" called Cressy.

"Lynch, no!" Orson grabbed Lynch's bridle.

"What? Whassamatter?" Lynch raised his visor and glared at Orson, then at Woborn, then back at Orson. "Your Majesty does me disworship . . ."

"No, he doesn't," said Buller. "He does you a favour. Not only will that beast gobble you up for all your best efforts . . ."

"That me concerneth!" snapped Lynch, tugging at his reins. "For rather than I should be faren withal to such shenship of arms, I would rather be slain manly in plain battle!"

"Yes, yes, old chap. Calm down and have a cheese puff," said Lucas the Butler.

"Lynch, just look!" insisted Orson, pointing with his free hand. "That worm, for whatever reason, is winning the battle for us! If it turns on us, well and good. You can do what you like with it, but just at the moment . . ."

"Just at the moment," said Woborn quietly, "you place the kingdom in great jeopardy by so much as distracting the creature in its work."

Lynch glowered as his eyes scanned the battlefield, but, at the last, he sighed, nodded and raised his visor again. "OK," he said. "Gissanother puff, then."

It is axiomatic that worms will turn, and this one was certainly not original enough to disobey a good axiom. The Horde had been scattered and had fled into the hills thoughtfully provided for that purpose or lay scattered about the plain. Some of these groaned. Others were better off. These looked very surprised, and always would.

The worm released something that might have been a sigh as it gazed about its handiwork. It swivelled around then, and slithered towards the Logrian army. The air was riven with cries of "Uh oh!" and "Blimey!" and the sound of running feet as the bulk of the foot soldiers, with a lamentable lack of interest in Natural History, headed for the hills at their end of the plain.

The Riders, however, stood their ground. Their horses did not approve this plan, and many Riders found themselves in consequence sitting their ground whilst their mounts careered off to the hills. The hardcore of noblemen around Orson, however, held their coursers firm and prepared to do battle.

Now Lynch had his way. He rode forth at a canter, lance held high, to cheers from the remaining ranks. Even as the lance slowly and smoothly fell to the horizontal, he crouched and spurred his courser to a snorting, bobbing wallop. He aimed, even as he would with an aurochs, at a point just behind the head.

The spear-point struck.

And slithered up and over the worm's flank.

The horse hurtled headlong and head first into the beast's side. The horse's hindquarters arose, and Lynch was flung forward, scrabbling and kicking at air. There was a loud crunching, clanking sound as Lynch hit the worm and, spreadeagled against it, slowly slid to the ground. His horse had already picked itself up, turned away from the horror and, reeling slightly, headed back to the relative safety of the ranks.

Lynch groggily pulled himself to his feet. The worm lumbered on.

Cressy giggled.

Orson swung around on her. "It is not funny!" he barked. "We are under attack!"

"No, you're not," said Cressy. "Look at the beast. You saw it attacking the other people. Now it's just crawling. It seems to know where it's going, too . . ."

"She's right," said Woborn. "It probably just wants a bit of treasure. They like that sort of thing, I believe . . ."

Orson stared after the beast. He was forced to admit that Cressy was right. There was something very intent about the worm's progress. It looked neither to right nor to left. It was headed . . . for . . . Orson's . . .

Maybe, as Woborn suggested, it was like the dragons of ancient legend – rather than the real, modern variety beside him

- and it liked to hoard gold. Well, if all that it wanted was Orson's war chest, it was welcome to it.

And indeed, as, to gasps, the worm slid straight through the rear of the pavilion, which collapsed upon it, swathing it in white hides, it appeared that that indeed was its target. For, a moment later, the entire pavilion billowed up again, billowed high, high above the Riders' heads, and there, like an improbable bride, crowned with the gilt finial and trailing a veil of white, was the great worm, and in its maws a portmanteau of carved wood.

"Ah, that's it," sighed Woborn.

"Typical worm," Buller nodded. "Read about it once."

"Well, I wouldn't complain," said Ran with a massive Deedong shrug. "He kill our enemies, he want a little booty. Is fair, no?"

"Always like a little booty after a battle meself," said Buller. "There was one called Enid after St Alban's, I remember . . ."

Fear was rapidly dispelled by relief. Boris even laughed. The remaining riders cheered. The worm wriggled at high speed away from the camp and towards the centre of the plain.

"Three cheers for the worm!" called Cressy. "Hip hip!"

"Hooray!" bellowed the Riders.

"Bad luck, that," said Woborn as Lynch lurched up to him.

"Where's His Majesty?"

"What?" Woborn glanced around him.

"Hip hip!"

"Hooray!"

"He was here a moment ago. A bit stonied, you must be, I should think . . . Oh, there he is!" He pointed at the former site of the royal pavilion, where Orson, now dismounted, was opening the lid of one of three chests.

"Hip hip!"

"Hooray!"

Suddenly, Orson looked up. He shouted something. He remounted his courser and urged it into a canter. His cheeks were pink. He pointed. "It's . . ."

"Yes, yes, old boy," said Buller. "It's got a few millions in gold and jewels. So what? Plenty more where that lot came from. Calm down."

"Some gentlemen find these cheese puffs very soothing, sire," said Lucas the Butler.

"It's . . . !"

"Orson, what's the matter with you?" Cressy laid a hand on his arm. "It's only got a bit of treasure."

"No, it hasn't!" Orson managed at last. "It's got Cantiger!"

"Oh, well, then," said Kes smugly. "We've got a real bargain."

"Come on!" called Orson with a great sweep of his arm. "Come on! Get that worm!"

The Riders exchanged significant glances in amaze.[76] Then, knowing which side their trencher was gobbeted, and seeing their young king unslinging the famed X-Calibre as he rode, hands-free, at the wallop after a worm, they followed.

Orson's problem, amongst others, was that he dared not discharge X-Calibre's magic bolts at the worm's head, which contained, amongst other things, Cantiger. As for other vulnerable parts of a worm's anatomy, he was frankly ignorant. Did a worm have a heart, and, if so, where did it keep it? Did it have genitours, and if so, where were they secreted? Riding only with his legs, as every good horseman should, he released a bolt at the upper left-hand side of the beast, but it was writhing so frantically that he doubted that he had hit it.

The worm was now on the very banks of the stream that wound through Downy Bottom. Orson urged Demeter on. He aimed another magic bolt with all his might at the upright section of the beast's sinuous body.

This time, he knew that he had hit it, for blood splashed from the great beast's side. It turned back with an expression of outrage and dropped the wooden chest on to the dry mud. With a long, flickering tongue, it licked the wound. The chest now lay

[76]If you should be reading this aloud, I would be grateful if you would explain to your listeners that I do not here refer to "a maze" as in "a totally pointless plantation of yew" – and I do not mean "you" as in "you and me", but "yew" as in "tree or bush" – "or box" – not as in "rectangular container" but as in "hedge or bush not unlike yew in its density", not that I wish to imply that you are, as it were, dense, by which I mean "thick" rather than "indentations" – "designed to occasion befuddlement and confusion", but rather "amaze", as in "befuddlement and confusion", conditions which I am always, as you are aware, at great pains to avoid.

on its side. Its lid swung open. Tousle-haired and plainly groggy, Cantiger crawled from it. He shook his head. His dewlaps flapped. He blinked up at the towering beast above him, said, "Oh, bugger. You again!" then, "Ohdearohdearohdear!" scrambled back into the safety of his mobile home and pulled down the lid.

The beast looked smug. It stuck its long tongue out at Orson, picked up the chest once more, and plunged into the stream.

Orson reached the river bank to see one last thrash of a tail-tip a hundred yards downstream. Then worm and magician were gone.

Woborn reined in beside his king. "Ah," he said. "Shame."

"Funny little chap," said Buller.

"Pink and white," agreed Kes. "Not his fault, I suppose, though I don't hold with it myself."

"Probably why the worm went for him," said Magsin. "Ah, well . . ."

Orson stared downstream. He blinked. "I don't know what I'm going to do without him," he croaked. "It was because of him . . . I shouldn't have brought him here. It's my fault. And now . . . He's gone . . . He's gone . . ."

"Yes. He is, rather. We shall not see his like again," said Woborn.

"Lugh," murmured Buller. "I hope not. Bit worried about the worm. Won the battle for us, really. Deserves better. Can worms vomit?"

Orson just kept staring after his lost friend and mentor, the man who had brought him X-Calibre and a kingdom. He suddenly felt very alone.

Tears glazed his eyes and he made great dole out of measure. "Ah, Cantiger," he breathed, "thou wert head of all sorcerers, and, howbeit thou wert a boystous villain and fulfilled of bobaunce and orgulyte and much missaid for thy greed, covetise and passing flatulence, yet me repenteth this thy mishappy and grimly fate. I had liefer than the stint of my land a year that thou wert alive!"

The Riders exchanged baffled glances. Buller shrugged. "Well, a month, perhaps."

'Yes," said Skinner consolingly. He sat upright and with due solemnity declared, "Cantiger will be remembered as a . . ." He winced and struggled to find the apt word.

"Person?" suggested Cressy.

"Person," Skinner nodded and snapped his fingers. "Yes. Yes, that's it Person. He will be remembered as a person." He paused. He frowned. "Well, roughly, anyway . . ."

And so, with barely a backward glance and with this moving epitaph ringing in their ears, the Riders of the Court of King Orson turned from the stream and from consideration of the magician who had given rise to that Court and that King, and Orson rode into a daunting future without his boon companion and counsellor. He rode from the past into the future through the portals of the present as no one had ever done before or will do again.

And he rode alone.

(*To be continued*)

Appendix One

KING LEAR
by
PLETE WORKS

Rendered in portable form by Milo Snugsnuffler, poet
Rhododendronate to Bos Buller Delamere Maudite.

"Ruling and reigning are frightfully draining,"
Protested a weary King Lear,
"Campaigning is straining, but oh! Entertaining's
"The bit that I principally fear!

"Ambassadors bore me, and matters of state
"Have a fearful effect on my bowels;
"These merciless banquets would make any man quit;
"Why shouldn't I thwow in the towel?"

Now Lear was a pampered and silly old man
Who dearly loved praise and flim-flam;
His daughters once summoned, he sat on his bum and
Said, "Tell me how super I am."

Girl number one said, "Look at the sun!
"I'll swear it just blinked at your brilliance!
"And on a reliable scale," said sweet Goneril,
"You're tops, pops; now give me my millions."

"Naughty old daddy," purred Regan,
"You've ordered the day to be bright;
"Please be so kind as to change your great mind
"Before we retire tonight!"

Then up got the youngest, his fav'rite,
Who said, "You're not bad, for a dad;
"For all that I feel you want more from Cordelia,
"I've nothing more fawning to add."

So Lear gave his lands to the first two,
And banished the crusty Cordelia,
But sometimes the crusty prove somewhat more trusty,
Whilst toadies prove harsher and steelier!

KING LEAR (PART 2)

When designers move into the castle
To make it all modern and merrier,
It's just so *uncool* to play host to a fool
Who smells like the old Border terrier.

Lear wasn't perturbed when his firstborn
Declared that she found him fatiguin'.
He still had this dumb thought that he'd live in comfort
With darling, delectable Regan.

But Regan said, "Sorry, pops, sweetie;
"Awfully sad and all that;
"We're infested with guests, so I would suggest
"That you doss in the yard with the cat."

At this, the old king got neurotic,
And scampered about in a storm,
In scant *deshabille* with a fool at his heel,
Declining to keep himself warm.

The fool said, "Now, nuncle, you see,
"You get cold and wet just like me!
"Forget pomp and grandeur; you're only a man, dear;
"Tolderol, fiddlededee!"

At length, much sadder and wiser,
Lear died, thanks to wicked intriguin',
And so did Cordelia, if somewhat genteelier,
And likewise with Gon'ril and Regan.

And that (excluding some business
With Gloucester, his sons and his eyes)
Is the tale of *King Lear* (note the pity and fear),
In which just about ev'ryone dies.

(Curtain)

Appendix Two

Obviously any decently brought up Logrian has no more need of this appendix than of tuition in archery or venery or carfing biforn his fader, but, since my scribes, Friars Constable and Robinson, are looking to break into the Sotis, Wogglish, Ochtian, Deedong and even Saracen market (and Boss Warhawk has ordered a copy), I am obliged to supply this little list of common, self-explanatory terms.

GLOSSARY

adoubted . . . . concerned, frightened
alaunt . . . . large, heavy black-and-white boarhound
an . . . . before
avoid . . . . leave, dismount
bisene . . . . appointed, apparelled
bobaunce . . . . pomp, bombast
boystous . . . . boisterous, rough
brachet . . . . small hound, like a beagle
clip . . . . embrace
courser . . . . warhorse
dole . . . . sorrow
embushment . . . . ambush
fewter . . . . a rest for a spear, to place a spear in the rest
forbled . . . . having lost much blood
foyne . . . . thrust
gramercy . . . . thanks a lot
lief . . . . dear, welcome, gladly
liefer . . . . more gladly, rather
lymer . . . . large scent-hound
miscreature . . . . monster
missay . . . . abuse
or . . . . before
orgulous . . . . proud
palfrey . . . . a light saddle-horse
pillier . . . . squire, attendant
raze off . . . . cut off
samite . . . . a rich silken fabric

sendal . . . . a fine, thin silken fabric
shenship . . . . disgrace, dishonour
syker. . . . . secure
sythen. . . . . since
to-rove, to-riven. broken or torn to pieces
truage . . . . tribute
undorne. . . . . mid-morning, from 9.00 to midday
wallop. . . . . gallop
ween . . . . deem, think
worship. . . . . honour
wood . . . . mad, demented
wood-shaw . . . . copse, thicket